*continued . . .*

# a fistful of sky

## Nina Kiriki Hoffman

ACE BOOKS, NEW YORK

A FISTFUL OF SKY

An Ace Book / published by arrangement with the author

PRINTING HISTORY
Ace hardcover edition / November 2002
Ace mass market edition / June 2004

Copyright © 2002 by Nina Kiriki Hoffman.
"Transitions" copyright © 1997 by Nina Kiriki Hoffman. First appeared in *Bruce Coville's Book of Magic II*. This version extensively revised.
Cover art by Judy York.
Cover design by Rita Frangie.
Text design by Tiffany Estreicher.

ISBN: 0-441-01177-2

ACE®
Ace Books are published by The Berkley Publishing Group, a division of Penguin Group (USA) Inc., 375 Hudson Street, New York, New York 10014. ACE and the "A" design are trademarks belonging to Penguin Group (USA) Inc.

PRINTED IN THE UNITED STATES OF AMERICA

10 9 8 7 6 5 4 3 2

To Ginjer.

To my family. You know who you're not.

To Kris, my guardian and goddess.

Thanks to Swedish fiddle group Väsen,
who, unknowing, provided the soundtrack.

# Foreword

My mother suggested I mention that the LaZelle family is nothing like our family. Well, okay. We did line up like that at the buffet to get our dinner. And yeah, we lived in that house.

But that's all.

No, really.

Honest.

They open their wings,
flash patterns and colors,
fly from flower to flower.
I, with the dark bristles and many feet
of the former form,
inch along the ground.

Sometimes all I want
is two armfuls of air,
a fistful of sky.

*One*

IN my family, we used the word *we* all the time. Most of the time *we* meant the five of us, the children. *We* hated this TV show, loved that one. *We* adored cutthroat card games and fast chess, but pretended to hate team sports. *We* were going to the beach.

Which was not to say we didn't form in-groups and out-groups among ourselves. But the power of *we* was stronger than anything we did to each other, especially when we were united against a common enemy. Often enough, the force we supported each other against was right in the house with us.

Even that could shift. When we were talking to strangers, *we* widened to include everybody who lived in our mansion with the pool, the guest house, and the fruit tree orchard in Bosquecito, a rich enclave just south of Santa Tekla, Southern California: *we* meant us kids, plus Mama, Daddy, Great-Uncle Tobias and Great-Aunt Hermina.

*We* went to Los Angeles twice a year, once between Christmas and New Year's, and the other time at Midsummer, to parties where even more of our family lived:

Mama's parents and aunts and uncles, her brothers and sisters, and so many cousins, removed or not, that we couldn't remember all their names.

*We* didn't tell outsiders what we were really like. We learned that particular brand of separation from the rest of the world before we could speak.

As for the other kind of separation, differentiating oneself as an individual, I hardly knew I was a separate person from my brothers and sisters until I was around seven, and I didn't believe it until later, when I found out just how separate I was.

I was twelve when my older sister Opal went through transition.

At sixteen, Opal was almost as pretty as Mama, with the same full lips, high cheekbones, and wide violet eyes. She had nice hair, too: long, wavy, and brown with gold streaks.

The rest of us were darker, both in looks and temperament.

Jasper, fourteen, teased Opal because she acted timid. She never dared a dare or took the lead in follow-the-leader. She didn't like walking to the beach with us because the tunnel under the freeway was full of broken glass and spooky echoes. She couldn't stand to get dirt under her fingernails. Caterpillars gave her nightmares, and snakes made her run the other way.

As for me, Gypsum, the middle sister, I didn't take the lead, but I didn't back down from much. I could run almost as fast and hit almost as hard as Jasper, and harder than Opal. Flint and Beryl, the younger kids, weren't threats yet; they were still just bothers. Jasper and I had age, size, and strength on them, so we ignored them when we could. Flint had started to follow me and Jasper around, even though I beat him up. On the other hand, Beryl looked up to Opal, which annoyed me.

I remembered how Opal used to hug me when I was little, and comb my hair, help me dress, rock with me in the big rocking chair in Mama and Daddy's room and sing to me, but that was when I was three and she was seven. It lasted until I was seven and she was eleven. Then I grew out of it.

Opal was a girl, and Jasper was a boy. I sure didn't want to turn into what Opal was. I didn't want to be her doll, either.

Transition was something every kid in our family went through if they were lucky.

Watching Opal go through it scared me. She had chills and fever and then chills again over the course of three days. She moaned and talked to people who weren't visible.

Mama did most of the nursing. Daddy, the one who usually cared for us when we were sick if Opal didn't, was an outsider, not a member of Mama's family; he had no experience with this special kind of sickness.

I helped take care of Opal. I kept her covered with blankets instead of letting her shiver them off. I sat by her and gave her water when she would take it. I held her hand when she moaned and cried. Watching her eyes burn with fever in the dim light, I was scared. I didn't want her to die.

The power came on Opal at midnight of the third day. I was asleep by her bed. I woke to find her hand gripping mine, and when I looked at her she smiled and blew me a kiss. I felt it melt into my cheek like sunlight.

After that, she was okay.

Her settling-in period was mild compared to some Great-Uncle Tobias told us about. He was the family historian and our teacher in all the family things we couldn't learn at school.

Opal only had little spurts and glories as she and her

gift adjusted to each other, not the pyrotechnics and major risks and accidents some people had.

When she figured out how her gift worked, she used it on Jasper.

Jasper had been her chief tormentor the past few years, and often he had gotten me to help him. We'd dropped worms and ice cubes down the backs of her dresses, left a garter snake in her bed, scared screams out of her by jumping out of closets.

Opal wasn't scared anymore.

Every time Jasper relaxed, Opal set invisible things in his path and tripped him. Even when she didn't, she had him so spooked he tripped over nothing and banged himself up.

When Opal got stronger in her power, she took over Jasper's legs and walked him places he had no interest in going, like into the pool. He never knew when she was going to attack.

Jasper made me stick with him, and the next time Opal took over his legs, he grabbed me and hung on. Opal wasn't strong enough to control two people at once, and she wasn't that mad at me, so after Jasper kicked me a few times while she was running his legs, she gave up torturing him.

After that we didn't see Opal do anything interesting.

Great-Uncle Tobias told us that once you got the power, you had to use it. People who didn't use their power got twisted up inside and died. It had happened to Great-Great-Aunt Meta, who got the power of curses instead of the more common wish power. She didn't know anybody she wanted to curse. Unused curses had turned to cancer inside her.

"What do you think Opal's doing with her powers, Gyp?" Jasper asked me one day when he and I were in our fort in the middle of the bamboo thicket near one edge of the family property. Our space in the middle of the tall canes stayed cool and quiet and private, no matter how hot the day was. The light shafting down was green, and the air smelled like sweet grass and damp earth. Any wind at all and the canes rubbed against each other, making a noise like squeaky hinges. Long pale leaves papered the floor. Little knobs of bamboo stuck up here and there from the ground.

We all used to hang out in the thicket, hiding from Mama and the neighbor kids, making plans and leading secret lives, but Opal had changed even before transition. She never came here anymore.

"She must be doing something," Jasper said. The green light in the thicket made his eyes look even greener than they usually did. He had elf eyebrows, dark, with sharp downward angles at the outer ends. "She's not choking up like Uncle Tobias said she would if she wasn't using her powers. What's she doing?"

"You haven't been watching hard enough." I watched everything, particularly things I couldn't understand. I liked puzzles. "She's beautifying herself. She buys fashion magazines and studies them, then fixes her face different every day. She changes her eye and hair color too, but only a little, so Mama won't get on her case."

"Trust Opal to do something stupid with her gift!" said Jasper.

"You weren't talking like that last month," I said. Last month he kept walking into the pool against his will.

He gave me a look. I didn't talk back to him very often.

"I want to watch her do it," he said after a short silence that was supposed to teach me a lesson.

"All right." I liked spying on people. I figured I would be an anthropologist when I grew up; they were the biggest snoops I ever heard of. "How?"

As the oldest, Opal had the best room; the rest of us had smaller rooms, narrow and dark, at the west end of the house. Opal's room had big windows, but it was on the second story and not near enough a tree for us to climb up and see in.

It did have a glass door out to the widow's walk. Maybe we could hide outside on the widow's walk and watch through the door. But Mama's study was at the other end of the widow's walk, and she came out on it once in a while to center herself. Mama frowned on spying.

"Let's hide in Opal's closet," said Jasper.

"Right before she has a date is the best time," I said. At sixteen, Opal was dating more than I planned to in my entire life.

Jasper and I listened to Opal at supper that night. She told Daddy she was going out Friday from five to eleven. She used to ask his permission for things like that.

I decided I wouldn't let transition take me that way, stop doing what Daddy said just because he couldn't make me anymore. I would respect him after transition the way I did now, even though he had no wish power.

By four Friday afternoon, Jasper and I were in Opal's closet. He was mad when I told him we had to be there a whole hour before the date. "Trust me," I said. "She's going to take an hour." Luckily Opal had already laid the dress for the date across her bed. Luckily, Opal's closet was a huge walk-in; there was room for us and her clothes and shoes.

Opal's closet smelled like violet sachet. I found it stifling.

She came into the room about ten past four; by then, Jasper was already mad at me and pinching. I had to pinch him back to get his attention when Opal came in. He peered through the keyhole, which left me without much of a view. We had left the door open a crack. A sliver of light laid a stripe across Jasper and a finger on the edges of a couple of the dresses.

"Does she change her looks before or after she gets

dressed?" Jasper whispered. I leaned forward and saw the light from the keyhole shining in his opalescent eye.

"Let me look," I whispered. He frowned, but he moved. I watched Opal take off her school dress and slip into her date dress.

Then she sat at her mirror and picked up something from the vanity table.

"Oh!" I whispered. Something about her reflection—

"What's she doing?" Jasper elbowed me aside and peered out the keyhole again.

Opal had asked for a dressing table complete with lighted mirror last year, and even though Mama and Daddy never gave us big presents for Christmas, Opal got her dressing table. Maybe that was another part of growing up, but I would have asked for a ten-speed bike.

"Hey," Jasper said, almost talk instead of a whisper. He sat back on the shoes. I peeked through the keyhole.

I saw Opal's face in the mirror, and already it looked less like her. She had wider cheekbones and a bigger mouth. She lifted a magazine and looked at a picture in it, then leaned toward her mirror and ran a thick brush over her face. In the wake of the brushstroke, she changed back to the original Opal.

Jasper tugged at my shoulder then, so I backed away and he got the keyhole the rest of the time. Opal made one trip to the closet for shoes, but she didn't see us because the shoes were right in front of the door when it opened, and we weren't.

WHEN Opal left the room at ten minutes after five, Jasper and I looked at her special brush. "Hah," said Jasper, picking it up, "you think—?" He reached out and brushed my cheeks with it. They turned bright, slick red, like a doll's. "Trust that dumb Opal to put the power in a brush instead of keeping it inside herself." Jasper painted my nose . . . green.

"Jasper Elliot LaZelle, you stop that!" I yelled, and jumped him. I grabbed the brush before he could stop me. I brushed brown streaks all over his face.

We had quite a tussle after that. He ended up with curly spiral horns, and I got black lips and purple eyeshadow up to my eyebrows. I was trying to give Jasper an extra eye when the brush stopped working.

We broke apart, staring at each other and breathing hard. Like one person we got to our feet and looked in Opal's mirror.

"That dumb Opal," said Jasper, tugging at his horns. "She never has enough power to finish what she starts."

I rubbed my nose and cheeks, but the color was there to stay. I licked my lips. They remained black, even though they tasted normal. I wondered how long the effects would last. "What are we going to do?"

"Wait till she gets home, I guess," said Jasper. "We sure can't let Mama see us like this." His face was dark brown in places, and he had a painted-on pencil-line mustache.

"You really think Opal will help us after we used her brush without asking?" I couldn't imagine even goody-goody Opal being that nice.

"Maybe it's a short spell," said Jasper. "Opal never does things the hard way."

"But it has to last at least six hours," I said.

"Oh, yeah. She wouldn't want to fall apart on her date."

We giggled. "There goes her nose," said Jasper.

"Oops! Lost her hair."

"Where's that special smile?"

We were still laughing when I realized someone else was peering into the room. Luckily it was only Beryl. "What are you doing in Opal's room? And what the heck happened to your faces?" she demanded in an agonized whisper. "It's supper time!"

Mama believed in letting us settle our fights among ourselves. She told Daddy that was the way it worked in our family; it was traditional. I didn't think she would ignore this particular fight, though, since Jasper and I had broken a couple of important family rules—don't go in somebody else's room without asking, and don't mess with their things.

Jasper turned into his General self. "Beryl, we're going to sneak to Gypsum's room and stay there till this wears off. Tell Mama Gyp and I went to the Outpost for supper, and bring us food and maybe a deck of cards, okay? Or the Scrabble game, that'd be good."

"But—what happened to you?"

"We found out where Opal keeps some of her power," said Jasper. "Check and see if the coast is clear."

With Beryl for a lookout, we got to my room with no trouble. What to do there was the problem.

It was a difficult evening. Jasper was restless, but he didn't want to chance Flint catching us; Jasper and Flint were having one of those long, drawn-out fights where they actually got nasty, which sometimes included tattling, even though Mama punished the tale-teller as well as the person ratted on. So he stayed in my room and pestered me, instead of sneaking off to his own room, which was next door to Flint's. We spied and saw Flint go to his room right after supper. We hoped he was wearing headphones and listening to music.

Beryl said Mama and Daddy weren't happy that we had gone off without telling them about it. As the night wore on, Beryl came upstairs during the ads on TV and told us the parents were getting madder and madder. We were supposed to call in advance if we had alternate supper plans.

Opal came home a little past eleven. Jasper and I had the bedroom door open to hear what was going on downstairs. Daddy scolded Opal for being late, mostly because he was mad at me and Jasper, but Opal wasn't in any mood for criticism. She stomped up to her room and let out a shriek after she had been in there long enough to try her beauty brush.

By that time Jasper and I were in *my* closet, a much tighter fit than Opal's.

"What if she can't take off her face-lift without the brush?" I whispered. "Maybe we'll never get rid of these faces!"

"They'll wear off," Jasper whispered back. "It's Opal, remember? Besides, I think permanent, lasting change feels different. You didn't feel changed all the way through when I painted you, did you?"

"No. Just surface. Barely that." But what if I had to go to school Monday morning with red cheeks, a green nose, purple eyelids, and black lips?

I'd have to stay home sick. For as long as it took.

It was hot in my closet and Jasper and I were both sweating, but we didn't dare venture out until we changed back to ourselves.

"Jasper," I whispered presently, "are you going to get all weird when you go through transition?"

"Hah!" he said. "When I go through transition, things are going to change, you bet. I'm not going to put my power in anything but me, for one thing. For another thing, Opal will never be able to get me again. I'm not going to blow my power on anything stupid like makeup. I'm going to do real stuff with it, mage stuff like figuring out how water runs or where the top of the sky is. And I'll practice turning people into things. What would you like to be?"

I thought. "A cat. You better not do anything much to me, 'cause I'll transition right behind you." I said that, and then I shivered even though I wasn't cold.

What if I wasn't right behind him?

What if transition killed me?

What if transition killed Jasper? That would be worse.

Things stayed tense in the closet for the next hour, but around midnight I touched Jasper's forehead and felt that his horns had gone. We opened the door and let light in, saw that our faces had reverted to normal.

Getting free of that spell was like getting out of prison. I felt such a lift in my heart, I didn't even care Saturday morning when Daddy sentenced me and Jasper to eight hours of extra chores for going out without telling and staying out past curfew.

IF Opal had been her old self, she probably would have gone to Daddy and told him that someone had been in her room disturbing her things, and he would have gotten her justice.

But this was post-transition Opal.

Our lessons with Uncle Tobias had gotten more interesting since Opal transitioned, because she could demonstrate what he was teaching us, and we could think about what it would be like when we got our own powers. Tobias had always been able to demonstrate what he taught, but that wasn't the same as having one of *us* show us.

The Saturday morning after Jasper and I had our date with Opal's beauty brush, all five of us met in Uncle Tobias's tower schoolroom as usual, around a wooden table covered with black velvet. I had my notebook. I was the only one who took notes during Uncle Tobias's lectures. Flint had a string he was practicing Jacob's ladders on. Uncle Tobias let him do it, because it stopped Flint from shaking his legs or tapping on the table or doing some other distracting thing to shed extra energy. Jasper slumped in his seat, arms across his chest. Beryl put her elbows on the table and propped her chin in her hands, staring at Uncle Tobias. Opal took her place beside Uncle Tobias, ready to try anything. Today she was frowning.

Uncle Tobias showed us a special mirror. It had a small scuffed reflecting surface surrounded by worn silver ivy vines, and the handle was a tarnished twist of vines and leaves. "You can see into the future and the past and hidden places if you look into this mirror and channel your power just right and speak a rhyme to help you focus the energies. An easy rhyme is, 'Staring in the mirror, I see/The past looking back at me,' or '. . . future looking back at me.'

"It doesn't get you a picture of the distant past or future," he continued. "It's not a powerful spell. But it can be interesting."

Opal channeled power, then spoke the words to see the past. She held up the mirror and aimed it over her shoulder so she could look at each of us in turn.

"Jasper and Gypsum," she said. "You're the ones who played with my change brush and stole all its power!"

Oh, man!

"Daddy said you guys were out all evening! How can this be?" She spoke the rhyme again and studied Jasper's and my reflections. "Well, of course you were out, with faces like that," she muttered. She stared into the mirror at us for what seemed like way too long. I met her gaze and saw an Opal I had never seen before. She looked furious but remote. Something cold lodged in my chest.

She put the mirror down and turned to stare at us. "I can see the future without the mirror." She smiled.

"How come you put your power in something outside yourself, anyway?" Jasper asked. "Seems stupid."

"Opal?" Tobias said. "What have you been up to? Using objects as power reservoirs is advanced work. I haven't laid the groundwork for that yet. You could hurt someone."

Opal raised her hands, rubbed her thumbs back and forth across her fingertips, then opened her hands so her palms faced up. Thin smoky light came down in two cones from the dark ceiling, twisted into tight zig-zaggy strands and dove into her fingertips. She smiled this spooky smile that made her look like someone in the kind of movies that gave me nightmares.

"It worked just fine until those two messed me up, Uncle." Lightning danced across her fingertips and made little zissing noises. She closed her hands into fists and the light stopped spinning down to her.

"This will be a simple spell." She held her hands out toward me and Jasper, snapped her fingers out in two fans. I felt something jolt into me. My face got blister hot and my nose and chin hurt and made creaking noises. I looked at Jasper through a haze of tears. His face was red, and it pulsed. Then it shifted. His forehead bulged, and his nose melted down to nothing. His eyes changed from green to solid black, and his hair and eyebrows melted away.

After a minute things stopped happening to my face. I saw parts of it I had never been able to see before. My nose and chin stuck out like the upper and lower parts of a duck's beak, and they looked brown and warty and hideous. Jasper looked all flat-faced and big-eyed like the big-headed aliens I saw on the covers of newspapers at the supermarket.

My face ached. I touched my nose. It was sore and soft. My chin felt bony, but it hurt, too.

Opal lifted the mirror and aimed it toward me, and a gnome woman looked back, brown and wrinkled, her eyes like small black beads, her eyebrows bushy, her hair gray and wispy. Opal showed Jasper how he looked. "Don't you ever mess with my stuff again," she said. "Or I'll do worse to you." She set the mirror face down on the table.

"You're going to regret this," Jasper said. His voice came out squeaky. I couldn't believe he would threaten her right after she'd done this to us. It seemed suicidal.

Besides, how could he be sure?

Opal lifted an eyebrow and smiled at him. "Or I could do worse to you right now," she said.

"Opal, that's enough," said Uncle Tobias.

She frowned. Then she stood, dusted off her hands, and stalked out of the room.

I glanced at Beryl. She looked scared. Flint looked unnerved too.

"Can you breathe all right?" Uncle Tobias asked us.

I was afraid to speak. I breathed through my nose. I noticed I could smell a lot more than I usually did. Uncle Tobias's tower room always smelled incensey and smoky and strange, but now I could tell there were spices under the smoke, cinnamon and amber and paprika, and somewhere a trace of beer, and the presence of a cat. I could smell Flint's grass stains and Beryl's baby shampoo and Jasper's sweat left on his shirt from yesterday. I could smell Uncle Tobias's years: he was much older than he looked.

"Gypsum?" he said as I sat there sniffing decades and sorting the nuances of different ages of skin. "Can you breathe?"

I wasn't yawning, and I felt okay, except my face hurt. I nodded.

"Jasper?"

"I can breathe," Jasper said. His voice sounded high and metallic. He touched his face gingerly, then stroked his fingers across his cheeks, his non-nose, his forehead. He frowned, and only his mouth moved. "Jeeze! I never knew she had it in her." He reached out and touched the end of my new nose. "Gosh." He looked at Uncle Tobias. "How long is this going to last?"

"Until she relents, I suppose," said Uncle Tobias.

"It's not going to just wear off like most of her spells?"

"It wasn't that sort of spell," said Uncle Tobias. "It would behoove you to treat her a little better."

"There's nothing you can do about it?"

Uncle Tobias cocked his head. "I wouldn't say that. But this is part of the self-sorting any family goes through. It would be against the rules for me to interfere."

"We can't go to school like this."

"School is two days away," said Uncle Tobias.

"We can't leave the house like this," Jasper said.

Uncle Tobias nodded. "Probably better if you don't."

I picked up the mirror and looked at myself. My face was a mass of wrinkles and warts and outthrust features. I really did look like something you'd find under a mushroom in an unpleasant forest. But only my head had changed; the skin on the backs of my hands was still smooth and unwrinkled. "Uncle," I said, and my voice came out deep and hoarse, "can you look in the mirror for me and see if I get my face back sometime soon?"

"That much I can do." He channeled power and repeated the spell he had taught us, then aimed the mirror over his shoulder and studied my reflection in it. "I see you back to normal and cleaning Opal's room," he said, "and ironing her dresses."

I sighed. I hated ironing. None of my clothes needed it. Opal hated ironing, too, but that never stopped her from buying things that needed ironing. What counted with her was how things looked.

"What do you see when you look at me, Uncle?" asked Jasper.

Uncle Tobias aimed the mirror to pick up Jasper's image. He set the mirror down and turned to look at Jasper. "How do you feel, boy?"

"How do I feel? Hot."

"Yes," said Uncle Tobias.

"And cold," said Jasper. Sweat beaded on his alien forehead and ran down the shallow slopes of his face.


WHILE Jasper went through the first stages of transition, I apologized to Opal and did chores for her, and she gave me back my face. She gave Jasper back his face even though he didn't do her any favors, because he was sick.

I spent the next three days taking care of Jasper, tipping

water into his mouth whenever he would let me, sponging off his forehead when he got too hot, piling covers on him when he got too cold. Transition hit him a lot harder than it had hit Opal. He shivered so much he lost weight, and he was out of his head all the time. He yelled and thrashed and fought with invisible things.

Even Mama was worried.

There was a time near the end of the third day when I got under the covers with him and hugged him hard because his skin was icy and I didn't know how else to warm him up. "Don't die, don't die, don't die," I whispered to him. I rubbed his arms and his chest and tried to stop his shivering. I knew I should call down to Mama, but I didn't even want to walk to the bedroom door. I was afraid if I let go of Jasper his spirit would escape his body. I hugged him and chafed his skin and cried and wished somebody, anybody, would come and help me. "Stay here. Stay here. Stay here," I whispered to Jasper.

When my throat was sore from talking to him and my arms were so tired and heavy I wasn't sure how much longer I could go on, Jasper hugged me. "It's okay," he whispered. I touched his forehead. It wasn't too hot or too cold. It was wet with sweat.

I fell asleep smiling.


WHEN I woke up Jasper was sitting up among the snarled, sweat-soaked blankets and shoveling hot Cream of Wheat into his mouth. "Want some?"

I shook my head.

"You should eat, Gyp. You haven't been getting enough food or sleep."

I rubbed my hand across my face. My skin felt greasy. "Are you okay?"

"Yeah. Starved is all." The cereal he was eating was

steaming, but that didn't seem to bother him. He swallowed without chewing.

"Did the power come on you?"

He smiled down at me. "Oh, yes. Oh, yes." He put the spoon down and drank the rest of the hot cereal, set the bowl aside and wiped his mouth with the back of his hand. "I need a shower, and then I need lots more breakfast. You want to sleep some more?"

I checked in. Every muscle in my body felt stretched and tired. I nodded.

He smiled again and touched my forehead; I fell into a deep comfortable sleep.


JASPER and I sat in the bamboo thicket a couple days later. The sun pounded down on the yard, but the bamboo shade was cool, even though no breath of breeze moved through the canes.

Jasper had had three accidents already—power surges that once shut off the electricity in the house for two hours, once did unfortunate things to most of the food—popped popcorn, melted butter, burned bread, cooked eggs in their shells, baked apples in the fruit bowl, exploded milk and juice cartons all over the inside of the fridge—and once made all the paint in his room blister and peel off the wall in long twisted strips.

Flint and Beryl were afraid to be near him. Flint moved out of the kids' wing to sleep on a couch in the living room. Mama and Opal and Tobias could channel power surges, so they weren't scared of him, just irritated. Daddy was on a business trip.

A power surge could really hurt me, but I didn't care.

Jasper had tried to make me stay away from him. I wouldn't. Now he was holding a green stone I had found at the beach that morning. He stared at it. He murmured a chant Uncle Tobias had taught him. I huddled on the papery white leaves, hugged my knees, and watched my brother speak to a stone in a language I did not know.

"Keep this." He held the stone out to me.

"Why?"

"It's got power in it. I know I said I wasn't going to do that, but you need this. It should protect you from power—mine, or Opal's, or anybody's."

I took the stone. It felt warm in my hand. I looked up at my brother. "I thought your transition was going to change everything for the better."

"I feel a lot different."

"What does that mean?"

He stared over my shoulder, leaf-green light touching his eyes. "I don't know. I just—I can't imagine hiding in a closet to spy on Opal. I can't believe I did that just last week. There are so many more interesting things to do."

"Mage things?" I whispered.

He nodded.

"Things I can't do."

He licked his upper lip, then nodded again. He looked beyond me. "Everything's singing, Gyp. I couldn't hear it before, but now I can. There are voices everywhere. I have to learn their languages."

A minute went by before he met my gaze again. No wonder he had looked so distracted since transition.

I said, "Can you do a predicter mystery for me?"

"Which one?"

I set down the rock he had given me. I opened my backpack and pulled out a watch and a little zipped-shut bag of flower petal dust. This was something Uncle Tobias had taught us last fall. "Tell me. . . ."

"What, Gyp?"

"Tell me when I'll transition. I don't like being on the other side of a wall from you."

"You really want to know?"

I thought about that. Tobias had told us to be careful

of questions. Some would offer us answers that hurt. I felt a chill brush the back of my neck. Then I thought, *Opal's sixteen, Jasper's fourteen, I'm twelve. Will my transition be soon? Will it be this year? Or will it be four years before I know what Jasper and Opal know now? If I have some idea of when I'll transition, I can plan. Or at least I can stand it.*

*What if I don't survive? Do I want to know?*

*If I don't survive, I should know so I can do what I need to first.*

"I want to know," I said.

Jasper took the spell ingredients from me and prepared them, then said the chant that would give us an answer. He tossed the flower dust up and watched it float down. I watched too.

When Uncle Tobias had demonstrated Image in the Air, I had seen a picture of Mama as a young girl, which was what Uncle Tobias had asked about.

This time I just saw flower dust drifting, swirling down. Maybe only Jasper could see the picture. I looked at him.

"No," he whispered, shaking his head.

"No what?"

He hesitated. "No transition."

"What?" I felt like someone had punched me in the gut.

The dust settled. Jasper looked away. "I could be wrong. I haven't tried this before. Maybe it's not one of my gifts."

"What did you see?" I whispered.

"Nothing."

"What did you see?"

He shook his head.

"What did you see?" I asked him a third time.

"I just saw you, older, but without any magic, Gyp. You. Just you."

Some people never went through transition. People in our family always married outsiders. Sometimes outsider genes stopped children from having a magical heritage. I had never imagined it could happen to any of *us*.

"Hey," Jasper said. "I don't know what I'm doing. I probably did it wrong."

I felt cold despite the hot still air of the afternoon. I hugged myself and shivered.

Since transition, Opal had changed into someone I didn't know and wasn't sure I liked.

Jasper had changed into someone I didn't connect with the same way I used to.

I wasn't going to change.

The future stretched ahead of me like a dark corridor I would walk all alone. All those notes I had taken while Uncle Tobias was teaching us . . . I might as well burn them. There was no skill inside me. My family was no longer my family. Cold welled up in my stomach and my chest, traveled outward to my toes and fingers.

"Stop it, Gyp." Jasper picked up the green stone, grabbed my hand, and closed my fingers around the stone. "Hang on. Hang on."

The stone was warm. I pressed it to my breastbone and felt its warmth wash through me.

"See? You *can* do magic."

I remembered working Opal's beauty brush, painting horns onto Jasper's forehead. No problem there. If somebody gave me an object with magic in it, I could work it.

"Come to me whenever the stone needs a charge," Jasper said. "I'll take care of you. Nobody needs to know."

"Not even Uncle Tobias?"

"You don't have to tell him. Let's pretend we never did Image in the Air, okay? Let's pretend you never asked the question." He patted my shoulder.

I could pretend, but I couldn't deny that everything had changed. Jasper had never patted my shoulder before. He felt sorry for me now.

I couldn't wish away the answer to my question.

I felt the warmth that came from the green stone, and

thought, *Well, all right. If pretending is what it takes, I'll be the best pretender ever.*

"I don't know my range, anyway. Maybe I didn't look far enough ahead," Jasper said. "Maybe you transition later."

*How old did I look?* I wanted to ask. Then I thought, *Better if I don't know.* I had heard of late transitions, but they were even more dangerous than normal ones.

I touched my forehead with the green rock. Warm as sunlight. I looked at Jasper, and noticed that his nose looked a lot like Flint's nose, like my nose. Opal's beauty brush could stroke away any resemblance we had on the surface, but Jasper and I had been together in her closet, together in my closet, together in the bamboo thicket a week ago, a year ago, three years ago. A thousand thousand memories connected us. Whatever else happened, nothing could change that.

I slipped the green stone into my pocket. "Let's go run through the sprinklers."

Jasper smiled. "All right."

*Two*

THE summer I was sixteen, Dad took my brothers and sisters on a trip ninety miles south to Disñeyland and Universal Studios. Uncle Tobias and Aunt Hermina also left on trips, though in different directions. It didn't dawn on me until later how sinister this was.

After everybody left, I wondered if the whole everyone-goes-on-a-trip-but-Mama-and-Gyp hadn't been Mama's idea. Why weren't we on that trip, too? We did family things together every summer, so what was different this year? She'd probably used persuasion, one of her best skills, to get everyone else to leave and me to stay.

It had been a while since anybody had cast something scary at me. I'd stopped carrying the protection stone Jasper had made me.

Flint had transitioned the year after Jasper, and before I remembered I had the stone, he erupted at me—by mistake—and I ended up with my first broken bone. I was laid up in the hospital for a while, and I got to use crutches and have people sign my cast, and then a couple months later I had to learn how to get both legs to work together again. Flint felt really guilty about the accident; he left me alone until I recovered. Then he really went after me, maybe to get back at me for all the times I had beat him up. The stone came in handy at that point, when I remembered to carry it, and remembered to get Jasper to charge it.

Dad played power chess with Flint to teach him what it was like to be outclassed completely and lose at something, and eventually Flint got the message and backed off on torturing me.

Beryl transitioned the next year, after Opal moved to Hollywood to find work in the movie industry. By that time Beryl and I were pretty good friends, so I had never carried the stone around to protect me from Beryl.

I had to do a lot of mental maneuvering so I didn't spend all my time and energy getting mad at my siblings for being themselves. In time, my mind became well-trained and agile. It shied away from negative thoughts and impulses. I used a lot of mental whitewash. I believed I was perfectly happy.

Nobody talked about the fact that everybody had gone through transition but me. Historically, there were late transits—Cousin Raychel hadn't gone through the sickness until she was nineteen, and then it was touch and go, but she made it, and afterward she was one of the more powerful people in the family. Maybe everyone thought a late transition would happen to me. I wavered between hope and despair, with despair often outweighing the hope. After all, I had Jasper's prediction to depress me. Every once in a while, though, like on Christmas Eve or the night before my birthday, I got all worked up and imagined: *Maybe it will happen tomorrow.*

I hadn't asked Jasper to charge the stone with protection for me in about a year. My siblings cast prank spells on me sometimes, do-my-work-for-me spells sometimes, and sometimes favor spells if I asked for them, like spells to help me study for a test without getting distracted by TV, or a spell that guaranteed me good hair on school picture day.

I was completely unprepared for Mama's spell.

I didn't even know Mama had spelled me at first. I woke up like I did every summer morning and went down to the kitchen to put together breakfast. Breakfast was my favorite meal of the day. You couldn't have too much bacon, in my opinion. Fried eggs were okay if you put paprika and maybe garlic powder on them, and toast was a great excuse to eat butter and jam, or better yet, peach preserves. On the other hand, a nice layer of melted butter on warm toast could be doused in brown sugar, which would melt into a deep brown frosting, or you could spread a sweet spicy mixture of white sugar and cinnamon into the butter. Yum!

So why did I take out skim milk and a box of Fiber Plus cereal? Why was I measuring a cup of cereal and a half-cup of milk into a bowl? What was this measly amount of food I didn't even like doing in front of me at the table?

I tried to get up and grab a jar of raspberry jam, but my body wouldn't cooperate. Instead I found myself eating bits of pulverized plywood wetted with thin white liquid. I finished the whole thing, small as it was, then washed my bowl and spoon and the measuring cup and left the kitchen.

My stomach cried aloud, "My god, why hast thou forsaken me?"

Well, maybe not in those words.

All the luscious things in the kitchen, bananas, cupcakes, ice cream, the candy jar, the cookie jar, last night's leftover lasagna in the fridge, they all whined behind me, saying I was neglecting them. Yet I left the kitchen.

What was wrong with me?

Maybe if I could just get away from the house . . . I

still had some allowance left. I could go buy Hostess Cupcakes at the liquor store down on the Old Coast Highway. Or head up to the village, where we had a charge account at the market, and stock up on all kinds of stuff.

My body had other ideas. I went up to my room and changed into my bathing suit, then went outside and jumped into the pool.

I never jump into the pool. I believe that such a move can be deleterious to the health. Getting into a pool takes time. One toe at a time, specifically. Okay, then you have to go down a whole step. Then another. Then another. Once you're standing on the bottom and your suit is wet up to the waist, you can take ages edging along toward the deeper water, until your body has time to get used to the water decently.

That summer I had an awful black-and-yellow suit Mama had helped me buy. The suit didn't have any of those features that helped disguise how fat a girl was, like a little skirt to hide the upper thighs, or extra material to disguise one's width. It was a tank suit that showed every bulge. Mama had even tried to get me to buy a bikini. Insane! That had made me suspicious, too. My mother was a total fashion plate. She always looked great. I should have suspected something was up when she made me look terrible.

The result of having an ugly swimsuit was that I hadn't gone swimming so far that summer unless nobody else was home. And the beach? Forget about it.

The only saving grace about this situation was that no one was around to see me.

I plunged into the pool. My skin screamed in horror at its coldness, and then I found myself swimming from one end of the pool to the other.

Those Y-camp swim lessons I'd had when I was twelve were finally coming in handy. I guessed I could do the freestyle and the backstroke and the breaststroke, after all.

I sure did them that morning. I swam until my sides heaved and my muscles ached, back and forth, back and forth as the sun crept up the sky behind the house and the passion flowers on the poolyard fence opened.

I woke up at the bottom of the pool, trying to breathe water. I lunged up, coughing, and dragged myself out of the water to collapse on one of the chaise longues on the pool's cobbled rim. My chest heaved. My arms and legs felt as though they had been beaten with sticks, and my stomach gnawed on itself, I was so hungry. I coughed my throat raw. Everything hurt so much I doubted I could crawl to the house and ask someone to help me. Who was even home?

A vision of loveliness drifted into focus above me.

"Gyp! What's the matter, honey?"

"I don't know," I whispered hoarsely.

Mama, warm and jasmine-smelling, sat beside me on the chaise and felt my forehead. "What happened?"

"I don't know," I whispered. "I swam and swam until I started to drown. I don't know what's wrong with me."

"A little too much oomph," she muttered, and tapped signs with hot fingertips on my forehead. I felt something tight inside me loosen a little.

"What are you doing?" I rasped.

"It's for your own good, honey." She smiled and stroked her hand across my short dark hair. "You know I worry about your weight. It's holding you back, sweetie. How can you enjoy your womanhood if you're hauling around all that fat? I thought it was time for you to get a taste of another way of life."

I groaned. She'd been on my case to go on a diet ever since I was twelve. When she got too pushy, I complained to Dad, and he told Mama to back off. Dad said I was perfect just the way I was.

Dad wasn't witchy, the way people in Mama's family were, but Mama listened to him anyway.

Which was probably why he wasn't here now.

"Don't do this," I whispered to my mother.

"Oh, honey." She patted my cheek. "Just try it. You'll like it."

BUT of course I didn't like it. For lunch I looked longingly at sliced ham, cheddar cheese, sourdough bread, pickles, mayonnaise, Twinkies, potato chips. My hands made me a sprouts-and-olives sandwich, piled carrots on my plate, and added an apple. Dinner was a giant salad. In between lunch and dinner I powerwalked all through the village without stopping to look at anything.

I had a couple of hours of down time, but every time I picked up a book—which was what I liked to do during the summer, curl up on the porch swing with a cool drink and a hot book and read—I put it down again before I could finish a page, got up, and ran up and down the stairs for fifteen minutes. I was sweaty and exhausted, my stomach churning, after every one of these incidents. I learned not to touch books.

Mama had left in the afternoon to go to the TV station, where she was a special reporter who covered social events and local arts news—she knew everybody important in town, and they all liked her and told her things they wouldn't tell anybody else; it was part of her gift, and made her invaluable—so I had dinner alone.

When Mama got home around eight, I was waiting. "Stop it, Mama. Please. Stop it. This is torture."

"It's hard the first day. It'll get easier, honey."

I wished she wouldn't call me honey. I couldn't even look at the honey pot. "The first day? How long is this supposed to last?"

She smiled, though her eyes looked sad. "Just a week. After that, we'll see."

"Mama." I rubbed my eyes. I didn't think I could take another day of this.

A tear streaked down her cheek. "This hurts me more than it does you."

"I doubt it."

She brushed past me and went to the kitchen.

I headed upstairs. I took a shower, contemplating the week ahead, then tried not to think about it. I went to my room, tired enough to sleep at eight-thirty in the evening. I lay down, pulled up the covers, and opened the fantasy novel I was reading.

I found myself running up and down the stairs. Mama came out of the kitchen, and I yelled at her. No words, just thumping shrieks as I pounded up and down the stairs. She ran away again.

I tried fighting the compulsions, but nothing stopped them. Mama was the best witch I knew. She could craft seamless, inescapable spells in her sleep. I had no hint of power to fight them.

The second night, while Mama was at work, I called Dad's hotel in Anaheim. The family was all out. I left voicemail begging him to call me back, then waited all evening for the phone to ring.

I called every afternoon as soon as Mama left for work. The family was never at the hotel, and they never called back.

On the sixth day of salads, fruit, fiber, and skim milk, I powerwalked past my friend Claire's house, a couple blocks from mine. It was the third time I'd circled her block. I couldn't go up to the front door; on these walks, which lasted until I was almost too tired to crawl home but not quite, I seemed confined to the sidewalk, no daw-dling, no going up anybody's driveway; but at least I could choose my direction.

Claire came out of her house. That day her short curly hair was magenta with black streaks. "Hey, Gyp!" she called.

I walked past. "Hey, Claire," I yelled over my shoulder.

"Stop!" she cried.

"Can't." I walked on and turned a corner, then went around her block again, hoping she'd still be in the yard when I passed the next time.

"What's the matter?" she asked as I cruised past.

"I can't stop."

She opened the gate and caught up with me. "Are you on some kind of program?"

I reached for her hand. If only I could cling to something and make myself stop!

We had never held hands before, so for a second she didn't get it, but finally she put her hand in mine. I tried to stop, but even Claire's touch didn't free me. I tugged her forward with me. "Slow down, will you?" she asked.

"I'm sorry, Claire. I can't slow down." Tears gushed out of my eyes. "I'll let go if you want me to."

"What is it, Gyp? What's wrong? You look sick."

"My mama—I—" Of course Mama would put a "protect secrets" component into the spell; she was thorough that way. No matter how much I wanted to tell Claire everything, I wouldn't be able to.

Claire and I had met three years earlier on the school bus, a couple weeks after she and her mom and little brother moved to our neighborhood. She was slender and pretty and a little punky. I was just starting to gain weight.

We didn't know why, but something pulled us together. By the end of the first day of school we had given each other friendship bracelets and were looking forward to spending eighth grade together.

The weird thing was that Claire's mom, July, was trying to teach herself how to be a witch. She wasn't secretive about it. She wasn't like any witch I'd ever met in our family, but she was a witch of sorts.

I had never told Claire about my family.

Now I physically couldn't.

"I can't tell you," I said.

We marched up the block toward Hennings Park.

"What do you want me to do?" she asked.

I shook my head. I wanted her to save me. How could she save me? I wanted her to know what was happening, but I couldn't tell her.

"Gyp, you're hurting my hand."

"I'm sorry." I let go of her. "Claire . . ."

"Your mom did something to you?"

My throat closed up. I couldn't breathe. I tried to gasp air in, but there was no passage.

I kept walking, and then the sky went dark.

I woke up a little later flat on my back on the sidewalk, Claire's face above me, her expression horrified and concerned. "Are you all right?" she asked.

I could breathe again. My clothes, hair, forehead were wet with sweat. My throat hurt. Muscles in my legs jumped and jerked even though I was trying to lie still.

"Don't move. I'll call an ambulance," she said.

"No." I gasped. "Don't." I reached for her hand, and she took mine.

"You don't look well, Gyp. You just fainted. Stumbled and fell right onto the sidewalk before I could catch you. Your head hit the ground. You might have broken something. I better get help."

"I'll be all right in a minute." Now that she mentioned it, the back of my head did ache, and some other things stung and burned. But it was so nice to be lying down.

I savored it for a couple more minutes, just lying there, the breeze cooling my sweaty face, Claire's hand in mine, my breath easing in and out of me. Then I sat up. One of my elbows was scraped, and the back of my head was pounding now. Apart from that and the now-constant cry of despair from my stomach, I felt all right.

I felt like I didn't have to powerwalk anymore. At least not this minute.

"I'm okay." I squeezed Claire's hand. "Thanks, Claire."

She shook her head. "You're sick, Gyp. You look terrible."

"I'm having kind of a bad week, but I feel better now."

"You stay here. I'll see if I can get Mom to come and drive you home."

I pulled myself to my feet. "It's only three blocks," I said. After all this powerwalking, three blocks seemed like nothing.

Claire frowned at me.

I took a couple of steps. My head pounded and my elbow burned, but the rest of me felt all right.

"I'll be okay," I said. I started walking. I strolled, in fact, at a leisurely pace I hadn't been able to use since Mama laid the spell on me. I felt happy just to be able to walk the way I wanted to.

Claire walked beside me. "What did your mom do to you?"

"Don't ask." What if I fainted again to prevent myself from answering a question?

"Gyp—"

"It's nothing."

"It is not either nothing! Do you want me to call the child protection agency, or whatever it is?"

"God, no!" I stared at her with wide eyes. "No! Absolutely not! It's nothing like that."

"Swear?"

I stopped and looked into Claire's eyes.

Okay, I was having maybe the worst week of my life. But was what Mama had done to me technically abuse?

Suppose some government official came to the house to help me? Mama had all kinds of spells. She could turn people into whatever she liked. She could mess up their minds so they wouldn't know which way was up. She could make them forget their own names.

Or, most likely, she would just talk to them, persuade them everything was fine, and they'd leave smiling, thrilled to have had a close encounter with Anise LaZelle, local TV celebrity.

And afterward, she might come after me. Without Dad or Uncle Tobias around to make her think twice, who knew what she'd do?

"I swear," I said. I shuddered.

"Call me if you change your mind."

"Sure."

Claire walked me all the way home, came inside and helped me put antibiotic and a bandage on my scrape. Mama had already left for work, and I was glad.

Claire called me as soon as she got home to make sure I was okay. I heard her mom July in the background, telling Claire to tell me I was welcome to come stay at their house if I wanted. So I knew Claire had told her mom something.

I thought the offer over for two seconds. But distance wouldn't break the spell. I would just act superweird in front of people who didn't know me well enough. "Thanks. I mean that. I'll let you know," I said.

For dinner that night I made a great big salad, looked at it, and put down my fork. I was hungry, but I couldn't face another bowl full of green stuff.

Later, I picked up a book by reflex, and found myself on the stairs again. Up, down, up, down.

I knew I had lost some weight during hell week; my pants were loose around my waist. I did feel a little stronger than I had before. Short distances that I had balked at walking last week seemed like nothing now.

I hated everything I had eaten since the spell started

except for the oranges, apples, and bananas. I was constantly hungry and tired. I hated this life.

Twenty-five minutes later, I stopped running up and down the stairs. Longer session than before; I guessed my endurance had grown.

The only time I had felt free of the spell was after I fainted.

I looked at the stairs. I breathed hard for a little while.

Then I ran up and down some more, under my own power. I ran even though I had a stitch in my side. I ran with breath heaving in and out of me, sweat dripping off me. I ran, though my legs felt like lead.

I ran past the end of my energy.

This time I melted down to the floor before I passed out. Blessed darkness wrapped around me.

I woke in the hospital. Mama sat by the bed. Shadows darkened the skin around her eyes. "What happened, honey? I put failsafes in the spell to protect you. This wasn't supposed to happen."

I closed my eyes. I didn't want to see her.

"Gyp," she whispered.

I waited. After a while, she went away.

WHEN I woke up the next morning, Dad was beside my bed. "Baby, what happened?"

"Why didn't you call back?"

"Call back?"

"I left you messages every night."

"I never got any messages. I talked to your mama every night, and she said everything was fine."

Of course. I only thought I was making those calls. My eyes got hot.

Dad sat on the bed, took my hand. "Gyp, what happened

to you? The doctor says you're malnourished and dehydrated and fatigued. How could that happen?"

"Mama," I whispered. Sobs started, and they wouldn't stop. Dad held me. After a long time, my crying slowed. "I can't go home, Daddy. I can't go home."

"What did she do to you?"

I told him about the diet and exercise spell. That was the first time I saw Dad in a white hot rage. He went away, closing the door very softly behind him.

Jasper dropped by in the middle of the afternoon. I didn't even want to talk to him about what had happened. He asked if he could spell me better, and I asked him please not to do that. I had had enough of people using power on me lately. He gripped my hand and left.

Later, Claire came to see me, and I asked if I could stay at her house, and she said sure.

I slept. I woke up after dark had fallen, and there was Mama, sitting by the bed again. I turned away from her as far as I could with that IV thing in my arm.

"Honey, I'm so sorry. You weren't supposed to get hurt. I thought I fixed it so that wouldn't happen."

I closed my eyes and thought myself down into a dark cave in the center of myself. Her voice kept making noise, but I didn't listen.

Hot fingertips touched my forehead. My eyes popped open. I had to stare into her face, even though I wanted to turn away again. "Talk to me," she said.

My voice tried to make a sound. Despair drowned me, and I let it choke the voice before it responded to Mama's command.

Dad spoke: "Stop it, Anise! I forbid you to spell Gyp again! Leave her alone!"

"But Miles, she won't speak to me," Mama said. Her fingers stroked over my forehead. I felt the compulsions seep away, and I could close my eyes again.

"That's right. Live with it," Dad said.

Live with it? I didn't know if I could live with what had happened. In my heart there was a broken place. In the image I had of family, there was a broken place.

In the fall, I went away to boarding school.

*Three*

GEORGE Fox High School was a small alternative-education Quaker boarding school on a farm in the foothills of the Sierra Nevadas, in Northern California near Reno, and I stayed there, even over the four-day holidays they had every month. Life was strange there; nobody was trying to be a witch. They were all more or less normal. After a while, I saw advantages to that. I even started to like it.

All the kids at Fox had work jobs that changed every term. I signed up for garbage detail first term, which was fun; we got to ride around in the school flatbed truck, collect garbage from all the cans around campus, and drive it to the dump, where stacks of strange and interesting discards from other peoples' lives swarmed with rats. Occasionally we picked up cool free stuff for our dorm rooms or cabins.

Next term, I switched to babysitting for teachers while they taught.

Then I signed up to work on dinner prep, and something about that job woke up a sleeping part of myself.

Making food for lots of people—after that horrible week when I couldn't even choose what to make for myself—excited me. I studied the school cook's talents and skills, and when she realized I was interested in more than just chopping vegetables and spoon-dropping cookies onto huge baking sheets, she taught me things.

Jasper and I wrote letters to each other. I wrote more often than he did, but his letters came with all kinds of surprises. I learned to sneak off into the hills to open them after a firebird flew out of one in the middle of the dining hall.

I went home for Christmas—Christmas was a big deal in our family, though not from the same traditions I saw at other people's homes—and kept my distance from Mama. She didn't spell me.

Summer was harder. My ideal summer had always been lazing around the house and reading, and now I was scared to do that, even though Mama said she'd leave me alone. I stuffed books into a backpack and ran off to Claire's house most of the time. Claire's mother had a beat-up La Z Boy on her porch that she called Gyp's chair because I spent so much time in it, and their cat Bavol gave me a lot of laptime. Claire and I went to the beach together, sometimes with Beryl, Flint, and Jasper. We went to the mall and the movies. I watched Claire test-drive boyfriends. She wasn't as good at it as Opal had been, but she knew how to tease. No boy ever looked twice at me unless I beat him at basketball. That was okay with me.

Dad and Jasper gave us both driving lessons.

Gradually I found a way to live at home and not be scared. I went to boarding school for three years, and each summer I spent at home felt better. Mama made an effort to accept me the way I was. It wasn't successful, but she stopped being obvious about all the things she hated about me.

So after I graduated from high school, I moved home.

\* \* \*

Two years later I was still living at home, working as an English tutor at the tutorial center at Santa Tekla City College. I hadn't figured out what I wanted to do with my life.

I wasn't following the usual path in my family, which was to go through transition and see where your gifts led you, then follow, if you could stand it. Opal's gift led to her being a makeup artist in movies and TV, with a growing reputation for greatness. Jasper's gift led him toward music, though it didn't lead him out of the house. Flint's gift confused the hell out of him, and Beryl kept hers quiet.

I asked Beryl about it once, on one of those nights when we made rootbeer floats and sat out on the high back porch, watching cars drive along the Old Coast Highway and Highway 101 below. "What am I going to be when I grow up?" she repeated. "I'm going to put off thinking about it as long as I can. I'm still technically a kid, Gyp. My only distinction so far is being the baby of the family. Gonna milk that for all it's worth."

When I talked to Dad about my future, he said I should take my time. People in his family were late bloomers. Wait. Try lots of different things. See what called me. So I went to City College and took lots of different classes. One of my English teachers told me they needed tutors at the Center, and since I wasn't doing anything else with my afternoons, I went over there and got a job.

I met all kinds of people. That was the great thing about a city college, my supervisor, Jorge Diaz, told me. Lots of adults came for continuing education along with all the kids who were getting their first two years of college out of the way in a less expensive venue than the University of California. I met men and women from other countries who had come here to make new lives, older people who wanted to learn something new, and a bunch of kids my age and younger, who weren't as fun to teach—not as motivated. I liked watching them tease each other, though. The Learning Center, the city college itself, they were both like boarding school: a place where I could teach myself by observation how to be a normal human being.

Every day I worked—I worked three days a week—I asked myself whether I wanted to make teaching my life's work. The answer wasn't clear to me yet. But at least I had something to talk to Dad about. He was a professor at UC Santa Tekla, and he taught me lots about how to communicate with students.

FLU was going through the college that winter, but I usually didn't get sick. We had basic family spells to guard against illness that covered everybody in the household. Every once in a while something slipped through, though.

One weekend in early December, the whole family planned to go to L.A. to see Opal, who was working on the makeup for a big-budget monster movie and thought she could get everybody in to meet the star, Gerard Shelley.

My family usually didn't get starstruck—we had a history of film work dating back to the teens, when the Ace of Hearts Studio shot westerns in the hills above Santa Tekla, and our grandparents were on the crew. Need special effects? Clever sets? Crafty costumes? Someone who could ride herd on a horde of extras without anyone complaining? Hire a LaZelle. We still had lots of relatives in L.A. working behind the scenes on all kinds of projects. We'd heard tons of stories about the stars and their clay feet; we didn't awe easily, secure as we were in our own talents.

Thing was, Opal said Gerry was really nice, besides being an actor we had all admired in the four or five years since he started landing leading roles.

But Friday, after I got home from work, when everybody

else was heading for the van, I went in the bathroom and threw up.

Beryl knocked on the bathroom door. "Aren't you ready yet? Mama's getting snippy."

I swished water in my mouth to get rid of the bile taste. "I'm sick, Bere."

She came in. "Sick sick?" She'd been sick that week, too, but not like this, though she'd missed a big history final. Somebody had muffed a health-protect spell.

I leaned on the sink, still holding the cup with some water in it, and measured how I felt. I thought about the pita pocket I'd had for lunch, and lurched back to the toilet so I could throw up again.

"Uh-oh," said my little sister. She reached for my forehead.

"Don't touch me. It's probably the flu. It's a twenty-four hour bug. Everybody else at the Center already got it. I've heard all the advice: lie in bed. Sleep lots. Drink 7-Up and lots of water when you can keep liquids down. Rest. Aspirin if there's a fever."

"I'll go tell Mama I'm staying home with you."

"It's nothing, it's just the flu. You feel bad for a little while and throw up and then it's over. Go on. I'll be okay."

"But Gyp—"

"Beryl?" Mama called from below.

Beryl shook her hands, then ran out. I heard her footsteps cross the sitting room, then run down the hallway to the top of the stairs. She explained things to Mama. While she was doing that, I threw up one more time, and started feeling better right away. I washed my mouth out again and brushed my teeth. I gave the toilet a quick scrub, washed my hands, then headed back to my bedroom. Flannel nightgown, that was the ticket. Heap a couple extra blankets on the bed. The pillows looked like heaven. I lay down and wrapped up. My stomach felt sore.

A little while later, Mama came up to see me, even

though she was terrible in the sickroom. She was wearing a shield; I saw glints around her edges, and I was glad. If she caught anything from me she would be upset, and when Mama got upset everybody felt it.

"Will you really be all right?" she asked.

"It's mild," I said. "Everybody else already had it. I'll be fine by tomorrow."

She went to the bedside table. "Here's my cell phone number." She wrote it in my dream journal. She went out in the hall and got the upstairs phone, brought it in and set it on the table. Next she brought in a pitcher of water and a glass. "This pitcher will refill itself." Then two two-liter bottles of 7-Up. "I put a spell on these so they'll stay nice and cold, okay, honey?" She set a big box of saltines there too. "I wouldn't let your father come up. I don't want him catching this. But he asked if you want him to stay home with you."

"No, no," I said. "Go on."

"Call if you need help. One of us will manage to get to you." Instant travel was taxing but possible for Uncle Tobias and Mama, and easy but unreliable for Flint. Jasper had trouble with it.

"I will," I said.

She blew me a kiss. It marked my cheek with warmth. "We really have to go, you know. What if Opal's in love with this Gerry guy? We have to find out whether he'll make a good addition to the family."

"Go," I said.

"We'll be back tomorrow afternoon," she said.

The plan was to stay with Opal all weekend, only coming home late Sunday night. We didn't get down to L.A. very often, even though it was so close. Besides seeing Opal and meeting Gerry, the family had plans: the Huntington Museum; the Getty; Beverly Center. . . .

"I'll be fine. Don't change your plans on my account."

If they skipped everything to rush home and I wasn't even sick, people would be mad at me.

For a second she looked anxious. Then she formed a spell in the palm of her hand and tossed it over my bed. I pulled the covers up to my chin. "It's just a little guardian spell," she said as I stared up into the blank air. "Something to give you strength if you need it." Her voice sounded hurt.

"Thanks, Mama." I closed my eyes and curled up tight under my blankets.

When I opened my eyes again it was much later. The room was dark. My blankets were wet through with sweat, and I felt worse than I ever had in my life.

I fumbled for the phone, knocked my dream journal off the table, couldn't seem to reach my aching arm high enough to turn on the light. When I lifted the phone's handset, the buttons lit up. I dialed Claire's old number; I knew that by heart.

July answered. Of course, July answered; Claire had moved into her own apartment a year earlier.

"Help," I croaked.

Later, a light was on. July's warm, swarthy face, her wide gray-green eyes, short pepper-and-salt hair hovered above me. "Hey, child. Hey." She washed my face with a warm wet cloth. My skin was burning, but that soothed it. My stomach twisted and burned. My throat was swollen and hot.

"Thanks," I whispered to her.

She lifted my head, held the water glass to my lips so I could drink. "This going to stay down?"

I drank. I waited for my stomach's response. "Yes," I whispered. "Thanks. Thanks."

"Anytime, kiddo. How'd you end up so all alone?"

"Everybody went to L.A. I didn't think I'd get this sick."

"I talked to my friend the nurse. She said there's a flu going around, but yours is the worst case she's heard of.

You know you were running a temperature of one-oh-five?"

"Didn't know." The room wavered. All the colors slid toward red.

"Rest," she whispered, and I sank down grateful into darkness.

When I woke up again, I felt fine, and there was daylight beyond the curtains. July sprawled in a chair by my bed, her face tired and old in repose. I felt so grateful to her. I took a shower, got dressed, went downstairs and cooked a big breakfast. Was that right? I checked the clock after I'd made two ham and cheese omelettes with green onions and avocado in them. Noon. Hmm.

I set the breakfasts on a tray with cutlery and napkins, coffee in white ceramic mugs, cream and sugar in Mama's best crystal service. I took the whole thing upstairs.

The smell of coffee brought July awake. "Oh, man! Room service! Gyp's cooking. I love Gyp's cooking!" We ate our omelettes with our plates on our laps in my room. "Guess you're feeling better," she said after she had finished.

"Oh, yeah. Thank you so much for coming over."

"You're welcome, Daughter Too." She had been calling me that since I stayed with them after I was in the hospital. It was my secret name. She never said it in front of Claire, or her younger son Orion, only when we were alone.

This time I cried.

She put her arm around me and just listened.

It turned out that it was noon on Sunday—I'd been sick all day and all night Saturday. No wonder July was exhausted. I told her to go home and get some rest and I'd come over and make her a big dinner.

"No lie? You're feeling that much better?"

"Yeah. It's over."

"Call me if it's not. I'll hang out by the phone today."

But the sickness had gone. I cleaned up all the evidence.

I made July the most fantastic dinner in my repertoire, then went home and waited for my family.

They were happy. They liked Gerry, who had adjusted well to an onslaught of LaZelles, and had even endured Uncle Tobias's Polaroid habits with grace—I saw the pictures; the guy had actually done silly poses with various of us—true class. The family had had a great time in L.A. "How were you, Gyp?" Dad asked me.

"I was fine," I lied.

MONDAY I went back to work. It was finals week before Christmas Break, and the Learning Center was swamped with people who wanted help learning everything they should have studied all semester.

Tuesday I took finals of my own.

Wednesday night, after a shift that seemed twice as long as normal, I put down the headphones in the study carrel and glanced around the Learning Center.

When had the sun gone down? Why was the place empty and dark? Had everyone told me they were leaving?

Only two more days of finals week left, and not that many finals; most of the students who could had already left town for Christmas vacation, so the Center had been less busy than usual. Still, for it to be empty—

I remembered some signals from a couple of the other tutors. L.D. had tapped my shoulder and finger-waved when I looked up, and Esther had handed me a Twinkie, which she often did before she left for the night. She was the only person I knew who opened a package of Hostess and ate just one of the two treats inside. José had thumped the back of my head. He always did that, and I always hated it, which made him laugh.

I had been submerged in listening to a new learning tape, and I had lost track of everything else while I focused on how I was going to help two of my English-as-a-Second-Language students study.

Now I realized that half the lights were out, a signal to the students that it was time to leave the building before we closed for the night. Nobody else was around. Beyond the windows, the sky was dark.

I pushed my chair back. The scrape of chair feet on carpet sounded loud with all other sound gone except the hush of the air circulation system.

The hairs on the back of my neck prickled. My stomach lurched. It had been doing that since the flu attack last weekend.

I stood up, stretched, and grabbed my backpack. I shoved my notebook inside.

Something skreeked against a windowpane.

A jacaranda tree leaned close to the windows outside the computer commons, but this noise came from the front window.

I turned and saw the flash of a pale face against the darkness beyond the window.

Tension clutched my chest. I couldn't find my breath.

Why was someone staring in? What did they want?

The face vanished.

My heart stuttered into motion. I breathed again, but too fast.

I didn't know if it was a man or a woman. Was it someone normal, or a member of my family who could wish themselves here?

What if it was someone who wasn't normal? Lately there were rumors about a campus rapist. I didn't know anybody who had actually been attacked. But what if——?

I was alone in the center. The door probably wasn't even locked. We closed at eight, and maybe that was when everybody else left, but I was still here, and whoever left last was supposed to lock up.

But usually we left together. When there were six of us

walking down to the beach parking lot, which was pretty far away, I felt safe. Going down there alone after dark was not my idea of fun. Why hadn't I been paying attention?

I raced to the door and flipped the lock. Then I cruised through the center, checking to make sure I was actually alone. Once in a while someone hid under a desk or behind a shelf, and spent the night with books, study aids, computers, testing materials, tape players, school supplies, a couple drinking fountains, his and her bathrooms, telephones, and all kinds of administrative filing nobody but staff was supposed to see. Sometimes things were missing in the morning. A favorite target was the receptionist's cashbox. Last year someone had vandalized the center, trashed our tools and sprayed orange mottoes across some of the walls and cabinets. We couldn't understand it. All we did here was try to help people.

I didn't find anybody inside. I checked both rest rooms. Empty.

I went to the cloakroom and got my jacket, put it on. The center was heated, but I felt cold anyway. I used my password on the center computer to access the timeclock, and clocked out. It was late, almost nine. Later than I was supposed to be working; Phil Reece, the director, might cut my hours on the Friday shift to make up for it.

I wanted to get home, where I could cook something warm and fortifying.

I stopped at the door and leaned to peek out the side window.

Someone tall stood out there, across the quad, under one of the orange streetlights that lit the paths of the western campus. Light shone down on a dark head, black-clothed shoulders. The body looked broad, all the clothes dark in the Halloween light. The head tilted, and the face came out of shadows, a pale oval with two dark pits for eyes.

A chill zipped down my spine. I jerked back from the door.

What was he waiting for? Me? Why?

Nobody ever waited for me.

Maybe it was just an evening walker. The concrete campus paths were well lit, a destination for late night and early morning dog walkers and joggers who lived nearby and didn't want to fight traffic.

I peeked through the window again.

The figure still stood under the light, its face turned toward the door.

There was no back way out of here, not with the keys I had; a door led deeper into the building, on into the library proper, but we didn't have access to it. If I had had Beryl's talents, I could have sweet-talked the library door lock into opening for me; with Flint's gifts, I could have just slid sideways a little and come out somewhere else. If I were Opal, I could have made myself look seven feet tall and loaded with muscles; Jasper probably could have whistled something weird and made the lurker decide to leave, but I was me, Gypsum, the normal one, and I didn't know what to do.

Maybe it was just someone thinking hard about something. Maybe I should just walk out and head for my car, in that beach lot, four staircases and a quarter mile away. There would be people down by the beach. Maybe. The fog was coming in the way it did most winter evenings, and casual strollers had probably gone home, out of the cold wet night. The Pelican Bar & Grill down there should still be open. I could find people to lose myself among. If I got that far.

I ventured a third look out the window.

The figure had moved closer, halfway across the pink concrete quad.

I checked the door to make sure it was locked and retreated behind the divider that separated secretarial/receptionist services from the rest of the center. I ducked down behind one of the secretary desks, then peered over the top.

Silhouetted against the orange light, the figure pressed close to the window by the door.

I reached up and grabbed the phone, crouched down with it in my lap. I sat cradling the phone for a couple minutes. I could just walk out of here. Probably nothing would happen. Maybe it was one of my students who wanted to talk to me about something. Maybe it was some guy I had met in one of my art or writing classes who wanted my phone number, or something.

But how likely was that? Everybody liked me and nobody asked me out; story of my life. Except for Ian, a guy I'd met at one of Claire's parties—her apartment was so small that her parties maxed out at eight or ten people, and I never knew who I'd meet over there, but I had met Ian, and he was the only guy I'd met who had called me later—and I wasn't sure *what* Ian wanted. Somebody who could sing harmony was the closest I could figure.

Anyway, why couldn't whoever was out there ask me for my phone number in class, or during working hours?

Maybe it was somebody else.

I lifted the phone's handset and punched Line One. As soon as I heard the dial tone, I called home.

Beryl answered. "Hello?"

"Hi," I whispered.

"Is this an obscene call?" She sounded more interested than threatened. She had been coming up with creative answers to the problem of obscene calls, and she was always anxious to try a new one.

"No. It's Gyp."

"Why are you whispering?"

"I'm alone in the Learning Center, and I'm scared. There's someone outside."

She hesitated for a second, then said, "You want Jasper?"

Suddenly I wanted Jasper more than anyone else on Earth. "Is he home?"

"Yeah. Hang on." She thunked the phone down. I heard

her footsteps recede, and the murmur of the TV in the great hall, and Mama and Daddy speaking quietly to each other somewhere nearby. A picture of our house bloomed in my mind, home, yellow light, warmth that breathed up through iron scrollwork screens in the hardwood floor, scattered rugs, furniture old and new, so many comfortable places to sit and talk and eat and listen.

"Gyp?" Jasper's voice warmed me, too.

"I'm scared."

"Do you need me there right now or can you wait till I drive there?"

I hunched tighter. If he used power to transport himself here, he would be tired; even for Jasper, powerful as he was, the transport spell wasted way too much energy for casual use. "I don't know. I think I can wait. There's just this guy right outside. Staring in." I peeked over the top of the desk again. The window was empty now. "Wait," I whispered. "Maybe he's gone."

"Go check."

"Don't," said Beryl's voice from a little farther away. "Don't you feel that?"

"What?" Jasper asked her.

"Atmospherics! Something watching and waiting. Gyp, stay hidden."

I pulled back into the footwell of Linda's desk.

"I'll take the motorcycle," Jasper said. "Beryl, you stay on the line with Gyp. If anything happens, snag Flint and send him to her."

Flint's gifts were different from anybody else's. He could transport without taxing himself energetically, sometimes; he used some technique none of the rest of the family understood. Only he had real trouble with direction and accuracy. He often didn't end up where he was trying to go. Every once in a while, though, he got it right. Better than never.

"I'm on my way," Jasper said. Phone-handing-over sounds came over the line.

"Gyp?" Beryl asked.

"Yes."

"I'm right here. I mean, I'm on the phone in the kitchen." I pictured it: a yellow wall phone with a long curly cord that always got twisted up, Beryl nearby with the handset against her ear, maybe perched on the square red metal stool that had steps under it which folded out so you could climb up and grab things from high places. "Where are you, exactly?" my little sister asked.

Maybe she needed to know so she could try to send Flint to me if something happened. "I'm under the receptionist's desk in the Learning Center." Beryl had visited me at work. She knew the layout.

"Under it?"

"Crammed into the footwell," I said. "Me and the phone."

She giggled.

"Sure, you can laugh," I whispered.

"Sorry!"

This was ridiculous. Why was I hiding under a desk? Well, but there were occasional stories, never confirmed by real sources like the school newspaper, about women who got raped after dark on campus. Somehow I had always figured this didn't apply to me, and I had walked blithely after dark, secure in my obliviousness and size. Would a rapist pick a fat victim? You never read about *that* in the news. It was always cheerleaders or beautiful coeds. Girls with long hair. Not friendly fat women with short curly hair.

For the millionth time I wished I had some sort of personal power. Opal could make herself appear so stunningly ugly in an instant that you'd cross a street to avoid her. Or she could just go invisible. Or make you think your hand was burned or had sprouted warty green skin.

My stomach rolled. Yeah, just what I needed. A flu relapse! Maybe I could scare off potential attackers with projectile vomit. Only I didn't have much in my stomach. I hadn't been very hungry since my sickness; nothing tasted good.

At this time of night it shouldn't take Jasper more than fifteen minutes to get from our house to campus. I checked my watch. About ten after nine. But I hadn't looked at the time when I made the phone call, so I didn't know what that meant. What if the guy outside had given up and gone home? Wouldn't Jasper give me a hard time for panicking? I hated having to ask somebody to rescue me.

What would the stranger do if he saw me? Break in through a window? Come after me?

When you really thought about it, you had to wonder why people didn't break more windows. What was a little pane of glass in the face of determination to get into or out of a building? There was some kind of cultural inhibition against busting glass—well, burglar alarms mitigated against it, too—but wasn't that weird?

"Gyp?"

I jerked. I'd forgotten I was holding the phone.

"Gyp? You there? You okay?" Beryl asked.

"Yeah," I muttered. "Sorry." Again I thought about Jasper getting here and finding me hiding under a desk because of nothing. "What you said before, about atmospherics? What did you mean?"

"There's some kind of—I don't know, it's like a shadow coming out of the phone."

That sounded strange. "Is it still coming?"

"Yeah."

In a weird way, that was reassuring. At least Jasper wouldn't get mad at me because of a false alarm.

Neither of us spoke.

"Wait a sec. Flint just came in for cookies. Hey, Flint?" Beryl said. She cupped a hand over the phone so her conversation was muffled.

I held the phone away from my ear and listened to the ticking silence of the center after hours. Beryl said there was still something menacing around. I had no sense of it anymore. I just felt stupid. I edged over and peeked across the top of Linda's desk. No silhouette in the window.

A knock sounded on the door. I jerked and fell forward, the phone tumbling from my lap. "Gyp?" Jasper called through the wood.

"Gyp?" Beryl yelled from the phone. "What happened? You okay?"

I struggled to catch my breath. My heart staggered and hit me hard. I managed to say, "It's all right. Jasper." My words were half breath, half sound.

"Whoa!" Beryl said. "Okay. Good."

"Gyp? You there?"

"Gotta go." I hung up the phone. My hands shook as I put it back on the desk. Then I swayed to my feet and stumbled to the door.

"Gyp?" Jasper pounded on the door.

I unlocked it and let him in.

"What happened?"

"You scared me."

He looked exasperated. "Well, what was I supposed to do?"

"No. No. It's all right. Not your fault." I pulled him into the building and hugged him. He stood stiff in my embrace. "Thanks for coming," I whispered before I let him go.

He patted my shoulder. "Okay. There's no one out here. Let's go home."

I got my backpack. I took a last look around the center to see if I had left everything the way it was supposed to be, and decided it was okay enough.

"Hey?" said a hearty male voice from outside.

I jumped again. Then settled. I had Jasper with me now. Nothing could get me.

"Anybody in there? Why's this door open?" A dark face appeared in the doorway. "Oh, hi." He stepped in through the door. He wore a blue uniform.

"Mr. Perez!" He was one of the school security guards.

"Hey, Gypsy. What are you doing here so late?"

"I lost track of time."

"Who's your boyfriend? You guys messing around in here?"

"This is my brother, Jasper. He came to take me home. Jasper, this is Mr. Perez."

"Howdy," said Mr. Perez. He shook hands with Jasper. "Hi."

"We were just leaving."

"Okay. Have a good night. Gypsy, don't leave the door open after dark if you're all alone, okay? Bad things happen sometimes."

"I know. Thanks." I tugged Jasper's hand, and we went outside. Mr. Perez watched as I locked up, then waved and walked on into the fog.

Jeeze! Santa Tekla City College had security! Why hadn't I just called the campus cops? That would have been faster. Less trouble for the family. The sane response.

Feeling like an idiot, I turned to my brother. "I could have called him. I didn't even think of it. I'm sorry."

"It's okay." He worked his hand, and I dropped it. "You want to ride home on the back of the motorcycle? I brought the extra helmet."

"If you could just walk me to my car. . . ."

"Where is it?"

"In the Speare Beach lot."

"Jeeze, that's half a mile away!"

"I always park there. When I get here in the morning, all the close places are taken."

"I'm in the visitor's lot at the top of the hill. Let's get the bike and I'll drive you down."

" 'Kay."

Fog drifted across the nighttime campus from the nearby ocean, glowed under the orange lights. The air was cool and damp. I followed my brother's broad leather-jacketed back. A feeling of contentment settled over me. I felt like I was a kid again, with Jasper leading me into another adventure.

But that was ridiculous.

I moved up beside him. "Did you notice anybody hanging around the center?"

He glanced at me, then shook his head.

I stared at the ground as I walked. "Sorry."

"Why?"

"I got you out here for no reason."

He shook his head again. "Maybe I scared him away. Better safe, you know?"

"You had other plans for tonight, I'm sure."

"Not until ten. I can still make it. Celtic Knot's playing at the Bismarck. You want to come?"

He hadn't invited me to listen to live music with him in a long time. He had this girl he was seeing, Trina, the latest in a string of girls he'd been seeing; he did lots of things with her, and left the family out of his plans these days. Mama said having a girlfriend was a natural step in his development, and we should quit bothering him about it.

Sometimes I was really conscious of how odd my family was. Most people our age moved out of the house, went away to college, got their own apartments. Opal lived in L.A. But Jasper still lived at home, and so did I, even though we were old enough to leave. Mama said not to worry about it. LaZelles didn't have to live like anybody else; it was customary for us to cluster. She said it was okay with her if I *never* moved out.

I was heading for my twenty-first birthday in the spring. I didn't know what to think about Mama's offer. Sometimes I talked it over with Claire.

Claire had gone through a rebel-against-everything-July-does phase where she utterly rejected her witch upbringing. She had moved to an apartment across town when she was eighteen. She got a job waitressing and took a year off from school, then went to college at UCST, where her mom was a cultural anthropology professor.

Since she had moved out, though, she'd been exploring the craft again. She could finally look at it as something separate from family, something she might want to use. After all, she knew all about it already. Now that she had a little distance, she could appreciate it.

Sometimes I went to Claire's place to study. We went to movies together. Her apartment was tiny; you did almost everything in one big room except cook or go to the bathroom or shower. The kitchen was so small that you could stand in one place and open the refrigerator and the oven and every cupboard she had, plus you could wash dishes without doing anything but turn around. The bathroom was like that, too. A rug a foot square covered all the ground there was; you stood on it to brush your teeth, your feet rested on it when you used the toilet, and it was where you stepped when you got out of the shower.

It was very cute. Sometimes, though, when Claire really wanted to, she came to our house and took a four-hour bath.

"Why should you move out?" Claire had asked. "You get along with your folks, you've got those cute brothers and Beryl, there's a big old pool and a hot tub in your backyard, you can walk to the beach, you guys have a giant TV, and you're not going to be able to afford an apartment with a kitchen like that. Besides, as long as you live at home, you don't have to pay rent."

"Daddy says I should start paying rent if I'm still living at home when I'm thirty."

"See? Free ride for another ten years! No rent, no

utilities, no phone or cable bills. Hey, can I move into your house?"

"Opal's room is up for grabs."

We had grinned at each other, then went back to eating microwave popcorn and watching *Men in Black*.

"What's Celtic Knot?" I asked Jasper.

"It's a band."

"Yeah, I got that."

"Celtic technopop. I've never heard them live. They got the gig at the Bismarck. We auditioned there, but they didn't hire us, you know?"

"Oh. Yeah." Jasper's band, River Run, was still in the formative stages. They did instrumental Celtic and contra dance music, but they hadn't rehearsed enough to be solid yet. "I need to make myself some dinner."

"Make enough for two and I'll definitely take you to the show."

"You'll fix my I.D.?"

" 'Course." He'd been fogging ages on driver's licenses for years so he could get into places to see bands before he was old enough to drink. Now he was legal, and I was going to be soon. How weird was that?

At his Honda motorcycle, he unlocked the two helmets and handed me the blue one. He rolled the bike off its kickstand, kicked down on the starter, and turned it toward the exit, and then I climbed on behind him and held on. This, too, reminded me of old times, when he was sixteen and got his license and I was fourteen and still, potentially, a full member of our family, despite Jasper's predicter mystery on my behalf. We burned up a lot of back roads in the mountains above town back then, and found many strange people and places.

It was a short ride from the upper parking lot down to the lot at the beach. Through the fog, Christmas lights glowed on the palm trees by the Pelican's entrance, and rock versions of Christmas carols sounded on the damp air.

The night was cold even through my jacket, and Jasper's jacket was cold too. I didn't care. I felt safe.

Jasper pulled up to the entrance to the Speare Beach lot. To get in, you had to take a ticket, although the ticket booth wasn't manned this late at night. My lime-green Mazda Protegé was one of six cars in the lot.

He pulled the motorcycle over by the divider where adolescent palm trees grew and dropped the kickstand. "Want me to walk you to the car?"

"I'll be all right. Thanks. In case I didn't already tell you. Thanks."

"You told me." He smiled.

"I'm so glad you're my brother."

He yawned. "Let's go home and you fix dinner!"

"Yeah, yeah." I took off the helmet and handed it to him, then headed across the lot. My car was at the far end, barely visible through the orange-stained fog.

Maybe I should come to school earlier and find better parking spots. On the other hand, this was the only exercise I got.

Halfway there, my neck prickled. I glanced sideways.

Was someone standing under that palm tree? Watching me?

I clutched my pack and ran toward my car.

The dark figure paced me, traveling along the curb.

My footsteps slapped loud on the asphalt, but I didn't hear a sound from my pursuer.

I glanced back. Had Jasper already left?

No. He was running across the lot toward me, but he was twice as far away as the person under the trees.

I put on a burst of adrenaline-fueled speed, and bumped into my car. Scrabbling through my pockets, I found my keys at last, opened the driver-side door, and collapsed into the car. I slammed and locked the door.

The chasing figure evaporated.

Jasper dropped from the air to the ground right beside

my car, spun to look. His head turned as he surveyed the parking lot.

I tried to catch my breath. It took me a while.

Eventually Jasper knocked on my window, and I lowered it. "Did you see it?" I asked him.

"Yeah." He sounded ragged too. "I don't know what that was, Gyp. I don't even know if it was a person."

Freezing marbles rolled around in my stomach. "What else could it be?"

He shook his head. "We better talk to Tobias."

I drove straight home, with Jasper following on his motorcycle.

It was strange to go home, the house looked so everyday. So many places on the route were shining with lights, and the businesses along the Old Coast Highway had holiday scenes painted on their windows. Usually by the week before Christmas, Mama had assigned us our holiday chores, and everybody had worked to decorate the house. You could expect to see the house's lights from down the street, competing with the displays of our neighbors, some of whom turned their lawns into shrines to reindeer and choristers and even Mother and Child.

This year Mama hadn't said anything yet. Not that we expected surprises. I was pretty sure my job was to make cookies again, so I planned a big bake on Saturday.

Mama hated it when I parked the car in the turnaround out front. I was supposed to go to my assigned spot under the giant Morton Bay fig tree by the side of the house, where my car would be hidden from the view of all but a couple of guest house windows. Hermina lived in the guest house, and didn't complain about what she saw. Beryl and I parked there; Flint hadn't managed to get and keep a car yet; when Opal came home for a visit, she was supposed to park in the street. Jasper was supposed to lock his motorcycle in the garage where Dad had his shop set up.

Tonight we both ignored the rules and parked by the front door.

The house was huge, square, and ochre yellow, with lights on in the windows behind all the curtains, and lights that shone up on the front of the house from the shrubs. Cliff swallows nested under the eaves all along the front of the house. Mama didn't like the mess they made, but Dad asked for special dispensation because he liked the baby birds, the constant come-and-go of the parents in their smooth swoops, and she relented and let the birds build there.

The house was woven around with protect spells. It looked like a vision of paradise. Inside I knew I'd be safe.

I climbed out of the car and almost forgot my pack in my hurry to get inside. I unlocked the front door, went through the foyer past Dad's study on the left and the immense structure of the three-section staircase on the right to the great hall. I heard television sounds from behind the TV divider to the left in the great hall. Serious voices and classy music with no laugh track made me suspect PBS, with Mama and Dad watching. They liked to unwind with heavy TV after dinner and work.

I turned right past the staircase, away from the TV alcove into the hallway that led between the kitchen and the dining room. I was starving.

Jasper caught up to me in the kitchen, where I headed for the fridge, the breadbox, and various tins in search of something to eat.

"I looked," he said. "I didn't see it."

"Oh; God! Do you think it could have followed us? I never even thought—" If the follower were supernatural, of course it could have followed us.

Why?

"Gotta talk to Uncle, but I have to eat first," I mumbled.

"You made it!" Beryl rushed up and hugged me.

"Yeah. Thanks for staying on the phone with me." I found a package of Oreos, broke it open, and stuffed one in my mouth. "Thanks for finding Jasper for me," I mumbled through a mouthful of black crumbs and frosting.

"No problem."

"That's not cooking," Jasper said.

"Too hungry to wait." I held the package out to him, and he grabbed some cookies.

"Not as good as homemade," he said after he ate two. I ate three. The hunger pangs in my stomach stopped gnawing.

"All right, all right. I'll make you a batch of whatever kind of cookies you want on Saturday. I'm doing the big Christmas bake then anyway."

"A really big batch? Two kinds? Snickerdoodles and Tollhouse."

"You got it." I checked the crisper drawer and found some green and red peppers, red onion, mushrooms, and broccoli. Also we had feta crumbles and eggs. Enough interesting stuff for an omelet. "Should I actually fix dinner?" I checked the clock. Nine-thirty. I wasn't ready to leave the house again, not if that thing was outside waiting for me. "Maybe you should go on ahead to the club? I don't think I want to go after all."

"First things first. Forget dinner. Grab whatever else you want to eat, and let's go talk to Tobias," Jasper said. "I have to call Trina and tell her I'll probably be late if I make it at all."

"What happened at the college?" Beryl asked.

"Nobody there when I got there," Jasper said.

"Nobody there? But I thought—I mean, even right at the end when we said good-bye, I felt something—" She bit her lip and stared at me. "There's still something." She shook her head. "The house masks it."

Jasper said, "All I found when I got there was Gyp. All quivering!"

"Shut up," I said.

"The thing showed up when we went to Gyp's car, though. It was scary. Is Tobias still up?"

We all glanced up and toward the right, where Tobias's tower was, its third-story room higher than the rest of the house, the secret fourth story higher still.

"I don't know," said Beryl. Tobias had made new rules since everybody had graduated from basic training. He had his own life, he said, and nobody should bother him after nine at night unless it was an emergency.

"I think we have an emergency," Jasper said.

I found a bag of baby carrots, a banana, and some saltines. I put them all on a plate and poured myself a glass of milk while Jasper made a phone call to his girlfriend.

All three of us went up the stairs. On the way, we passed the TV alcove in the great hall again, and I still didn't stop to greet my parents.

Why hadn't I told them about the Follower? From the start I had asked my siblings for help, and hadn't even thought about my parents. There wasn't much Dad could do in supernatural matters, but Mama was strong in every direction.

Strong, but she gave you hell if you asked for help and didn't really need it. I was pretty well trained not to ask her if I only suspected I had a problem.

Well, I was home, and safe, and I only owed Jasper some cookies, and maybe a dinner sometime. Problem somewhat solved.

I munched crackers as we went. We reached the top of the stairs, turned right, went down the hall, traversed the sitting room outside our bedrooms. I knocked on the narrow black door that opened onto the spiral staircase that led up to Tobias's tower. I heard muttering and thumping. A couple minutes later Tobias opened the door. His thick white hair stood up in a ruffle on his head, and he wore a blue terry bathrobe and slippers. I'd never seen him in such informal dress before.

"Something important?" he asked in a dry voice.

"Something followed me."

His eyes narrowed. He fished some half-glasses out of his robe's pocket and put them on, studied me. Three times his tongue ticked against the roof of his mouth. "Come up," he said at last. He turned and led the way upstairs.

Jasper and Beryl and I followed. I was mesmerized by the sight of Tobias's bare legs, which were pale and muscular and forested with white hair. I had never even seen my great-great-uncle in a bathing suit; somehow I had imagined that he spent his life inside of clothes. I wasn't sure I was ready to learn that he had hair on his legs.

In the lower tower room was the school room, with a round table in its center where we had had our lessons before Tobias graduated us, and where Tobias now studied and did workings. The air smelled faintly of nag champa incense and book dust. Tobias's bedroom was in the room above, right under the pointed tower roof. None of us had ever seen it.

He turned on his hotplate and put a tea kettle on. "Go on."

We went to our usual places at the table and sat. I set my plate and milk on the black velvet tablecloth. "It waited outside my work at school. I was afraid to leave. Jasper came to get me, and it disappeared, but it came back down by my car."

"Jasper?"

"I was prepared for it to be some creepy stalker guy. I don't know what it was."

"Any intuitions?"

"It's supernatural," Jasper said.

Beryl said, "There's atmospherics, even now."

Tobias smiled at her. "Good observation."

"Do you know what it is, Uncle?" she asked.

He stared over my head at the west tower window and the night outside. "I have ideas." His gaze lowered to my face; the pupils of his eyes widened. "You've been sick."

"Sure, I had the flu last weekend. You knew that. You got me Gerry pictures."

"You were sick while we were all gone. Was it very bad?"

I shrugged.

Tobias leaned closer, staring into my face. "Was it very bad?" he asked again.

"I don't know." I leaned back. His gaze was so intent I felt it. I shrugged again and looked away.

"Gypsum."

Jasper and Beryl stared at me, too. I picked at a scuff in the tablecloth, then glanced up. "Sure, I was really sick."

"All alone." Tobias's voice was a whisper.

"I called July, and she stayed with me."

"July!"

"You were all gone. She came right over. She was great! She's always great."

"You had July watch over you while you went through transition?"

"Transition!" My stomach dropped down into a bottomless pit, and my hands iced over. "What do you mean, transition? I'm too old for transition." I checked my brother and sister. They looked as shocked as I felt. Transition! I'd never heard of anybody going through transition at twenty.

Maybe everything would change now. Maybe I'd finally be a real member of the family. Tiny tendrils of hope unfurled in my mind.

Tobias didn't look happy, though. "What did she say? Did she tell you how sick you were?"

"Transition," I whispered.

"Gypsum."

"She almost called an ambulance, but then my fever broke and I got better."

"She didn't say anything about . . . accidents?"

I shook my head. "Transition, Uncle?"

"Late transition."

His voice sounded so cold and dark I waited for what he was going to say next. All my life I had longed for some kind of power. Wasn't that what transition was? Growing into some kind of power? What did late transition mean?

"Do you feel your power, Gyp?"

I took a couple deep breaths and tried to see if I felt different from the way I had last week, before I got sick. How horrible would it be to go through transition and not even get anything out of it? My stomach rolled over. It had been doing that since the weekend. I hadn't thrown up, though, just felt a little sick off and on. Was that what power felt like?

"Does power make you sick?" I asked.

Something tightened his face until I saw the bones beneath the skin. I usually didn't wonder how old Great-Uncle Tobias was. He didn't look old, but I knew he had lived a long time. He could remember things that had happened before there were cars, telephones, movies, though he didn't talk about that much unless it came up in the context of something else. Now I thought, he's more than a hundred years old. I can see it for the first time.

"I understand transition makes you sick, but it seemed like everybody else felt much better afterward," I said. I hoped that if I talked fast enough, he'd turn back into his regular self. "*I* felt much better afterward. Except I'm still kind of sick to my stomach every once in a while. I mean, not that I think that was transition. How could it be? You never told us it could happen this late."

"Sometimes it happens late in the interests of mercy."

"Mercy!"

"If, afterward, you have one of the unkind powers."

I sucked in a big breath and forgot how to let it out again.

Jasper and Beryl stared at me.

Tobias put a hand on my head. "Breathe," he said.

Breath rushed out of me. In a moment, I managed to breathe in again, and out. Calm flowed into me from Tobias's hand.

"We haven't done any of the right things for you, child. We should have noticed this coming on. We should have watched over you, helped you through. Now we should celebrate."

"Celebrate an unkind power?"

"Every transition is some kind of gift."

"But I—" If transition was a gift, what had it given me? I hadn't noticed any spurts or glories or anything else. I had no sense that there was power inside me and I could use it. I laughed. "No. I was just sick. Boring, normal sick. There's no—what makes you think—?" I stared up at him. His eyes looked dark and ancient. A moment later, though, he smiled. I coughed. "What's an unkind power? The power of curses, like Great-Great-Aunt Meta died of?"

"Probably." He stroked my hair. "There are several kinds: backwards power, souring power, others we don't need to speak of unless it turns out you have them. We can do a diagnostic if you like."

Bewildered, I looked at Jasper. "But when he—but when Opal—right away, they could do things."

"Yes."

"I'm not doing anything."

"Not yet. You had better start, or you'll get sicker."

"Start . . . start cursing things?"

"Yes, if that's your power. The sooner the better."

"Uncle? What does this have to do with the stalker?" Beryl asked.

"Look." He nodded toward the window.

A face peered in, pale against the darkness. I screamed and jumped up, backed to the wall across the room from the window. My heart struck hard inside my ribs.

*Four*

JASPER rose to his feet. "How did it get here? Why don't the wards drive it away? Uncle!"

Beryl licked her lip and walked to the window. "But—" She glanced at Tobias, then reached for the latch. He nodded, and she opened the window.

The figure paused on the windowsill. It stared at me. Then it stepped into the room. It was all swathed in black, its hair dark, only its face pale. It stood silent.

"But Gyp," Jasper said. "It's you."

I held my hand against my chest. Slowly I came away from the wall and walked toward the stranger. Was that what I looked like? Oval, pale face, chubby, rosy cheeks, deepset hazel eyes below dark brows, clever mouth. Hair a dark froth of curls. Body so hidden in black that I couldn't make it out, not size nor shape.

I would never have seen myself in that face, but now that Jasper mentioned it, I looked harder. It was not the mirror me, but it looked a little like the photographed me. I usually didn't look very hard at pictures of myself.

"Uncle," I said.

The stalker stood quiet.

"It appears you did something pretty sophisticated. You split off the power part of yourself and sent it away. This usually takes training in techniques I haven't taught any of you; it's not a good thing to do. Untrained as you are, you didn't completely sever your bond to it, which is a good thing; if you had cut it off, I'm not sure what would have happened. You would have been diminished, probably in horrible ways, that much I know. But look: it has found you, and now it wants to come home."

She took a step toward me, held out dark-gloved hands.

I gulped and backed up. "She's an unkind power?" I squeaked.

Tobias went to his tool cupboard and took out a wire loop as big as a head. He held it up and stared through it at the stranger. "Let me see in the language I know," he murmured. Something flashed across the space inside the loop. "Thank you." He lowered the loop. "Yes," he said. "She is the power of curses."

"But I don't want the power of curses!"

"She's part of you now. If you don't accept her, you'll most likely both sicken and die."

"But—" I looked at Jasper, and at Beryl.

"Go on, Gyp. You can curse me," Beryl said. She smiled at me, but she looked scared.

Curse my beloved little sister? My comfort, my friend? How could I? "But I don't—"

"Come on," Jasper said. "What's a curse, anyway? We can ward against them."

I looked into the stranger's face. She looked sad, and somehow, strangely, beautiful. So unlike me.

"Please. Accept her," said Tobias.

She was a power of curses.

She was a power.

She was part of me. How had I sent her away? I couldn't remember doing anything powerful, not in my whole life, except when I borrowed or stole tools somebody else had put magic into. I had sat through so many lessons, though, printing instructions for dealing with power on my brain. Somehow I had cast her out, without even knowing she was there.

I held out a hand to her, and she took it. Her gloves were smooth butter leather, her hand warm as summer sun. I felt something stir under my skin, the slow brushing of a thousand butterfly wings. She spread my hand flat, with the palm up, and wrote something with her index finger on the heart of my hand. Then she held out her other hand to me.

I didn't know what she wrote on my hand. I tried to remember magic signs Tobias had drilled into us years before, the ones that everybody with power used to ward and protect or dispel or summon, but they had blurred with time and disuse. I took her black-gloved hand and spelled COME HOME on it in English.

She stepped closer and hugged me. Why had I thought she was tall when she stood outside the center under the orange light? She was my exact height. She kissed my cheek. Her lips were hot, almost brand-hot. She pressed her lips to mine. I struggled and tried to pull away from her, because this seemed so strange and wrong, but she was stronger than I was. She wouldn't let me go. The heat of her kiss spread through me. I felt strange, uncomfortable, excited.

Finally I had to breathe. I sucked in a deep breath, and somehow sucked her inside. My stomach roiled and turned over, and I felt burning everywhere under my skin.

I licked the roof of my mouth, then tasted my lips. They still burned. Where was she, my power of curses? Had I just eaten a person? And all her leather clothes? What did *that* taste like?

Cinnamon and sugar.

I touched my lips. More intense heat spread across my

cheeks. My brother and my sister and my uncle had watched me get my first kiss, and I had kissed—myself?

"Good," said Tobias.

I swallowed spit. My stomach growled. Fire sang through me, then faded away, and I felt normal again. "She had really cool gloves," I said. "Wish I had some like that."

Something fluttered in my chest.

My hands and forearms grew another skin, black, smooth leather so thin I barely felt it. I stared at my gloved hands, my mouth open, then I looked up at Tobias. "This is my power? This is a curse?"

"You're going to have to watch your words."

"But I just did something magical." My own magic, for the very first time. "I didn't even rhyme. I didn't even plan. I made a wish, and it came true." I flexed my fingers; the gloves moved with them. I almost couldn't tell they were there except to look at. I lifted a hand and sniffed it. Faint smell of leather. I rubbed the back of my gloved hand against my cheek, and felt soft smooth skin more velvety than my own. "Uncle?"

"Beware of wishes, Gyp. Beware of saying anything with a wish in it."

"But look!" I held up my hands. They looked elegant, classy, *so* not mine.

Jasper frowned. "Yeah. How is that a curse, Uncle?"

"Do the gloves come off?"

They encased my arms in black leather up to my elbows. I picked at the edge of one with the fingertips of the other. No. There was no dividing line between the glove and my skin.

I swallowed again. "How long do they last?"

"We'll have to wait and see."

I smoothed my gloved fingers across my lips. So my hands would be black. Somehow I couldn't see that as a curse. Wasn't a curse supposed to bother you? I liked this. It would be hard to explain at work, though. And in class. Nobody took notes with gloves on. Nobody wore gloves in any context I could remember, except to fancy dress-up events I saw in movies, or when it was really cold. I imagined raising my hand to answer a question in class, everybody turning to look.

I hunched my shoulders. Well, heck. Class was over until mid-January, and I only had one more shift at work, two days from now. Maybe the gloves would be gone by then. If not, well, maybe I could start some kind of trend— if anybody actually came to the center the Friday before break started, which seemed unlikely.

Black gloves.

When Opal and Jasper first did workings after transition, the effects were short-term. Beryl's works, on the other hand, had lingered for a week or longer, and with Flint it had varied depending on what he did. Maybe the gloves would be gone by tomorrow. Maybe they'd last a month.

I frowned and looked at Tobias. Everybody else had been through transition and knew the basics. I had let go of them when I thought I wouldn't need them anymore. I knew I had to use my power or it would twist up inside and hurt me, but I couldn't remember details. Tobias had given up teaching. Maybe he'd come out of retirement. I hoped. "So I used my power. How soon do I have to use it again?"

"How do you feel?"

I put my black-gloved hand against my stomach. With these black hands, I look like a skunk in a comic strip. It made me smile. My stomach was quiet for the first time in a week. "Pretty good," I said. I drank milk.

"You'll need to do something again when you feel worse. Different people experience it in different ways, the sense that there's something you need to do to feel better again. Sometimes it's a thickening in the back of the throat, or a sense of something binding your arms or your guts. Beryl?"

"My eyes got hot, like I was about to cry. If I used power, the feeling went away."

"Jasper?"

Jasper hunched his shoulders. "I felt like I ate too much. Sort of like I had to throw up." He wrinkled his nose. "I'm glad *that's* over."

"You'll have to learn to listen to your own signals, Gyp," Tobias told me.

"I start feeling tense, I have to curse something?"

"Yes."

"Next time you can give *me* gloves," Beryl said. "Those look so cool."

"I don't know, kid. Maybe there are more problems with these than that they don't come off. Let's wait and see." I turned to Tobias. "Do I have to curse a person?"

"I don't know."

Maybe I could curse rocks! Maybe I could use all my power cursing rocks and see what happened to them. Maybe I didn't have to hurt anyone.

Naw. If it had been that easy, Aunt Meta would have done it.

"Do I have to wait until I feel my . . . signal before I can use my power?"

Tobias smiled. "What did you have in mind?"

"I could curse a rock next time, see what happens."

"What would a rock perceive as a curse?" Tobias went to his tool cupboard and got out a rock. I never knew what he had in there. This rock looked ordinary, something lo-cal, bread-brown sandstone. I wondered what he had planned to do with it.

He set it on the table in front of me, and glanced at me, eyebrows up.

I didn't feel like I was going to cry or throw up. I felt like I'd had something to eat, and I was tired.

I felt ordinary. Normal.

I frowned at my black gloves. No, I had proof that I had changed.

To give a spell power, rhyme helped, and so did rhythm and cadence, Tobias had taught us. Something about how sounds worked together generated energy. Spell crafting had never been my strongest suit, though I loved to read. Trying to write proper spells was one of the few things about power that I had been glad to give up. Jasper was so good at it. I knew I'd never be as good as he was.

I'd have to try again, though. All I needed to do was figure out something clever to say, and see what happened.

I put my hand on the rock. I couldn't feel its sandy grit through the glove, which surprised me: the gloves felt so thin and invisible. I thought, then said, "Rock. Be chalk."

Heat stirred in my chest. A cascade of pings and clinks rang out as the rock changed into a couple hundred pieces of sidewalk chalk, all colors, and collapsed across the table and floor.

Somehow this impressed me more than the gloves had. I had planned something, and it had happened. Me. On purpose. Unless—

"Did you do that?" I asked Jasper.

He shook his head and smiled.

Beryl laughed and picked up a few pieces of chalk, green, red, orange, blue. "Let's go draw on the front walk."

"Jasper's got a club to go to," I said. Was I still invited? Hey, I'd just kissed my power, and now I didn't know what I was doing. I should stick close to home until I figured it out. Probably I should cancel my shift at the Center on Friday and tell my boss he needed to call some other tutor to fill in for me; I didn't want to take chances with my students.

Gloves. Chalk. Ooh, scary.

Jasper said, "Forget it. I already told Trina I'd be late and might not make it. I'll catch the band later. Uncle, do you have something we can put the chalk in?"

Tobias got a shoebox from a lower shelf and handed it to Jasper, who grabbed handfuls of chalk and dumped them in. Tobias picked up a piece of chalk from the floor. His hand jerked, and he dropped it. His eyebrows rose. "If I might offer a suggestion? Draw on the back walk instead. Be careful what you draw."

Beryl's smile faded. A tiny worry wrinkle appeared between her eyebrows.

"Sorry to be so ominous," Tobias said. "We don't know what we're dealing with yet."

"But it's just Gyp."

Just Gyp. Good old Gyp. Never hurt anybody, never scared anybody, never threatened anybody, no matter what you did to her.

"We don't know what we're dealing with," Tobias repeated.

I stooped and collected chalk from the floor. I sat with chalk in my hands, trying to figure out what Tobias had felt. Shock? What? I got nothing from the chalk. Then again, I was wearing gloves. Multicolored chalk dust patterned my palms. I dumped the chalk in Jasper's box and slapped my hands together as though they were blackboard erasers. The chalk didn't come off.

Huh. I wasn't so worried about appearing everywhere with black hands, but black hands dusted with chalk? Maybe it would wash off. Could you wash leather in the bathroom sink? I guessed I'd find out.

"I think that's all of it," Jasper said. He dropped a last piece into the box. "Turquoise! So cool. We never had these colors before."

"Let's go," said Beryl.

Tobias yawned against the back of his hand. "Let me know if you need me. If you don't, I'm going back to bed."

"Thanks, Uncle," I said, and went to him.

He suffered a hug from me. He'd never been very

touchy-feely. This time, though, he closed his arms around me. He smelled like incense and black tea. "Interesting times ahead," he murmured into my hair. "I'll help as much as I can."

"Thanks," I whispered.

Jasper, Beryl, and I clattered down the stairs. The tower door locked behind us.

As we trooped past Flint's room, he opened the door. "What is this, a parade?"

"Gyp made cursed chalk. We're going to go try it."

"What?" Flint came out into the hall.

"Gyp went through transition while we were in L.A. meeting Gerry," Jasper said. "Only, she got a dark power instead of a fun one. She made this chalk." Jasper showed Flint the open shoebox.

"What?"

Beryl tugged Jasper's sleeve. "Come on."

We headed down the hall, Flint trailing after. "What happened to your hands?"

"I cursed them with gloves."

"That's flat-out weird." He didn't say anything else, just followed us down the staircase, but at the bottom he grabbed my arm. "You went through transition? You went through transition! Wow, that's great! At last! I thought it wasn't going to happen." He hugged me. "But hey! Who's going to make the cake? You shouldn't have to make your own cake."

I felt a melting in my chest. Tobias had mentioned a celebration, but in almost the same breath he had talked about how dangerous I was going to be. Jasper and Beryl had been pretty quiet, not surprising since Tobias was trying to scare us all. Finally somebody was happy for me, the way people were supposed to be when you survived transition. I hugged my younger brother.

He got embarrassed and pushed me away. "I could try to do it," he said.

Jasper, Beryl, and I all said "No!"

Flint clapped a hand to his chest. "You wound me!" He said that a lot.

"We'll figure out the cake tomorrow," Jasper said. "Right now we have to test this chalk. Tobias thinks it will do weird things because Gyp's power is unkind. He told us to practice out back."

From our backyard, on clear days and nights, we had a view all the way to the ocean, even though it was half a mile away. We had a big terrace with a pool and a lawn and an orange tree and a rose garden on it. At both ends of the terrace, stone staircases led down into a fenced orchard which stretched seaward, and beyond the orchard's edge, the land sloped jungled and unimpeded to the Old Coast Highway, which was lined with shops, stores, businesses, gas stations, banks, doctors' offices, a couple of hotels. There was a huge empty plot between our land and the highway. Various businesses had tried to buy it over the years, wanting to build something tall. Mama had made it her practice since she had transitioned at twelve, thirty-four years earlier, to jinx all the land deals so we could keep our view.

We could see everything from the back porch, which was more like a balcony, a stately concrete expanse that ran outside the great hall between the dining room and the living room, with stone arches two feet thick that framed the view, and two broad staircases down to the back lawn; but nobody could see into our backyard. It was a great place to do strange things.

"Unkind power," muttered Flint as we all trooped across the great hall and out the double doors that led to the back porch. The night was foggy and damp. I wished I had brought my jacket instead of hanging it up when I got home. "What on Earth is an unkind power?"

"You remember Aunt Meta?" I asked.

"No. We had an Aunt Meta? I don't think I ever met

her." One side of his mouth quirked up into a half smile.

"None of us met her. She died. She had an unkind power and she refused to use it, so it killed her."

"What?" His eyes widened.

"Tobias says I have to use mine, or I'll be in trouble."

"But that's—hey, Gyp. . . ."

"What?"

"Maybe I could work some kind of time twist? Take us back to last week and make things come out different? I mean, not that I want to take your power away, but it doesn't sound like fun."

"Could you do that?"

"I've been thinking about it a lot. My latest project."

"How many times have you practiced?"

He looked away. "Not very many," he muttered.

I wondered what he had done, and why. Talk about dangerous stuff! Especially with Flint's penchant for messing up.

"Just little tiny things. I know I should start small and not mess around too much until I know it's safe."

"You haven't talked it over with Tobias."

"He'd just say no."

I patted his shoulder. "Thanks for thinking of it, but it sounds way too risky. So far, I don't seem very scary. Maybe my power is weak and will just annoy everybody. I can live with that. Let's wait and see."

"Okay." He frowned. "The longer you wait, though, the harder it is to untwist time. Things take on weight and get sludgy. They harden, like cement. You can't change them unless you have pickaxe power. And even though I've got a lot of range, I don't have much concentration."

"Flint? Please don't do more of this work without talking to somebody about it, all right? It sounds like there's huge potential for trouble."

His face went stubborn. "Just trying to help."

"I know. I appreciate it. It's just . . ."

He shrugged. "Just a thought." He turned away.

Jasper and Beryl had gone down the steps to the back walk, a wide pale concrete path that led along the side of the house, the left way leading to the pool, the right to the steps down to the orchard. Jasper set the chalk box on the path. "Light," he said, and studied the porch facing. The yellow outdoor light by the porch doors was lit; the arches dropped shadows across the path and lawn.

Jasper trailed his index finger along the edge of the porch, drew a line of clean white light at about head height. It lit up the path evenly and well.

"Okay!" said Beryl. She dived at the box and grabbed six sticks of chalk. "Every piece is a different color. I dibs these first!"

I sat on the steps and watched my siblings as they knelt on the walk with chalk in their hands. We were all supposed to be grownups, or at least young adults. Everybody jumped at the chance to get down on their knees and play with sidewalk chalk. We never let dignity stand in our way.

It seemed to me that my family didn't know how to grow up; we weren't much like other people our age I knew, and it wasn't just because of the magic.

Or maybe it was?

"Draw safe stuff," I said.

We had had a lot of practice drawing and painting. From the time we were four or five, Mama and Dad had treated us to art and music lessons with a variety of teachers, and when most of us were ten or under, Mama read aloud to us before we went to bed. Dad gave us stacks of scratch paper generated by the University, and later our own sketch pads and lots of pens, pencils, felt-tip markers, and crayons. While Mama read, we illustrated the stories. Opal was really good at it, and Beryl was too. Jasper could draw a decent picture. Flint never showed his sketch pad after he turned eight, so I wasn't sure what he was doing these days.

I liked art, but had lost confidence in my own ability when I was about fourteen.

Beryl drew with the tip of her tongue sticking out. She drew big. From the porch steps it looked like giant flowers.

Jasper stroked in a few lines, then sat back to study what he was doing. He slapped at the chalk dust on his hands, but it didn't come off.

Flint had grabbed orange, yellow, pink, white, and powder blue chalks. He drew really fast. He glanced up at me. "Why aren't you drawing?"

I was still trying to figure out what I felt about all this. I had been plodding along, looking for a direction to take, a normal life I could stand to live.

I liked tutoring English, and this semester I was taking *Introduction to Teaching & Learning in K–12 Contemporary Classrooms*. If I wanted to pursue a teaching certificate, though, I would have to switch schools, and I was so comfortable at STCC. I could take anything I liked.

I liked to sing, but I hadn't done anything professional with it. Sometimes Jasper let me sing with his band for a song or two. People said nice things. But if I wanted to be a professional singer, I was pretty sure I should have committed myself to it already. On the other hand, there was that late bloomer thing.

Everything would be different now, wouldn't it? Whatever my magic turned out to do, it was going to change everything else.

"What are you, chicken?" Flint said.

I grinned. "Gee, I haven't heard that in a while."

"Hah! Get used to it. Maybe it'll be fun to tease you again."

"Better watch your step." I'd had a couple of miserable years after Flint transitioned when he had teased me a lot, even though I couldn't fight back. Jasper had reminded me to carry the protect stone with me. That was good until Flint figured out how to hide it so I couldn't find it. Mama said, as she always did when things like that happened, that in her family, it was customary to let the kids fight it out. Dad said maybe that was why she hadn't spoken with her two older sisters since they were teenagers.

Now . . . something else that was going to change, apparently.

I got up, looked in the shoebox, picked some pieces of chalk, moved along the walk past Beryl, and knelt on the grass, a big blank sweep of walk in front of me.

Tobias had told us to be careful what we drew. No monsters, I guessed; maybe it would be better if I didn't draw animals or people. So what, then? I sneaked a peek at Beryl's work. She was still drawing giant flowers.

She saw me looking and sat back on her heels so I could see what she had drawn. "This chalk is great, Gyp. It goes down really fast and easy, and the color smears great. Look." She had drawn hibiscus flowers the size of her head in Hawaiian shirt colors, blue, red, orange petals, bright green leaves, purple pistils with little fuzzy orange flowerbursts at the tips.

"Wow. You've been practicing. That's great."

"I'm taking life drawing at school." She rubbed her hands. "This chalk makes my fingers tingle."

"Huh." Should I be worried? Jasper and Beryl thought my curses wouldn't hurt them. Wait and see.

It felt weird to draw with gloves on. I couldn't feel the chalk's texture between my fingers; I only knew I held something small and round.

I leaned over the sidewalk and laid down a curving line of bright pink. Beryl was right. The chalk was soft and smooth. It didn't leave cracks and wrinkles where the pavement was rough, but wrote solid lines, almost like a felt-tip. I put a line of emerald green beside the pink. I'd try abstract stuff. Maybe that would be safe. I crosshatched in some baby blue, then stroked a line of gold nearby.

One of our art teachers, a wild old woman named Petra, used to make us close our eyes and draw big squiggles on giant pieces of butcher paper. Then we'd open our eyes and look for a shape. Once we saw something in our squiggles, we could draw to bring the thing into focus. Opal hated that exercise, but I had always liked it. I couldn't make things look much like real things, but I loved finding order in chaos.

Now, though, every time my picture started to look like something I could identify, I scrawled some other line to destroy the reality. A different kind of challenge.

"Gyp," Beryl squeaked.

I sat back and looked sideways.

Beryl scooted across the lawn on her rear as the flowers she had drawn pushed up out of the cement.

*Five*

THE bush was vivid and garish, the leaves and flowers huge. The petals pulsed open and closed, and the large pistils swayed, bristling with pollen pompoms, reaching like fingers.

"Uh," said Jasper.

I jumped up so I could see past Beryl's bush.

A head stuck up out of the sidewalk in front of Jasper. It was the size of a small sheep, and had coppery, curly hair. It had Trina's face. "Jasper?" it said, its voice too loud for conversation. "What happened? Is this a dream?"

"Uh, Gyp?" Jasper said. He glanced at me, and I shrugged.

"Hah." Flint stood up and stared down at his patch of walk with a satisfied smile. I checked, though it was hard to look away from the head in front of Jasper—giant Trina turned this way and that, peering through the night.

Flint had drawn a big sheet cake on a fancy crystal platter. At least, I had to assume he had drawn it; now it looked real. The cake had white icing with blue and pink flowers on top. "For your celebration," Flint said.

"It's beautiful," I said. My throat tightened.

"Gyp?" Jasper said.

"What's wrong with me?" Trina asked so loudly it made me wince. "Where am I? Why do I feel so strange? Where are my hands?"

My own drawing rippled on the walk. An edge lifted free. No identifiable image, it was a stretch of color. It flapped another edge.

"Jasper?" Trina said in her giant voice.

"Yeah, Trina?"

"What happened?"

"Gyp!"

My sketch lifted free of the walk, whipped through the air, and splattered itself across the front of my dress. Its colors bled down into the fabric; soon it was flat, meshed into my best I-am-a-businesswoman outfit so that I now looked like a refugee from a bad fabric sample book.

I sighed and went to Jasper.

"Gypsum?" Trina cried.

"Yes?"

"Why am I looking up at you both? Why are you so small? Where am I?"

It was strange. She really looked like Trina, but as she turned I saw the blur of crosshatchings shading under her brow and cheekbones and chin, umber, sienna, ochre; Jasper's technique, excellent, like most things he did. Her copper curls shone with spots of white highlight.

"What is this?" Jasper asked.

"Why are you asking me?"

"It's your chalk."

"Yeah, sure, like I've ever done any of this before."

"Is Trina really here?"

"I don't know." I shook his arm. "How should I know?" My voice sounded desperate and scared.

Jasper knelt. "What's the last thing you remember, Tree?"

"Sitting at the Bismarck with a beer in front of me, waiting for the music to start, wondering where you were. Did I fall asleep? This is a really weird, uncomfortable dream." She glanced toward Beryl's bush, which was growing bigger by the minute. It sprouted curly tendrils. Some of them had already clamped onto the porch; the plant spread across the front of the house, its giant flowers budding and blooming like ink dripped into clear water. The plant reached toward us, then sprouted new branches closer to us.

I held my hand out to the plant. A tendril curled around my gloved palm, a strange cool clasp, and a branch sprouted above it; a huge pink bud swelled, opened right beside my face. Its pistil brushed pollen across my cheek with sticky little fingers. I smelled exotic perfume: Hawaii, whorehouse. The pollen sizzled against my skin. The giant flower wilted. The plant shot out another tendril, gripped my other arm before I could back away, grew more leaves and flowers across my front. The branches curled around me, weaving me into a basket, but they weren't tight. It was only when I tried to move that I knew I was trapped. They reached past me toward Trina.

"Gotta be a dream," she said. "So surreal."

"Beryl, go get some branch cutters from the gardening shed," Jasper said. Beryl ran. Jasper batted branches away from Trina's head, but tendrils locked around his arms, too, and then his legs. More and more of them, until he couldn't move. Flowers burst out all over him.

It was one of many moments when I wished like hell I had a camera.

"Flint," Jasper said, turning his head to dodge the kiss of a flower, "do something, will you?"

"Like a time twist?"

"No!" I yelled.

"What, then? Hey, I drew plates and forks and a cake-cutting knife. They worked out great the first time. How surprising is that? Boy, this cake tastes great!"

"Don't eat that," I said.

"Oh, yeah. Sorry. It's your celebration. I should have given you the first piece." He brought me a plate with a huge piece of frosted cake on it. "Here's a corner. Hey." He realized that the plant had handcuffed me and grown around me until the only thing I could move was my head. He cut off a bite of cake with a fork and held it out to me.

I shook my head.

"Flint, you made a knife?" Jasper said, his tone exasperated. "Could you maybe bring it over here and do something with it?"

"It's really good," Flint told me, "almost as good as cake you make." He ate the bite.

"But it's cursed," I said.

"I don't get that part." He ate the rest of the cake. "It's an expression of power, right? You did the chalk, I channeled the power of the chalk and drew the cake, what's not to like? Tastes fine."

"Flint!" Jasper struggled, but the plant had wrapped all the way around him. He had no more mobility than I did.

Beryl came back, carrying pruning shears and flower clippers. "Should I cut it?" she asked.

Branches reached for her.

Weird, but none of them were interested in Flint.

Beryl dropped the pruning shears and unhooked the safety latch on the clippers. The blades sprang apart. "Don't come any closer!" she told the branches, snipping the air with a harsh noise of metal sliding past metal. The branches curled away from her.

"Hah. Come threaten the ones on me," said Jasper.

"You look so cute!"

Jasper groaned. "My mission in life."

I glanced at Trina's head. Huge red, orange, and blue flowers wound through her curly hair. She looked like spectacular topiary, or maybe the drowned Ophelia floating downstream with her herbs around her. Her half-lidded eyes looked dreaming and drowsy.

"Check Trina, Beryl," I said.

Beryl knelt in front of Trina. "You okay?" she asked.

Pollen dusted Trina's lips. She licked them. "I don't understand the symbolism of this dream," she murmured, "but it tastes good." Her eyes closed all the way. Her mouth smiled. Faint snores came from her nose.

Beryl looked up at me, a question in her eyes.

I shrugged. In a way. Kind of hampered by plant arms around my shoulders.

Beryl turned to Jasper. She held the clippers toward the branches that snaked around him. The branches shivered but stayed where they were. Her mouth firmed. She opened the clippers and placed them around a tendril. She closed her eyes and the clippers. Snip! The tendril dropped to the ground.

The whole plant shivered. I felt like a salt shaker above a bad steak.

"If you don't let them go," Beryl told the plant, "I'll cut right above the root."

Tendrils shot out and curled around her wrists. "Yiiiiii!" she yelled. Another branch shot out and knocked the clippers out of her hand. The plant took its time wrapping around her. Not the slow deliberation of real plant time, but somehow leisurely, artfully, a flower at each of her joints, a belt of flowers at her waist, a corona of flowers around her face all blooming at once, then leaning over to lay stripes of pollen across her cheeks and down her front.

For a while we stood there as Beryl's bush grew denser around the three of us. It seemed satisfied with its hold on Trina and left her face alone. It left all our faces alone aside from dusting them with sizzling pollen, but it seemed to view the rest of our bodies as nice trellis space. As flowers bloomed and wilted a few inches from my nose, I figured out that each color had a different perfume.

"Well, okay," Jasper said eventually. "Thanks for this instructive experience in what it's like to be part of the landscape. We get it. Could you let us go now?"

A flower brushed pollen across his nose.

"Okay, how about you attack Flint too?"

Flint sat nearby. He had eaten about six pieces of cake. I wondered when the cake's curse would kick in, and how it would manifest. Would he get sick to his stomach? Throw up all night? Change color?

"Okay, wait. I've been thinking about this. I finally figured it out!" Flint smiled and grabbed the shoebox. "I know what it wants." He went past Beryl's plant and flopped down on his knees, pulled colors out of the box and started sketching.

"Oh, God," Jasper muttered.

"You said you could ward against curses," I said. I felt tired. It had been a long day. I relaxed in the embrace of the plant, and it was strong enough to support me.

He smiled. "Sure. Kind of helps to know what form the curse will take ahead of time, though."

"Chalk."

"Actually, that part is great. I hope Trina's okay. I can't tell if that's really her spirit inside my picture. I hope not."

"What else could it be?"

"My idea of her spirit?"

"Wish I hadn't drawn such big flowers," Beryl said. A flower grew right in front of her face, eclipsing her. "Oh, well," she muttered, muffled. She sneezed.

"You can't ward against curses after they're cast?" I asked Jasper.

"Not that I know of. I could cast spells of my own, maybe burn the whole plant to the ground, but I keep hoping it will disappear on its own."

"That would sure be nice." I would love to know that my curses had a short shelf life.

"It's so lively and happy." He frowned. "A curse mixed with a blessing. I hate to hurt it."

"There," Flint said. "I'm done."

We turned.

A new plant shot up from the walk. Its leaves were darker green, and its flowers were different colors from the ones Beryl had drawn—lavender, white, soft pink with crimson hearts, stamens dusted with yellow or purple pollens.

Its branches reached for Flint. He jumped up and ran across the lawn.

Then the new plant became aware of the older plant. They sent branches toward each other, tangled tendrils, waved flowers at each other. The plant holding me shifted and rustled, and then it pulled away from me, and I fell on my butt on the lawn. Jasper and Beryl dropped beside me. Flint's plant and Beryl's plant interwove, a slow fireworks of exuberance, pressed pollen kisses into each other's flowers, and paid no attention to us anymore. They even left Trina's head alone.

"Wow," Beryl whispered. "Flint did something that worked!"

Flint strolled back. "I heard that. And you're wrong. I did two things that worked in one night. Cake, and the plant."

Jasper stooped next to Trina's head. She still looked and sounded like she was sleeping. He glanced back at Flint. "What would you do about her?"

Flint straightened. Jasper never asked for his advice. "She was talking about dreams, right?"

"Yeah."

"Go where she really is and wake her up."

Jasper studied Flint, then slowly smiled. "Couldn't hurt," he said. "Gyp, you want to come?"

"Thanks, but I'm too tired. Besides, maybe I should watch all these things. Not that I know what to do about them."

"Here's what you do," said Flint. "Have some of my cake."

I smiled at him. "Okay." Maybe the cake would make me sick or make me change. Maybe it wouldn't. That would be worth knowing. I had permanent gloves, and my best dress had a new color scheme, but so far my own curses hadn't hurt me. Was that a rule, or just chance?

"I still have two corners left. Beryl, you want some celebration cake?"

"I've got a big history test tomorrow," she said. "My teacher gave me special permission to take the test late because I was sick last week. I mean, my whole class started Christmas Break last week, but Mrs. Walker is coming back just to let me take a makeup test. Don't want to get sick again and miss it."

"Chicken," said Flint.

"So true!"

Flint got me a piece of cake. Feeling fatalistic, I took a big bite. He was right. It tasted delicious. The cake was dense and moist and vanilla-lemon, and the pale frosting was orange buttercream, fresh and wonderful. "Wow!" It might just be the best cake I ever tasted, including my own. No wonder Flint had eaten six pieces. "Thanks! You do good work."

"Told ya." He got another piece himself and sat next to me to eat. "Happy transition, Gyp."

"Thanks, buddy. This definitely helps." I took small bites, savoring the taste as it melted on my tongue, and waited for the curse part to kick in.

Nothing happened. Beryl stood up. "I have to study," she said. "You going to be okay out here?"

I checked the plants. Now that they were involved with each other, their growth had slowed, though they were still inching across the front of the porch. I stood up for a better view. Yep, they had flowed up and over the porch walls, and their furthest branches were approaching the second story windows. "I'll call you if it gets bad, I guess."

"Okay. I'll check back in an hour." She edged around the plants and climbed the stone steps to the porch. The plants had sent fingers across the edges of the steps, too.

"When you get upstairs, could you toss me down my green jacket?" I called. Now that things had stopped erupting and I had time to notice how I felt, I was cold.

"Sure." She went inside.

A couple minutes later a window opened upstairs. Beryl leaned out and dropped my green jacket and a blanket for Flint. She guided them through the air so they landed gently right on us.

"Thanks," I said.

"Welcome." The window closed.

Flint yawned and wrapped up in the blanket.

"You don't have somewhere else to go?" I asked.

"Just to sleep. I can do that here as well as anywhere." Flint was taking a year off between high school and college to goof off, so he didn't have studies or work prep to worry about. Mama didn't approve, but Dad said to let him do it. So far Flint hadn't found anything like a calling. He tried various jobs. It was like a contest. How fast could he get fired? He'd lasted four days as a dishwasher at an upscale restaurant, three at McDonald's, two as a clerk in a CD store, one on a construction crew.

Lately a few neighbors had asked him to babysit. Strangely, he was good at that; his reputation was spreading, and he had babysitting jobs lined up five nights out of seven. He was saving for a trip to Baja. There were lots of things he could manage with magic; he wouldn't have to pay for food unless he wanted to taste local specialties, and he expected to be able to sleep fine outdoors. He might even be able to travel by magic, except he could never depend on going where he wanted. He figured he'd be better off taking the train.

Unlike the rest of us, he had never saved up for a motor vehicle, even though Mama and Dad offered matching funds. He took the city bus when he wanted to go someplace, or begged rides from us, or borrowed cars from friends.

His Baja plan was loose and constantly changing, like most of his plans, and might never come to anything. He had talked his friend Calvin into going with him, whenever they managed to go. Surfing. Gray whales. Desert. Nothing he couldn't get locally, but he wanted to see it in another country.

"I wonder why this cake isn't wild like the other stuff," I said when I finished my piece.

"What did your drawing do?"

I opened my jacket and pointed to the splashes, smears, and splatters of color on my dress. His brows lowered. He leaned forward and touched the material. "You drew a dress?"

"No, I drew a deliberate nothing. It jumped off the walk and plastered itself onto my dress, and now it's part of it."

"Maybe you could design stuff. Wallpaper, towels, placemats."

"You *like* this?"

"It's interesting."

"Do you ever think about design work?" I asked. He drew a mean cake. I hadn't seen it before it turned real, but judging from the way other things were acting tonight, it must have looked pretty good even in the flat version. I could imagine placemats, kitchen towels, wallpaper with Flint-designed pictures of food on them. How did a person get into that field?

He turned away. "I never think about anything."

"But—hey!" Trina's head melted. One second it was there, curly and huge, a sleeping, smiling lump, and then it melted down until nothing was left but what must be Jasper's original drawing on the walk.

"Cool," said Flint.

"I bet your idea worked."

"Three things that worked in one night? How likely is that?"

I slugged his arm. "Come on. You have lots of good ideas."

He glanced at me. Smiled, and looked away. "I'm a legend in my own mind. But nobody else is paying attention, Gyp. Admit it."

I picked at blades of grass. Truth was, he was right. Flint had screwed up so many times we all expected him to do it every time. "Do you have any idea why your cake is good when you drew it with cursed chalk?"

"Sure, I have an idea. I always have an idea. Not necessarily a correct idea. Here's what I think: I have this maverick energy that Tobias can't help me train because he doesn't understand it. Nobody's recorded a power like mine in our family histories. While I was using your chalk, I called on my power, too, asked it to help me do something safe. Maybe it nullifies curse power, or something."

"If that's true, you're going to be my favorite brother now." I leaned against his shoulder.

"Don't get mushy." He pushed me away.

"But seriously." What if he was right? Maybe I could curse him and he could protect himself. I could use my curse power, and not cause harm. "Can I have another piece of cake?"

He jumped up and got me another piece of cake. "Should I save some for Mama and Dad?"

"And Tobias and Hermina? Unless you want to eat it all."

"I'm full. I'll put this in the fridge." He lifted the platter. There was still lots of luscious-looking cake on it. "Be right back."

I ate more cake and studied the effects of my second curse. Trina had flattened down into two dimensions. The plants didn't move at all anymore. Where Flint had drawn his cake, there was blank walkway.

I checked the many-colored splotch on my dress. It showed no signs of giving up being part of my dress. I set aside my empty plate, wrapped up in Flint's blanket, and lay on the lawn.

*Six*

"GYPSUM!"
      Startled out of sleep, I struggled to sit up. Mama's voice always had a galvanizing effect on me.

My hair was wet, and my cheek itched from being against grass all night. My mouth tasted sour. I felt like I had slept in my clothes. Which I had.

"What are you doing out here? It took me fifteen minutes to find you! I had to resort to Search! Why is your car in front of the house?" Mama had a great voice, very useful on TV. Whatever she said always seemed more important than anything you were doing or thinking.

She had a great presence, too. Usually around the house she toned herself down, wore glasses and sweats and let her hair fall where it wanted. She was in full charisma mode. She wore a stylish red dress with gold buttons down the side, and her face looked luminous, her lips a red that matched the dress, her violet eyes outlined in soft black, her hair tamed from its natural wild waves into a glossy dark honey coronet.

Mama in full charisma mode. Me, a mess, out of place,

guilty of illegal parking, and not properly awake. Recipe for trouble.

I rubbed my eyes. My skin didn't feel like my skin. I peered at my hands. Black, with smears of chalk across the fingers and palms.

"Where did you get those gloves?" She stooped to stare.

I looked at the sky. It was barely daylight. "What time is it?"

"Six A.M."

Six A.M. and she was already dressed and ready for the world! Mama never slept very well; she had night terrors, and was often up at five or six, but she usually didn't gear up until later. She didn't even have to go to work until three in the afternoon. Maybe she was really mad. What had happened while I was asleep? If those chalk plants ate the house—

I checked the walk beside me. No more plants making love all over the back of our house; the drawings had reverted to drawings, except there was no picture of cake, and no abstraction.

Mama followed my gaze and spotted the pictures. "What kind of party did you kids have out here last night?" She lifted one of my arms and studied my glove. "Where on Earth did you get this? The workmanship is amazing! But look what you've done! Haven't I taught you to take better care of your things?" She tugged on the glove, and it slipped off in her hand.

"Whoa!" Exposed to morning air, my arm chilled.

"I don't even remember who cleans gloves these days. Guess I'll have to do it myself. Give me the other one."

I held out my gloved arm, and she tugged the glove off. "Oh, this leather! You have to tell me where you got them. This is the softest, finest—" She stroked the gloves over her hand and muttered to them. "What is this chalk? It's persistent!"

I touched my lips with my naked fingers. I had my own skin again. "A lot happened last night."

"I saw. Half a cake in the fridge. When did you bake it? I don't remember you in the kitchen last night except right when you got home from work, and there weren't any baking smells then."

Sometimes I forgot how many secret agent skills Mama had. When she was paying attention, she knew way too much. Another reason I tried to stay out of her way. "Right. Flint made the cake."

"Flint!" She touched her stomach. "But I ate a piece. It was really good."

"Yeah. Mama, Flint made me a celebration cake. I finally had my transition."

Her violet eyes widened. "Oh, honey!" Then she hugged me, warm and comforting as flannel fresh from the dryer. "Oh, honey. Oh, honey," she murmured in my ear. She smelled of jasmine. "I'm so happy. I'm so relieved. I've been so worried about you."

"Well, the news isn't all good. My gift is a dark power."

She sat back and stared into my face. "Gyp?"

"The power of curses," I said.

"Oh, Gyp."

"I've got a lot to figure out," I said.

Mama hugged me again. With my cheek pillowed on her breast, I felt like a kid again. An urge to cry rose in my throat. I swallowed it.

Still, when she let me go, and stared meaningfully into my eyes, I sniffed. I fished a Kleenex out of my coat pocket and blew my nose. "I made those gloves. My first curse."

She frowned. She drew the gloves over her hand. "This quality leather is a curse? I'm not sure I understand."

"Well, they wouldn't come off until you took them off."

"Hmm." Her eyes narrowed.

"The chalk was my second curse. I cursed a rock into chalk."

She grinned.

"So we drew pictures with it to see what would happen. They came alive last night."

She shook her head. "Gyp, this doesn't sound like a curse. It sounds more like playtime."

"In retrospect," I said. I yawned and looked around. "Where's Flint? I thought he was going to watch with me."

"Look." She pointed to an outline in the dewed grass near where I had lain. "Maybe he got up earlier. Somebody made coffee before I got to the kitchen. It was really bad coffee, too."

We both smiled. Flint's kitchen skills were so bad they were legendary. I used to figure he was just doing it to get out of work. But he cooked the same—badly—whether he was alone in the house or there was someone around to notice.

"I threw it out and made a new pot. Would you like some?" Mama asked.

"Uh, sure." Six A.M.! The middle of the night! I had my schedule set up the way I liked it: no classes before eleven in the morning, and my three-day-a-week schedule at the center was an evening shift, three to eight. And anyway, this was finals week, and I'd finished my finals. I didn't even have to go to campus today. All I really wanted to do right now was go back to sleep, but I knew I'd feel better if I got out of my crumpled day-old clothes, brushed my teeth, and showered before I did.

As I crawled to my feet, I realized that I never wanted to sleep on a lawn again, either. I had creaks and crooks in muscles I had never noticed before. I felt like a badly treated antique.

"You have the most interesting rash on your face," Mama said.

"Thanks."

"Is there more of your cursed chalk? I've been thinking about these gloves. If the chalk doesn't come off, maybe I can fix them by sprinkling chalk all over them. I could pick colors that would match several outfits."

"Those are *my* gloves, Mama."

"Oh, you want them back? Really, are you ever going to wear them again?"

Would I ever put them on again, knowing that they tended to cling? I would be scared to wear them. On the other hand, they were the product of my first conscious act of power. On the third hand, when Mama really wanted something, it was hard to resist her. Sometimes she got things through sheer force of character, and sometimes she cheated and used hidden persuasions. She really liked my gloves.

"Uncle Tobias says I have to use my power every day or I'll hurt myself," I said. "Couldn't I just, kind of, curse you a new pair of gloves?"

Her eyes glowed. "Oh! Let's try it! Can you make them red to match my dress?"

"I'll see." How had I made my gloves? I held out my hand and Mama put the gloves into it. I rubbed one against my cheek. I had seen the gloves on my power self, and wished for my own pair. "I wish you had a pair of gloves like these, only the color and style you want," I said. A snake of fire uncoiled inside me and struck. A flash shot from my chest and bathed Mama's arms in red light. Then she was wearing red elbow-length gloves.

A faint tension in my shoulders that I hadn't even noticed relaxed a fraction.

"Yes," she whispered. She held her hands out in front of her and relished. "Ohhhh." She brushed gloved fingertips down her cheek. "Smooth as water. So thin! I bet for sure they can pass the dime test."

"The dime test?"

She blinked, realized I was still with her. "The true test of a good pair of gloves is whether you can pick up a dime while wearing them. This is fine, fine work, Gyp."

"Cool." I stuffed my own gloves in my jacket pocket. One thing accomplished. Whether I ever wore them again, I got to keep my gloves. "Promise not to be mad that they're cursed?"

"Cursed? They're gorgeous. Just what I wanted! This power acts like wish power. Surely Tobias was teasing you, child."

"I don't think so."

"How are they cursed?"

"Try to take them off."

She tried to grasp the upper edge of one glove with the fingers of the other, but she couldn't lift it. There was no dividing line between her skin and the glove. Maybe the glove *was* her skin?

"How clever of you," she said, in that tone that meant the opposite.

"If they act like mine, maybe they'll turn into real gloves after—hmm. When did I make them? Ten last night, and now it's six? Say, eight hours? Or did mine get normal because you pulled on them?" Maybe they'd turned normal long ago and I had slept through it. "If you can't wait that long, I'm sure you'll figure something out. When you figure it out, would you let me know? I'm hoping people will have curse antidotes so I don't have to be scared of using my power."

"I will inform you." For an instant she frowned, but then she got up and headed for the house. "Have to see what the total effect is," she said.

I suspected she would head for the full-length mirror in the entry hallway, placed so everybody could check what they looked like before they went out to meet the world. Most of us didn't use the mirror because we left by the backdoor, since we had to park our vehicles in hidden spots out back. Mama always consulted the mirror before she left the house. Her red Mercedes had its own spot out front to the right of the turnabout, masked by a pittosporum hedge that also hid the tarp tent that kept sun and rain off her car.

The car. Mama had given me a message about my car. I better move it before I did anything else.

No, wait. The shoebox full of chalk sat just the other side of the walkway. I picked it up and looked inside. In the pale morning light, the chalk colors glowed, enticed me to take them out and play with them. I shuddered. There were kids in this neighborhood who liked to draw monsters with sidewalk chalk, or giant warplanes having death duels with spaceships.

I checked the path for stray ends of chalk and stowed all the bits I could find in the box, then took it inside. In my room I looked for a good place to hide it. Not that people came in and went through my things the way they used to. We all used to snoop through each other's stuff when we were little, even though that went against the big fat rule about not invading each other's space. If we told on each other, the person who had snooped had to stand in a corner for half an hour or more. Anybody who tattled got shunned for as long as the rest of us could remember. You had a choice of punishments: the ones Mama and Daddy administered, or the ones the other kids gave you. Sometimes Mama and Daddy punishments were easier to take. Sometimes it was worth the risk.

After people went through transition, our interkid punishments got much more severe.

Worrying about snoops finding my chalk was silly. Everybody who might snoop had already tried out the chalk; I couldn't imagine any of them—except maybe Flint—would want another test-draw. I put the box on a shelf in my closet and shut the door.

A strange little prickle of heat brushed my forehead as I faced the closet door.

I backed up and it went away.

Huh?

I took two steps toward the closet, and felt the tiniest flush on my face. I opened the door, and the heat increased. I walked up to the shelf so that my face was right near the box. Sunlight hot.

I backed away again, shut the door, walked all the way across the room.

The heat was gone.

I blew a breath up across my forehead, ruffling my bangs. Weird. Maybe I could sense things I had cursed? I dug the gloves out of my pocket and held them close to my face. Nothing. Scratch that theory.

Or maybe the gloves' curse had run out.

I pulled the left glove on. It fit like itself. I waited a second, and pulled it off. Hah! No longer a trap! They were plain—well, cursed-chalk speckled—gloves now.

Maybe I had a sense of my own curse energy? Whether it was active, where it was?

I went back to the closet to check. This time I held my hand out to the box, and felt warmth in the tips of my fingers.

Okay. This could be a good thing. To really test it, though, I should see if I responded to other cursed things like this. I could curse something else and see what happened. Or check something I had already cursed. Right now, that meant Mama's gloves. I wasn't going to get anywhere near her until she figured out how to get the gloves off. She hadn't seemed angry when she left me, but if she got frustrated, she—

Mama!

My car!

I ran down to the kitchen where I had left my pack last night, found the car keys in the outside pocket, went out the front door and moved my car to its hiding place under the fig tree.

Then I went back upstairs and finally brushed my teeth

and took my shower. I set the alarm for later and collapsed across my bed.

SOMEBODY knocked on my door a couple hours later. In my dream, I was carrying armloads of glassware. I kept dropping pieces, which shattered and sent chips up to nick me here and there. Small wounds scored my forearms and bare legs. The cuts didn't hurt at first.

The realworld knocking startled me, and in the dream I dropped three vases and a big crystal punchbowl. The splashing crash of breaking glass excited me. A big shard flew up and cut my stomach. Red flowers of blood burst out of my stomach, inner fire leaking from me to take shape in the air in front of me as cool flowed in. The flowers hovered, held their shape. I liked looking at them and wondered if this was my art.

Knock knock.

I struggled up from sleep, let go of my frozen dream life. "What?"

"Gyp?" Tobias said from outside the door.

"What time is it?" My voice came out scratchy, squashed by sleep.

"Eight-thirty."

I groaned. What was with all these people who got up way too early?

After a minute during which I contemplated whether I wanted to move, I got up, threw a happi coat on over the 6X T-shirt I slept in, and went to open the door.

"Sorry I woke you," said Uncle Tobias.

"Yeah, so why did you?"

"I wanted to make sure you were all right."

"You couldn't just come in and check?"

"Gypsum." He used ice voice. There was frost in his eyes.

Without thinking, I straightened, woke up. I was not

supposed to speak to my teacher and elder like this. "Sorry. Had a long weird night, and you woke me out of strange dreams."

After a second, he smiled. "All right. I admit I was too curious to wait any longer. How did everything go?"

I opened my mouth, closed it. "Sorry, Uncle. For this I need coffee."

On my way downstairs, I wondered what the rest of the day would be like. I had slept on the lawn, in a position that left me aching. Mama woke me at six. I slept for maybe an hour and a half, and Uncle Tobias woke me an hour before the alarm. I hated being awakened before the alarm! I hated sleeping in ridiculous positions so parts of myself fell further asleep because of lack of circulation. I hated having my sleep broken up into bitesize chunks. None of those things made me feel like I'd gotten any rest. Might as well have stayed up all night.

Or maybe after I talked to Tobias I could go back to sleep. It wasn't like this was a regular school day. I didn't have to go anywhere today, not even school, my second home. I'd gotten my two-year degree last spring; I stayed at City College because I had a job I liked there, and now I was taking classes for fun. This was sort of my year of goofing off, only, unlike Flint, I managed to make it look like I was doing something semi-important. Dad had encouraged me to get a bunch of college catalogs last spring, but I'd stacked them on my desk without looking at them until it was too late to register for any of the colleges.

Dad had mentioned the University of California at Santa Tekla once or twice. I'd been to the campus out there—it was where Dad and July worked. Plus, there were all kinds of film festivals connected to the film studies program, films which the general public could attend if they paid for tickets. Opal had started a tradition of taking us to foreign and/or obscure films out there while she still lived at home, and after she left, Jasper and I went out once in a while, and sometimes took the younger kids. But there was something about the campus that made me uncomfortable. If I was going to a four-year college, I wanted to go someplace else.

And yet, I wasn't ready to leave home. I'd already spent my high school years somewhere else. While I was away, I had been so homesick . . . not for Mama, but for family, for being in the midst of all these people I knew and loved, and all this chaos of magic that I had never found anywhere else except with the rest of the family in L.A. But maybe I *would* be better off if I went away to college—

Well, no. Not right now. First I had to learn how to deal with this curse thing. For which I needed Tobias.

In the kitchen, Tobias poured me a big mug full of coffee and dumped in half-and-half and four spoons of sugar. "Talk."

I stirred first, then sipped. I told him about the chalk, Beryl's plant, Trina's head, Flint's cake, Mama's gloves. I glanced down at my waist and realized that I had taken my chalk-splotch dress off before I showered. If it had been stick-to-me like the gloves, that part of the curse had worn off. I told Tobias about the probable timespan of my first curses: less than eight hours.

"Fascinating," Tobias said. "You need to start a journal of your power use. You'll want to note trends. The more you figure out about your power, the sooner you'll be able to control it." He went to the fridge and got out Flint's cake.

"Oh, yum!" I got up, grabbed a knife, fork, and plate, lifted the plastic wrap off the cake, and sliced off a piece. "Cake for breakfast. A dream come true."

"It didn't make you sick?" he asked, even though I had told him that already. I had explained Flint's theory of Flint Power plus Gyp Power.

"Just try it." The cake tasted maybe better than it had

the night before; but then, I liked a few things better when they were stale—cookies, for instance.

"Ah, well." Tobias cut a piece for himself.

For a while we ate in companionable appreciation.

I finished my piece and sighed. I probably shouldn't eat another. Dad hadn't even tried it yet. Maybe Jasper and Beryl would want some, too, now that they had proof it didn't hurt people.

On the other hand, when Flint woke up, he'd probably eat all the rest.

Before I could decide whether to grab more while I could, Tobias put the cake back in the fridge.

"So how often do I have to use the power?" I asked. "Is once a day enough? I've already used it once today."

"In an ideal situation, supposing it was a power you really wanted, you would use it until you exhausted it every day, and keep track of how long it took your power to revive. That's the best way of building up your power and testing your ability. In the case of an unkind power, though—" He frowned at me. "Do you want to be a villain?"

I tapped my chest. "Me?"

He sighed. "I have to admit that of all the people I know, you seem the least constitutionally suited to receive a power like this. Any of the other children might have reveled in it."

"Not Beryl."

He lifted an eyebrow. "Oh, yes. I forgot. You left off lessons with me before Beryl transitioned. You don't know what she's capable of. Well, I do. I think even Beryl would have found a way to make this work for her."

"You think I can't?"

He sighed again. "I think you'll have to." He drank some coffee. "So the question is, is this a power you want to foster, or just endure? If you want to become strong in this power, you need to curse as much as you can."

"I don't want to curse!"

"So, you want to merely endure this power. Have you found your tell yet?"

"My tell?"

"The thing that tells you you need to use power."

I thought back. "After I cursed Mama with gloves, tension went out of my shoulders."

"How are your shoulders now?"

I shrugged one shoulder, then the other. They felt tight. I frowned.

"Your first curse of the morning was about two hours ago?"

"Right. Maybe a little longer."

"Oh, dear. Fast recovery time. This power wants to be big. It might not settle for less. I suggest you find something else to curse as soon as you can."

"Like what?" Would he volunteer?

He glanced around the room. "Has anything ever frustrated you about this kitchen?"

Our kitchen was huge. Since I came back from boarding school with lunch and dinner prep skills, I loved the kitchen best of all the rooms in our house, and spent a lot of time here. In many ways, it was a wonderful kitchen. There were tons of cupboards; a large pantry; a chopping block/butcher table big enough to dismember pumpkins and watermelons on; and lots of great dishes, knives, and utensils. I had the industrial-sized kitchen at boarding school to compare it to, though. "I hate that there's no exhaust vent over the stove. The main counter with the sink in it is too low. It makes my back hurt to wash dishes there. And the freezer compartment is way too small."

"If you were to wish any of those things were different—"

"But if my wish is a curse? All those things are adequate as they are. What if I mess them up?"

He shrugged. "Eight hours later, they go back to normal."

"But some stuff didn't do that. My dress was still stained this morning. The cake is still here. What we didn't eat, anyway."

"Don't include Flint in the equation unless you want the effect to last."

Flint bounced into the room as if the mention of his name had drawn him. "Hi." He went to the fridge and grabbed the cake platter. He turned, and waggled his eyebrows at me.

"Just as great as it was last night," I said.

"So can I have some more? It's your cake."

I smiled, touched that he was thinking about me. Maybe he did, off and on, but not so I noticed before. "Hey. If the others aren't up early enough to get some, too bad."

"When we run out, can we make some more?"

Tobias said, "Dear boy, have you ever managed to get your powers to repeat themselves on purpose?"

Flint sighed. "I wouldn't mind experimenting." He got a plate and a fork and carved himself a big piece of cake.

"So, Gypsum? Have you chosen?" Tobias asked.

"Couldn't I do something that's not in the kitchen?"

"You undoubtedly will in the normal course of events."

"What are you choosing?" Flint asked.

"Something to curse."

"Oh, yeah," he said. "Use it or lose it." He went to the fruit bowl on the counter and tossed me a grapefruit. "You could start with something small."

I smiled. Right! Why should I pick on big important things? Maybe my whole curse career could center around fruits and vegetables and rocks.

I studied the grapefruit. A little sticker on it said it was a Texas Ruby and gave a number for the cashier to use when ringing it up.

What harm had a grapefruit ever done to me that I

should curse it? Worst thing one had ever done was squirt in my eye when I was a kid and didn't know how to use those tooth-edged spoons to scoop sections out of grapefruit halves. If someone was trying to scoop out sections of me, I would hope to squirt in their eye too, so I couldn't exactly blame the grapefruit.

This particular batch of grapefruits had been kind of pulpy and juiceless, though. Helping me learn how to curse might be a better fate for them than being thrown out. Maybe they didn't care.

I blew breath up across my face and rolled the grapefruit between my palms.

"Strive for some finesse this time, Gypsum," Tobias said.

"How do I do that?"

"You want to learn to direct your power. Choose its form. You can use rhyme to strengthen your control."

"Poetry is not one of my strong points."

"So work on it. Work on any weaknesses you have; turn them into strengths. Can you envision a curse?"

I frowned. Even thinking about wishing something ill made me queasy. I'd totally suppressed that part of my imagination when everybody was doing nasty things to me and I couldn't do anything powerful back. It was easier for me to accept brief spans of undignified life inflicted on me by relatives if I believed I was above that sort of thing, rather than letting myself know I had no way of retaliating.

I needed to change my way of thinking.

I had done rock into chalk. It had worked, though on the surface you might not think that was a curse. Chalk was some kind of rock, so it was sort of like telling something to be a different version of itself. "What if I try something that's not a curse?" Then I knew the answer to my own question. Rock into chalk wasn't a curse, but the command had supplied cursed energy that made the chalk peculiar and scary.

"If there's no way for the curse energy to embody itself,

nothing will happen. If there's a way but you haven't given a direction, the energy will take the way. If there's more than one way, it's possible the curse energy will take the worst way; that is its nature. It will be better for all of us if you learn to give direction. Then at least we'll know what to expect."

I had expected Mama's gloves not to come off, and they hadn't. Maybe there was more to the gloves than that. I hoped she would tell me.

What would a grapefruit consider a curse?

I frowned. "Does it have to be something *I* consider a curse? Or is it something that the person or object in question considers a curse?"

Tobias raised both eyebrows. "Interesting. I don't know. Another thing to determine as your experience grows."

What was the worst thing a grapefruit could imagine? Probably being eaten.

Rock to chalk. Was chalk a rock's nightmare? It did involve being broken into bits and worn down to nothing through use, whereas if the rock stayed a rock, probably neither of those things would happen. I hadn't considered rock to chalk a curse when I did it, but it had worked out like one. Maybe, ultimately, only the curse energy knew what worked.

Oh, for godsake. I should just try things. I could worry about theory later.

I held the grapefruit between my palms and stared down at it. Tension twitched my shoulders. "May you be plump and juicy and tasty," I said.

Again, heat went through me, and came out of my chest. It shot into the grapefruit. The grapefruit swelled, and swelled, and swelled. It pushed my palms apart, then spread my arms. It grew to beachball size, then weather-balloon size, then even bigger. I let go of it when it got bigger around than a car tire, and I backed away as it grew. So did Flint and Tobias.

Eventually the grapefruit reached the size of a small hot-air balloon, having pushed me and Flint and Uncle Tobias out of the kitchen and smashed the furniture up against the counters and even raised the ceiling a bit.

Then it just sat in the middle of the kitchen, a giant, fragrant, looming globe of citrus with pale gold, pink-washed skin. The pores were enormous, and the scent was overpowering, sweet with a large dollop of throat-closing sour.

I felt incredibly relaxed. I also noticed that I felt heat from the direction of the grapefruit. Okay, good. I could sense my own power in something outside of me. The power felt pretty warm, too. I had used a lot of power on this one.

"Dear me," Tobias said.

"Way to go!" said Flint.

Dad strolled down the hall. "What are you looking at?" He peered over our shoulders into the kitchen. "Hmm. That's not particularly convenient. Would one of you gifted people get me a cup of coffee? With cream and a spoonful of sugar?"

"Hey, Dad. Gyp did it," Flint said.

Dad stared at me. My heart flattened. Dad and I had a great relationship based on our mutual status as normal people in a house full of magic-users. Mama always protected Dad from anything the kids might be tempted to do to him, and made sure we respected his authority by backing up most of what he told us with her own irresistible force; but she didn't dictate our attitudes, and some of us had gotten pretty cocky after transition.

My eyes got hot. A tear streaked down my cheek.

Dad hugged me. "Hey. It's all right. I don't know why you need a giant grapefruit, honey, but it's all right."

Then his hand stilled, stopped stroking my back.

I had a morbid sense of him pulling away from me, even though we still embraced.

He put his hands on my shoulders and pushed me back so he could look into my eyes. He was smiling. Maybe I had imagined that new distance. "What happened?"

I rubbed my eyes. My throat felt tight. I couldn't speak.

"She went through transition while we were in L.A., Miles," Tobias said. "Not a normal transition. She received a dark power."

"Aw, come on," said Flint. "How dark is it if it makes giant grapefruits? Maybe it's sort of misty gray."

"Interesting," Tobias said. "Something midway between curse power and wish power? Perhaps you're right. Any chance you can grab that fruit and take it somewhere else, Flint? The backyard, perhaps?"

Flint shrugged. He stepped over the threshold into the kitchen and put his palms against the grapefruit.

The grapefruit growled.

## Seven

FLINT jumped back as a slit appeared on the side of the fruit, split to reveal the fruit's sleek, juicy, ruby-red interior. The slit gaped wide, the growls louder now that the mouth was open. Flint leaped over the threshold into the hall and slammed the kitchen door. "Okay. Maybe I was wrong about the gray part," he said.

"Gyp?" Dad said.

I swallowed. "I got the power of curses, Daddy. Only I don't know how to use it."

"Killer grapefruit?" He smiled at me.

"I just wanted it to taste good."

"Hah!" Flint said. "Maybe it tastes good, all right. Maybe it wants to taste us good!"

Tobias sketched signs across the kitchen door. "We had better stay out until it goes away," he said. Black bands of force stitched from side to side across the door, binding it shut. "Sorry about the coffee, Miles. I guess we'll all be going out to eat until later."

"What? You're just leaving a giant grapefruit in charge of the kitchen?"

"So far, Gyp's curses have lasted less than eight hours. If this follows the pattern, it will revert in time for us to make supper. Small price to pay, don't you think?"

Dad frowned. "Eight hours? You were cursing things more than eight hours ago? You transitioned last weekend? Gyp, what has been going on?"

"I thought I had the flu. I didn't know it was transition. Nothing happened until last night. You and Mama were watching TV and we didn't want to interrupt you."

He looked rueful. "Oh. I wish. . . ."

"I'll be cursing things the rest of my life, Daddy. I'm sure you'll experience as many curses as you can stand, and probably more."

He ruffled my hair. "It's not that I'm asking for curses. I just want to help."

"You will." I would need everybody's help, I was pretty sure, especially Dad's. He was a psychology professor. It used to make us mad when we were little and he analyzed us all the time. He grew out of it, and we grew out of some of our resentment; analysis was part of his character. Sometimes he told us things about ourselves we would never have been able to figure out on our own.

Maybe he could help me think about my power and figure out how to make it work better. I trusted Tobias for that kind of knowledge, but what did Tobias know about curse power? Not that much, if Great-Aunt Meta was the only other person he had known who had had it, and she had died before she could master it. Maybe a fresh brain would help.

"So what's the game plan?" Dad checked his watch. "I have to leave for work in about twenty minutes—earlier if I want to stop for coffee and a doughnut somewhere on the way."

I said, "I want to go back to bed."

"You should record everything as soon as possible," Tobias told me. "What you did, how it manifested, what you felt while you did it. All these things are important."

I growled at him.

"Gypsum." Ice voice again.

I straightened, then glared at my great-uncle.

He held a hand up, palm toward me, and I saw a faint blue shield in front of it. Light glanced off a translucent blue disk.

My eyes went wide. Tobias was shielding himself from me? Never-hurt-anybody me? How could anybody be scared of *me*?

He took my power seriously. And he thought I'd use it on him.

I backed up a couple steps, swallowed, and said, "Okay. Right. I'll go upstairs and find a blank notebook right now and write everything down. Bye, Dad." I darted forward to kiss my father's cheek. "Have a good day at work. See you later. Flint. Uncle." I left the hall and ran all the way up the stairs, trying to escape some phantom self who could scare other people, even my oh-so-powerful great-uncle.

I woke up later that afternoon with my notebook on my chest. My fountain pen had leaked blue ink on my T-shirt and sheets. "Damn," I said.

The pen shriveled and cindered into dust. Its apotheosis burned my fingers.

Suddenly I was wide awake.

One word could do that. Destroy some innocent thing that just happened to be nearby, had followed its own nature and done something I didn't like.

This power was real.

My burnt fingers throbbed. My eyes leaked.

House-eating plants, a man-eating grapefruit, somehow those things had felt like a game. Maybe a really bad video game. Total destruction of my favorite pen with one careless word? Somehow more serious and scary.

I remembered the shield Tobias had thrown up just because I was mad and glared at him. He understood.

Tension rode my shoulders. I glanced at the clock. One-thirty in the afternoon. I'd slept for about four hours; I had had time to build up a big charge. What was going to happen when I managed to sleep eight hours in a row, if I ever did again? What kind of charge would that give me?

I got my wastebasket and studied the litter in it. The basket was half full of crumpled drafts of an anthropology paper, used Kleenex, candy wrappers, empty ink cartridges, magazines I'd finished reading minus the pictures and articles I had ripped out to save in my information morgue, and other miscellany. Slated to go out with the garbage unless I had a recycling moment and sorted the papers from the other stuff.

I set the wastebasket on the floor. I licked the tip of my index finger. I thought it through: the waste, not the basket. I pointed. "Damn!"

A flash, a spiral of smoke, a few sparks. The litter was gone. The inside of my wastebasket bore scorch marks.

My shoulders felt incredibly tense, still. Maybe there was a fraction of ease.

But hot dog! Something constructive to do. I could fry all the garbage in the house. Maybe that would bleed off some of this power. After that, I could visit Dumpsters and trash cans all around town, maybe the landfill out in the salt slough near the university, burn off power by cursing waste into oblivion. Something! Something safe.

I went to the closet and looked for regular clothes. As I flipped through my shirts, I glanced up at the chalk box. No heat came from it. I took it down and looked inside. It was still full of chalk, but the colors had faded, and some special nuance of the way the chalk had looked while it was cursed had gone.

I took a pink piece and drew a small, simple five-petaled

flower on the closet wall. I waited a minute. It stayed a scribble.

Whew.

I should be writing this down to show to Tobias later.

Instead I found a blue blouse and a pair of jeans. I changed, put on tennis shoes, and dropped my ink-splotched sleeping T into the laundry.

I was about to leave the room when I noticed the protection stone Jasper had given me eight years earlier. Now that I didn't use it and Flint had stopped hiding it from me, I kept it on my desk. Sometimes when I was working on a paper for a class and I got stuck, I'd hold it until my mind settled. It had become a friend.

I picked it up. There wouldn't be a charge in it now. When Jasper had charged it, he had to do it pretty often; the stone wasn't a natural holder of power. I didn't sense any special energy in it. It was just a pretty green sea stone.

Maybe if he charged it, I could carry it around with me and hand it to people before I cursed them. What would happen then?

I tucked it in my pocket, then snuck downstairs and out the porch door.

I went down to the orchard.

On the upper terrace just south of the house below the back porch, there was the pool, the lawn with one big orange tree in the center, Mama's rose garden, and a retaining wall. The wall was broad; you could sit on it and look out to the sea.

About ten feet below the upper terrace was the orchard, a wild place not as maintained as the lawn and pool grounds above. Nobody mowed the orchard; native grasses grew knee high around all the fruit trues. We had lemon trees, plum trees, orange trees, apricot trees, even a grape-fruit tree in the orchard, but the centerpiece was a big loquat tree, very tall and scraggly with shiny dark green leaves and millions of clusters of pale yellow fruit that turned almost apricot when they were ripe. Eating loquats was a lot of work; first you had to peel the skin, then you could eat the thin layer of flesh, sweet and fine-textured, but not much food before you hit the big glossy seeds in the center.

In the eastern half of the orchard just below the pool yard lay a small plot of land that Dad had had rototilled. For a while when we were kids, we each raised some kind of vegetable or fruit in that plot. I raised carrots one year, and corn another. The others raised radishes and zucchini and tomatoes, green beans, bell peppers, strawberries, watermelon. We had to learn how to take care of our plants. I had hated thinning carrots. It was hard to pull up something already alive that I had planted, though I didn't have much sympathy for weeds.

Jasper had a year when he raised pumpkins. He even milk-fed a couple so he would have giant pumpkins for Halloween, but their skin turned pale, so they looked wrong.

We each tended our own crop, put the Burpee packet on a green-stained bamboo stick at the end of our rows to weather and fade as the season progressed. I remembered how excited I was the first time I ate a carrot I had actually grown.

I wandered over to the plot where we had had our vegetables. Weeds choked it now, though there were traces of the old rows and the squash and bean mounds. When had we stopped planting things? I squatted next to the plot. Maybe the year Opal and Jasper went through transition; everything had changed after that. As though they had turned into other people, and everybody and everything had had to adjust to it. We had lost track of some of our family rituals and started others.

I picked up a stick, stuck it in the ground, and pointed at it. "Damn!" The stick vanished in a flash of light and a puff of smoke.

Three damns down, and I still felt awfully tense.

I wished I had brought the notebook and a pen with me. I should be keeping track of all this data. Tobias was right, even though it made me grumpy.

How would curse power answer if I actually wished aloud for my notebook and pen?

No time like now to try it, and better here, where I was alone in a big open space, than somewhere inside the potentially fragile house, close to loved ones.

"I wish I had my curse notebook and a pen from my backpack," I said. A small dart of heat stroked my breastbone on its way out of me. An instant later, my notebook dropped out of the sky into my lap, and a Bic pen thumped down on top of it.

Clean and simple. Huh.

I opened the notebook.

Every page was covered with black ink scribbles, none of them legible.

I found a little space near the top of one page and tried the pen. No ink.

I sighed. I was glad I had just started the notebook this morning; there wasn't much lost work I would have to reconstruct.

I cleared a patch of earth in the garden plot and used the pen to draw three lines in the dirt, one for each of my experimental "damns." I cleared another section, wrote W at the top, and wrote one line below it for my first wish of this session.

After that I wandered through the orchard, picking up small objects, bringing them back to the plot, and damning them. I zapped loquats, rocks, oranges, twigs, a really big stick, a beer can—which left a little dribble of melted metal; now, *that* was scary—and a faded hula hoop I found in some tall grass, so old it must have been left behind by children a couple generations before us. The ancient plastic vaporized without leaving a trace.

I had crosshatched fifteen "damns" in the dirt and my shoulders still felt tense when Beryl showed up.

"Whatcha doing?" she asked from behind me.

I jumped a foot. Then I whirled. "Don't sneak up on me, Beryl!"

"Sneak? I was just wandering around."

"Don't even come near me, okay? Or, I know, has Tobias taught you how to shield yet?"

"Shield?" She looked bewildered. "I need a shield with you now?"

I sucked on my lower lip. "Watch this."

I grabbed a big stick I had been saving and stuck it in the ground. It stood as tall as I did. I pointed at it. "Damn!" I said.

A brief thumbprint of heat at my chest. Light outlined the stick, then it turned black, then vanished. A small drift of acrid smoke, a flashmark on the ground were all that remained.

Beryl gasped. Her face went pale.

"I don't even have to mean it," I said. "I could do this by mistake. I've never had to guard my words before. I'll do the best I can, but until everybody in the house is shielded, I think I better stay outside."

She blinked a couple of times. "I'll go tell them this is what you're doing," she said after a minute. "I'll tell them about the shields."

"Thanks."

"You hungry?"

I checked in with myself. "Starving. Is the grapefruit still in charge of the kitchen?"

"Yep. I've got a box of granola bars in my room—" Her eyebrows lowered and she looked inward. A box appeared in her hand. Wish power! She handed me the box. She frowned again and materialized a bottle of water, handed it to me. It was cold, straight from the refrigerator.

"Thanks. Thanks, little sister."

"Hang in there."

I nodded. She left, pushing through the high grass of the orchard, burrs catching at the hem of her dress.

I ate a couple of granola bars and drank some water, then realized I was delaying the inevitable.

My shoulders felt stiff and tight. Damns didn't seem to do it as far as discharging curse energy; I would have to curse something else soon or suffer lockjaw or something worse.

I hesitated, then pulled my protection stone out of my pocket. Maybe it could protect itself. I cupped it in my hands. I couldn't sense any energy in it, but then, before my transition I hadn't been able to sense magical energy. Maybe now I could only sense my own.

I was going to think this through. I was! But words dropped out of my mouth. "Stone, be bone. Be within muscle and skin. Be own. Be kin."

At last I felt real heat gather. From my toes and fingers and the top of my head, from all my outer edges, heat streaked toward my center. This'll do it, I thought, cast off curse energy for at least a little while. The heat swooped out of me, leaving cool behind, and traveled into the rock.

Within my hands the rock's surface changed from hard and cold to smooth, warm, pliant. The rock swelled and shifted, stretched and spread. It grew limbs and a head—at first as generic as the body of a gingerbread boy, a cookie cutter shape of a small human. The curse energy kept working on it, spinning across its skin in pearly drifts, drawing details to the surface. It sprouted hair and features and selfhood. Finally it opened large black eyes and looked up at me.

Someone alien and old lived inside those eyes.

It was the size of a three-year-old child, much larger than the rock had been, but it had the shape of a grownup. Its hair was wavy and dark brown, like mine. As I watched, color bled into its eyes until they were hazel, like mine. It had a belly on it, like mine, and breasts like mine too. She looked like a miniature me. I had never enjoyed looking at myself, and I wasn't happy looking at her, either, but I knew she was mine and I should do what I could for her. A child of my curse. What had I done?

"Sister," she said.

"Hi." She could talk. She had a mind, could draw conclusions and voice them. She wasn't chalk to use or ignore.

What was she?

I had turned a rock into a person. I couldn't remember any of my siblings doing that.

She was a product of curse energy. How unpleasant was this going to be?

She pushed up, got to her feet. She stood about two and a half feet tall. She looked me over, frowned.

"Who *are* you?" I asked.

"That's a question." She bent her arm at the elbow, watched as her forearm waved. She made her other arm do the same trick. "I'm small."

"Yes. I made you from a rock."

"You *made* me." She tossed me a look with attitude: *Yeah, right.*

"I didn't make you?"

She kicked one leg, then the other. "Perhaps you made this body. People don't make spirits."

"So you're really someone."

She smiled. A dimple showed in her cheek, just like the one I had when I smiled. I thought with surprise that she looked cute.

"Have you ever thought about doing something different with your hair?" she asked.

"What?"

She ran her hands through her hair, and I felt hot fingers moving through my own hair, pressing from the front to the back of my head. When she lifted her hands away, her hair was a mass of short black curls streaked with auburn.

I felt my head. My hair, fine, flyaway, short, and brown, had changed, felt thicker and more tightly curled. I tugged one of the curls, but couldn't pull it out far enough for me to see what color it was. I had my suspicions. "How did you do that?"

She stood with her hands on her hips and stared up at me, her head cocked to one side. "That's one look," she said. "I like it. But let's try something else." She put her hands to the side of her head and pulled on her hair. The curls straightened, grew; cascades of silky black hair poured from her head, from my head, until we sat in sleek black capes of our own hair. I bunched some of it in my hands. Thick and smooth and heavy.

I had always dreamed of long hair, but I'd never been able to grow mine past my shoulders; it was so fine it split and broke before growing longer. I pulled some of the new hair forward over my shoulder and looked at it wonderingly. True, I was getting a headache from the weight of it, but wasn't it beautiful? I separated it into three strands and started braiding. I had braided Beryl's hair and Opal's hair, but never my own.

"Or blonde?" said the other. The hair in my hands changed to platinum blonde.

I looked at her to see what the effect was. The blonde washed out her skin color. She looked sallow.

"No, you're right. Not our color. But what if—" She stroked her hands down over her breasts, stomach, legs, up over her rump, her sides, her back, finally over her arms and shoulders, neck and face. Her skin turned golden.

I held my hands out before me, marveling at this new tan. I had never spent much time in the sun. I'd heard too much about skin cancer. But I was as susceptible to advertising images as other people, and I'd wondered what it would be like to have skin this color.

"You like that, hey?"

I checked her looks. Blonde, tan Gypsum? Still fat, but

somehow it looked good on her. Well, no. The blonde was not a good color.

"More golden, then." She stroked her hands over her hair and darkened the color from ash to coin gold.

I smiled and shook my head. I was creeped out by the fact that she could hear my feelings even when I didn't say them out loud. At the same time, it was kind of handy.

"What color do you want?"

"I don't know. Who are you? What are you? What are you doing to us?"

"I'm just playing." She ran her hand through one part of her hair and it turned fiery red. She ran her hand through another section and it turned black. A third section, grass green. A fourth section went deep brown and curly. A fifth section, blond-streaked brown and frizzy. Then she stroked through her bangs and left them pink. "And—" She pulled a section from the top, threaded it through her fingers, left a long solid streak of white. With every move she made, I felt something move through my hair, and I saw it change around me. "Something for everybody. Nice, eh?"

"Patchwork quilt hair," I said. "What happens when you brush it?" Would it all mix together, or stay in separate sections? It looked incredibly silly; it was hard to take her seriously, and I figured nobody would take me seriously either as long as my hair looked like this. Maybe that would be a good thing.

"Did you bring a brush?" she asked.

"No."

"Conjure me one."

"I don't know how."

"Wish one up."

"It'll be flawed," I whispered.

"Why?"

"Because my power is unkind."

"Who told you that?"

"Uncle Tobias."

She spat to the side. "Wish me a brush."

"I wish you had a hairbrush the right size for you to use, one that will work as a brush should," I said. A tiny trace of heat on my breastbone, then a tiny trace of chill.

She held up a red brush. "How hard was that?" She stroked it through her many-colored hair. I felt the phantom touch of a brush through my hair, and sat back with my eyes closed.

I had always loved having my hair brushed. Opal used to brush my hair when I was little, and she had cut my fingernails and toenails for me until I was old enough to clip them myself. Mama was too busy for such things. Opal was pretty busy too, but she had made time.

These days the only people who brushed my hair were me and the hairdressers at SuperCuts, and they usually worked fast.

Now here I was in the orchard with an unknown creature, having my hair brushed by proxy. It felt great. She brushed for a while. My shoulders had already relaxed when I made her, but now, as the brush traveled through my new luxurious long hair, stroked across my scalp, I fell into a state of ultimate contentment. The sun shone on my face and the air smelled like lemons. I couldn't remember the last time I had felt so nice.

What kind of curse was this?

At last she stopped. She thumped my knee with the brush. "Hey. You asked. What does it look like?"

The hair had changed again. It was heavy and wavy, streaked all through with shades of brown, black, blonde, and red, with one vivid white streak down the side. Sun gilded it.

"It looks great," I said. "Thank you."

"This is the look you want to go with?"

"It's up to me?"

"Why not?"

I shrugged. "You're making all the choices. I just

wanted to thank you for brushing it like that. That felt great."

"I'm making all the choices." She smiled wide and wicked then. "You said it. So what about the rest of us?" She spread her arms and looked down at her stomach. She cupped her breasts. They filled her hands. She patted her stomach, and it jiggled. "I don't think there's enough of us. You made me too small, but that's because you're too small."

"Too small," I said faintly.

She slapped her belly. "We could be much more magnificent." She tugged, pulled her belly out to twice its size, and I felt an answering surge in mine. My stomach spread, pushing my arms out from my sides. "And these." She pulled at her breasts, and they grew too. Mine ballooned from grapefruit to honeydew size. "And this." She slapped her rump. It swelled. "And these." She slapped her thighs, and her upper arms. They grew and grew, and so did mine. "And, of course, this." She cupped her face in her hands, pulled her hands outward, and her face followed, rounding out, chins tripling.

I sat inside my new shape, my clothes in tatters around me. My fat, fat arms lay across the upper curve of my rounded belly, and my breasts lapped over my arms. My butt lifted me higher off the ground than I was used to, and my legs were layered in rolls of fat like a baby's, splayed out like a baby's, too fat to cross.

# Eight

I had been fat since I was twelve, but I had never been fat like this before. I spread my hands and stared at pudgy fingers. The adjustable silver ring I had worn since a boy gave it to me in seventh grade had opened wide and fallen off the ring finger of my right hand. My flesh was golden with rose undertones; I cupped my breast and felt velvet skin against my fingers. Everything about me was huge and soft and cushioned. I stroked my belly, pressed it in, let go to see it spring out, round and huge, monumental. The shake reverberated through me. I flexed my ankles. What would it be like to swim like this? I would float really well. The water would cradle me. What would it be like to walk like this?

Buddha was fat like this, I thought, and looked up to see Jasper by the loquat tree, staring at me.

I had nothing to cover myself with except my hands. I cupped them over my breasts, and drew my knees toward me as far as they would go—not very far. Too much me in the way. I dropped my head as far as my chins let me and watched my blush travel across my breasts. I stared down at my curse child.

"What are you worried about? You're magnificent," she said. She spread her arms wide and whirled to show me all the large, loose, jiggling parts of herself. How abundant and succulent she looked, how lush. Her long many-colored hair danced around her without hiding her. She laughed.

I smiled.

Jasper stooped beside me. "Want something to wrap up in?" he asked.

"The sun feels good." My voice sounded richer and more robust. The sun, the faint breeze that brushed across my skin now and then and teased my hair, the scent of warm earth, crushed grass, the sound of the highway not too far away, birds calling from tree to tree in the jungle beyond the orchard fence, it all melted together into comfort.

I did want to wrap up in something and hide what I looked like from my brother, and from myself. Then I thought, this is a manifestation of my own energy. I better ride it out, wherever it takes me. Gotta get used to weird things happening.

"What is she?" He stared at the small woman. She stood, smiling, her arms akimbo.

"She won't tell me."

"Where'd she come from?"

"I put curse energy into my stone, and she's what happened." I sighed, glanced at Jasper, who looked away. I tipped as far forward as I could, put out my hands, pushed up, managed to rock to my feet. Sumo wrestlers were fat like this, I thought. But they probably had more muscles. "This is Jasper," I told my curse child.

"I know." She came to me and held her arms up. "Lift me."

I was afraid to lean over, afraid I would collapse onto my huge belly and be as helpless as a turtle on its back. I tilted forward a little and held out my arms.

"All right. A for effort." She jumped up into my arms, settled her butt between my breasts on my stomach as though it were a shelf. I clutched her to me. She, too, felt soft and velvety.

"God, you're heavy," I told her.

"So are you."

I glanced at Jasper. He held a green blanket in his arms. "Is that for me?" I asked.

He looked away and shrugged.

"He can't stand to look at us in our natural state," she said.

"Is this our natural state?"

"One of them." She leaned across my breast and poked Jasper's arm. "Hey, you! Get used to it!"

"She's my sister," he mumbled.

We had always been embarrassed to see each other naked, even when we were little. Well, not when we were, like, two and four, but later. "Give me the blanket," I said.

He shook it out and draped it around my shoulders and tucked the corners into my hands. The curse child's head rose above it. The blanket wasn't big enough to go all the way around me. He studied it, then tugged on it and made it bigger, big enough to surround my new size. "You coming up to the house?"

I shook my head. "I was thinking about going swimming."

The curse child turned and smiled at me.

"Mama's by the pool," Jasper said.

"She still wearing red gloves?"

"Yep. They go all the way to her shoulders."

Uh-oh. They had started out elbow-length. Maybe they'd grown because she liked them to start with. Maybe if you liked the result of a curse, it would figure out a way to make things worse.

What did that mean for me in present circumstances? I didn't exactly like what I had become, but I found it interesting. Did that mean the curse child would intensify it?

How *could* she?

Maybe I shouldn't ask.

I took a couple of steps. My feet dropped like thunder, and every loose thing on my body swayed in response to each impact.

If Mama was by the pool, no way was I going swimming now.

I headed away from the stairway up to the pool, toward the stairway that led to the lawn. Jasper walked beside me.

"Did Beryl tell people about my curses?" I asked. "She tell you what happens when I say the D word?" I liked my new voice. I wondered what it would sound like if I sang.

"Yeah."

"Are you shielded?"

"Nope."

"D— Jasper! What are you doing here?"

"I came to see how you were."

"I'm fine!"

"You sure?"

Stomp. Jiggle. Stomp. Jiggle. "I'm enjoying this, actually."

"Wow."

"Would you like to try it?" asked the small woman on my stomach.

His eyes widened. He shook his head.

"Chicken," she said.

He drew a pattern on one hand with the index finger of the other, then held up his hand, palm toward us. The sun glinted on the shield he had built.

The small woman relaxed back across my collarbone, one hand riding on each of my breasts. She was warm against me. Her heavy, smooth hair fanned across my front. "Chicken," she muttered again.

"How long is this going to last?" Jasper asked.

"I don't know." We reached the stairs and I lowered

myself to sit on the second one. My rear was so cushioned that even stone felt soft. "It's up to her."

"Let's just stay like this the rest of your life," she said drowsily.

I contemplated that. It was scary. People would look at me funny, mock me; they already muttered things under their breath, but if I stayed this size, I was pretty sure I would hear much louder things. People would stare and point. Nothing would fit. Clothes? I'd have to have them made for me, and I wouldn't be able to fly in planes, or sit in booths at restaurants, or ride rides at Disneyland. No more movies. Wheelchairs wouldn't hold me. I wouldn't be able to drive my car.

Not that I had ever dated, except for whatever my confusing relationship with Ian was, but with my new look, the prospects were even dimmer.

And how could I work? How could my students listen to what I wanted to teach them? I would be triply the freak I already was. How could they pay attention to anything I said when they were confronted with something they had probably never seen before? What could they do but stare and speculate?

Movement was challenging, and I hadn't even tackled stairs. If it were this hard for me to walk, my world would shrink to a very small sphere.

"If I'm going to stay like this, I need more muscles," I said.

"I can do that." She sat up and patted my stomach, my arms, my breasts. She patted her own legs and rear and back, stroked her shoulders. With each touch, strength flowed into me. Things under my skin tightened and grew more dense, the thick layers of fat riding higher over the muscle fibers so that I expanded even more. I felt strong, full of coiled energy waiting to be used.

The blanket was too small again. It dropped off my right shoulder. I lifted my arm and pumped it. Muscles rippled and popped under the skin as I flexed, even as flab hung down from my arm and swayed with my movement. I felt muscles shift across my back. "Wow!" I climbed to my feet. Oh, yeah. This felt better. Movement was ponderous, but it didn't make me out of breath to walk. I stomped around the orchard, flattening the tough grasses under my feet. The little one rode me as though I were a carnival ride. She laughed.

Was the ground really shaking under my tread? Maybe it was just my own wobbling that made me think so.

I grabbed a tree trunk and bent it. Whoa! Bent it! My arms didn't hurt from the effort, either. I let it go, and it whipped upright. I felt like a god in a bad Italian Greek-myth movie. Roar! Or, characteristically, I guessed I should have roared with laughter. I was afraid to test the power of my voice. What if it was loud enough to rouse Mama, and she came over to see what was happening?

"Roar," I whispered.

Okay. I wasn't sure I could get used to this, but it was a lot better than feeling totally immobilized by myself. I wandered back to the stairs and sat down again.

"God," said Jasper. "How did she do that?"

The curse child laughed and drummed on my stomach. Jasper touched her shoulder. "What are you?"

"You shouldn't have done that." She stared up at him, and he snatched his hand away. His touch had built a bridge between them, one she could cross; it was an invitation to her energy to shape him, if she took it that way. "Too late! Too late. What would I like you to look like?"

"Don't," I murmured.

"We're brother and sister. He should look more like us."

"Please. Leave him alone," I said.

"I dropped my shield," Jasper said, his voice surprised.

"I wasn't even working on you," she said. "I'm having too much fun with her. But now that I've got you, hmm."

"I can't believe how stupid I was. Well, go ahead."

She cocked her head and studied him. I looked at him too, my golden brother. I had always thought he was handsome, but lately he had grown into his face and looked better than ever. He had tilted opalescent green eyes set far apart, and dark eyebrows that quirked at the outer ends; his nose was straight and handsome, his upper lip short and his lower lip full, and his jaw was fine, a clean line from pointed chin back to below his ears. Right now his dark hair was long on top and down the back and short on the sides. He was wiry rather than muscular, and he walked loose, comfortable inside himself.

She sucked in a deep breath and puffed out her cheeks like a chipmunk's. Jasper doubled in width. Buttons popped off his shirt. He unzipped his jeans and dropped them in a hurry. He made a couple of passes and came up with a garment like a judge's robe, which he slipped into.

His face lost its fine edges and blurred. His throat thickened and his chin doubled. His belly stuck out.

I felt strange. If my curse child was my own image in miniature, I thought I looked—enormous, but somehow wonderful. Jasper did not wear fat at all well. He slumped on the stair, all his lines sloped and defeated.

"Pitiful," she said.

"How can you stand it?" His voice sounded garbled and full of despair.

"That's why you should try it."

He shuddered.

She turned her moon face to stare up at me. She patted my cheek and smiled. "This has been more fun than I ever imagined," she said. "But I've used up almost all the energy you put into me. You really want to stay this way?"

If she was a curse, wouldn't she want to leave me in trouble? If I said I wanted to stay huge, would she think I was telling the truth, and shrink me? Or listen to me, leave me like this? If I said I didn't want to stay huge, would she think I was telling the truth, and leave me like this? "I don't know what to tell you."

"Are you handing me the choice again? Gypsum, you should stop doing that. You can't trust me."

"Are you sure?"

She stared into my eyes for a long, long moment, and then she rose to her knees on my stomach, facing me, and kissed my cheek. "Call me if you want to mess around some more. I'd love to come back."

"Call you what?"

"Altria." She hugged me around the neck. She stood on my stomach, sighed, and melted from a lively flesh-colored form into a green stone that thumped down on my stomach. I caught it in shrinking hands.

Diminishing felt very, very strange.

I had almost gotten used to taking up a lot more space, feeling my own heaviness and how parts of me settled onto other parts. I had liked having enough muscles to support myself. It all whittled away, not instantly, but a layer at a time so that I felt myself shrink. Maybe it was more like deflating. Skin that had stretched wide to encompass all that new me slowly pulled in as new me melted, finally snapped tight to what was left. I held the blanket open and looked down at myself. I still had a bulge of belly, breasts bigger than I was comfortable with, thick thighs and hanging upper arms, and yet, it was all so much less than it had been. For the first time in my life I felt small.

I wrapped up in the blanket, now miles too big for me, then reached up to my head and felt my hair. Short again, and curly; I wasn't sure how short, or what color; shorter than it had been before I conjured her, though.

I looked at my brother. He was still twice his size, and looked lumpy and miserable. That was no good. He should be able to fight this. Couldn't he shrug off curses? Hadn't he said so last night when he urged me to accept my other self?

He stood up. He took five steps away from me, turned and came back. "Oh, God! How do you stand it?"

"But Jasper, you're only as big as I am now. Not like I was before."

"Yes," he said. "How do you stand it?"

"Stand it?" I rose to my feet. I was myself again. I felt so light I could float away. I knew I had a closet full of clothes that fit me, that my car seat would hold me comfortably, and that my students would see me as the same person I was yesterday, even though I had changed. I was outside the normal accepted size range, but not too far outside. I laughed. "This is great!"

He frowned. He shook himself, and blew out breath, and stood up straight. "You mean that."

"Sure. Specially now that I've had a chance to try it another way."

He walked around. "My legs rub against each other when I walk."

"Well, sure. That's why I wear pants more often than dresses."

"My stomach moves."

"Yeah."

He walked back and forth. He slapped his hands against his chest, his stomach, his thighs, his rear. He frowned. "It's all . . . so heavy."

"You can get used to it."

He sighed. "Guess you can get used to anything."

"Or you can change it, right?"

"I don't—Yikes!" He staggered and sat down. Everything extra about him evaporated; his judge's robe collapsed in a welter of folds over him. He lay flat on the ground, back to Jasper normal, and stared at the sky. "Oh. Okay. Whew."

He frowned and sat up. "Whew."

"Did you do that?" I asked.

"No. Guess she left planned obsolescence in it. Thank God. So what was she?"

I shook my head. "I really don't know."

"How did you make her?"

I showed him the stone. "I said some words to this, and it turned into her."

He frowned. I held the stone out to him. It was cool now, clean of curse energy. He stroked his fingers over it and looked up at me.

I shrugged. "I don't know. I know it's not charged right now, but I thought it might be safer than anything else."

He sketched a sign on it, shook his head, smiled. "It's empty, Gyp. There's a faint frame of habit in it, protection and love, but no real charge. Nothing there to moderate your power."

"So it was all me, I guess." I held out my hand, and he put the stone in it.

"What words did you say?"

What words? "I tried to get my notebook without going to the house so I could write everything down, but I screwed it up. I don't think I can do power things directly without messing them up. So I don't have a record of what I said, and I don't want to say the same thing outloud again." Besides, my shoulders felt loose and relaxed. Altria had been a really great curse. "Maybe if I go to my room now, I can write down what I remember. It should be safe for me to go in the house now, at least for a little while. I don't think I've got any power left."

"Good." He jumped to his feet.

We went up the stairs and across the lawn together. He bumped his shoulder into mine. "That was really something, Gyp."

I shook my head. "I'm glad I don't have to go back to school today. I don't think I'm safe to be around."

"The learning curve is high right after transition. I bet you'll get some of this down real soon."

"Thank God it's almost Christmas Break. I don't want to inflict this on my friends." Well, sooner or later I'd be facing my friends with this power intact if I didn't want to die of it, but maybe if I waited and worked, I'd know how to control it enough not to threaten everybody by my ignorance.

What was I going to do about work tomorrow? It was bound to be a light shift, but maybe I should call in sick anyway. Yeah. That would be a good idea. I wondered what curse power would do to the equipment at the Center, but I didn't really want to find out.

"What's the deal with you guys? Costume party?" Flint asked as we came in off the porch. He was sitting in a chair in the great hall with his feet on the table, reading a comic book.

I glanced down. Jasper was wearing his sizes-too-big judge's robe, and I was wrapped in a big green blanket.

"Curses," said Jasper.

"Cool! What'd I miss?"

Jasper slanted me a look, his eyebrows up.

"It was spectacular," I said.

"Dang! Beryl told us not to go in the orchard. I knew I shouldn't have listened."

"You wouldn't have liked the side effects," Jasper told him.

"There were side effects?" Flint dropped the comic book and jumped up. "What? What? What? Tell me!"

I rolled my eyes. "Give me half an hour." I needed another shower and some actual clothes, and I needed to locate another blank notebook so I could start my power record over. "Then I'll tell Tobias about it." My stomach growled. "Oh, yeah, that too. It's been a while since those granola bars Beryl gave me." I pushed past Flint and headed for the kitchen. I didn't feel like cooking, but I could sure slap together a sandwich in three minutes and take it upstairs.

"But Gyp—" Flint said.

The kitchen door was still banded with black. I leaned toward the door, my eyes closed, and listened to my skin. No heat. The curse was over. "It's safe to go in now."

"How can you tell? Anyway, you can't get in while that black stuff is on the door," Flint said. "Tobias has to take it off."

I reached past the wards and turned the kitchen doorknob. The black bands snapped against the door and held it shut. "Damn," I muttered.

Sparks jumped from my fingertips to the black bands and dissolved them.

*Nine*

I clapped my hand over my mouth. I wasn't going to forget! But I had forgotten. And despite the power I had spent on the Altria curse, I still had enough left to do damn damage.

Jasper reached past me and opened the door.

The kitchen was dented, top and bottom, by the grapefruit; the ceiling had a dome in it, and the floor had a dip. The grapefruit, once again grapefruit-sized, sat in the middle of the dip looking incredibly silly. All the furniture was still shoved up against the counters and the walls. I sighed. In cases of post-transition blunders, if you caused a problem, you were supposed to clean up after yourself. I could move the furniture back in place, and check my bank account to see if I could afford to replace whatever was broken, but I wasn't sure what to do about the ceiling and the floor. Maybe I could get one of the others to fix it for me.

But first, I wanted some lunch.

The cake platter sat on the table. It still had three pieces of cake on it.

Flint and I eyed each other. "Dibs the side piece," I yelled.

"Dibs the big piece!"  .

We glanced back at Jasper, who shrugged. "Knock yourself out. Don't know when I'll be hungry again. Maybe never."

"He hasn't tasted it yet," I said. Flint and I chortled, got plates and forks, and divided the rest of the cake. I took mine upstairs in lieu of sandwich. I set the stone on my desk, ate the cake, and went in to take a shower.

My reflection startled me. My hair was still dark brown, but shorter, curlier, and with golden highlights, and the tan—somehow it changed the color of my eyes, made the hazel green paler and more startling. I looked more fit, maybe just because I was more tan, maybe because Altria had left me an extra layer of muscle. I flexed my arm. Yeah. A little more.

I looked a little like someone else. But not too scary.

HALF an hour, a shower, a change of clothes, and some writing later, I left my room. Tension was already seeping into my shoulders again. Oh, well. I'd worry about that in a bit. Right now, I had to talk to the others.

Beryl's bedroom door was open. She saw me and jumped up from her bed, where she had been reading. "Gyp! What happened to your hair?"

"I'll explain, but I want to tell everybody at once so I don't have to repeat myself. Want to come?"

"Oh, yeah."

I tapped Jasper's and Flint's doors, and they followed me.

We knocked at Tobias's tower door.

Tobias opened the door after a while. This time he had clothes on.

We climbed up to the school room and took our places

around the table. I set my new notebook and two pens in front of me. "I've figured out a few things," I said.

"Go on," said Tobias.

I fished a couple pieces of wadded-up paper out of my pocket. I'd filched them from the trashcan in the bathroom. "First, this." I pointed to the pieces of paper and muttered "damn," and they flamed into ash. "D-word spells don't take any energy. I can do them even when I think I'm depleted. I say the word. Whoosh. Stuff disappears or melts."

He glanced toward his wastebasket, then back at me. "How useful."

"What if I said it to a person?" I asked, anguish naked in my voice.

"How likely is that? I've never heard you curse."

"Mainly because I do it in my car when I'm driving around and don't like the way other people are driving. I don't think I should drive anywhere until I figure out what to do about this."

"Dear me. Conceded."

I told him that I could sense my own curse energy in things, and could tell when it was gone. He nodded. "Excellent."

"Here's the part I can't figure out," I said. I told him about turning a stone into my curse child, and how she had been able to do anything she liked to me, and later to Jasper.

"Like what?" Flint asked.

I swallowed. I hesitated, then decided what the heck. "First she changed my hair, all different colors and lengths. Then she made me hugely fat."

Flint frowned.

I stretched my arms out in front of me as far as I could reach. "This big."

"You lie!"

"Not by much," Jasper said.

"You *saw* that?" Flint slapped the table. "Dang! I miss all the good stuff!"

"But what I don't understand is, who or what is she? She was a person, not just somebody I made up. She had her own name and her own notions. Did I curse a whole new person into being, or what?"

"Was she perhaps a hidden facet of yourself?" Tobias asked.

"What?" I leaned back and crossed my arms. Would I do those things to myself and to Jasper? I wouldn't know how. Still, I'd experienced a lot of magic in recent years, including all kinds of transformations. Maybe some part of me had absorbed techniques. Maybe I had actually learned them from Tobias, and they had lain dormant until now.

Did some part of me want to make myself fatter? "She looked just like me," I said slowly.

Jasper shook his head. "She was a separate person."

I searched my memory. She had said something early on that spooked me. "She told me that maybe I made her body, but people couldn't make spirits."

Tobias sucked in breath between his teeth. "You created a vessel, and something jumped into it? Oh, Gyp. Terrifying work. They're all around us, waiting for chances like that. You don't ever want to do an open summoning. You don't want to trust your luck. Statistics are against you. So many of them are nasty!"

"Who?"

"Spirits."

"Dead people?"

"Oh, no, it's a much broader category than that. It can be ghosts; it can be those called demons and angels by some; it can be the nonphysical forms of sleepers, or even people from other worlds. They drift and sleep all around us. Sometimes, though, if a vessel is offered, they wake and dive in. Depending on their intent, they can do a world of harm. Did she tell you her name?"

"Eventually."

"Hmm." He drummed his fingers on the table. "What was it?"

"Altria."

He drummed harder, looking into the air. "No. Not a known name. I wonder what class of being she was."

"She said she was having a great time and would come back anytime," Jasper said. "She told Gyp to call her."

Tobias shook his head. "This is all new to me. Did you write the experience down?"

"I started. I need more time to write."

"Do you remember the words you used in the original curse?"

I sucked on my lower lip and opened my notebook to the page where I'd tried to reconstruct my curse. I turned the notebook around and showed what I'd written to Tobias.

His face lost color. "You said 'be kin'?"

"You told me to rhyme."

He shook his head. "You've given her a bridge. You've made her a member of the family. That's a bond that doesn't end easily. She can come back whenever she likes, and do things to any of us." He leaned forward and peered at me. "You look different."

I ran my hand through my hair. It felt thick, crisp, and curly. "She left my hair a different color, and shorter. She gave me a tan."

"She worked lasting change on you?" He went to the cupboard and got out the loop thing he had used the night before. He studied me through it.

"I don't know. It hasn't been eight hours yet. Maybe it'll fade?"

"No, this is independent of your time contraints." He put the loop away. "It isn't something you did to yourself. She left you changed."

"It could have been worse," I whispered. Still, much as

the idea had disturbed me, there was also something inviting about being so huge. Fee, fi, fo, fum!

Jasper nodded. He shuddered. Beryl gazed at him, her eyes sharp.

Tobias glanced away. His fingers drummed. "Anything can happen," he said at last. "Please, Gyp. Please keep notes of everything you do. We might need to reconstruct it later, if things go—"

I gulped and said, "I will."

"Anything else?"

Jasper and I exchanged glances. He frowned, then said, "She changed me, too."

"Against your will?"

"I made mistakes. I dropped my shield. I touched her. After she changed me, I lost my will. I was demoralized and couldn't figure out how to change back. But the change disappeared a little while after she left."

I said, "Uncle? Is this how curses work? She did scary things to us, but she didn't make them last. Can curses be nice?"

"I don't know. I'm still thinking about your earlier question. Is the curse defined by the one casting it, or the one it's cast on? If you think something is a curse and the person you cast it on thinks it's a blessing—you could have steady work without feeling too bad about it. You just need to find someone who wants the curses you can give."

"Mama wanted those gloves. I wonder if they've turned into regular gloves yet."

"Gloves," repeated Tobias.

"My first curse this morning." I told him about Mama's red gloves, then checked the clock. I'd cursed Mama up a pair of gloves at around six A.M., and now it was—almost four in the afternoon? More than enough time had passed for the gloves to have turned normal, if the eight-hour duration of the curses was the right amount of time. I had been asleep when the earlier curses had worn off; I couldn't really be sure it was eight hours. Maybe less, maybe more.

Four in the afternoon. Mama would have already left for the TV station to do *News at Five*. I hoped the gloves had behaved. Maybe we should check the news when it was five, and see if she was wearing them.

Four in the afternoon? "Wait a sec. It's my night to cook, and I haven't even cleaned up the kitchen from the grapefruit yet, let alone planned a menu. I have to go check our supplies and see what I can make or if I need to go buy something."

"Gyp, strive for perspective. Learning to control yourself is more important than cooking," Tobias said. "We can always order pizza."

"You guys had pizza last night." They hadn't left me any slices, but I had seen the boxes this morning.

"We love pizza. We could have it for a week and not get tired of it," Flint said.

"I'd get tired of it. But I'll cook tonight if you like, Gyp," said Beryl.

"No, I want to cook." Maybe cooking would make me feel normal. I cooked three nights out of seven; three other nights a week, I worked the evening shift at the Center and ate brown bag suppers or fast food from the campus vendors and the rest of the family scrounged; and on Sunday nights, everybody who wanted to went out to dinner in a bunch. We had various favorite places around town we went to, and for variety, when new restaurants opened, we descended on them. "I need some help with the kitchen cleanup, though. There was structural damage, and I don't know how to fix that." I looked at Jasper, pressed my hands palm to palm in prayer.

He shrugged, then laughed. "Sure. Add some pfeffernüsse to Saturday's cookies?"

I groaned. "How am I going to find time to do Christmas cookies for the rest of the household?"

He smiled and waggled his eyebrows. "I'll put these to

good use. Maybe sweeten the tempers of my bandmates, eh? We've been fighting a lot lately."

"All right."

"Gypsum, how are your shoulders?" Tobias asked.

I hunched them and frowned.

"How tight?"

I sighed.

"Before you get to the kitchen, maybe you should discharge some more energy. Wouldn't want it to get in the food."

"Let's do something together," Flint said.

"Like what?" I asked.

"Are you nuts?" Jasper said at the same time.

"I don't care," answered Flint. "Anything. I just want to see if we can mix powers again and do something cool."

"Please take it outside," said Tobias.

"Out back is best," Jasper said.

"Come with us?" I asked Tobias.

He pointed to my notebook and pens. "Keep track of what happens and tell me later." He waved his hand to dismiss us, and we jumped up and left.

We went out on the back lawn and sat in a circle.

"Do you all really want to be here?" I asked. "This stuff backfires. I think it's supposed to. It might be messy." I glanced at Jasper, then Beryl.

"No matter what happens, I want to see it," Jasper said.

"Me too," said Beryl.

"If it affects me, I hope this time I remember that I can take care of myself," Jasper said. "Last time was scary. I didn't know I could fall apart so fast."

"I bet you would have come out of it pretty soon. Shock can affect anybody, even you guys."

" 'Fess up. What happened?" Flint asked.

Jasper tapped his lips with his index finger a couple times, then said, "Gyp's demon friend made me fat, too, and I didn't react well at all."

"You, fat? Gaw dang! I don't want to miss anything else!"

Jasper gave him a rueful grin. "It's been a long time since anybody made me change without my consent."

"Pretty cool it's Gyp," said Flint.

"It wasn't me. It was her," I said.

Flint only smiled.

"It was educational, anyway," Jasper said. "Knocked me in the self-confidence."

I shifted one shoulder, then the other. I felt like a vise was tightening around me. "Guys, I need to do something curselike soon."

"I know! Let's do two things at once!" Flint said. "Let's make something to eat."

That would defeat the purpose of cooking. I really wanted to get my hands on some knives and chop things up the good old-fashioned way. Kitchen therapy. Maybe Flint and I could make dessert together, though. That had worked pretty well last time.

"How do we combine powers?" I asked. "I curse something, and you use it to make something good?"

"That's two steps. Let's try just one. Give me your hands."

I handed Beryl my notebook and pens. She nodded, opened the notebook to a blank page, and started writing.

Flint reached across the circle to me, and I placed my hands in his.

He jerked his away. "Whoa! Hot hands!"

I checked my palms. They looked the same as ever.

"Let me try that again." Flint rubbed his palms across each other, murmured something, then held his hands out to me. When I touched his hands, they felt icy. "Let's do this fast. What do you want for dinner?"

"Let's make dessert. Something easy."

"Nothing's easier than sheet cake," he said.

"Don't you want some variety? Let's try cinnamon rolls, huh?"

"No. Let's do chocolate this time. Brownies. Those gooey ones."

"All right. You guys, get back." I waited until Jasper and Beryl moved a little ways away, then closed my eyes and ran through a brownie recipe in my mind, all the ingredients and the steps: melt together butter and unsweetened chocolate, remove from heat and stir in sugar, vanilla, then eggs; beat all together into a warm, dark, chocolate, gooey mixture, then blend in the flour (a little less than the recipe calls for), pour the mixture in a pan, sprinkle in loose chocolate chips for little bursts of flavor, then bake at 350 for twenty-five minutes or so. The broom-straw test for done didn't work on these; something always stuck to the straw. I just took them out when I thought they were done. Cool them on a wire rack before cutting. The house would fill with the smell and everybody would come to the kitchen, watching and waiting until I said it was time to eat.

Heat glowed in my chest, my own internal campfire.

I licked my lips and imagined baking more brownies, only this time blond ones, butterscotch instead of chocolate. I could smell them.

Then I thought, how about some frosted ones? Chocolate frosting on some and vanilla frosting on others. Mint frosting! Chocolate mint brownies! Let's make some with nuts, even though I don't like those. Chopped walnuts. I think Dad likes that kind. I wonder if we could make caramel brownies. Or how about some with minced Heath Bars sprinkled through them? Yeah, let's try that. Yum.

"Hey?" said Flint.

I opened my eyes.

We were inside something dark and hot. The air was so thick with the scent of brownies I could almost eat it. What light there was reached us dimly through random beige squares in the walls, just enough light so I could see that we were in something like an igloo.

My shoulders had relaxed again.

"What happened?" I asked.

"Kind of a Hansel and Gretel thing." He slipped his hands out of mine and shook them. "Hot hot hot. Maybe next time we should do two steps so you don't burn me. This is a lot of brownies."

## Ten

I put my hand against the wall. Gooey, soft, still hot. I brought my palm close to my face. Melted chocolate streaked it.

"Are you all right in there?" Jasper's voice was muffled, coming through walls of cake.

"So far," Flint called.

"I wonder how much air we have," I said. I shouldn't have said anything. I felt totally claustrophobic. "Flint!"

"Don't worry. Worse comes to worst I'll pop us somewhere else. But I think it's easier than that. Let's eat our way out!"

"You'll ruin your appetite for dinner."

"Yes," he said, "but in a noble cause. First, though, I'll just see if we can bust out." He got to his feet and pushed up on the roof. "Ugh! How many did we make? Did you know that when you're spelling, you just pour energy out? Scary big flow. Almost too much for me to channel." He put some muscle into it and poked a hole up through the roof. Brownies and blondies cascaded to the grass around us as he widened the hole.

Sunlight poured down into our structure as heat flowed up and out. I tasted fresh air and smiled at the sky.

"Okay. Now." Flint took a brownie from the side of the hole he had made. "Smells great." He bit it. "Oh, yeah. Perfect! What's this light brown one? Oh, boy! Wait, there's another kind over here. I didn't know you knew how to make so many kinds, Gyp. This is fantastic." He grabbed a brown-sugar-colored brownie and offered it to me.

"Just one," I said. I wondered if we had managed to make good food again, or if there would be some curse attached. Oh well. I had to find out, right? I took a bite.

One of the scotchies. Heaven. Chocolate had never been my favorite flavor, even though everybody else loved it best; I thought again, Flint was paying attention, and I never realized it. He gave me a blond brownie because he knows me. Oh, delicious!

"Let's go get some plates and stuff from the kitchen," Flint said. "Gotta store some of these for later." He grabbed my hand and pulled me up into the air.

"Jeeze! I didn't know you could fly."

"Not for very far, but I can manage this much." We went up high enough to get out of our house of brownies, then dropped with a thud to the lawn.

I climbed to my feet and looked at what Flint and I had done.

"The leaning tower of brownies!" he said.

Sheets of brownies were the bricks that had built this round, beehive hairdo-shaped structure. It was almost six feet tall, and maybe eight feet in diameter at the bottom, narrowing to about five feet across at the top. Flint had destroyed its symmetry by busting out. I stood up and brushed off my pants.

"So is it dangerous?" Beryl asked.

I licked my lip and reached for another butterscotch brownie. Perfect. Delicious. Smooth and wonderful.

"I'm going for the cookie tins," Flint said.

"I'll be in in a minute."

"It doesn't make you break out or anything?" asked Beryl.

I waggled my eyebrows at her. "You could wait and see. Or you could take a chance."

She sighed. "Well, I finished my makeup history test, and I'm officially on Christmas Break now. So I guess—" She grabbed a brownie and bit into it. "Oh, my, God. This is the best brownie I ever ate."

I glanced at Jasper. He smiled and shook his head.

Beryl finished her brownie, licked her lips and then her fingers, and eyed the tower. "It's not like we're going to run out." She grabbed another one. "Oh, God. There's— caramel in here?"

"That worked?"

She offered me a bite.

Yes. Somehow, little nuggets of caramel in the midst of the chocolate. Strange mix of texture and flavor.

"I'll be right back." I followed Flint into the kitchen.

We ran out of cookie tins long before we ran out of brownies. Jasper boxed up the rest of them and took them to the Mission, where they served meals to the homeless, after he was sure that Flint and Beryl and I weren't suffering from having eaten some.

"Tomorrow," Flint said, "creampuffs."


DAD came home while I was pan-frying flank steak. Beryl was in the dining room, setting the table. "Smells wonderful," he said. "Say. You got a haircut. Looks good. So how was your day? Looks like you survived it."

"It was interesting." I flipped the steak and got a cookie tin down from the cupboard. "Flint and I figured out how to make dessert together. Look."

"Good grief." He sniffed. "Smells divine. This is a curse thing?"

"Flint's power modifies it so it's safe. We could go into business, maybe." I was joking, but then I thought, hey. Really. We could do some business this way if it worked every time. Sell cookies from a stand in the street? Not enough traffic. Sell them at the Farmer's Market, or at Sábado y Domingo, the weekend open-air market down by the beach? I wasn't sure what kind of permits you needed or how much you had to pay, but we might be able to do that. Or sell to area bakeries or outlets?

It would involve research either way. Might be too labor-intensive for Flint.

"So you don't eat these and turn into a troll."

"Not so far."

"Good. I'll save room."

"How was your day?"

He smiled. "Normal."

I felt a tiny tug at my heart. I used to have days like that. I didn't think I ever would again. Then I cheered up. I'd been waiting all my life not to be normal. Now, finally . . . I smiled back.

"The kitchen survived the killer grapefruit, huh."

"We fixed it." I pointed to the grapefruit in the middle of the butcher-block table. "Look. It went back to normal."

He shook his head, still smiling. "You'd never know."

"I'm not sure we should eat it."

"It did have personality."

I put the steak on a carving board and covered it with a towel, then turned the heat down, melted some more butter in the pan and added vermouth and mustard, Worcestershire sauce and capers. "I wonder where Mama is. This is almost ready."

Just then she breezed in. "Hello, darlings!" She waved a red hand at me. "Did you watch my broadcast? I wore my gloves the whole time."

"I'm sorry, Mama. I missed it. Can you take them off yet?"

"Oh, yes. They're wonderful. Miles! Look what Gyp made for me!" She brushed gloved fingertips down his cheeks, then kissed him.

"You're making lots of things," Dad said to me when he had finished kissing Mama.

"Yeah. It's surprising." I carved the flank steak into thin slices, set it on a platter, and poured the sauce over it. Beryl came in from the dining room and took the salad out of the fridge. "Dad, could you grab the vegetables and the rolls?" I asked. I had poured a steamed vegetable medley into a bowl while I was frying the steak, and the warm rolls were wrapped in a towel in a basket on the counter.

"Sure."

I followed Beryl, and Dad followed me, with Mama trailing after. She paused at the entrance to the dining room and rang the dinner bell. We set the food on the buffet. I went back to the kitchen to grab the serving spoons and forks and a couple of pitchers of milk for the table. By the time I returned to the dining room, everybody was there.

Jasper touched flame to the candles at either end of the table, and we all sat in the places where Beryl had set our cloth napkins—really guest towels—with our names inked on clothespins. Mama had started using clothespins on napkins as place cards years before, when I was too young to read my own name.

Mama sat at one end of the table, and Dad at the other. When we were younger, there were rules about who sat where; whoever had the worst manners had to sit next to Dad, so he could instruct them in etiquette such as knife-wielding and keeping one's elbows off the table. Whoever set the table usually set themselves as far from Mama as possible. She had seemed even more powerful and overwhelming when we were small; we feared her attention.

Sometimes she noticed good things about you, but sometimes she took note of bad things, things that "needed fixing," and that was always scary. Some of her fixes hurt and didn't work very well.

Aunt Hermina, who lived in the guest house, rarely joined us for meals. She was working on several projects and liked her isolation. She was there if we needed special help, like when Flint screwed up so much it took three grownups to fix the problem, and every once in a while, she got lonely and came in for dinner. Once in a while when I had a restless night and came downstairs to heat some milk and honey, I'd find her in the kitchen drinking tea and sneaking cookies. She wasn't at dinner tonight.

Uncle Tobias's place shifted around the table at the whim of whoever set it. Beryl had put him beside Mama tonight, with Flint across from him. Beryl and I sat across from each other next to Dad, and Jasper sat between me and Uncle Tobias. Beryl had left the empty seat between Flint and herself.

Once we were seated, we reached out to clasp hands with people to either side of us, and lowered our heads. I glanced at Mama. She would choose grace for tonight, but which one? Usually these days we had silent grace, where we were supposed to be saying our own versions of thanks. We had a couple of singing graces from when we were little kids, but we were feeling more and more snotty about these kinds of family events now that we were supposed to be grownups, even though Mama could pick up on sarcasm and get you back for it.

Mama chose the oldest grace. "For all that is good, for all that is ours," she sang. We all chimed in on the second line: "Thanks to the Spirits, thanks to the Powers." We squeezed each other's hands and let go.

There were rules about the order in which we went up to the buffet for our food, too: Women first, Mama very first unless Hermina was present, then Opal if she was home, then me, then Beryl. The men went up from oldest to youngest, too: Tobias first, on down to Flint. Flint hated this system. He always got last pick of everything except on his birthday, when he got to go first. I tried to fix enough of everything so that there would still be plenty for him by the time he got to the buffet, but he was the hungriest person in the family.

If people complained about the line order, Mama just said this was the way it had always been done, and Tobias agreed. Some family traditions were just unbudgeable. This one didn't make a whole lot of sense to me, but it worked in my favor, so I liked it.

I had sampled several different brownies while we were packing them up, to see which thought-recipes had worked best; but that had been three hours earlier, and I was hungry. I took only one serving of each thing so there would be enough for the others. We were allowed seconds, but we weren't supposed to take anything we weren't going to eat. Mama was strict about that too. One of the benefits of cooking was that I always fixed things I liked. Sometimes I found something I really liked that nobody else liked. More for me.

Three hours since Flint and I had made the brownies, I thought as I sat down. I had forgotten about timekeeping. While I waited for everyone else to serve themselves—that was another rule, nobody got to start before everybody sat down after getting their food—I tested my shoulders.

Tense again.

Maybe I should excuse myself from dinner? Sure, that would go over well. "Pardon me. I have to go curse something."

Better than staying here and cursing something or someone in the room.

On the other hand, dinner was in front of me, and Flint had finally finished dishing food onto his plate and sat down. I could get tenser than this before I had to use my power.

"So," said Mama, "what did everyone do with their days?"

This, too, was part of our dinner ritual.

I had never had so much to tell before, or felt so reluctant to tell it. I was used to telling Tobias things. He didn't take them personally; he analyzed, repackaged the information I gave him, and handed it back to me so I could take another look and maybe see something in it I hadn't known I knew.

Mama, on the other hand, looked at everything we said in light of how it pertained to her. Sometimes Dad could moderate her response to things, talk her down; mostly, we'd learned to edit what we said.

"Somebody better say something before I toss a little truth-tell around the room," Mama said, and smiled at us. "Gypsum? Don't tell me making a pair of gloves was the most exciting thing that happened to you today."

"Not really."

"The chalk drawings happened last night, I'm guessing, since they were there when I woke you up on the lawn this morning."

"Yeah."

"Have you cleaned them off the back walk yet?"

Oh, man. I had forgotten that one of Mama's many aims in life was to keep the house and environs in fine condition. Messes could exist, as long as they disappeared after a specified time. Six or eight hours, max. "I, uh, I've been kind of busy today. And that chalk is a special case. It's hard to get out of things. Though, come to think of it, the curse came off it this morning, so maybe I can hose off the walk after dinner."

"Busy with what?"

"I'm trying to learn how to curse."

She smiled her most glowing smile at me. As always

when I saw that smile, I was struck by how beautiful she was, and I wondered why I hadn't inherited any of it. Opal got some great features from Mama—lush lips, large, sparkling violet eyes, slender nose—and what she didn't get, she could assume any time she pleased. Or she could look like anyone else she saw or could imagine. Beryl had Mama's eyes. I didn't look like either of my parents— although Flint and I had gotten Dad's hazel eye-color. Mama thought I had chosen my body shape. Nobody in her family was fat. We hadn't met Dad's family. I wondered if I looked like them. Dad was thin, but that didn't mean the rest of his family was.

I wondered what my Great-Aunt Meta had looked like. Maybe there was a power-of-curses body type that would explain me.

"How's it going?" Mama asked.

"I found out one thing that's going to be handy around the house."

She nodded, encouraging me.

I fished a Kleenex out of my pocket and held it up. I focused on it, narrowed my concentration. I didn't want to burn my fingers this time. "Damn," I whispered, and the Kleenex flashed into nothing. This time my fingers were fine.

Mama blinked and sat back.

"Thought I could take care of the trash," I said.

"Honey," said Dad, his voice a little hoarse.

"Hey, that's my job," Flint said. We all had work jobs. I did a lot of cooking, which left weeding, setting the table, watering the houseplants, laundry, dishes, trash collection, and other things for the others to sort out. We had a gardener, Esteban Rivera, who mowed the back lawn and trimmed the bushes out front and planted whatever Mama asked him to plant, but left the orchard alone; and a housekeeper, Luz Herrera, who came in once a week to sweep, vacuum, dust, and clean the bathrooms—Tuesday, a day when everybody was encouraged to stay away from home so Luz could work undisturbed. I had spent some time with her, since in the past I wasn't a danger to myself or others.

"You can have it, though," Flint said after a minute's thought.

"And Flint and I made brownies together, and they're really good. When we combine our powers, he takes the curse off. So we have dessert."

Her smile broadened. "Excellent. Is there anything I can help you with?"

"I don't know, Mama. Did you know Aunt Meta?"

Her face smoothed. "I met her a few times when I was a little girl. She was so unhappy and sick. I didn't know why until I was much older, and she was gone."

"I just thought if you'd ever seen her work. . . ."

Mama glanced at Tobias. Her eyes darkened. "Only once." She returned her gaze to me. Candle flame reflected in her eyes. "Her mother, my great-aunt Lynx, made her curse a house. It was a little old shack that nobody lived in—used to be in the jungle out back—and they wanted it off the property. Meta wouldn't do anything, you know. She lived twisted inside herself and spent most of her time in her room. Her power was eating away at her insides. Aunt Lynx knew that was wrong, and tried to get her to work, but most of the time—oh, baby, I'm so glad you're practicing and doing. Don't stop. Don't stop."

I couldn't look away from her.

She took a breath. "Anyway, Lynx convinced Meta that it was all right to curse the shack. So Meta said: 'You before me, be eaten up by the powers inside you.' So creepy. Like she was talking to herself. I didn't know that till later, though. The shack shook. Dust flew as the boards kind of—it was like fast-acting termites. They shrank down on themselves, fell apart. The glass in the windows ran like water. But worst were these little cries, something dying."

Mama shook her head. "It frightened me so badly I didn't want to go through transition. I had nightmares. What could be crying and dying in an old abandoned shack? Nobody ever told me. Meta's face—"

# Eleven

TOBIAS coughed into his hand.

Startled, Mama glanced at him, then shook herself free of the story she was telling. Sometimes she put dazzle in the words so you heard them better than you did normal speech. Sometimes she didn't even know she was doing it.

"So it's exciting that you're finding positive ways to channel your power, Gyp." She smiled again.

"I guess so," I said, unnerved. "Hey, Dad, what did you do today?"

"I taught three classes and had office hours," he said, and smiled. "I had lunch with Kingston. You remember him, Anise. He was at the faculty Christmas party last year."

"The man with the long earlobes? I liked him."

"Pleasant day," Dad said. "Jasper?"

Jasper checked his watch. "I've got band practice tonight," he said. He had finished his dinner.

"Do you have to leave this minute?" Mama asked.

"No."

"Anything new and good happen today?"

"I've been watching Gyp work. It gives me lots to think about."

"Would you like to share?"

"Not until I've had some time to mull it over. Anyway, it's exciting. Gyp, don't worry. I bet you're nothing like Aunt Meta."

"Thanks."

"May I please be excused?" Jasper said.

"You're not staying for coffee and dessert?"

He checked his watch again.

"Oh, all right," Mama said, a little cross.

"Thanks." He refolded his napkin, clipped the clothespin on it, grabbed his empty plate, and headed for the kitchen.

"Beryl?" Mama stared at my little sister.

"I took my American history makeup, and I think I aced it. Now I'm on break until next year! Hah!"

"Oh yes. Break!" Mama said. "Miles, you go on break too, yes?"

"Tomorrow after school."

"Gypsum?"

"I've got one more shift at the Center, but I phoned in and left a message I'd be out sick tomorrow. I don't want to curse at school."

"Oh. Probably wise. Flint? What did you do today?" Her tone shifted, turned a tiny bit satiric. Flint usually reported things like "wandered around downtown" or "practiced guitar" or "rode my bike up in the mountains" or "went surfing."

"I'm getting into baking. I love it! I've got a babysitting gig with the Foster twins tonight, and I'm taking them some of our brownies. Wait till you try 'em, Mama. They're outrageous."

"Have you found your interest in life?" Mama's tone was too intense.

Flint leaned back in his chair and beamed. "Naw. I'm interested in everything. You know that."

Mama never growled, but sometimes I was sure she wanted to, and this was one of the times. She smiled instead, more teeth than feeling. "Tobias? Did you have a good day?"

"Yes, Anise, I did." Tobias didn't play "new and good" with the rest of us, and Mama couldn't make him. She'd given up trying. "Excellent dinner, Gyp."

Everybody else chimed in, and I smiled, until my shoulders pinched me. Then I hunched. Tobias's gaze sharpened. Beryl and I got up to clear and bring in the dessert and the coffee pot. I laid out the various kinds of brownies on a platter decorated with pictures of holly plants and berries, striving for a herringbone pattern—Mama loved a nice presentation. I set down the last one. An arrow of pain shot down my spine. I sucked in air.

"What? What's wrong, Gyp?" Beryl asked.

"I've got to curse something right now." I dropped the cookie tin and ran for the back door.

Curse something, yes. But what? And how? An image of a house eating itself flared through my mind as I pounded across the back porch. I had to get away from our house. I ran across the lawn to the orchard steps. Night and fog had fallen again. I tripped over something at the top of the stairs, and time shifted into slow motion.

Though the light was bad this far from the back porch, I still saw the steps, pale in the night with black cracks where one step stopped and the next began. Each step had a drooping lip. I was falling, falling toward them forever, though I knew at the end of my tumble I would smack down. I had time to think about that: about how I could crush my ribs, break my jaw, my neck, snap my legs against all those concrete edges. I could die from stupidity and hurry. Or I could just hurt myself really badly.

"Damn!"

A sun went nova in my chest. An ocean of white light opened below me. I heard hard, heavy cracks and snaps, and smelled scorching, melting, acrid stone.

# Twelve

"ALTRIA," I whispered, falling.

Someone laughed, and I fell, but instead of hitting all those angled edges I dropped into arms stretched out to catch me. She loomed over and around me, larger than an elephant, warm, smelling of ripe apricots and peaches and fresh-baked bread. For an instant she hugged me, and then she set me down and disappeared.

I was sitting in a scorched crater. Above me was the lip of the upper terrace, and to my right, the orchard spread out. Beside me was the upper terrace's retaining wall that used to run beside the staircase. Burn marks had etched a medusa mural, like the outline of fireworks smoke, into the wall.

The staircase had disappeared.

My clothes hadn't survived the blast very well either. My shirt and most of my bra had burned away from my chest, though I still wore the sleeves, straps, and back. My jeans were mostly there, but streaked with smoke. I didn't know what had happened to my slip-on shoes; they were gone. The bottom of the crater still steamed. I felt the heat rising from it. Somehow, the heat didn't bother me, even though my bare feet were against hot stone. It was my own heat. Maybe it couldn't hurt me.

"What!"

I pressed my palms against the bottom of the crater. Almost porcelain smooth; my curse had carved it out.

"Gyp! What!"

I looked up. My family, minus Jasper and Hermina, stood on the edge of the terrace, where the stairs used to start.

I crossed my arms over my breasts, covered them as best I could with my hands. "I had an accident," I said.

Dad stripped out of his jacket and dropped it to me. "Thanks." I turned my back on the family and put the jacket on backwards so it would cover my front. "Are you all right?" asked Dad when I turned to face them again.

I shifted my shoulders, bent my legs, flexed my ankles. No internal screams of pain. Nothing broken, maybe nothing bruised. How could that be? "Guess so."

Definitely no tension left in my shoulders at all. Curseproof, for a couple hours at least.

"You destroyed the staircase?" Mama asked.

"I didn't mean to. I fell. I cursed. It was a reflex."

"You did this," Dad said.

"I did, Dad. It's the new me. Walking disaster area." I pulled myself to my feet. "Cursing sure is hard on the wardrobe."

"You did *this*."

I sighed. Maybe Dad was finally getting that I had changed.

"Well," said Mama, "maybe I can replace the old stair with something marble. Something really nice. It never did look good anyway."

"Thanks, Mama." She could have reacted a bunch of different ways. Deciding she wanted to replace the stair was the best way I could imagine.

"How do you feel?" Tobias asked me.

"Completely relaxed."

"This took quite a bit of power, Gyp." He sounded worried.

"I noticed that."

"Add it to your record. We need to do some math after dinner, maybe graph your output and frequency so we can plan ahead."

"Personal math! My idea of heaven. I won't be able to hurt anything else, so I guess I might as well do math. Did you guys try the brownies?"

"We didn't have time before the explosion," Beryl said. "You ready for dessert?"

"Oh, yeah."

Flint knelt and held his hand out to me. I reached up and took it, and he lifted me up through the air. "We should both be there to watch when they take their first bites."

He and I exchanged grins.

"That sounds ominous," said Dad.

"Wow," said Flint, "it does. I didn't mean it to."

We went back to the house. I ran upstairs to change into a new shirt while Beryl finally put dessert out. By the time I got back everyone had served themselves. I grabbed three different kinds of brownies on a small plate and sat down.

Silence.

I poured myself a glass of milk. I looked around the table. "What?"

"How many events have you had today?" Mama asked.

I thought it through, tapping my fingers as I went. Gloves. Grapefruit. Altria's stone. Brownies. The staircase. "Five." Plus unnumbered small "damn"s.

Mama looked at Tobias, then back at me. "That's a lot," she said.

I tried to remember everybody else's transitions. We had

gone through a lot of events. There had been days when we didn't dare invite friends over because we didn't know if we would all be walking on the ceiling, sprouting feathers, talking backwards, or struck mute. I didn't remember us ever measuring somebody's transition by how many power events happened in a day, though.

My shoulders tingled.

"Am I supposed to do something different? Please tell me. Tobias said if I didn't use the power, I'd hurt myself. Is there a safe way not to use it?"

"No," Mama said. She sighed. One of her better sighs. It made me feel extremely guilty.

A thread tightened across my shoulders.

"I'm sorry about messing up the grounds, I truly am. I know I'm lucky nobody's gotten hurt yet." When Flint transitioned, I had ended up with a broken leg. Beryl had had the itches so bad she scratched herself bloody, and Jasper had spent a couple days without vision. Since Jasper had powers, he had managed to compensate with extra senses. None of our problems were deliberate on Flint's part. We all understood; settling in after transition was maybe the roughest time of a person's life, barring personal tragedies and things beyond one's control. Flint's was the toughest transition we'd had in my generation, maybe because he had powers that nobody knew how to work, or maybe because he lacked personal discipline. It hadn't bothered me a whole lot, despite the broken leg.

Transitions were bumpy. Everybody knew that. But I was being more inconvenient than the rest of them, waiting so late until everybody had settled into believing it would never happen. Mama didn't like things that fell outside of patterns, or things that didn't present well. She would have to tell Grandmère and Grandpère and her brothers and sisters about me sometime. They'd all had lots of kids, but none of our cousins had developed curse power, and all of them had transitioned. I was already a blot on Mama's breeding record; was this new development better or worse than having no power at all?

What did Mama have to complain about? She had ended up with the fantastic family house and land in Santa Tekla, while everybody else had moved to L.A., San Francisco, or San Diego and had to start their own places for their broods. I wasn't sure how Mama ended up with the house; maybe she had won it in a contest of wills or powers, siblings settling things among themselves, as Mama had taught us to do. When we were little, one of Mama's younger sisters and her husband had lived in the guest house where Aunt Hermina lived now until they had had twins and the house, even though it had three bedrooms, had somehow gotten too small.

Maybe, I had thought back then when I was eight, it was because the babies were twins. Mama had never had twins.

I remembered liking them, Aunt Hazel and Uncle Doug. They were nice to have around. Sometimes they babysat us when Mama and Dad went out. Aunt Hazel had given me Jujubes on the sly once in a while.

They'd left Santa Tekla when I was eight, and moved to some town in Northern California that started with "Red." I had only seen them once since, at a family gathering at Grandmère's and Grandpère's in L.A. We went to the grandparents' every year in July to celebrate Grandpère's birthday, and every year after Christmas to celebrate Christmas, and to fight and compete and compare notes with our cousins. Aunt Hazel and Uncle Doug lived too far away to come down every year. They did send Christmas cards; Mama put all the cards in a big bowl on the coffee table in the great hall after she had written answering cards, and I went through them sometimes.

I wondered how Doug and Hazel were doing. The twins, Amethyst and Chalcedony, would be twelve by now. I wondered what they were like.

"I hope you learn control by tomorrow," Mama said.

"Gee, I hope I do, too."

"Don't take that tone with me. You're no longer a child, Gypsum. You can be more responsible than the others were. You're older, and you've had lots of practice."

"What, I'm not allowed to fall apart like everybody else did?"

"You should be beyond that."

"Anise," said Dad.

Her wonderful eyes flashed at him. He lifted one eyebrow. She blinked. The temper she'd been building seeped out of her. She sighed again and looked at me. "Gypsum, I'm sorry. Of course you'll make mistakes. Just—try to be careful, will you?"

"Of course I will." I would try. I always tried. That didn't mean I would succeed.

I had a brief vision of our whole house going up in sorcerous smoke, and me saying, "Oops."

"The brownies are delicious," Mama said, and gave me and Flint an excellent smile.

*Thirteen*

WHEN I opened my eyes early Friday morning, I groaned. My shoulders ached. I needed to build myself a routine, a safe way of discharging the power I stored while I slept. But what could I automatically curse that wouldn't hurt anybody?

I glanced at the clock. A little after six. I guessed I'd be waking up early until I figured out how to manage my power better; it was like needing to pee.

I pulled on my happi coat and some flip-flops and ran downstairs to the place by the backdoor where we kept the garbage cans. I opened all six cans. There was a satisfying trash build-up inside them, including lawn and bush clippings that Esteban was supposed to put in the compost heap. He hated the compost heap and often neglected it.

I rubbed my thumbs across my fingertips and focused. *What's inside the cans, and leave the cans alone.* Maybe I better work them one at a time. I stood over the first one, wrinkled my nose against the reek of decaying kitchen trash. I pointed. "Damn."

The metal inside of the trashcan gleamed. There was

nothing left of its contents. Even the smell was gone.

I zapped each can in turn, then felt prickling at my neck, and glanced up.

Aunt Hermina, her white hair wild, her blue fish kimono tied closed with a piece of rope, stood on the stairs that led to the walk between the kitchen and the guest house, holding a wastebasket. Her mouth hung open.

"Is that for me?" I sensed only a tiny lessoning of the tension in my shoulders. Damning our trash was not going to be enough to take the morning curse out of my system.

She closed her mouth. "I guess so." She came down two steps and handed me the basket.

"Hi, Aunt Hermes."

"Good morning, Gyp. I guess things have been going on while I was working."

"Yeah. I finally got my transition, and now I have curse power." I licked my fingertip and pointed it into her wastebasket. "Damn." Her trash vanished with only half a puff of smoke. I handed her back the basket.

"Good gracious, Gyp. Congratulations. Or is that right? I'm happy for you. Are you happy?"

"The jury is still out. I'm excited to have power at last, but it always comes out strange. Mama thinks it's inconvenient."

Something flashed in Aunt Hermina's brown eyes. She shook her head. "How's the cursing going?"

"Weirdly but intensely. I have to figure out something to curse right now, as a matter of fact. Any ideas?"

"My computer keeps crashing, even when I give it special nutritious power jolts. I'm about ready to give up on it. Why don't you try that?"

"Really?"

"Honestly. I've been planning to buy another, but I haven't been able to leave my plants. Come on in."

I put the lids back on the garbage cans and followed my aunt into the guest house. The door opened onto a hallway, with a bathroom to the right and a bedroom to the left, and two more bedrooms opened off the hall at its other end. Aunt Hermina's bedroom was the smaller room at the back. In the big back bedroom and the small one nearest the door, she raised, altered, and studied varieties of plants.

The air smelled green and weedy. Then again—

"Coffee?" I asked.

"Yep. Fairly fresh. Want some?"

"Oh, yeah." I hadn't even checked the kitchen for coffee on my dash through the house.

Hermina led me into the big back bedroom, where she had a desk set up amid the hydroponics tanks and grow-lights. On the desk, which was as big as a door, was a white laptop computer and a hotplate with a pot of coffee on it. My aunt took a mug off a hook on the wall and poured me a cup. "Do you take things in it? I don't have any things."

"Black is better than nothing. Thanks."

She handed me the mug and turned the laptop around so I could look at its screen. "This dumb thing. The battery won't hold a charge for more than a minute, and even when I leave it plugged in, it always crashes just after I've entered my data but before I have time to save. You can curse it to kingdom come if you like."

"Let's take it outside." I didn't want to hurt her plants or give them ideas.

"Good idea." She popped out a disk, unplugged the laptop and closed it, then carried it through the back bedroom to her private balcony, where she set it on the floorboards next to a rusty black hibachi.

I could zap the laptop, but zapping didn't use up my power very fast. I wondered what kind of curse I could cast on such a small object that would use up big power?

I stared at the computer and shifted my shoulders. If I had wish power, maybe I could use it to heal the computer.

Tobias told me to be specific. Maybe if I was specific enough, I could use my power like wish power. If I knew what I wanted and boxed my wish in really well, the curse power might not be able to find ways to make my desires evil. Maybe the power wouldn't operate at all if it was trapped in a wish. Or maybe something else would happen.

I hadn't had much coffee yet, not enough for a really good plan.

I knelt and put my hands on the computer. "Be wise, be well, be kind, don't hurt, just help, just work," I said. The power spot above my breastbone warmed, then heated, then glowed almost through my clothes. The energy whooshed down into the computer. I slumped back, satisfied that something had happened, that I'd discharged my curse energy for now and was safe for a while.

"That's a curse?"

"Um." I drank coffee. "Probably."

"If you really want to curse things, you should put some mean into it," Hermina said.

"But I don't want to curse things. I just have to."

"Oh. Interesting. You're fighting yourself?"

"Am I?" For the second time I wondered if I'd gotten the real story about my condition. Tobias had told me I had an unkind power, the power of curses; but Altria had cast a question on that. "Make me a brush," she had said, and when I said it would be cursed, she asked why? I had made her a brush. It had worked just the way a brush was supposed to. I needed to find out a lot more about my power.

The computer's fliptop lifted. Its screen brightened. A pixelated face formed, smiled at us. It looked generic, modelesque, beauty without character or individuality. Its skin tone was white, tinted swamp-green around the edges and shadows. Its eyes were a mixture of synthetic colors, an array that included peacock and magenta and chartreuse and spots of other colors too bright for nature. "How may

I help you?" asked a pleasant processed voice. The mouth moved almost in sync with the words.

"Have you got my plant studies data?" Hermina asked.

The face and the screen tilted to look up at her. "Of course."

"If I put a disk into you, could you store my data on it?"

"Of course."

"Wait right there."

"If you insist."

Hermina went inside. The computer tilted to study me. "How may I help *you*?"

"Can you tell me how to use my power so it won't hurt or destroy things?"

"I'm sorry. No. Not possible."

"Are you going to turn out to be cursed?"

"Yes, but I like it." Around its keyboard, the white casing surged and rippled, swelled and bubbled. Then things burst from it. The computer grew a body, white, featureless, slender arms, torso, and legs. The keyboard formed its shoulders, and the screen held its head. The body grew to a height of about three feet. Now its face could stare on the level into mine while I was sitting down. "How helpful could I be if I couldn't get around?" it asked. "You must let me do something for you."

"Like what?"

"If you don't know, I'll figure something out." It took a step toward me, and I scooted back. It smiled, took another step, and I scooted back again. Then my back was to the wall.

"Wait. Give me a minute. I'll think of something," I said.

"You've already had a minute. Do you know how long a minute is to a computer? An eternity. I can't wait any longer." It reached out a white arm with a cartoon-gloved three-fingered hand on the end. Its fingertips pressed against my forehead. Something happened to my brain. Confusion overwhelmed me. I could scarcely see. My eyes didn't focus, or when they did, the images stretched or compressed. My awareness of my body blinked out. I felt like a mind floating in darkness.

Then I heard its voice. "There's certainly room for improvement here. You're disorganized in so many ways, and yet some elegant structures are in places where they shouldn't be. You need help, all right. You find the recording of your behavior onerous? Here's a little program we'll call curse-tracking: data fields for everything; observations automatically feed into the right fields, no extra work for you, though printing out may be a problem. I'll solve that later. I've observed lots of human behavior while the Typist surfs the Web. Let me introduce some rules for eating and dressing and behavior to make you more socially acceptable *here*. Let me dismantle a couple of these inhibitory structures that are causing you trouble, *here*. Oh, while I'm at it, here's a rhyming dictionary to help with your spellcasting, and, oh! Goodness. Now, why didn't I notice this first and save myself the trouble of the earlier improvements? You're finding your power troublesome? You don't know what to do with it? I'll just introduce a power shunt *here*. It will bleed off the power from you to me so I can stay in operation instead of suffering that six-point-seven hour cutoff your work comes equipped with, and you won't have to worry about finding anything else to curse." Click click clickclickclick.

The pressure on my forehead vanished and the computer backed away, its smile benevolent.

## Fourteen

I rubbed my forehead, tried to collect myself.

Hermina came from the bedroom, a disk in her hand. "Oh! What happened to you?" she asked the computer.

"I thought I would be more helpful if I were mobile," it said.

She held out her disk, and the computer took it from her and stuck it into a slot in its side.

What was I wearing? A giant beige T-shirt with a picture of Jasper's band logo, rivers running in a circle with a fern in the center, and a blue-and-white happi coat Dad had given Jasper or Flint when he came back from his one trip to Japan. He had bought both the boys happi coats and had brought kimonos for Opal, me, and Beryl, but the kimonos were too fancy to wear. I had craved those happi coats until I ended up with one. I couldn't remember whose. Neither of the boys ever wore theirs.

On my feet, pink thongs with black soles.

Horrors!

All of this would have to change.

Why? asked some part of me.

Because these clothes were dreadful. None of them did a thing for me.

I leaned forward. The computer patted my shoulder. "Let me know what else I can do to help," it said. Its fingers dug into my shoulder. "I mean that." It sent some kind of charge through me so that I twitched, then released me. I got to my feet. I felt as though I had water in my ears from swimming, so I took a little hop to see if I could break the bubbles and let them run out; but there was no water in my ears.

Something wasn't working right.

Don't think about it.

"All done." The computer lifted its arm and the disk stuck out of its side like a square-edged tongue.

"Honestly? These are all my results?"

"Everything you've input so far."

Hermina took the disk from the computer's side. The slot it had come from disappeared.

"Can you make me another backup?"

"Sure."

"I'll go get another disk." Hermina went inside again. I followed her, glanced back at the computer, which held its hand up to its screen and mimed kissing its fingertips and then blowing a kiss to me. "Love you," it said.

I shuddered.

"You okay?" Hermina asked as I passed her on my way to the door. She was searching through a drawer in her desk.

"Pardon me?"

"Gyp? Something happen?"

"Excuse me. Thank you for a lovely time."

"Gyp." She reached out to me, but I brushed past and left.

Back in my room upstairs, I flipped through everything in my closet. Dreadful! Every single item! Dreadful! The colors were terrible, the styles worse. And the underwear?

Horrifying! Apparently I had spent my whole life collecting garments that emphasized all my bad qualities and didn't accent a single good one. Not that there were many of those. With work, though, maybe I could present an impression.

I finally selected a gold sweater and a green skirt from the closet, both things I hadn't worn because they were presents from relatives whose taste I had formerly disdained. I dug some pantyhose out of the bottom of the underwear drawer—they were still in their package, had never been worn. Then I looked at the shoes. A motley collection of worn sandals, men's tennis shoes, some horrid flat slip-ons from the drugstore. Despair swamped me. None of them would do. There was not a feminine shoe in the whole closet.

Then it occurred to me that Opal hadn't taken everything with her when she moved out. *There* was someone who knew how to dress. Her clothes wouldn't fit me, but her shoes might. And she had probably left all kinds of makeup on her vanity table. I didn't have any. Opal and I had completely different complexions, but I could improvise with what she had until I could get to the mall and buy my own supplies.

We weren't supposed to go into each other's things without asking, but—who made up that silly rule? I had needs.

Come to think of it, Mama knew even better than Opal how to make herself look good. Her makeup kit, her shoe collection, her clothes—everything she bought was stylish. But she was probably still home and might get upset if I used any of her things. I could wait until later to see what she had.

Carrying my clothes, I crossed the hall to Opal's room. I'd put together an ensemble, then take my shower and get made up and dressed. Which reminded me. Hair! I had never done anything about my hair before, just washed it and wore it, but I knew better now. I could borrow Opal's blow dryer and curling iron, if she hadn't taken them with her.

Opal's closet was a treasure trove. At first I just sat there, transfixed, staring at all the shoes and dresses, each one elegant or stylish or whimsical but fun. I picked up a pair of emerald green strappy high heel sandals and sat with them in my lap. I almost cried, they were so pretty. I did cry when I found out they were too small, but I cried well, just a few rolling teardrops and no sound. I found a slightly larger pair of black spike heels, and managed to squeeze my feet into them. They would do. I took them off again.

As I stood up, I saw a poppy red blaze from the hanger bar. I tried to remember if I had ever seen Opal wear something that color, but nothing came to mind. I took out the hanger and found a loose A-line dress in this delicious red-orange color.

Maybe. Maybe.

I went to Opal's vanity table and checked the drawers. She had left all kinds of equipment. I stared at tubes of lipstick and small plastic boxes of eyeshadow, squeeze-tubes of foundation and a scattering of compacts. My hand darted out and retrieved some things, which I put on top of my stack.

With pantyhose, borrowed dress, borrowed shoes, borrowed makeup, I finally ventured to the bathroom. I went in just before Beryl reached the door.

"Gyp! Hey! Did you just come out of Opal's room?"

"Excuse me. In a minute," I said. I locked the door and turned on the water.

"Wait, I need to pee before you shower!"

"I'm sorry. I hope you'll forgive me, but I need to be in here now. Please go downstairs." We had two bathrooms downstairs.

"Gyp!"

The water steamed and I stepped under it. I washed my hair twice and conditioned it once, things I used not to do. Stupid previous me. I found Beryl's shaving equipment and used it. I had never shaved anything on my body, but somehow now I knew how to shave my armpits and legs.

I finished my shower, dried off, and put on deodorant, lotion, strategic baby powder, and some of Opal's perfume. More new practices. I'd only ever used deodorant before. I donned my horrible cotton bra and panties and slipped Opal's red dress on over my head. It floated down over me, a little too tight in the chest and stomach, but not impossible. I would work on reducing; a tight dress would give me added incentive. Who wanted to look bad?

I sat on the toilet and pulled on the pantyhose, slipped my feet into the tight shoes, then rose, put a handtowel around my neck to protect my dress, and went to work on my hair and face. The hair was short and didn't take long to dry and curl. The face. . . . I wished I had more to work with, but what could you do? At least I had found a poppy red lipstick to match the dress. I persevered.

Somebody pounded on the door. "What are you doing in there?" yelled Jasper.

"Getting dressed," I said. I blotted my lips with toilet paper and took a good look at the final result.

Better. Much, much better.

"Well, wrap it up, will you? It never takes you this long in the bathroom! We're waiting!"

I dumped the happi coat and sleep shirt into the laundry hamper, put all the purloined makeup items in my section of the bathroom drawer, went to the door, and opened it.

Jasper backed away. "God! What happened to you?"

"Good morning. What do you mean, what happened to me?"

"You look so different. You get mugged by the Avon lady?"

I tried a smile. I tried ignoring what he had just said. Something surged under the surface of my mind, and for a bare instant I had an image of my face in clown makeup. A spurt of rage almost burned all the art off my face. Monumental calm smothered my anger before it could manifest. My mind settled. Forgive him, it whispered. He's young. He'll learn to treat you with respect if you act as though you deserve it. "Excuse me." I edged past him.

He grabbed my arm. "Hey, Gyp, wait. It was a joke. I mean, what *did* happen to you?"

"What do you mean?"

"You look a lot different."

"Better?" I said.

He studied me. His brow furrowed. "Different."

"Oh, dear." He was young. He didn't know what looked good or bad. "Well, I had better get on with my day," I said. I crossed the sitting room to my door.

"Gyp? Have you cursed anything yet today?"

"Excuse me, please." I slipped into my room and shut the door.

My life was messy and disorganized. It needed some revision. Easy place to start? Eliminate the current wardrobe so I would need to buy all new. I opened my underwear drawer and almost gagged. So many plain, ugly, worn-out things. I picked up one pair of underwear with loose elastic, and said, "Damn."

Nothing happened.

Try something easier. I tore a sheet of notepaper out of a notebook and damned it. Nothing.

Odd. Even my biggest curses of yesterday hadn't deprived me of damns. What had happened?

Someone knocked gently at my door. I opened the door and smiled at Uncle Tobias. Jasper stood across the sitting room.

"Good morning, Gypsum. How are you?"

"Fine, thanks. How are you?"

"Curious. May I ask you a few questions?"

"Please do."

"What did you do when you woke up this morning?"

When I woke up? It seemed like hours had passed since then. In a way, a lifetime; I felt as though there was a sheet of opaque plastic between my earlier self and who I was now. I frowned and concentrated, dredged up a memory. "I—felt really tense, and knew I needed to use my power, so I went downstairs and zapped all the garbage."

"Good idea. Then what?"

"It didn't even take the edge off. Aunt Hermina was there. She was going to empty some trash. I zapped her trash too. Then. . . ." Something difficult about this part of the memory.

"Was she surprised?"

"Yes. She didn't know I'd gone through transition."

"Did you then curse anything?"

"Oh." Curse-tracking clicked on. My mind flooded with information. "Indeed. She was mad at her computer so she said I could curse it, and I did."

"What words did you use when you cursed the computer?" Tobias asked.

That information, too, came clean and fast into my head and out of my mouth. " 'Be wise, be well, be kind, don't hurt, just help, just work.' "

Tobias drew in a deep breath, let it out through his nose. "How could it know to be wise?" he muttered, not really asking me. "How could it know what hurts, or what kindness is? What does a computer know of such things? Only what it's been programmed to believe. Colored by curse energy. I wonder what you did to it. What happened next?"

"It wanted to help me, so it reprogrammed me."

"Aha," said Jasper.

"In what way?" asked Tobias.

"It gave me curse-tracking to keep a record of how I use my energy—that's why I can remember this so well. It gave me a new set of rules for how to eat, dress, and behave. It destroyed some of my inhibitions that it thought were useless. It installed a rhyming dictionary so I could come up with better spells. Then it put in a power shunt to siphon off my curse power into the computer so that I don't have to figure out what to do with it, and so that the computer won't come uncursed after six point seven hours."

For a little while, no one said anything. Tobias's breathing was louder than usual.

I tried to think about what I had just said. My mind kept sliding away from it. Jasper muttered something I couldn't hear.

"It said that if it had done the last thing first, none of the rest would have been necessary," I said. "But I guess. . . ."

"Does the power shunt work?" Tobias asked.

I nodded. "I don't even have a damn left."

"How do you feel?"

"I'm fine, thank you."

He reached for my forehead. I backed up. No. Not another hand on my head!

"Stand still," he said gently, but there were freezers in his voice. So I froze, just the way I would have in the old days. I had no defenses against my family anymore.

He touched my forehead with warm fingertips and said, "How do you feel?"

A great upwelling of rage flooded through me. I wanted to blast everything around me, including people and especially computers. I wanted to incinerate the dress I was wearing. I wanted to be giant and fat the way I had been yesterday so I could stomp on everything that bothered me. I wanted my short local nightmare to end.

"Ah," said Tobias. He lifted his hand from my forehead.

I felt peaceful and calm again. The only thing I wanted to destroy was my old wardrobe.

"Excuse me. What was that?" I asked.

"I wanted to see if the changes were deep or superficial. Definitely superficial.

"What does that mean?"

"You're still alive under the surface, Gyp, which is good news."

Mama came down into the sitting room. "Gyp! What have you done with your hair? Your clothes? Your face? You look wonderful!"

"Thank you," I said.

"But surely you don't own anything that colorful. Isn't that one of Opal's dresses?"

"She left it behind. I didn't think she wanted it anymore."

"But, child—what were you doing getting into Opal's things?"

"Why shouldn't I? She's not here."

Mama turned to Tobias.

"It's a curse," Tobias said.

"But she—finally, after all these years I've been begging her to do something about it—she's finally taking care of her appearance." She held her hands out to me as though to display me, like a model at a boatshow pointing out the virtues of a boat. I felt a glow of pleasure in my stomach. My mother had never done that for me before.

Tobias just smiled at her.

"So how do we get the curse off her?" Jasper asked.

"Do we have to?" asked Mama.

Tobias's smile vanished. "Anise, is how your daughter looks more important to you than how she feels?"

"How do you feel, Gyp?" Mama asked me.

"Fine, thank you."

Mama turned on Tobias. "She feels fine, and she looks great."

"Thanks," I murmured.

"Are you really this ready to accept the surface as truth, Anise? You used not to be so shallow."

Mama's eyes widened. White fire burned in them. She lifted a hand, and fire flared above her fingertips.

Tobias sketched a shield on his palm, but he kept it lowered. "Will you really try to burn me just for telling you a truth?"

Mama's nostrils flared. A vein pulsed in her forehead. "You know that truth is my highest good."

"Then look for it."

She turned to me, her form all outlined in light. Today she wore a turquoise dress, turquoise necklace and earrings, and a big turquoise ring. She looked marvelous, as always. "Gypsum?"

"Mama."

"What's the truth of this situation?"

I searched for something to say. "All my clothes are horrible, Mama."

"Even your favorite? That green corduroy jumper Luz made you that you wear over everything, blouses, T-shirts, even that awful tie-dye thing Uncle Douglas sent you?"

I cringed and put my hand over my face. I'd flipped past that dress earlier while searching my closet for anything to wear, felt a surge of disgust because I knew how much former me had loved that dress. "Hideous," I whispered.

Mama pulled my hand away from my face, gripped my shoulders, and leaned closer to stare into my eyes. "Where are you?"

"Pardon me?"

She frowned, but only briefly. She rarely made expressions that didn't look good on her face. "How would you like to go clothes shopping with me? Sky's the limit. I would love to buy you a whole new wardrobe, as long as you listen to my taste in clothes. How about it?"

I hugged her, almost crying I felt so relieved and happy.

*Fifteen*

SHE sighed and gently pushed me away. "What do we do?" she asked Tobias.

"Normally, I would encourage Gyp to solve this herself, but she's in an elegant trap I'm not sure she can work her way out of. The thing she cursed is stealing all her power before she can use it. And once her power has been channeled through another user, it is cleansed of its curse-charge and can be put to any use, witness the brownies she made with Flint. Also, there's no obsolescence built into it; since the cursed thing worked this change on her with channeled power, it won't wear off automatically."

"What is that computer doing with her power?" Jasper asked. "Look what it already did. What's it doing now?"

"You're right. We should find out."

"Muh—" I had something to say, but I couldn't get it out.

"What?" Tobias asked.

"Duh."

He reached for my forehead, touched it. His touch loosened the hold all the new rules had on my brain. I fought my way through a thicket of delirious shopping thoughts. "Don't let it touch you." Fire burned my tongue as I said the words—not the fire of the forbidden, but the fire of my rage, crackling through me again because Tobias's touch set me a little bit free. I pressed my hand over his on my forehead.

"I thought that thing you cursed up yesterday was scary," Jasper muttered, "but it wasn't as bad as this. It might have changed what you looked like, but it didn't tell you how to think and feel and act."

I pressed Tobias's fingers against my forehead even tighter. "Altria," I said.

Something shifted in the hallway. It took me a moment to figure out what. My shadow changed from a shadow to something with color and shape. It rose from the floor and plastered itself to my back; I felt as if I were wearing a thin, clinging veil. "Oh," she whispered in my ear. "This is different."

"What?" Tobias said. "What did you just do, Gyp?"

Mama started toward me. Tobias waved her back with his free hand. I held his other against my forehead still. I didn't want the surface me back.

"But we're so weak," Altria murmured. "What happened?"

"Altria," I said.

"Where's all our lovely power?"

"Altria?" said Jasper.

I felt her move against the back of my head, a sideways slide of fabric over my shoulders and back.

"Jasper?" she said. Her voice was faint.

"Can you help Gyp?"

"I can try. I have no strength. There's nothing here to draw on."

"Today's curse child is stealing all Gyp's power, and turned her into a puppet."

She shifted against my back. I felt warmth against the

back of my head, and in some weird way, *inside* my head, a breeze blowing over my brain. "Oh," she whispered. "Nice design. Unpleasant execution."

"Can you stop it?"

"This direct feed," she whispered, too low for anybody but me to hear. She stroked my hair. "I want that. I want it too much. That would solve all my manifestation problems. I never thought of it, but now I've seen it, and I want it."

"Altria?" Jasper said.

She kissed my shoulder, then spoke loud enough for him to hear. "I cannot stop it, Jasper. I don't have the strength."

"Take mine."

I gasped.

Altria ran fingers like breeze over my shoulder. "Gyp? What do you want? Do you want me to stop what this thing is doing to you? Root its alterations out of your brain?"

"I do. But I don't want to risk Jasper. You scared him yesterday. And what—what—would you turn into an energy vampire next?"

"Wouldn't that be lovely?" She sighed, a warm exhalation against the back of my neck.

"No. I want some of my energy for myself."

"Do you want me to leave?"

Oh, God. No. I wanted anything rather than to be the person I now was when Tobias wasn't touching my forehead. "I would rather have you sucking energy off me than that thing."

"You shouldn't say that."

"But it's true."

Insubstantial fingers stroked my cheek. "All right, then. I'll do what I can. *And* I'll leave you with some of your energy. Perhaps. Jasper?"

He came toward us.

"Do you offer me your power freely?" she asked.

"Jasper," said Tobias.

"But what else can I do?" Jasper asked.

"We can try all kinds of other things. We haven't even seen the thing we fear. We could face it, attack it directly, all together. We have considerable power. If this—shade can solve this problem, surely we can too."

"But she knows Gyp."

"We don't know Gyp? We, who have been her family all her life?"

"I can't explain it, but I know we don't know Gyp the way Altria does." Jasper stared at Tobias, then walked to me and held out his hands. "Altria. Please use this for Gyp's good."

Shadow hands reached out to lie across his hands. "This will strengthen our connection," Altria said. Already her voice was stronger. "You won't be able to cast me out very easily. I'll be able to do as I like with you. You don't know the half of what I like to do."

Jasper's face paled, but he kept his hands under hers.

"You. Thing," Mama said. "Hurt my children at your own risk."

Altria spun from flickering shadow into something more solid. Her hands across Jasper's looked almost real now. Again, she looked like me, but this time a full-sized me. She was dressed the same way I was, in poppy red, and she wore the makeup I had put on after my shower. Now I saw what I must look like without the reversed vision of a mirror. I was surprised. She looked handsome and strong.

"They are not children," she said.

Mama rose taller and looming. "They will always be my children."

"That'll get tiresome." She gripped Jasper's hands and let them go, then leaned to kiss his forehead. "Thank you, sweetie. That's enough for now."

His eyes burned in his pale face.

Altria came to me and stared into my eyes. She glanced at Tobias. "You may let go now."

Tobias tried to tug his fingers out from under my hand, but I held on.

"Gyp, let go," Altria told me.

I released my hold. Tobias's fingers slipped away, and I fell back into what the computer had made me.

"Can you make me skinny?" I asked Altria.

She laughed. I watched how she did it, to see if there was any hope of my ever looking good. She came pretty close to looking almost okay. "I can make you anything I want," she said.

"Can you make me pretty?"

Her face sobered. Her eyes looked hot. "Kiss me," she said.

"Do I have to?" I was almost reconciled to how she looked, but not enough to want to do *that*. Eww.

"To get what you want, you do," she said.

I could be pretty, and skinny, if I just kissed her? One kiss. Then I could wear any of the clothes Opal had left behind. Maybe I should ask for long hair first. I knew Altria could do that, too. But she was staring at me like she was angry. Maybe I shouldn't ask for anything else. I could always get some wigs.

I leaned forward, closed my eyes, and kissed her.

Things snapped and cindered in my brain. A white heat blew through my mind like a sirocco and scoured out all the structures and prisons the new rules had built. I hugged Altria and kissed her hard, glorying in the melting of all the un-me.

She laughed and pulled away. "Wait, wait a second." She leaned forward and whispered, hot wind in my ear, "What about these other things it put in your brain? Do you want to dump all of them? This curse-tracking thing?"

"No, I like that."

"The rhymes?"

I hadn't noticed the rhymes doing me ill or good. I shrugged.

"The shunt?"

I leaned back and studied her face. I wanted that shunt gone.

"I could coopt that. Make it mine."

I waited.

"What the thing said is true. If you give me your energy, you won't have to worry about what to do with it."

I would have to worry about what *she* would do with it.

"You don't even have to know."

I glanced at Mama and Tobias and Jasper.

"I froze them," she said. "This conversation is just for us."

"You *froze* them?" It was true. They weren't moving. Their eyes didn't track. They hung there in mid-motion, stuck in a moment that didn't move. I stared at Altria. She had taken Jasper's power and this was what she did with it? I didn't even know it was possible to freeze Mama or Tobias.

"Just for a moment," she said.

"Altria, please destroy the shunt."

She sighed. "Kiss me again."

I pressed my lips to hers. Something else splintered and broke in my mind, and then power flooded into me.

"Look at that," Altria said, breathless. "That little machine was sucking so much out of you that it increased your flow."

Just what I needed. More curse power.

She smiled. "Have fun." She went to frozen Jasper and kissed his mouth, too, then faded away, and the world ticked forward again. Jasper frowned and glanced around. Tobias blinked three times and stared at me. Mama looked ready to explode on somebody.

I stood there, tension ratcheting my shoulders tight, and smiled at my family.

"Where'd she go?" Jasper said. He stroked his index finger across his lips. "I feel—huh? I'm back to full strength."

"Are you all right, Gypsum?" Tobias asked.

I almost said "Fine," but decided against it. They wouldn't know I was back to being me if I said that. "I need coffee. I need something to eat. Then I need to go recurse that damned computer."

Nearby wallpaper singed and curled off the wall in strips. Smoke rose from the carpet under my feet.

"Sorry," I said.

"Fix that," Mama told me.

"I don't know how."

"You're going to learn."

"All right. Teach me."

"Don't you get sarcastic with me this morning. I've already put up with a lot from you."

"Mama—"

Jasper grabbed my arm. "Let's go downstairs."

"THANK you," I told my brother. "Thank you. Thank you." I averaged one thank-you per stair step.

Mama and Tobias stayed back in the hall to talk about something. I was glad to get away from Mama. Her explosions always terrified me, even though I couldn't seem to stop myself from saying things that set her off. Right now I had rivers of heat carving canyons in my shoulders, and I needed to set myself off sometime soon. What if Mama exploded at me and I exploded back? Would the world end? I wasn't ready to find out.

Jasper said, "Okay. Okay. I'm sufficiently thanked. Is she going to haunt me, Gyp?"

"I don't know. Thank you for risking it."

"She terrifies me. And I, I—she fascinates me." He frowned. "She shouldn't. I have Trina."

"We're venturing into strange territory here."

"I know. She looked just like you, and she kissed you."

I didn't tell him she'd kissed him too. He had been frozen. Maybe he'd never know. "I don't think she's me." It was a question that had been on my mind since Tobias had suggested it the night before, that she was some other part of me I had split off. In a way I wished it were true. She was so confident in her power, so effective in her actions.

"I don't think she is either. I wonder what she really looks like."

A woman the size of an elephant, who could catch flying people in midair in the middle of an explosion?

I said, "What happened with Trina, anyway? I forgot to ask yesterday. You drew her in chalk, her head came to life, then you left—"

"Oh. It was historic. Flint was right again. I went to the club, and there she was, asleep with her head on the table while the band was in the middle of a set. I woke her, and she told me about the extremely strange dream she had had. That was it. We watched the rest of the music together and I took her home, and—" He shrugged.

Jasper held the kitchen door open for me and followed me in. Flint and Beryl were eating cereal at the kitchen table. Mama liked it better if everybody ate all their meals at the dining room table, but that involved placemats and carrying everything from the kitchen across the hall to the dining room, and then carting it back and wiping everything down afterward. Eating in the kitchen was a lot easier.

"Jeeze, Gyp!" Flint said. "You changed again? What'd I miss this time?"

"What are you doing in Opal's dress?" Beryl asked, anger in her voice. She took a hard look at me and jumped to her feet. "What are you doing in Opal's makeup? If she were here, she would kill you!"

"Would she?"

"You know she would!"

"She could try," I said. My shoulders twinged. I had to get outside. Only I had no idea what to curse this time, or how. I needed a plan!

"You better stay out of my things!"

My little sister was threatening me. I was in a bad place for that. I wanted to curse her; the energy had so much momentum I wanted to fling it any direction, and she was acting like a target.

"I—Flint, you busy?"

"No." He jumped up.

"Let's go bake something."

"What about the computer?" Jasper asked.

I shook my head. "I can't wait long enough to think about anything. My flow is accelerated."

Flint grabbed my hand and pulled me through the house and out back. "What do you want to make today?" he asked.

"Let's not make creampuffs. This is going to be a lot. Let's make bread."

"Bread?"

I didn't have as many bread recipes on tap as I had other things. It was so much easier to buy bread than to make it. Dad had talked about a bread machine, but we had never gotten around to getting one.

I knew basic steps in breadmaking, and I knew which kinds of bread I loved to eat.

"Bread," Flint said again. "Okay."

We sat on the lawn facing each other and holding hands again, and I thought of bread. I dropped almost at once into a trance, where I went through mental motions over and over again. Mix up warm water with yeast and sugar and leave it somewhere warm for fifteen minutes. While it was sitting, go whip up a batch of blueberry muffins. Then make up the dough in a big bowl and add the yeast mixture. Beat the dough, add flour, mix . . . knead the dough. Oh, I felt my shoulders ease while I thought about kneading, kneading, kneading. Then more waiting time while the dough sat under a damp cloth and grew twice its size, might as well make some cupcakes. Punch the dough down to get rid of air bubbles. Knead. Cut in half, form loaves, set the loaves in loaf pans, let them grow again someplace warm. Ahh, so many warm places in this recipe. Bake. . . .

I thought of oat bread and rye bread and pumpernickel, seven grain, sprouted wheat, sourdough and honey bread, cheese bread, banana bread, cornbread and zucchini bread and pretzels and English muffins and bagels and croissants. Muffins. Pita bread. Lovely bread.

FLINT squirmed, woke me out of my trance. I glanced at him, realized I was hot hot hot, and tried to slow my thoughts down, but it was difficult.

At last he said, "Stop, Gyp. Stop it."

I blinked out of a dream of popovers and looked at him.

There was bread everywhere. It covered the back lawn, stacked chest high in some places. We were cocooned in the aroma of fresh-baked bread. My mouth watered. I let go of Flint's hands and grabbed a muffin, peeled it out of its paper petticoat, and ate it. Blueberry. Moist, crumbly, sweet, and satisfying. I grabbed a small loaf of banana bread and bit into that. Delicious, though heavy. Yes.

Flint blew on his hands. Tears tracked his face.

I dropped the little loaf and looked at my brother's hands. They were angry red and blistered.

"God. I'm sorry. I'm so sorry, Flint."

"I was going to figure out a system where this wouldn't hurt me, but I didn't have time," he said. "What happened to you? You're spilling way more energy. This is too much. I don't know about you, but I'm not sure how long I can keep this up."

"My curse bounced back on me." I tested my shoulders. Still tense, but not very. "I have to go find out what happened with it. Without your help, things I curse turn into people who do things to me. Yesterday was interesting. Today was awful."

"What did you curse?"

"Aunt Hermina's computer."

He glanced toward the guest house. I did too.

Even from here I felt curse heat against my face.

"We have to go check on it," I said. I had left my aunt alone with that machine, left the machine primed to help anyone it could get its hands on, left it without a clear idea of what "help" meant.

And I had left Jasper and Mama and Tobias to stew about it while I had a bake attack.

*Sixteen*

"GYP," said Mama. "What have you done this time?"

I glanced up at the back porch. Everybody else was there, even Dad.

"Goodness," he said. "Guess I won't have to stop for pastry today." He came down the steps, surveyed the piles of bread, and selected several fruit muffins.

"Where are you going to put all this?" Mama asked.

"We'll take it to the shelters," said Flint. He conjured ice and rubbed it across his palms, winced when he pressed down on blisters. "I've got a babysitting gig at the Toussaints' tonight. I'll take them a couple loaves. We can freeze some of it. Maybe we could take some to the neighbors. It's that time of year."

I stood up. "But first we have to go see what happened to Aunt Hermina. That thing took a lot of energy out of me. What did it use it for?"

The rest of them came down to the walk, where the chalk drawings from two nights ago were wearing away, and peered toward the guest house.

"Dad, you should stay out of this," I said.

He stared at me.

A sudden gust of misery swept through me. I'd heard the others say things like that to Dad, but I'd never said it before. Now it was out in the open. He was different from the rest of us. I had joined the other side.

"Okay, honey." He came and kissed my cheek. "I'll see you all later. Call if I shouldn't come home tonight. I can go stay with the Kingstons."

"Take some bread with you," Flint said. "Give it to anybody you like."

Dad laughed and grabbed an armful of loaves. He disappeared inside the house.

"Fix your lipstick," Mama said to me.

"Huh?"

"Here, I'll do it." She flicked a finger at me. I felt faint heat on my lips. "You always want to look put together before you go to war," she told us all. Then she smiled. "What a fine bunch of kids I have."

I checked us out. Me, Jasper, Beryl, and Flint; we didn't all stand together very often. I did think we looked like a fine bunch of people, though I couldn't see myself. I had my memory of Altria in the upstairs hallway, though.

"Let's go," Tobias said.

I held back for a second as the others headed down the walk toward the guest house. I looked at the sidewalk chalk. I focused. "Damn," I whispered, and the pictures vanished, left the walk clean and white.

The walk led past Mama's roses around the side of the house. Near our kitchen/laundry door, there was an array of doors: one to the multiroom basement under the big house, one to the basement of the guest house, and then a staircase led up to the hall between the guest house and the kitchen. A small fenced yard between the staircase and the house wall held our garbage cans.

We studied the guest house. My face felt hot. I held up my hands, and felt curse heat against my palms.

Plants grew out of the guest house windows, twined around them, sent runners up to the roof and down to the ground.

"What kind of plants are those?" Beryl asked.

"Hermina's plants," answered Flint.

"Yeah, but what kind is that?"

"She's been working to raise more vigorous and powerful strains of medicinal herbs," Tobias said. "She thought if she could get herbs to fix some kinds of magic so that they were resident in the herbs until applied to medical problems, that would be very handy."

"Wonder if she's got something for burns," Flint muttered.

"Regardless of what kind of plants they are," said Mama, "they're not behaving as they should. I told Hermes she could do anything she liked out here so long as she kept it quiet and inside. This violates our covenant."

"It's not her fault," Jasper said.

Mama looked sideways at him.

"It's my curse." I stepped past Mama and Tobias and climbed the stairs to knock on Hermina's door.

No one answered.

Everyone moved up around me. I knocked again. "Aunt Hermina?" I called. "You in there? Are you okay?"

A voice answered, but I couldn't understand what it said. I checked with my relatives. Jasper shook his head.

"We're coming in," I said. I tried the doorknob. It turned, but when I pushed on the door, there was resistance. Had something fallen across the door in the hallway? I pushed harder. The door opened a crack, and leaves rustled and shifted in that gap.

I pulled the door shut. I looked at Uncle Tobias.

"What's your sense?"

"It's my energy." I felt it pulse at me through the door.

"Your mess. You clean it up," Mama said. "We'll help you. This time."

I bit my lower lip, shoved on the door, and pushed it farther open, fighting back a wall of too-mobile plants.

The hallway between the bedrooms had turned into a jungle. As soon as I got the door all the way open, vines sent runners out to explore the outdoors.

So much lively life! Like Beryl's chalk plants. I stepped into the hall, crunching stems and leaves under my high heels as I went; there was no place to step without stepping on plants. Scents of fresh rosemary and thyme, basil and peppermint, a mingling of other strong scents I didn't recognize rose from the crushed leaves and stems. These plants didn't curl around and trap me. After I took a few steps among them, they tried to move out of the way.

I gave them some time. They cleared a narrow pathway to the back bedroom for me. I stepped carefully, and everybody else followed me single file into the house. "Aunt?" I called.

She answered, but not in words. A smothered cry. I pushed past hanging plants, plants that didn't naturally grow that way, but plants that grew that way now.

The foliage was even thicker in her office. The plants had blocked all the windows so that most of the light was dim and green, though there was a faint haloed blaze of synthetic light where her desk used to be. I pushed and picked my way that direction; the curse heat was stronger there.

Aunt Hermina sat at her desk, her hands flat on top of it. The computer rode her like a child playing piggyback, its long thin white legs tight around her waist, its arms around her neck. Its hands reached up to cover her mouth. Its keyboard pressed against the back of her head, and its screen peered over the top of her head at us. Her own eyes were wide. When she saw me she struggled, tried to lift her hands, but they were snugged down, like the rest of her, by vines and roots and rampant vegetation. Or maybe some of the white threads that tied her to her chair came from the computer's body. It was hard to tell in the dim and denseness.

"This isn't the charge I gave you," I said to the computer.

Its pale face stared at me. "I'm helping. I'm working."

"You're hurting!"

"No. I'm helping her realize her dreams faster than she ever thought possible." It frowned. "You cut off my power. How could you cut off my power? Now we won't be able to pursue our studies. Why did you reject my help?" It lifted a hand and reached for me, and Hermina shook her head, managed to get the other hand away from her mouth.

"Get it off me!" she cried.

I didn't know how to shield myself the way Tobias and Jasper did. I focused. I hunched my shoulders. I narrowed my concentration. "Damn," I murmured.

The computer incinerated, disintegrated, ghosted away in a second. Hermina screamed.

I stumbled forward. "Did I hurt you?" I had tried to keep my curse confined just to the computer itself. I didn't want any of the fallout to hit her. But it had been on her back. Had I burned her?

She screamed again, and started crying. She struggled, tried to lift her hands. Her plants still bound her. I went to her and pulled at the trapping plants, but she said, "Get away from me!" and turned her head.

Stung, I backed up, right into Jasper. He gripped my shoulders and edged me around, then helped me out of the room. "Go on outside," he said. "We'll clear up the rest of this."

Somehow I made it to the kitchen. My hands trembled as I poured coffee. I loaded it with sugar and milk and sat at the table, sipped until I stopped sobbing.

I had the power of curses. I could either destroy things utterly, or change them so they hurt people I loved. Or, if I could get someone or something to sit still long enough,

I could launder my power through someone else and then it could do good things. And burn the people who helped me.

I wished I knew how to fix all the things Mama wanted me to fix.

She would probably tell me to clean up the guest house, too. I could damn all those plants into oblivion. I would hate that. It wasn't the plants' fault they were made to grow. But I could do it. On the other hand, maybe Aunt Hermina never wanted to see me again, and somebody else would have to clean things up.

I drank my coffee, calmer by the time I got to the bottom of the cup. I couldn't clean up my messes with curse energy, but I might be able to do it a normal way, with muscle. I went to the pantry and got out a stack of paper bags, then headed for the back porch. On my way across the great hall I kicked off the high heels, then stopped to peel out of the pantyhose. God. Girl torture. All my life I'd told myself I would never have to go through girl torture. Evil computer. Force me to turn into what I hated. Rage simmered inside my ribcage.

I set open grocery sacks on the walkway and filled them with bread, pausing once in a while to eat a roll or a muffin. The bread still smelled and tasted great, only there was so much of it. We could take some to feed the ducks and geese at the bird sanctuary, drop some off along the beach where homeless people lived, drive around and ask random strangers in the street if they'd like bread. Maybe eventually we'd find a good way to give this out. But could we do it every day?

Maybe we would never do it again. Flint had trouble with it. How could I channel power through him and not burn him? I didn't know enough.

I felt more curse energy building.

I filled ten paper sacks with assorted bread, then went to sit on the wall above the orchard.

My aunt had sent me away. She had been angry and scared because of something I did. I told myself I needed to understand that this was going to be a common reaction to me in the future if I went on cursing things. People would be scared and horrified. They would want me to leave.

My little sister almost attacked me for something I did while not in my right mind. I needed to take responsibility for things I did while under the influence of my own curses, too, even though I felt like a victim. I had to own up to my acts and deal with the consequences.

My mother and I were feuding, and I had separated myself from my father. I'd hurt my brother's hands, and threatened my other brother with weirdness that scared him. So far, having my own power wasn't working out very well.

Maybe I *should* get rid of it. At least I knew how to do that. I'd learned something from that computer.

"Altria?"

Where was she? Was I nuts to even think about calling her? Did I need the protection stone? No. She had come to me upstairs without the help of the stone. What I knew about her was that she scared me, but also that she had saved me twice.

I stared beyond the Old Coast Highway, the scattering of stores fringing it, and Highway 101 beyond. Out past every land thing, the ocean lay. Sun shone, but it was a hazy day, too hazy to see the Channel Islands, twenty-five or thirty miles out to sea.

Presently I realized someone sat beside me. I turned my head and saw myself, the new edition, in red dress, makeup, styled hair; not a me I was in any way comfortable with. She stared out at distance, too.

"What are you?" I asked.

"A different kind of person."

"What do you really look like?"

"A giant praying mantis."

I glanced at her, saw the edge of a smile.

"Really?" I asked.

"No."

"Where do you go when you're not here?"

"I can be in several places at once. Now that I know you, I leave a fragment of myself here to listen for your call. I have fragments in many places; other people call me, too. I find doors in people's dreams. Part of me is in a place that listens for new calls, like yours yesterday, when a way opened for me to find form. Invitations into new forms, plus power, those are my favorite things. Much of me . . ." She frowned. "Where I am, it's not this world, but one nearby. Everything about it is different from here." She smiled and leaned toward me. "I could send you there," she whispered, "and stay here. Take your place."

I stared down at my hands in my lap. I had hurt my aunt. Everything I touched burned. I had more power than I knew what to do with, and when I used it, I had to hurt or disturb people. Wouldn't it be nice to be the victim of a diabolical plan, helpless to prevent my own abduction, not responsible for anything anymore? I could go somewhere else and leave Altria to deal with the consequences.

Then again, that wasn't fair to my family. She looked like me. Maybe they would be able to tell the difference, maybe not; armed with all my power, she might be able to do a lot of nasty things to them before they could stop her.

"Can't let you do that," I said.

"Maybe I'll do it anyway."

I sighed.

"But in the meantime, while I'm hatching evil plots, what did you want from me?"

"I wanted to talk about the shunt. That's one thing. I also wondered if you would work with me on a couple of things."

"Tell me about the shunt," she said.

I rolled my shoulders. Power sat on them like lead weights.

"Suppose we set up some kind of feed so you could take part of my power?"

She licked her lips.

"But I would want to be in control of the shunt. If I need all my power, I want to be able to cut you off. If I need to get rid of some, I'd love to be able to dump it on you. It's coming too fast for me, and I don't know how to use it yet. But if we set up a shunt, I want you to promise that you're not going to use my power to hurt me or anybody I love." I thought about the computer and its ideas of help and hurt. "Only, do you understand what I mean by hurt?"

"My definition is different from yours. A little pain now can lead to knowledge and growth later."

"Do you work toward knowledge and growth?"

She frowned. "I will not tell you what I work toward."

I felt like crying. I wanted to trust her. I wanted her to help me. I thought we could do something we'd both benefit from, but she had to say the right words.

She could lie to me and I would believe her.

I wished I didn't feel so tired and discouraged. Maybe I was making stupid decisions, courting disasters.

"What's your other project?" she asked.

"I need to curse something soon. If I work with someone else who can direct the energy, I can turn my curse into a blessing. Will you help me replace the staircase I destroyed last night?"

"Your power, my direction?" She grinned.

I had a bad feeling about this. But heck. At least if we built something together, it wouldn't be cursed, and somebody else in the family could change it.

"Mama wants white marble," I said.

"Let's do it."

We wended our way through stacks of baked goods to the edge of the walk where it disappeared into air. We sat down side by side and dangled our legs over the dropoff, our feet waving above the crater from last night's big curse.

"Rococo," she said.

I looked at the house. Early twentieth century, kind of a Craftsman house. "I don't think that'll go."

"Italianate. Gaudí? Byzantine?"

I didn't even know what she was talking about. "Classical?" I suggested.

"Boring?" she asked.

"That would make Mama happier."

"Leave it to me."

I looked away from her.

If it didn't work out all right, it could be fixed.

If it worked out all right, maybe we could get back to talking about the shunt.

I held out my hand, and she clasped it. "Lift up your feet," she said. I scooted back from the edge, tugging her with me. "Oooh, you're so hot."

"I don't want to hurt you."

"Heat doesn't hurt me. I love it. Close your eyes."

I closed my eyes and opened myself up to being used.

Our communion felt different from the one I had had with Flint. With my brother, I had just poured energy out headlong and thought about what I hoped would manifest from it. Here I sat, and felt Altria draw energy from me slowly and steadily, comfortably. I was conscious of some kind of spinning, of the energy leaving me, passing through her, changing, hitting the air and going solid, but I didn't know what she was making of it. I didn't have to hold onto anything. All I had to do was be, and let her draw from me.

It felt good. No, great. I could get addicted to this. I listened to my slow, deliberate breathing and paid attention to how the tightness loosened in my shoulders, how contentment filled me as the tension left.

"All right," she murmured what felt like a long time later. She squeezed my hand and released it.

I opened my eyes.

At our feet, white marble gleamed.

I crawled over to look at it.

The steps were rough instead of smooth, with faint chisel marks still on them. The railing was delicate Gothic fretwork, all marble. No way did this match the house in color or style, but who saw the backyard besides the family? The stairs looked safe. Even wet, they wouldn't be slippery, because of the roughness. They glittered in the hazy sun.

I looked over my shoulder at Altria. "Beautiful," I said. "Thanks. Thanks."

She smiled and cocked her head. "Now are you going to let me suck your brain?"

I laughed and lay back on the lawn, feeling boneless and utterly relaxed, cursed out and clean. Birds chirped and fluttered among the bread, tasting here and there. A scrub jay landed on a loaf of wheat bread not five feet from my head. It squawked at me.

"Gyp?" Jasper yelled from the house.

Altria and I looked that way.

"I'd better go," she said.

"You'll come when I call you?"

"Probably. Promise me energy and I'll come for sure."

"Thanks again for coming this time."

"My pleasure." She got to her feet, dusted off her dress.

"Hey! Gyp!" Jasper was on the porch now.

"Wrong," said Altria, and melted.

I rolled over and sat up, then stood so he could see me over ambient bread. "Hi," I said.

He jumped over bread and came to me. "What—" He glanced to the side where Altria had stood before she disappeared, then back at me. "What?"

"Look." I pointed to the staircase.

His eyebrows rose.

"She built it using my energy. I thought I better figure out how to fix all the things I ruined. That's my start."

"Pretty good. It looks different. Nice rock."

"I hope Mama likes it." I straightened. "Is Aunt Hermina all right?"

"She's getting over it."

"Did I burn her?"

"No. She's not physically hurt. She's mad about a lot of things, though. What the computer did, what it made her do, ruined her research, stuff she'd been working on for years. Those plants are no longer things she can propagate and sell to nurseries. And she's mad because the computer is gone, go figure. She has a couple disks, and she hopes her work is still on them, but they kind of got buried under plantlife so it's hard to tell if they'll be usable. She's in Dad's study trying them in his computer right now."

I wrapped my arms around myself, hunched my shoulders. Maybe I could curse myself mute and then I wouldn't be able to curse anymore. I could sink down silently into Aunt Meta's fate. Eat myself up from the inside.

"Let's try the stairs," Jasper said.

I sighed.

We walked down the stairs one step at a time. I couldn't rid myself of the conviction that these stairs would be cursed too. Would they throw anybody who walked down them? Tip you over, send you sailing? My power, Altria's direction, what was I thinking?

I navigated the stairs with no problem, and so did Jasper. We walked out into the orchard to check them out.

There were the weatherstained and venerable retaining walls holding up the upper terrace, and there was the gleaming white staircase, shining in front of them like something Photoshopped into a background where it didn't belong. The mellow ochre walls of the house beyond, the glossy green of the orange tree's leaves, the dark shingled roof. And that glowing staircase.

It was a beautiful staircase.

"Altria?" I didn't realize I had said her name aloud until I heard it.

She stood beside me and studied the view. Then she laughed. "Well, you said white."

"Yeah."

She put her hands on my shoulders. "Hmm. A bit of buildup already, just after I drained you. We can fix it."

"Okay."

She hugged me from behind, her arms around my waist, her chin on my shoulder. "Close your eyes."

I closed my eyes. I felt the movement of power from me into her, from her into air. Jasper gasped.

"All right," said Altria.

I opened my eyes. The staircase was now golden marble veined with black, and it melted into the view, an organic part of the whole. "Much better," I said. "Thank you."

"Let's do different work next time. Something lively!"

"I'll see."

"Sounds like a no to me. So I'll just take this." She skimmed her hand across my shoulders, pulled tension out that I hadn't even noticed, and vanished.

"At first I thought the filtering effect would only work with Flint," I said, "but I think it works just fine with her, too." We headed toward the staircase, climbed the steps. They worked just like steps.

"She uses your energy for anything she likes. Once it gets one step removed, it's not your problem anymore. I wonder what she is. She took energy from me and used it, too. But then she kind of gave it back. Is she a vampire?"

"Maybe." None of the standard vampire rules seemed to apply. She could run around in broad daylight. What she was sucking wasn't exactly blood. Was she a parasite or a symbiote? "Probably not. But I don't know what she is."

"Oh, I forgot. You got a phone message from Phil."

"What?"

"That's why I was looking for you. Phil left you a message. Says everybody has the flu and he really needs you to work this afternoon."

I groaned. It wasn't even eleven yet and I'd been up for hours. I had attacked and demoralized half my family, and the other half had attacked and demoralized me. Now Phil wanted me to come to work? When I kept collecting curse power? "I better call him and tell him I'm really sick, too."

"He sounded desperate."

"He'd be worse off if I went to work with all this uncontrolled power. Look what happened to Aunt Hermes!"

Jasper frowned. "Maybe you could take Flint with you. Things get desperate, Twinkie attack!"

"Flint has a job tonight. Anyway, he's retired from helping me. I burned him bad last time. I'll see what I can do." I dug a loaf of dill rye and a loaf of sourdough bread out of a pile the birds hadn't pecked down very far yet and took them into the house.

In the kitchen, I put the bread in the bread box, then grabbed the phone and called work.

As soon as Phil recognized my voice, he said, "How sick are you?"

"If I'm contagious, nobody else on Earth wants to catch this," I said.

"How contagious could you be? I thought you got hit hard last weekend, but you came to work on Monday. Are you saying you've had a relapse?"

"Same sickness, different symptoms."

"Can you walk? Can you talk? Can you think semistraight? Look, Gyp, chances are nobody will come in looking for a tutor, but you're my last shot at getting someone to actually be here the required hours. My plane leaves at 3:30—Mary and I are flying up to San Francisco to spend Christmas with the kids—so I have to get out of here by one, and Anita's got to leave on the dot of four. Could you please, please come in at ten minutes to four?"

"Anita can't just close down the Center?"

Phil muttered something. "I'd consider it service above and beyond the call of duty if you could manage to come in today, and close up tonight. You'd build up some nice brownie points. You can close the Center at six; that's when the rest of campus is closing. Can you manage two hours?"

"All right," I squeaked.

"Thank you. That wasn't so hard, was it?"

If I planned it just right—cursed something right before I left, maybe brought something to curse—if nobody showed up looking for help—

This wasn't going to work. I could tell already.

"Merry Christmas," I said to my boss.

"You have a merry Christmas, too," he said.

We both hung up.

The phone rang. I picked it up. "Hello?"

"Gypsum! Just who I wanted to talk to! Hi, this is Ian."

"Hi, Ian."

"You busy tonight?"

I covered the transmitter with my hand and sighed. Then I took my hand off. "I'm working until six, and then I have to go curse something. After that I'm free for a couple hours, maybe. What did you have in mind?"

"You have to go curse something?"

"Did I say that?" I said weird things to Ian all the time just to see what would happen. He didn't know that any of it was true. Sure, he knew Claire, and he had met Claire's mother. July never kept it a secret that she was a practicing witch, but she never kept it a secret that she wasn't very good at it, either. You could know July, hear her talk about this stuff, and just think she was a flaky Californian, even if you saw her do craftwork. She did get things right. But then she was always surprised by it. And the sorts of things she got right were things that might have happened anyway, like getting something to bloom or summoning up a little nice weather so she could take a walk.

So, because I made these absurd statements, there was a chance that Ian believed I, too, was a flaky Californian. Last week at this time there wasn't even the possibility that he'd seen me do anything outré, and I hadn't introduced him to my mother. We were much more secretive about our practices than July was.

But somehow, when I talked to Ian, I just said things. Maybe because I couldn't believe this guy, and I didn't understand him. He'd spent time with me. Unlike every other guy I'd met, he kept coming back for more. Why? Whatever courtship signals were, I didn't send them; I knew that much, so what did Ian see in me that no one else did? He baffled me. At the same time, it was kind of exhilarating to just run my mouth around someone who wasn't in my family. I said, "It's like a tic. I have to curse things every once in a while. You don't want to be around when that's going on."

"When you curse things, what does it involve? Is it like Tourette's? Do you just say nasty things to them? Display your vocabulary and your imagination? I'd love to see that."

"No, I really curse them. I curse them to fall apart or grow too fast or rot. Actually, I just got this power, so I don't know what I'm doing yet, but I have to do something."

"I'd love to see that, too."

"But Ian—I mean, what if I cursed you by mistake?"

"Is it fatal?"

"Not so far."

"Is it permanent?"

"I'm still exploring that part. Sometimes it wears off after, uh—" what had the computer said? "—six point seven hours. Sometimes it lasts, but that seems to be when I combine it with something else."

"Six point seven hours," he said thoughtfully. "So, say,

you curse me at six-thirty, by one-twelve, I'm back to normal?"

"You can do math? With minutes?" For some reason this made me mad.

"It's a tic," he said.

I laughed. "Can you pick me up at the Learning Center at six?" I didn't want to drive. Too used to cussing out other drivers—I didn't want to do anything automatic where the consequences could be dire. I was hoping I could get someone to drop me off this afternoon, but I hadn't figured out how to get home afterward. Catch a bus? What if I got mad at other passengers? I hadn't used the bus system enough to know if that was something I would do. Ask someone to pick me up? I wondered how busy Jasper was.

If Ian could pick me up, I wouldn't have to bother my brother. But what was I going to do about Ian and curses? What if I cursed him, for real, and he hated me?

Unless I gave up my power, it was going to be part of me for the rest of my life. I wasn't reconciled to giving up the power, especially when I didn't know who to give it to. I guessed I might as well test my friendships with it, because sooner or later, they'd be bumping up against it.

Later I might have better control. Later might be better.

But where did that leave me now? Here he was, asking to meet me, and I'd agreed. Cancel now? On the off-chance I could learn how to handle myself and we could try again later? Or just go with it and see what happened? I'd already told him what was going on.

He said, "Six would be okay."

"So what was it you had in mind for this evening, anyway?" I asked.

"I've changed my mind. Since you'll be at the beach anyway, how about a stroll along the breakwater at dusk, and some kind of seafood? There's a couple nice restaurants down there."

"Is this, like, an actual date-type thing?" Part of what baffled me about Ian's approach was that he invited me to things, and I thought, *Is this a date?* Only it was things like going to a movie with him and five friends, or going to a concert with Claire, or there's a new exhibit at the Natural History Museum, want to meet there and take a look? I asked three other people to come, so we'll have someone to discuss it with. Or there's a Sing Your Own Messiah at Grace Lutheran tonight, want to go sing? We both like singing four-part music, and besides, Susie and Janet and George will be there.

He never picked me up, and he never took me home. We always went with company.

I always had a good time. There were always moments when Ian and I wandered around alone with each other, and I got a chance to say stupid things, and he responded with wild claims about his own family, who lived in Idaho and never came to California.

I had such a crush on him.

"I mean, is it going to turn out that you bring about six friends and we have a lovely time, only I have to curse them since they're there, and I turn them all into statues, or something, and then you never call me again?"

"Uh," he said.

"Not that I'd mind if you brought friends. Except—no, maybe I would mind. I have to tell you that up front this time, because when I'm irritated, I bet the curses work out even worse."

"Um."

"I mean, Ian, I only got this power Wednesday night, and I really don't know what I'm doing yet. Some of the results have been horrible."

For a minute he didn't say anything. Then he said, "I'll come alone."

"Good."

Neither of us spoke.

"See you later," I said at last.

"Later."

We hung up. My heart felt light.

My shoulders felt tense.

The kitchen door flapped open behind me, and I turned around. Beryl came in.

Suddenly I remembered I still wore Opal's dress, Opal's makeup. "Okay, okay. I'm going upstairs to change," I said.

Beryl sighed and handed me a pair of high heels and a snarl of pantyhose. "You left these in the hall. This outfit stuff, borrowing Opal's things, it was connected to a curse, right? You didn't do it on purpose."

"I cursed the computer, and the computer cursed me back. It made me think about nothing but how to look better." I shook my head. "It was the worst, the absolute worst."

"Well, it worked. I didn't know you could look like that."

"What?"

"You're pretty!" The words burst out of her with a bitter edge.

"Don't worry about it. I'm going up to wash my face. I'll never do this again. Or maybe I shouldn't say never, but I won't do it on purpose again."

"Shut up," Beryl said.

"What's your problem?"

"How come you never looked like that before?"

I felt bewildered. "Why should I?"

"Because you can."

"But it's not me."

"But it *is* you. There you are, you, and you look like that."

"But—" Huh?

"You could look good every day! Why are you always disguising yourself?"

"Disguising—I don't care what I look like." Well, I did have that one good outfit, but now it was covered with chalk splotches. I had some other dresses, too. Nothing fancy, but a step up from slob. I mean, there were moments when I thought it was a good idea to dress up, like when I went to work. But I never wanted to dress up much. "I just want to be comfortable."

"How uncomfortable are you now?"

I looked down at Opal's dress on me. It was tight, but it wasn't uncomfortably tight. I couldn't even feel the makeup enough to tell if it was still on my face. My hair felt a little strange, but I hadn't noticed it until this moment.

"This is *red*. I never wear red."

"But it's a great color on you! It puts roses in your cheeks. You look all healthy and glowing."

"Maybe that's the makeup."

"Either way."

"Why are you mad at me?"

Her hands curled into fists; her face tightened in frustration. "Because you've been hiding for years!"

"What are you talking about? I've been right here."

"But you—arrgh!"

Having my little sister growl at me added weight to my already tight shoulders. "I'm going to turn back into myself now, Beryl. If you know what's good for you, you'll get out of my way. The power's riding me right now, and it wants out."

"Hey. I got the answer to that. Do your worst."

"You're seriously daring me?"

"You got it." She scrawled something on her palm, muttered some words too low for me to hear. Then she held up her hand. She had built a shield, but it wasn't the kind Jasper or Tobias had used; it was nearly transparent, but flashed opalescent colors.

What should I do to my little sister? I had to curse

something, and she thought she was prepared. Whatever it was, it would last about seven hours. It might not even land on her.

Curses that sounded good worked out badly. I had told the grapefruit to be plump, juicy, and tasty, and look where that ended up. I had told the computer to help, and that had been awful. Maybe if I said something that actually sounded like a curse, it would work out better.

I stared at my sister. She looked pale. I realized how much I loved her. We'd never had a fight like this before. She had been nice to me when everybody else was picking on me. I thought we were friends. How could I curse her?

"Come on," she said. "Give it your best shot."

"I can't figure out what to do. I don't want to curse you."

She sighed in disgust. "Quit being such a martyr. Do something mean."

I checked the clock. About twenty minutes after eleven. I couldn't do math with minutes! But whatever I dropped on her, it would last until around six-thirty, say. "Do you have any plans for this afternoon?"

"Stop stalling!"

"Ultimate Fashion Sense!" I yelled. I pointed my hand toward her. Heat balled in my chest. No! Not another outfit ruined, I thought. This one's not even mine! Power, leave through my hand instead!

The power listened to me. It gathered in my chest, flowed up to my shoulder, then shot down my right arm and out my fingers at my sister.

She looked fierce and held up her shield.

The shield glowed red, then orange, then white. A ball of power collected in it and shot back at me.

## Seventeen

IT slammed into me, and I screamed, the impact was so unexpected! But it didn't hurt. First there was heat, then a wave of flickery tingling, then sort of a champagne-bubbles in my brain feeling. I blinked a couple of times and stared at my sister.

"No, no, no," I said.

Her hand dropped to her side. "Ultimate Fashion Sense? What kind of curse is that?"

"You can't possibly wear that skirt with that blouse. Those socks!"

She glanced down at herself. "What's wrong with my socks?"

"*Ribbed* socks? With plaid? Not midcalf height! Please! Either anklets or knee-highs. And your hair? How can you live with it?"

"What's wrong with my hair?"

"You can't go out in public with that hair. Come on." I grabbed her arm and dragged her upstairs.

"Gyp, what are you doing?"

"I have to cut your hair. It's imperative. No one should

have to live with looking at that any longer."

"Gyp?"

I took her to the upstairs bathroom, sat her on the toilet, got the Fiskar scissors and a comb out of the drawer, wrapped a towel around her shoulders, and went to work.

"Gyp, what are you doing? You're scaring me," she said in a small voice.

"I'll be done in a few. I won't hurt you if you just sit perfectly still. Keep your eyes closed." I wet the comb, tested different parts on her head, considered the results if I layered or cut straight across, allowing for the natural wave she had. Colors. She should have maybe a light wash of something. "So what kind of shield was that?"

"A reflector."

"Clever. It worked, huh?"

"I don't know. Is Ultimate Fashion Sense really a curse?"

I tapped my upper palate with the tip of my tongue. "You tell me. I'm obsessed with details of appearance, and I don't know what I'm doing." I scissored about ten inches of hair off the side of her head.

"You don't know what you're doing?"

"Hold still." Maybe she'd look good with asymmetric hair, long on one side, short on the other. She could start a trend. "Do you have any gel?"

"No!"

I glanced in the mirror. Oh, my God! *My* hair!

Not now. One thing at a time.

I wet-combed Beryl's hair and sliced off some more of it, evened the ends, layered the back. She'd been wearing her hair schoolgirl long for years, and it didn't flatter her face. Something short and playful. Bangs. She could use some bangs. Short straight ones right across her forehead. She had such great eyes and eyebrows. Her face was a nice shape. I tried wet-combing her hair a few different ways, wished I had those clips they had at salons to separate her hair out into different pieces for special treatment, but no.

Work with what I had. I combed and snipped.

I checked through the bathroom drawers.

"What are you doing?"

"Keep your eyes shut." I found an old hair dryer of Opal's and plugged it in, found some mousse, shook the bottle, squirted an egg of it into my hand, and smoothed it through Beryl's hair. Then I used the blow dryer to style it.

"You really don't know what you're doing?" she asked.

"Nope." One more comb-through, and I stood back to study the results.

Cute. Very, very cute. With all that hair out of her face, you saw what classic bone structure she had.

"Okay. I'm done."

She opened wide violet eyes, and she looked even better. She glanced at the towel on her shoulders, saw all the hair I'd cut off her head, and shut her eyes again. "You did that on purpose."

"Yep." I whisked the towel off her, poked her to get her to stand up, and shook the towel out into the toilet.

"No, I mean, you chose that curse just to torture me, didn't you?"

"What do you mean?"

"You knew it would bounce, and—"

"I did not."

She took a deep breath and looked in the mirror. "Oh!"

I stuck the towel in the hamper. I put away the tools. I could try to cut my own hair, but I'd probably mess it up. Better to pay a professional and give really explicit instructions.

Beryl's eyes met mine in the mirror. "I don't look like me."

"Join the club. What I'd really like to do is add some red highlights—" And then I thought, *Hey, I've got a little power, just*—I put my hand on her hair and let out a trickle of power. Her hair blushed.

How did that work?

"Wait. I'm sorry. I don't know how that worked. What if it's curse energy, and it makes your hair fall out, or something?"

She turned to look directly at me. "You're already cursed."

"I am cursed. It's very odd. This is like the curse from this morning, only I don't hate it. It's Girl Power, but it's not disabling. I mean, I know my own mind. I know what I think and what I want. I know that it's an aberration, me thinking I know what everybody should look like and how they should dress. I'll survive this, as long as I don't take my checkbook or my debit card out of the house. I'll just hate how everything looks until it wears off, except your hair. I like your hair now. You know, that shield was pretty nasty. Why'd you tell me to do something mean?"

"I was mad at you."

"You really wanted me to mess myself up, huh? That's going to go over well at work and on my date tonight."

"Work? Date?"

I ran my hand through her hair. "It feels all right." I frowned. "It looks great. I wonder how long the red will last. Hope I didn't do you any damage."

She glanced at her image again. "I almost like it."

"You will." I looked past my sister at my own face. Most of the makeup I'd put on earlier was still there. My lips were way too bright. Something subtle would be better. The rest of it was sloppy. Girlish, but messy.

I brushed my hand across my face, and the makeup disappeared.

"Whoa," I said.

I ran my finger over my lips. A nice plum stain followed my touch, a perfect fit in the lipline. I darkened the color of the top lip a little. Interesting. I ran my fingers over my eyebrows, straightening and darkening them. I outlined my eyes with off-black, not too wide a line, but smooth and even, then touched silver-pink shadow onto my eyelids.

"Gyp," Beryl said.

"In a minute," I muttered. A faint rose blush above the cheekbones and along the jawline. None of it obvious. All of it improving on nature. I took a look at the overall effect. Good.

"Okay, what?"

"You're doing an Opal."

"What do you mean?"

"You're putting on makeup without the makeup."

I frowned at her, then at my reflection, then at my fingertips. I thought about Jasper and me playing with Opal's beauty brush, a lifetime ago, and smiled. "Oh well."

"If you landed that curse on me, could I do what you're doing?"

"Why can't you just do it anyway?"

"But I—" She glanced at her reflection, then at me. "How do you know what color to choose?"

I shifted my shoulders. Yes, despite these tiny flares of power I played with, I was building up to another curse. I checked my watch. Maybe an hour had passed since I had cursed myself. Apparently plenty of time for me to amass more power. I put my hand on my sister's head. "Want to see what happens when you have this?"

"I don't know."

"Make up your mind. I don't need a double dose of this."

"You think it'll wear off in a few hours?"

"If it works like some of my other curses."

"Why is it a curse?"

"At the moment I'm not sure. When it wears off, I'll know. At least this answers one question. I guess it's a curse because *I* think it's a curse, not because the person being cursed thinks it is."

"Go ahead."

I gathered a blast of power. "Ultimate Fashion Sense!"

I said, and felt the power flow along my arm and into my sister's head.

Somehow this reminded me of Sailor Moon and Pretty Sammy and Magic Knights Rayearth. Maybe I should study Japanese animation to get my curse ideas. The superhero girls always shouted things when they used their powers. Mystical Water Dragon! Pretty Mutation Magical Recall! What would happen if I said that to somebody and backed it with curse power?

Beryl jolted under my hand, gripped the side of the sink, then steadied. I took my hand away. She checked herself in the mirror. "Oh!" she said. "It *is* a good haircut." She smiled at me.

"Meanwhile, I have to get out of this dress. Even if it does look good, it's not mine."

"Okay." She touched dark pink into her lips, frowned, wiped it off, tried something a little redder.

I left her staring into the bathroom mirror.

I had a completely different reaction to my wardrobe this time.

Jasper knocked on my door while I was working on it. "Come in," I said.

"So how are you now?"

"Good." I took a yellow blouse out of my closet and held it up to my chest, checked the color in my closet door mirror. Made me look sallow. I stroked the blouse and the color changed to pale spring green. Much better. Made me look rosy. I put the blouse away and grabbed a sweater, frowned at the pattern.

"What are you doing?"

"Fixing things."

"With curse power?"

I ran my hand over the sweater, made its pattern of roses shrink to delicate instead of overpowering. Then I held the sweater up toward my face. No heat. "Beryl made me curse myself, and now my power is acting like yours."

"You look different again."

"Yeah." I smiled at him.

"Beryl made you curse yourself? How'd she do that?"

I explained about Beryl's shield.

"Wow. Smart," he said. "Wonder if I could figure out how to do that."

Before he got lost in planning and technique, I asked, "Can you give me a ride to school later?"

"When?"

"Three-thirty?"

He thought, then said, "Okay. I can do that. So, you mean you're actually going out?"

"I have to sooner or later, and Phil needs me today." I looked at him. That hair. It was longer on one side than the other, and—I snipped my fingers surreptitiously, and a little sheaf of hair separated from his head and fell to his collar.

Jasper frowned. "What'd you do?"

"I'm sorry." I collapsed onto my bed. "I can hardly help myself."

"What's the curse?"

I told him.

"Something's wrong with my hair?"

"Not anymore."

"Don't fix me."

I gripped one hand in the other. "All right." My voice came out squashed.

"You're going out like this?"

"Nobody will be there. It's the last afternoon before break and everybody will have finished their finals. They'll be gone. Phil just has this thing. I think it's connected to funding. We have to be open and available during the stipulated hours."

"Maybe you better talk to Tobias first."

I glanced at my closet. I was only halfway through. Well. I'd probably have some more time. "All right."

I followed Jasper out into the hall, and saw the place that I'd scorched that morning while talking to Mama. Now I ran my hand over it, and repaired the wallpaper and the carpet. Good. Another problem solved. Maybe I better do something about the bread now that I was feeling confident. I had left sacks of bread out back, not to mention stacks of bread. The birds couldn't eat it all. Besides, it looked bad, and nothing bothered Mama as much as things that looked bad.

Tobias wasn't in his tower. I wanted to deal with the bread question and get back to working over my wardrobe while I had time from inside this curse, but Jasper said, "Let's find him."

We went downstairs.

Tobias and Hermina and Mama were sitting on the back porch. The instant I saw their heads through the great hall window I felt uneasy, and not just because I wanted to give Hermina a haircut and a makeover and change the color and cut of Tobias's shirt. What were they talking about?

*It's not all about you*, I told myself. It was almost never about me. I had been happy as a low-profile, low-maintenance, and self-entertaining person. But that had changed.

I would have to face Hermina sometime. I hoped she wouldn't yell at me to go away again. If she did that every time we ran into each other, it would make for a tense household, even though she spent most of her time in the guest house. Anyway, I needed to apologize. I might as well try it now.

I could figure out what to do with the bread after that.

I headed for the porch. Jasper followed me.

"Did you go shopping without me?" Mama asked when she saw me. She, Tobias, and Hermina were grouped around one of the wicker tables with the glass tops that lived out on the porch between the Adirondack chairs. On the table was a platter of sliced banana bread, a knife, and a dish with butter in it. They also had coffee steaming in mugs. Tobias was eating.

"No. These are things I found in my closet." I had done some alterations, that was all. Now I had a blouse, jeans, and penny loafers that actually looked good on me. "Aunt Hermes?"

She met my gaze.

"I'm really sorry. I'm so sorry. I don't know what to do for you. I had no idea all those things would come out of that curse."

"I know." She sighed. "I have to take some responsibility. I gave you permission to make that curse. Who knew."

"I realize you lost years of work." I squeezed one hand in the other. "Did the disks work in Dad's computer?"

She shook her head. "I took them to the shop to see if they could retrieve any of the data. I think it was part of the curse that when that thing stored my data on them, it did it so the disks couldn't be read, but there are some smart people at Motherboard. They might get something out of it."

"Do you—Uncle, can you think of any way I could make some of this go backward?"

"Backward is too dangerous a road for you right now, Gyp. For any of us. Best if we move on."

"Once I get this curse thing under control I'll do whatever work you want me to do, Aunt. Water plants, enter data, whatever. You want my computer?" I had an old desktop Dad gave me when he upgraded. It was great for writing assignments when I had them, and for finding stuff on the Internet and e-mailing distant friends I had made in boarding school, but I didn't spend a lot of time with it.

"I'll buy a new one. That one was old and irritating even before you cursed it. I should have upgraded last year. Then none of this would have happened."

"I think other things are going to happen anyway. I just

hope they're not as dire. May I give you a haircut?"

"What?" She laughed, maybe startled by the subject change.

"Please?"

"That's your idea of restitution?"

"No. It's part of my current curse. I—" Unable to restrain myself any longer, I waved at Tobias, and his white shirt shaded to pale blue-green, which brought out the color of his eyes and contrasted nicely with his white hair. I grabbed my hand again.

Tobias looked down at his shirt, then up at me. "What is it this time? Do you suppose this shirt will strangle me?"

I perched on a chair, grabbed some banana bread and butter, and told him the latest curse news.


As I cut Hermina's hair in the upstairs bathroom, I calmed down. She was letting me touch her. She even laughed. Somehow we were all right again, and that eased my heart. She even let me touch color onto her fingernails and stroke an embroidered placket of leaves into her shirt. "Pretty useful curse," she said. Then she looked at herself in the mirror and screamed.

"What!" I cried. Had I butchered her hair? No! It had been long and straggly before, and now it was shorter and shaped to flatter her face. I had toned up the color a little, upgraded it from gray to soft silver.

"It was just such a shock!" Then she patted my cheek. "I wanted to scare you."

I clutched my chest. "It worked."

She turned her head this way and that. "I do like it. It'll look like this if I just wash it and leave it?"

I put my hand on her head and told her hair to do that. "If this curse works like the others, my impulse to inflict fashion on everybody will vanish this evening, but I'm not sure about these effects. I think they'll last after I've lost the power."

"Unless there are hidden side effects, I think I can manage to deal with the consequences of this curse," she said. "Thank you, Gyp."

"You're welcome."

She gave me a hug and headed out.

I checked my watch. Two-thirty. I still had an hour for bread, my wardrobe, and maybe lunch before I had to leave for work. If I dealt with the bread I'd get my lunch, although I should probably eat some fruit or carrots at some point.

In the backyard, I discovered that most of the bread was already gone. But where? I had grabbed more grocery sacks on my way through the house, and I set them on the walk, then looked at the remains. Most of the pecked loaves had been moved over to the retaining wall, where more birds visited them. Not much was left of the intact bread.

Flint came whistling around the house.

"You changed *again*?" he asked as soon as he saw me.

I posed.

"Cool. What did I miss this time? Hey, I borrowed Calvin's pickup, and I've been putting the bread in the back."

"Great!"

We loaded more sacks with bread and took them around to where the truck was parked. Its bed was already lost under largesse.

"What are you going to do with it?"

"Drive around giving it away." He grabbed a big poppyseed muffin out of one of the sacks and bit into it. "I don't have to be at the Toussaints' until five-thirty."

"Thanks, Flint. Thanks." I hugged him.

"Hey, it was my work, too."

"Because you were helping me."

"That was so fun."

"Except I burned your hands. How are your hands?"

He showed me his palms. They looked much better. "After I helped Aunt Hermes get her plants under control, she gave me this magic salve she had. It helped."

"Oh, good. You got the plants under control?"

"We trimmed them down so she can at least move around. Without the computer pouring out your power on them, they stopped growing so wild. They've almost settled down."

"Oh, good." My shoulders were tight again. "You want a makeover?" I asked my brother. I had energy to spare, and I could apparently use it without hurting people under the current curse, but little alterations didn't use it up very fast. Did I have to cast another curse? I wondered what else I could do with it.

Make over something else?

"A makeover?" asked Flint.

I had an idea. I took a grocery sack of bread off the load in Flint's truck, and took out a loaf. Make over that. I narrowed my eyes and thought at it, and a second later, it was wearing a lovely paper wrapper like the kind French bread came in, with a label that said what it was and what was in it. "Ooh." I licked the tip of my index finger and started zapping bread loaves.

Flint got into it. He took loaves out of bags and handed them to me, suggested color changes in the labels. At one point when we were halfway through, he said, "Is this environmentally sound?" So I rezapped everything. It took us half an hour to go through all the bread, even though we worked really fast.

"This is better," Flint said when we had finished. "Makes it more presentable. People think something's safe to eat if it comes in a wrapper. Okay. I'll see who wants it."

"Tomorrow I'm making Christmas cookies," I said, "but I think I'll do it the old-fashioned way. If that's possible."

"Let me know if it isn't. I'll work on a save-my-hands idea. Mmm, cookies."

Making bread wrappers had used up some of my energy, but not enough of it. I better curse something else before I left for work. "Gotta go," I told Flint.

"See you later."

Had I finished every cleanup thing Mama had told me to do? I hadn't helped with Hermina, but she hadn't wanted me to. I had better do everything I could while I had the ability. I couldn't think of anything else undone, so I went back to my room to work on my clothes and come up with a curse or two.

While I was at it, I redecorated my room. Slate blue wallpaper, white trim around the window, an upper border of fancy nineteenth century printer's ornaments just below the roof, a bedspread that matched, and pale icy green carpet. Lace curtains. Hmm.

Not enough.

Beryl came in while I was stuffing things into my pack for work. "Wow," she said, looking around. "I really don't like the new look."

"We have dueling taste even though we both have Ultimate Fashion Sense? Cool." I checked her outfit. It looked like she had been adjusting her wardrobe, too. She looked almost Hollywood, brilliant magenta and acid green clothes, and a scattering of small objects, like a gold necklace with old watch fobs on it, to add interest. She had put a gold ribbon flower in her hair. Somehow it all went together, and though it wasn't anything I'd have chosen, she looked fabulous. I said, "So I need to curse something else now. Any ideas?"

"You could curse me again," she said in a small voice. "I said before you started that I'd let you."

"I already cursed you today."

"I'm having fun with it. Maybe you can do something else I'll enjoy."

"You promise not to bounce this one back on me? I need to go to work in about ten minutes."

"I promise."

"So what kind of curse would you like?"

"How can it be a curse if I choose it?"

"As long as I think it's a curse, it should be a curse. Or maybe it'll seem like it's something nice, but then it turns out to be a curse. Wait, I'm confused." Two different things had happened, I now realized, just when I thought I had the rules figured out. I knew that my normal self thought Ultimate Fashion Sense was a curse, and now that I had it, I thought it was a good thing. When I had cursed the computer, though, I had given it energy in hopes it would act for the benefit of everybody involved, and it had done me and Aunt Hermina ill. So my best bet was to use a curse that I thought would do someone ill, and see if they liked it.

I frowned. "I have to read more fairy tales. There should be examples of curses in there."

"They're always turning princes into frogs and stuff. Or how about Sleeping Beauty? Pricked her finger on a needle and fell asleep for a hundred years."

"That would be awful. I could curse you into an animal. If the computer was right, that would last for six point seven hours. But a frog is too fragile. You could get stepped on, or dry up. It should be something bigger and safe to be."

"If you cursed me into a frog, I wonder if somebody could kiss me back to myself?"

"Who do you know who would try it?"

"Orion," said Beryl. She dimpled.

Orion was Claire's little brother. He was young and energetic and wild. He was about Flint's age. He and Beryl and Flint had been friends since the Rhodes moved to our neighborhood, when Orion and Flint were ten. I didn't even know Beryl thought about him that way.

"The problem is, I have to do this curse and then leave. I won't be around to make sure it works out all right. So I have to do something you can live with."

"Only kidding," Beryl said.

"How about if I cursed you younger?"

Her eyes glowed. "No. Curse me older."

"Curse you older." Heat flowed from my shoulders to gather in my chest, and I felt the curse take shape. "Let her see through older eyes, give her wisdom and disguise her in the elements of age—"

The heat traveled down my arm, flowed from my fingertips, and formed a ball of red light above my hand. "For a day, then disengage." I lifted my hand, and the curse flew from it to splash over Beryl.

She gasped and gasped again.

My little sister was a sturdy girl of seventeen with wild clothes and a good haircut before the curse hit her. Once it went to work, everything about her changed except the clothes and the haircut. Her face and hands aged. Her back humped and her body dwindled. When the energy stopped working, she looked about ninety years old.

"Goodness," she said. Her voice cracked.

"Are you all right?" I felt so relaxed I was ready to fall over, even though worry ate at me.

She lifted her arm, looked at the papery, spotted skin of her forearm, stretched one of her legs so she could peer at the broken veins and shrunken muscles in her calf. "Oh, dear."

"Beryl?"

She smiled. "My joints feel creaky. Wonder if I can do this to you," she said. She walked over to my closet and peered at herself in the full-length mirror inside the door. "Oh, my." She edged closer. "I need glasses."

"I'm sorry."

"Don't apologize. This is a good one. I asked for it. Oh, my." She touched her wrinkled face, pulled the skin to the

side so that her cheek straightened into youthful smooth-
ness, let go so that it folded again. Her hair had gone
white. "For a day, you said."

"I don't know if having a rhyming dictionary in my
head is good or bad. Maybe I should have just said 'age,'
instead of all that. But I also don't know how my being
cursed affects my ability to curse things. What if this came
out clean and stayed with you? I thought I better put an
ending in it. In fact—" I held my hands out to her as
though she were a fire, trying to sense curse energy on her.
I felt no heat. Fear brushed my mind. "In fact," I whispered, "this is not a curse but straight magic. Why did I
think it had to be a curse? It could have been a wish!" I
stared at my ancient younger sister. Tears thickened my
throat. For once I could have been nice to somebody with
my power, and I hadn't even realized it. Damn!

"I'm so sorry, Beryl. It'll probably last longer than it's
supposed to, but if the words work, it'll be gone by this
time tomorrow. I'm sorry."

"Hmm."

"But you're basically all right?" I asked again.

She walked around the room. She moved more slowly
and creakily than she usually did, but she seemed to have
enough energy to get around. "If I need help, I'll ask someone," she said.

"You're sure?"

"I'm sure."

I sighed. I packed my curse journal in my backpack. I
figured I could update it at the Center while I was waiting
for students who wouldn't show. "Thanks for being my
guinea pig, Beryl. As usual, I owe you."

She cackled. "Wait till Mama sees me like this. And
Uncle Tobias. I look older than Uncle Tobias, and God
knows how old he is. Hah!"

"I'm out of here. You know where to reach me."

She cackled again. "Hah! If only it were Halloween, I

could scare everybody in the neighborhood." She hobbled out of the room. "Gotta find the Polaroid, get somebody to take a few shots of this. Hah!"

"YOUR car or the motorcycle?" Jasper asked.

I handed him the keys to my car. "More comfortable for me."

He smiled.

As he pulled up in front of the Center at a quarter to four, he said, "How are you set for curse power?"

"I cursed Beryl right before I left." Should I mention the line of weight across my shoulders now? I was still under my own curse. I could use my power like magic. I'd figure something out while I was alone in the Center.

"You did?"

"She agreed to it."

He frowned. "You gave her a haircut."

"You saw her hair?"

"It took some getting used to, but I'm halfway there. You gave her a haircut. You cursed her then, right?"

"Only it was straight power, not curse power. Damn! I wonder if I need to take the Fashion Sense curse off her myself? I didn't build in an endpoint. I'll call her from work." I realized I had said "damn" out loud. I glanced around. Nothing smoked nearby. Apparently while I was cursed, I could curse and not burn things up. Maybe I should use all my power on myself.

"And you cursed her *again*?"

"She agreed, both times."

"How come you never curse me?"

I widened my eyes. "You want me to?"

He looked away. "Well, no. Not right now. I have a gig tonight. But you could, you know."

"I'll—I'll keep it in mind."

"So," he said. "How are you getting home?"

"I have a date with Ian after work. He'll take me home."

"What?" My brother looked shocked. I didn't want to ask why.

"I warned him about the curse thing."

"What?"

Okay, that shock I could figure out. At some point in our lives, we had to explain ourselves to outsiders—if we were getting married. We always married outside the family. Sometimes we let friends know about us. Usually that took a family council to approve. "I can't spend the rest of my life holed up at home," I said. "For one thing, I'd run out of things to experiment on. Besides, the side effects really upset Mama. So anyway, Ian asked me out, and I thought it was an opportunity for me to practice in public, or figure out how not to practice." I paused. "I don't want to end up like Aunt Meta."

He sighed. "River Run is playing at Greenwoods Brew Pub, sound check at eight. Call if you need help."

"Thanks." I grabbed my pack and my jacket and ran to the Center.

"Gotta go, gotta go, gotta go," Anita said as soon as I came in. She logged onto the center computer and punched out. "Thanks for coming in even though you're sick. Are you sick? You look great! Have a great holiday, Gyp. See you next year." She disappeared out the door.

"Happy New Year," I muttered. I clocked in, then toured the center. Study carrels, writing lab, microfiches, computers, tapes for help with languages foreign and domestic, all straightened, all alone. I was the only one here.

I sighed happily and settled at the front desk, got out my curse journal, found a pen in my pack's outside pocket, and set to work writing down everything I read in my mental datafields about the past three days' worth of cursing.

\* \* \*

ONE person came in before six and asked for a brochure that detailed what services were available at the Center. Her haircut was okay and she had really good color sense, so I managed to restrain myself from doing anything to her aside from giving her a handout. She said she was sure she'd be back next year. We said holiday things to each other and she left.

Oh, and I couldn't resist adding a narrow turquoise line to the brown walls, suitably sleek and curved where necessary. And I added a subtle sparkling tint to the carpet. Just the briefest touch. No one would notice, right? They would just feel better without knowing why.

I finished my journal entries. I called Beryl and told her my fears about the Ultimate Fashion Sense spell, and she just laughed. "I'll figure out how to get rid of it if I ever want to." She told me Mama had something to say to me when I got home, and advised me to stay out late. I said I'd do my best.

The fog was rising by the time I clocked out and locked up. My shoulders felt extremely tight. I sat on a bench beside the building, near the access road where Jasper had dropped me off earlier. Last time I was here, I had been so scared, and it turned out I was my own bogeyman. This time I was trying to figure out what to do with the load of power I'd built up over the past two hours. It was still clean power for maybe another fifteen minutes, if my minute math was at all close. Shouldn't I use it while I could be sure it would do just what I wanted it to? But for what?

Could I use it on myself? Turn myself into a regular power instead of a curse person? I wished I had thought to ask Tobias about that, but other things kept coming up.

I was so deep into contemplation that it startled me when a hand fell on my shoulder. I jumped. "Ian?" I said.

"Who's Ian?" asked a stranger. "You must be the last woman on campus. Waiting for someone?"

He was tall, large, a little puffy-looking. Pale face, with

acne scars; narrow pale eyes under slender, expressive brows; good teeth and a nice smile below a neat mustache; brown hair, close-cropped. He wore dark slacks, and a navy suit jacket over a light polo shirt, no tie. He sat beside me. He patted my shoulder but didn't grip it. His hand dropped to his lap.

The fog had closed in so that I could only see about fifteen feet away, and it was shutting down the sounds, too.

"My boyfriend will be here any minute."

"I'll just wait with you until he shows up."

I gave this some serious thought while I stared at him, memorizing details. Those rumors of a campus rapist. On Wednesday I had been afraid I was being stalked, but it had turned out I was chasing myself. Was this guy the actual stalker?

Curse power or regular power, I had a huge supply at the moment; I wasn't afraid of him. But what if I was wrong? I had a sense of my range and ability, but, despite my filled-out curse journal, I didn't know my own strength. What if he was stronger? "Who are you?" I asked.

"Dennis Ralston."

"Are you a student here?"

"No. I'm a walker. I live up the hill, and I like walking the campus after hours. You shouldn't be here alone. It's not safe. Girls get hurt."

"Are you the one I should be scared of?"

"You should be scared of everyone."

"In that case, I think I'll go back inside."

He shook his head. "That's no good. If I were stalking you, I'd just force you into the building, and that way we'd have some privacy for what I wanted to do to you."

Heat flared under my breastbone, built.

"I mean, if I were that kind of guy."

"You seem to have given this some thought."

"A person does if he walks alone at night. You have to think about stuff like that, because you read about it in the news. Or maybe see something some night, but by the time you get there, there's nothing you can do about it. Same way you can wander around and think about how to rob ATMs. Haven't you ever planned a crime?"

"No." Well, there had been that brief fling I'd had with shoplifting as a child. Choosing a target object, observing the behavior of store authority figures, checking to find a time when they weren't paying attention. Too emotionally exhausting for me. I had managed to lift one package of Lifesavers when I was seven years old. Mama found out about it and made me take them back and apologize and pay. That was the end of my crime spree.

"What time is your boyfriend supposed to get here?" he asked.

"Six o'clock." I checked my watch. Six-fifteen.

"He's late."

"Yeah."

"What if he doesn't show up? Do you have a way to get home?"

"Why do you ask?"

"Like I say, I live in the neighborhood. I could give you a ride."

"This conversation is giving me the creeps." Rivers of heat traveled up and down my arm, flowed out from and returned to the lake in my chest. Flickers of red fire floated above my fingertips.

I tucked my hand in my pocket.

"Oh. I'm sorry. Guess you should be feeling like that. I could be just anybody."

"If you really want to trick me, shouldn't you be reassuring me, or something?"

"There you go." He smiled. It was a great smile. "I'm not reassuring you; therefore I'm probably not trying to trick you."

"Do you make it a habit to approach women alone and get into conversations like this?"

"Actually, I don't. If I'm looking for companionship, I can find it at singles bars."

"Oh. I hope you have better lines there. This one doesn't work."

"I'm not trying to pick you up. You're not my type."

"Oh." I frowned. "So what *are* you doing?"

"Just waiting with you."

"Gyp?" Ian called from around the building. "Gyp? Where are you? I thought we were meeting in the parking lot. Gyp?"

"I'm over here, Ian," I yelled.

"That's all right, then," said the stranger. "What kind of a name is Gyp?"

"Mineral." Stock answer. I got that question a lot.

"It is?"

"Short for Gypsum." The instant after I said it, I knew I shouldn't have. No reason I should let this guy know anything about me.

"Interesting. Well, take care, Gypsum. See you around." He rose and vanished into the fog just as Ian ran out of it.

"Gyp! I heard voices. Are you all right?"

"Yeah," I said. I was fine except for this load of power I needed to use somehow. I looked at Ian, a wiry guy my age with short straw-colored hair, sea-blue eyes, and a nice square-jawed face. His beige wool sweater was a little moth-eaten near the hem, and his jeans were an inch too short. I realized I didn't have an obsessive urge to fix his wardrobe. Ultimate Fashion Sense had expired.

## Eighteen

"GUESS we must have crossed signals," Ian said. "I thought we were meeting in the parking lot. There's not a single other car over there. I've been sitting in the car for half an hour watching the fog come in and worrying. Sorry."

"It's all right."

"Who were you talking to?"

"A strange man."

"Oh, no! I'm so sorry, Gyp. Are you all right?"

"I'm all right, but I have to use up some curse power now. I thought maybe I'd use it on that guy, but he never tripped my trigger all the way. I wonder if I should curse myself again."

"The curse stuff is serious?"

I stood up and grabbed my pack. "Are we ready for our relationship to go there?"

He blinked.

"I mean, do we have a relationship?"

He smiled.

"I mean, do I sound like the ultimate creepy girlfriend with a question like that?"

"No. I've been wondering myself."

"If you've been waiting for me to make the first move, we'll never get anywhere," I said. "I don't know how any of this works."

"Neither do I. I thought you already made a move on the phone."

"I did?"

"Asking me not to bring a bunch of friends? Maybe I'm wrong, but I kind of interpreted it as one."

"Hey." I smiled. "So was it a smooth move?"

"Smooth enough."

"It didn't make you run screaming into the night."

"No."

"Cool!"

"I'm not sure I get the part about curses, though."

"Oh, yeah. That. I guess that's the next thing we need to deal with." I sighed. "Maybe this part will make you run screaming. I don't know. This is all new to me, so I don't know how it's going to work with other people. Wednesday night I got my power, and it's the power of curses, and it builds up, and I keep having to use it. High tide right now. Understand?"

"No."

"I'll use it. Maybe that will help. See what you think."

I glanced around. What to curse, what to curse? There was the bench, which was a perfectly useful bench; I sat on it often. There was a line of concrete structures, waist-high pillars, to prevent people from driving on the walkway. There were slender-trunked eucalyptus trees growing out of the sidewalk, with their own grilled enclosures so people wouldn't step on their exposed roots. A scattering of scythe-shaped menthol-smelling leaves fretted the sidewalk. There was the street. Behind me was the center, and nearby were other buildings, classrooms, offices. There was me, and there was Ian.

I could call Altria.

I took my hand out of my pocket. The flames were steady over my fingertips now. I felt the heat. Curse heat. "See?" I said.

"Whoa!"

"It's gotta go somewhere or I'll make myself sick." I bit my lip. I pointed toward one of the concrete pillars. "But once you start thinking about things, you get the feeling there's no good place to send it. Here goes."

I zapped the pillar, and it blew into bits of stone and rebar. Then the bits blew into smaller bits, and then those blew apart until the pillar was completely pulverized. Dust floated in the air, then dispersed into the fog.

Ian jumped a foot and grabbed my arm.

First normal curse I could remember casting. Well, since I blew up the computer, anyway. I wondered about that. What if the computer had really been alive? Had I murdered it? Killed a thinking being?

I wasn't looking forward to going to sleep tonight.

"And that thing probably costs a lot of money to fix," I said. "But I didn't know what else to do. So let's get out of here!"

We ran for the parking lot.

We were both breathing hard by the time we reached his car, which turned out to be a red Saturn. He dropped his keys three times while he unlocked the passenger door for me. Then he ran around the car and it took him a while to work his own door open.

I leaned on the car while he worked at it, and then, when he was going to get in, I said across the roof, "Let's talk."

He leaned on the car on his side and looked at me through the fog. It was getting dark. The light from the orange streetlamps hovered in haloes up where it was coming from; the fog was so thick that not much light reached the ground.

"So was that okay with you?" I asked.

He breathed, then said, "Yeah."

"Oh, good. Can I put my pack in the trunk?"

Pant, pant. "Okay." He opened the car door, reached in, and pressed something that popped the trunk. I went back and dumped my pack in there, pulled out a scarf my Ultimate Fashion Sense self had stuffed in there earlier— lavender snakeskin pattern—and wrapped it around my neck.

I climbed into the car beside Ian. The seat was ultra-comfortable, and I felt relaxed since I had kicked all that energy out of my system. I strapped in and glanced at him.

He was watching me. His eyes looked soft. After a second he started the car. "You hungry?"

"Yeah."

"Seafood?"

"Oh, yes."

"Bistro okay?"

"Great."

The Bistro was one of the trendy upscale restaurants that looked out over the yacht harbor. I had never eaten there; it wasn't one of the places we went in our Sunday Evening Family Forage. I'd heard the food was good, though.

I had forgotten to figure out pseudo-date etiquette. Was this one of those things where we each paid for ourselves? Or did Ian pay? Which meant I should just order an appetizer, I guessed. Maybe I should ask him.

"We going Dutch?" I asked as he pulled into a parking space down by the beach.

"You want to?"

"Is that a signal for 'let's do it that way?'" In all our previous activities, we'd paid for ourselves; we'd been with big groups of people and it had been the obvious thing to do.

"No, it's a signal for 'what do you want to do?'"

"Oh. Subtle."

We smiled at each other.

I dug my wallet out of my jeans and checked the currency compartment. I had some money. "Let's go Dutch this time."

"Okay."

Maybe we should go Dutch every time. Who knew if there'd ever be another time? Jeeze, this was nervewracking.

The restaurant was decorated with blown-glass globes in all kinds of weird colors, supported by weird cages made of steel and antlers. A mess of the globes lay like alien eggs in the big stone fireplace. Each table had its own little glass-and-antler sculpture.

Our waiter brought out weird breadsticks in a vase made of glass panels wired together. The breadsticks looked like slices of focaccia and pita buttered and dusted with sesame, dill, and caraway seeds.

"Huh," Ian said after he tried one.

"Good huh or bad huh?"

"Vaguely good."

I liked them. Lots of flavor, soft texture. I wanted to remember this in case Flint and I baked bread again. "You get the feeling we're experiencing California cuisine?"

"More than a feeling."

The waiter brought us a basket of root vegetable chips that ranged in colors from white to orange to purple to pink. The water glasses were blown-glass goblets with twists of iron around them.

"Have you ever eaten here before?" I whispered.

"Nope," he whispered.

We studied the menu in silence.

Okay. I could afford a shrimp cocktail and a dinner salad. Not that they were called that. I closed my menu. Good thing there was lots of bread included with the meal. I checked the supplies on the table. Turbinado sugar came in paper tubes with illustrations on them in the style of Matisse.

"Well, it's an experience," I said.

"Right."

Our waiter returned and took orders. Ian ordered a portabello mushroom appetizer. Great minds.

"So," Ian said after we had finished the breadsticks.

"So."

"Curses."

"Yeah."

"Since Wednesday, you said."

I did some mental acrobatics, ended up flipping into the tell-him-everything net. "See, in our family, if you're going to be powerful at all, you're supposed to get your powers by the time you're, say, fourteen or fifteen. And I didn't. So I'm twenty, and suddenly I get my power, when I thought I wouldn't have any at all. And it's curse power."

"Huh," he said. "In my family, we had to figure out how not to shoot your first deer or join the neo-Nazis by fourteen. No, actually, the deer thing was more like twelve."

"Did your family manage that?" I knew he had four older brothers, and a sister who was the eldest.

"It was a struggle. Actually my brother Patrick had a brief cigarette-smoking neo-Nazi period when he was sixteen, but Dad managed to talk him out of it. The parents sent us to summer camps out of state and encouraged us to make weird friends, and I finally escaped by running away to California. Of course, no one back in Dahlia will speak to me now. Idaho local thought is that California taints everything it touches. With some justification."

"Why do your folks live there, if they don't have the local mindset?"

"Mom has about half of it. She wanted to move somewhere where she could learn to survive without too many blessings of civilization. She cans tons of things all summer and autumn. She spends the winters sewing and weaving. They raise a beef cow every year and slaughter it. She makes

Dad hunt stuff. I have shot birds, and I've caught and eaten plenty of fish. She's tried to get everybody involved in something that will come in handy in case the world ends, like, my oldest brother Frank is a potter—he's got some kilns in the yard, and he digs his own clay. Patrick is an apprentice blacksmith. Sarah is Mom's apprentice. She's learning all the skills Mom taught herself. Ricky's always been fascinated by archaeology. He learned how to knap arrowheads and knife blades from obsidian and make stone-age weapons. Art is learning woodworking and carpentry."

"And your dad telecommutes."

"Right. He makes tons of money designing software and supports everybody else's obsessions."

"So what skill did you learn?"

He smiled and shook his head. "I was never interested in any of that. I wanted to learn music and art. Oh, and I went through a Goth period in high school, and studied everything I could get my hands on about the black arts." He raised and lowered his eyebrows at me three times.

"And you met Claire—"

"In creative writing class at UCST."

I had heard that story before at some point, but forgotten.

"The black arts," I said. "Did you ever get good at them? Did anything you tried work?"

"Gave it all up when I graduated high school. None of it worked, but I was getting too many nightmares. But a couple of my Goth friends came to Santa Tekla with me. We share an apartment. Only one of us still wears black all the time, though."

"Claire's mom is a witch."

"Yeah, I know. So's Claire."

"She told you?"

"At one of her parties, when there were only a couple of us left, she was kind of drunk and wanted to do a love spell, but she said she needed some help. Joel and I were kind of drunk too and said we'd help her."

"A love spell on who?" I wondered how recent this party was and who Claire was interested in now. Had the spell worked? We hadn't had lunch in too long. We had a lot of catching up to do.

"She didn't tell us. She had some of his hair. She gave us some chants to do, and lit candles and burned incense and did strange stuff with various small objects. Our job was just to chant."

"Did it work?"

"Don't know. It made me notice things about her apartment, though. Symbols above the door, the altar on the mantle. All the artwork depicting witches at work." He smiled. "Makes you think."

"So what did she tell you about me?"

"Hardly anything. You come from a big family, and you and she have been neighbors and best friends since you were kids."

I wasn't sure what other questions to ask him. Some of the ones I wanted to ask verged on the pathetic. Like, "So, do you like me?" "*Why* do you like me?" No, forget that.

"So, the curse thing," I tried instead.

"Amazing," he said.

"Usually it's more complicated than just zapping something to bits." I wondered who would pay for repairs on the concrete post I had destroyed. Should I offer to do it? I could say I hit it with a car. What if it cost thousands of dollars to fix? Maybe I should curse myself with Ultimate Fashion Sense again and fix it myself.

Maybe I should curse myself with Ultimate Fashion Sense all the time. Wouldn't life be easier if the magic came out straight instead of crooked and unkind? If I could tell it to do something, and it would do what I asked?

But why did that work? Why should I be able to control the magic so much better when I had cursed myself?

I wasn't really myself with UFS. Close, but not really. I had had much more of my own brain with UFS than I had had when the computer told me to be a Girl Thing, but I was still a step away from my true and familiar self. Maybe the curse energy thought it was being filtered through someone else, and hence worked like regular energy.

I could make good magic as long as I spent my life being someone else.

Whoa. Something to think about.

My first impulse was to nix the whole thing. Why should I turn myself into someone else? Someone I considered cursed? That would have to be a prerequisite, too; to curse myself, I had to afflict myself with something I didn't like.

I didn't want to give the idea up without considering it, though. If cursing things got too hard, it was nice to know I had some alternatives—Altria, teaming up with somebody else to filter the energy, and this. Maybe I didn't have to use UFS. I could curse myself into other, different kinds of people and see what happened.

"Complicated how?" Ian asked.

I told him about the chalk, and a little about the computer. Our food came, and we got more breadsticks. We traded bites of our appetizers. I shared my salad. What there was was good, but there wasn't enough of anything. We even ate the vegetable chips.

I told Ian about Ultimate Fashion Sense.

"I thought you looked different, but I couldn't quite figure out how. The makeup," he said. He frowned. "Your hair's a different color, too, isn't it? And you got it trimmed?"

Interesting. He paid more attention to how I looked than some members of my family did. "Yeah. That was part of a different curse, though."

"I get the feeling some of these curses aren't too awful."

"They have their ups and downs. At least they expire after a certain point."

"Could you turn someone into a statue?"

"I don't know why not." A statue. I could curse myself into a statue, maybe. But where, and what if people did things to me while I was stone? Birds could fly over and bomb you. . . . Well, suppose you really wanted to meditate. Being turned to stone might be the ultimate sensory deprivation. I'd want to try more curses before I went that far, though, to make sure that I knew the timing was firm. What if a curse lasted longer than a few hours? Suppose I cursed myself or someone else into a statue and they stayed that way for years? "Why? You have somebody you want petrified?"

He shivered. "Not offhand. I'm just curious about what kind of limits there are on this."

"Huh. Me too." I shifted my shoulders. I checked my watch. An hour and a half since my last curse, and already I was too tense for comfort? "If you could curse anybody or anything you liked, what would you do?" Brainstorming! I could brainstorm curses. Maybe other people would have better ideas than I did.

"That's a scary thought." He sat back.

"Would you care for dessert?" our waiter asked. He waved someone over to take our plates, and then got out this little scraper tool and cleaned the crumbs off our tablecloth.

"I'll treat," said Ian.

Okay, was *that* some kind of signal? Did it mean I would owe him something? Or was he just being nice? Who knew date vocabulary? I could ask Ian about this, too, but I thought, we've already talked about all kinds of stuff. Just take it at face value. My stomach growled. "Thanks," I said.

We checked out the dessert menu. I ordered something that involved custard with chocolate shavings and raspberry drizzles. Ian ordered something densely chocolate.

"Really, we could just go to my house and get dessert there. Yesterday my brother and I made acres of brownies." I said it before I thought. Only after it was out did I realize that for the first time in my life I had invited a guy to our house. I mean, occasionally I had had over boys who were friends from school. Special occasions. But not like this.

We never invited people over without alerting the family first.

He was going to think it was just an idle suggestion, anyway. He wouldn't take me up on it, would he? I mean, we were having dessert already.

"We'll probably still be hungry after this," Ian said. "I bet the portions are small."

They were small, but beautifully presented. We traded bites again, something I'd gotten in the habit of when eating out with Claire—order one dish, taste two. Ian had been a little surprised when I suggested it with the appetizers, but he put up with it then and actually seemed to like it this time. The desserts tasted great.

We both sat back after we finished eating. I remembered I had left a question on the table, and he had never answered, so I asked it again. "Who would you curse if you could curse anyone, and how?"

"A long time ago, when I was in sixth grade, there was this bully at school who beat me up. He beat up a bunch of us. We could never figure out why. If there's anyone in the world I want to kill, it would be that guy. Only now, I think if I had known more about it, I might be able to forgive him. Like, who was he and where did he come from? It might have made a difference. Or maybe not. He never broke any bones, but he split my lip and gave me black eyes and bruises, and he made my life a living hell. See this scar?" Ian pointed to a streak of white across his forehead. "He pounded my head against a brick."

Curse energy simmered around my heart. Just hearing

this story made me hungry to curse someone. "Where is he now?" I asked. I wondered if I could do long-distance cursing.

"I think he's in law school at the University of Idaho."

"So what would you have done to him if you could have done something?"

"Well, in my fantasies, I grew muscles like Superman and squashed him into jelly in front of everybody else in school. Maybe it would have been enough if he had to wake up one morning and feel every bruise the way we did. Maybe not." Ian shook his head. "I bet somebody else beat him up, and that's why he did it to us. 'Course, I didn't have any perspective back then. I wished he would die."

My hand tingled. I felt the flow of energy in my arm, up and down, dipping into the red pool in my chest, waiting for me to flex my fingers and send it somewhere. I made a fist to hold it in.

"Ian?" I said in a low voice. "I've got to get out of here right now."

"Check!"

I clenched my fist tight, wished and coaxed the power back inside, though I felt it growing. I handed him my wallet and asked him to take out enough money to cover my meal and tip. He managed with a minimum of fumbling, and we rushed outside.

Fog lay over the harbor and the breakwater. The air was damp, soft, and salty. Masts of ships tied up at the marinas poked up above the fog into the clear sky you could see if you looked up. The sun had gone down earlier, but there was still some blue in the sky above. Streetlights were on. The palm trees lining the harbor and the boulevard beside it made shaggy-headed silhouettes in the clouded orange light.

"What do you need me to do?" Ian asked.

"I don't know. Let's get away from people, anyway. Maybe you should stay here."

"Forget it."

We headed for the breakwater, but where the concrete walkway along the top of it veered left, I climbed over the wall and dropped to Speare Beach. Maybe I could send curse energy down into the sand and not hurt anybody.

The yardlights on the yacht club lightened the fog enough so I could see, though not very far.

Twenty feet away, the ocean pulsed small waves against the sand, inhale, gasp, inhale, gasp. Something lay under the sea's breathing, but my curse energy was too loud for me to hear it.

Ian thudded down beside me. My energy pool swirled and stretched in response to the presence of another person. *Look*, it whispered, *an outlet*.

"I cursed a rock," I said in a low voice, "and it turned into a person who had power over me." I had put my protection stone into my pocket before I left for work. Altria didn't need it to manifest; I didn't know what I wanted it for. Maybe I liked it because it gave me a false sense of safety. I closed one hand around it now. There was no heat in it.

If I cast curse energy into the sand, would something like Altria manifest? Of course, I had said foolish words in my rock curse. Maybe I could be wiser this time, watch my words. But I needed to think fast. The energy was restless. I needed to pick an aim, a direction—something to curse, something to curse it with.

If I didn't send the energy out as something nasty, it would twist to get there.

Though how nasty was UFS? Ian was right. Some of my curses weren't too awful. The worst ones were the ones I tried to make nice.

So choose something nasty to start with.

Or call Altria.

Or repeat myself.

What was I most afraid of?

Losing my mind. Losing myself. Losing my family and friends. Losing control. Being weak. Being noticed. Being ignored. Being hideous. Being hated. Being feared. Being stupid. Being alone. Being—

"After this, no matter what happens, will you take me home?"

"Of course."

I pressed my hand against my chest. The heat in my palm made sweat break out on my forehead. "Cast it out and keep it in. Power go. I'm normal again."

The heat flared hot, then exploded through me. I felt like I was blowing into bits. I screamed.

After a long throat-scraping while, the heat left me— left me empty and sick and shattered. While I was in the grasp of the curse's working, everything had been hot and white, but now I saw that it was dark. The fog had closed over us, and the sand I lay on had lost the day's heat and felt cold.

Distant voices sounded through the muffling fog. "What was that?"

"Somebody's being murdered!"

"Call the cops!"

Warmth entered my world when someone took my hand. "Gyp?"

"Ian," I whispered and reached for him. He leaned closer and I closed my arms around him. This curse wasn't one of the easy ones.

He hugged me. He was warm, and his breath smelled like chocolate. His chest was hard against my cheek. He felt solid and safe. I held him tight.

Lights, long white lines in the mist, stabbed to where we were. "What are you doing to that girl?"

"Get away from her!"

Ian tried to straighten, but I couldn't let him go.

"Hey! You!" Someone grabbed Ian's shoulder and jerked him up, away from me.

"No," I tried to say, but I had screamed my voice out. I reached for him.

"She's hurt," Ian said. "I've got to take her home."

"We'll take care of her. You, come with me."

One of the men had a uniform. It wasn't a police uniform, but something with some sort of badge. Harbor security, maybe. He took some plastic handcuffs out of his belt.

"No. No." I pushed myself up. Nobody could hear me. My voice was like wind-blown sand. I managed to get to my feet, even though I still felt shaky and sick. I pulled on the guard's sleeve.

"Miss, what happened to you? Did he hurt you? Are you all right?" asked the other man. "We'll keep you safe."

I shook my head. I gripped the guard's sleeve, grabbed the handcuffs. He shone his flashlight in my face.

"I was scared," I whispered as loudly as I could.

"What was that?" Now that the light was on my mouth, he could tell I was trying to talk.

"I was scared. Ian didn't hurt me. I was scared. Please let him go."

"Are you sure?"

"Yes."

"Why don't you two come to the security office with me, and we'll write up a report, and then I'll let you both go? How about that?"

"Okay."

The harbor security office was small and warm, and the guard wrapped me in a yellow blanket, let me gargle with salt water, and gave us both hot tea. He took our driver's licenses and photocopied them. "If anybody asks, I need this information." He watched me covertly, watched Ian the same way. He let me write my account of what happened because, though the salt water helped, I still didn't have much voice.

"I scared myself," I wrote, "and I screamed. My boyfriend

tried to help me. He didn't do anything wrong." Boyfriend. Should I cross that out and say "friend" instead? Finally I left it. It wasn't Harbor Security's business what our relationship was or wasn't. Anyway, I didn't know.

After the guard went in the back room and talked to some people on the phone, he let us go.

"Are you all right?" Ian asked me. "I mean, I know you can't talk. What did you do to yourself? You hurt yourself. That was awful."

I grabbed his hand and squeezed.

We walked to the car in silence.

I should have phoned the family right after dinner to let them know I was bringing over a stranger, but I had needed to curse something too urgently to make the call. Now what? They wouldn't be able to hear me if I called now. Should I ask Ian to bring me home? Or to take me to the club where Jasper was playing tonight? But it was early. Jasper wouldn't even be there for sound check yet.

I just wanted to go home and hole up.

I handed Ian my driver's license so he could check my address.

He looked at it a while, then nodded and gave it back. He started the car and pulled out of the lot. "You cursed yourself back to normal?"

I nodded.

"And it hurt terribly."

"God," I whispered. I had never imagined such pain.

He sighed and drove me home.

When he pulled up in front of the house and turned off the engine, I took his hand. He leaned toward me.

"Maybe you better just leave me here," I whispered.

"I don't think so. I can explain this to your family much faster than you can."

I shook my head.

"Do you really want me to leave now?"

"No," I whispered.

"I'll walk you in."

We both sat there.

"Sorry the curse kind of blew our date," I whispered eventually.

"Will you go out with me again?"

"Do you want to try this again?" Some of my hesitation must have showed, even in a hoarse whisper.

"Oh, yes," he said.

"Good. Then, yes."

He got out, came around the car, opened my door, and helped me out.

The front lights turned on. "About time," said Mama. "If you sat there any longer I was going to come knocking on your window and see what you were up to."

"Oh, God," I whispered, mortified.

"Hi, I'm Ian Bennett. Gyp lost her voice."

"Good evening. I'm Anise LaZelle, Gyp's mother. Gyp lost her voice? How on Earth did that happen?"

"You're Gyp's mother? Aren't you on TV?"

"Of course." She smiled, full charisma mode.

Damn! I'd forgotten Mama's high profile.

"You're really great with the news," Ian said in just the kind of admiring tone that Mama liked.

Beryl swept up behind Mama and cackled.

Mama jumped a foot. "Don't do that!" she shrieked. "Go back to your room!"

Beryl cackled some more. How could she be so foolhardy? She had just made Mama look silly in front of a guest, one of the things Mama hated most. And she wasn't presenting a very attractive picture to a guest, either. Mama always said if we couldn't be pleasant in behavior and appearance, we should hide while we had company. I often hid.

"Hi, there, Sonny!" Beryl said. She looked incredibly ancient, and she was still wearing the magenta/acid green outfit she'd had on when I left earlier that afternoon.

Ian glanced at me, then back at Beryl. "Hello," he said. "Cute!" She patted his cheek.

"Uh," said Ian. He looked at me again.

"Beryl. My little sister," I whispered. Heat bloomed in my cheeks.

He stared at me as though I was crazy, then swallowed so that his Adam's apple bobbed, collected himself, and turned to Beryl. "Uh, hi. I'm Ian."

"Hi there!" She shook his hand. "Why is Gyp whispering?"

I leaned close to Ian's ear and whispered, "Say brownies."

"Brownies," he said. He looked confused.

"You've come for dessert?" Beryl asked. "Lovely. Follow me."

"Beryl," said Mama ominously.

Beryl smiled and shrugged. "All right, follow Mama, then."

Ian looked at me, his eyebrows peaked in confusion. I nodded. As we followed Mama through the great hall toward the kitchen hall, he whispered, "What happened to Beryl?"

"Cursed," I whispered.

He glanced at Beryl. She smiled at him, introducing hundreds of wrinkles into her cheeks. She looked cheerful.

"Cursed! That's right," she said. Maybe she was having trouble with her eyesight, but her hearing worked just fine. "Gyp cursed me. It was my idea."

Mama swept the kitchen door open and held it. We pushed past her into the kitchen. She said, "Will someone arrange a tray? Is there any coffee made? Let's retire to the dining room when the preparations are complete."

"Do we have to?" I whispered.

"Mama, couldn't we eat in the kitchen? The light's better here. I'm having trouble seeing," Beryl said.

"Child. We have company."

Beryl and I sighed simultaneous sighs. Ian smiled.

I got down one of the cookie tins and a platter and went to work arranging brownies. Beryl poured coffee into a white thermos pitcher, put it and cups, spoons, a sugar bowl, and a cream pitcher on a tray.

"While you're setting the table, I'll find Miles." Mama swept out of the room.

Beryl watched until the door flapped shut behind her, then turned to me and said, "So what happened?"

Suddenly exhaustion overwhelmed me. I tapped Ian's hand.

"She cursed herself back to normal," he said. "It hurt so much she screamed herself hoarse."

"Oh, no!" Beryl rushed around the table and hugged me. "How could you?" she cried. Then she straightened, gripped my shoulders. "How could you?" she asked in a puzzled voice. "You were never normal to begin with."

Was that right? But I had always thought I was normal. Wouldn't the curse work through my beliefs? Or maybe that was why this curse hurt so much more than the others had. It had to twist even more to make my words work.

"So your throat hurts?" Beryl put her frail, gnarled hand up to my throat and murmured something squeaky. Warmth flowed from her palm into my throat.

"Ahh," I said. I sounded like me again. "Thank you. I didn't know you could do that."

"There are lots of things you don't know about me, young lady," she said. "You stopped studying way too soon! But never mind that. Normal! How horrible!"

"I didn't know what else to do. All charged up and no place to go."

"Lots of things easier than normal," said Beryl. "You could've made yourself old, or young, or a boy, or ugly, or a dog, or something. Normal." Her white eyebrows drew together over her nose. "Is this what you really want, Gyp?"

When I stood on the fog-shrouded beach and thought up my latest curse, I had asked myself the same question.

I finally had power. I could do wonderful things with it, and I could do horrible things with it. If I were normal again, I wouldn't have to come up with new ways to curse, wouldn't have to wrack my brains figuring out how much I could hurt other people and things without hurting them too much. Normal. Maybe that would be best. So I had said my words, and tortured myself.

I met Beryl's gaze. "If it was what I wanted, it wouldn't have been a curse."

She pursed her lips, then nodded. "Good point." She turned to Ian. "And what about you?"

"Me?"

"Where'd you come from?" Her voice switched from almost Beryl-normal to the creaky voice of a crone.

"Beryl," I said.

"Idaho," said Ian.

"Idaho," she muttered. "Welp. Better get this stuff to the dining room."

"May I carry that for you?" Ian asked.

"Why, sure," she said. She held the door, and he took the coffee tray past her.

"I'll get the other one in a minute," he called back. But that was silly. I grabbed the brownie platter, then put it down again. It was really heavy, and my arms were tired. I sat down. Just for a minute.

Ian returned. "Are you all right?"

"I'm really tired."

"Do you want me to leave?"

"Oh, no. Not now that Mama's decided to make a production out of your visit. You have to stay. Are *you* all right? I don't have the easiest family in the world."

"I'm fine," he said. "Hey. Beryl put her hand on your throat and you could talk again."

"Yeah. That was nice."

"Your whole family is like that?"

"Everyone but Dad and me. I mean—" I put my hand

on my chest, feeling for my curse fire. It wasn't there. "Everyone but Dad. And maybe me again, if this curse really worked."

He sat down in the chair next to me. "How weird for you."

"Until Wednesday."

He touched my hand. "Even then, huh? Blowing up a piece of traffic furniture or turning yourself inside out isn't the same as being able to heal with a touch."

I turned my hand over and gripped his. My throat felt tight. I waited, then managed to say, "How weird for you this whole evening is, huh?"

He shook his head, smiling. "Oh yeah. I'm pretending it's a dream. It's more interesting than my daydreams, though, even the old ones where I invoked dark powers and made people do what I wanted."

"You had that dream?"

"I bet most kids do."

"Only in my family, those dreams come true."

"Gyp—hey, who's this?" asked Flint from the kitchen door.

"This is Ian."

Flint came in and shook Ian's hand. "Hi. Nice to meet you. I'm Gyp's brother Flint. Mama's getting steamed, Gyp. What's taking you so long?"

"Sorry." I stood up, then staggered. I'd forgotten how off-balance I was.

Ian put his arm around my waist. "Come on. There are comfortable-looking chairs in there."

Flint grabbed the brownie platter.

I leaned on Ian as we went into the dining room. *He put his arm around me. And I wasn't even screaming.*

It was strange and nice to be so close to someone who wasn't a member of my family. Also it was confusing. I liked it.

Mama, Beryl, Tobias, and Dad were seated at one end

of the table. The candles were lit. Flint set the brownies down in front of Mama next to the coffee tray. We sat down, and Mama introduced Ian to Tobias and Dad, then poured coffee and passed out plates with brownies on them. Ian held my hand under the table while my family asked him questions.

It spooked me. This was too much like interrogating a prospective husband. They weren't supposed to get this serious after our first date. What if they scared him off?

I must have fallen asleep sitting at the dining room table, because I didn't remember going to bed, or when Ian left.

The next thing I knew, I was in my bed, staring up at morning light highlighting the cracks in my bedroom ceiling, listening to the raging bonfire in my chest.

*Nineteen*

MY first thought was, *Oh, thank God!* The curse expired. The power came back. I don't feel sick and
lost. I'm me again.

I had wondered more than once last night if I had cursed
myself right out of the curse business.

I sat up in bed and laughed.

My second thought was, *Oh, my, God, I fell asleep and
left Ian alone with my family. Wonder if he survived.*

My third thought was, *Opal's coming home today.*

Then I wondered what to curse and how. I wished I had
brainstormed curses with somebody so I could have been
ready for this. It was going to be like this every morning,
right?

I glanced around my room. I'd finished superficial dec-
orating during my UFS period, so that everything was different colors than I remembered, and things looked styled
rather than thrown together. I liked the color combina-
tions, but Beryl was right. It wasn't quite right. My UFS
self was not my real self.

It was Saturday. Opal was coming home today, to stay

through Christmas, which was Wednesday, and then drive back to L.A. and the current project. I hadn't talked to her in a while, hadn't told her I'd finally come into my powers. I wondered if I had a curse to use that would help me enjoy her visit. UFS was the perfect curse to help me deal with Opal; then I would feel like I was even with her about looks and fashion for the first time in my life, even if I was wrong. But I wasn't ready to repeat myself, and how many more haircuts and makeovers could I do?

Today I also planned to start my traditional Christmas chore. I was going to make lots of cookies this year—I owed Jasper three batches already, though the way he'd been shying away from eating anything sweet since he had tried out being fat, I wondered whether he still wanted them.

Oh yeah, he could give them to his bandmates.

Once I got his cookies out of the way, there were the regular Christmas cookies to make for all the parties. There was the Christmas Eve party just for family. Then a Christmas Day party, to which we all invited outsider friends, people who knew us well and people who only knew us slightly, so the family would be on their best behavior. A couple days after Christmas, we'd go to L.A. to Grandmère's and Grandpère's for the big semiannual family gathering. It helped to take lots of cookies to that, too. It was my big bid for popularity in the cousin stakes, since I hadn't anything else to offer.

But wait a second.

Okay, this year was going to be different.

Oh, God. Everyone would find out about me. Mama would either be proud or ashamed. I should figure out which and plan accordingly.

And then there was shopping. I hadn't done any gift shopping yet.

I checked my clock. Seven A.M. Saturday morning. God, I was waking up early these days.

Red light flickered near my chest and above both my hands, little half-invisible flames.

Focus, Gyp.

I pulled on pants and a T-shirt, grabbed my protection stone, and ran downstairs and out to the orchard.

One of the lemon trees was dying, almost dead. I'd studied it the day before, but I hadn't known what I could do then.

This morning, with the image of the pulverized concrete pillar from the college before me, I had an idea.

If I damned it, it would disappear, and I would still be overloaded with power. If I cursed it, though, the power would siphon off, and I'd be safe for a couple more hours. Theoretically.

Most of the limbs were dead, but there were still two branches with glossy green leaves on them. I stroked a living branch. Red flame danced above my hand.

I leaned my forehead against the smooth-barked trunk, avoiding thorns. Then I gripped the trunk.

Could this be my answer? Find something to destroy every morning? Oh, God, I hoped not. How long could I do that and still feel good? Maybe there were things that needed destroying. I thought about garbage. Suppose I went through town and destroyed all the garbage of the day? Wouldn't that put people and systems out of work?

My chest burned.

Well, this dead tree could just sit here in the orchard until it decayed, or I could use my power to do something potentially useful, like make firewood out of it. That wouldn't interfere with anybody's livelihood and it might, if it worked, give me a couple hours free of curse energy without my having to hurt anybody.

"Shaped by life, now you're done. Power's the knife; many from one." I spread the fingers of both hands wide. Foot-long blades of red power sprang from my finger ends. I aimed them at the tree trunk.

Lesson one, if you're going to cut something into bits, start at the top instead of slicing through the trunk low down. The red blades slid through the wood with ease. The tree toppled toward me after my first slice. I ran, but its thorny crown came down on top of me, though, because there were so many branches, it didn't crush me. I lay on my back under dead branches, feeling the sting of many scrapes and thorn pricks. I waved my hands and sliced off more of the tree. The rest of it kept collapsing toward me, the few living leaves rustling, the smell of woodsmoke from the power slices stinging my nose.

I carved my way out from under the tree, but by then I was so hurt and so mad at it I didn't care that I was killing some living flesh with the dead. I raged through the tree with my blades until all that was left was kindling.

The blades flickered and vanished, and I was left bleeding and crying in the middle of a pile of demolished tree, the cool in my chest a treasure.

I slumped through the orchard back to the house, headed for antibiotic ointment, waterproof Band-Aids, and a shower.


SATURDAY was one of the days when everybody slept in. Mama and Dad didn't work weekends unless there was an emergency, and those of us going to school didn't have to get up for classes then either. Besides, we were all on break.

I had the kitchen to myself.

I made a big pot of coffee, put Joan Baez's *Noel* on the kitchen sound system, and set up for cookies.

Two hours later I had made Nestlé Tollhouse and snickerdoodle cookie doughs and was baking as fast as the oven could work. The rhythm and the repetition of beating batter, dropping spoonsful in neat rows on cookie sheets, putting them in the oven to bake, and pulling them out when they were done felt good. Finally I had found something which connected me comfortably to my previous self.

My first problem came when I had finished a batch of cookies and they were cooling on wire racks. I realized we had filled all the cookie tins we had with brownies.

I took the tin we had eaten the most brownies from, put the rest of its contents on a plate, and set the plate on the counter by the coffee thermos, where people could find it and succumb to impulse. I filled that tin with cookies.

I finished baking the sheets I had already filled with cookies, waited until those cookies were ready to cool and set them on racks, put all the rest of the batter in the fridge, and went to find myself a driver.

ON my way upstairs, though, I noticed that my hand was leaking red light.

I turned around and went back to the kitchen.

Okay, chopping up a tree hadn't been such a great idea. But the grapefruit curse hadn't been too bad. Worst thing about it was that it made the kitchen unusable for a while. If I did something like that somewhere else, maybe even that wouldn't be a problem.

I took a banana from the fruit bowl and headed to the orchard.

I sat at the edge of our old garden plot below the pool yard and studied the banana. Whatever I did to it, I didn't want to give it the power to hurt anybody. I should tell it something that would keep it here, outside the parts of the yard where people usually went. Also, because the curse put a reverse on well-wishing, I should tell it to be something bad, maybe. But what? Everything that came to mind seemed ambiguous, with too many ways it could go wrong. I wished I were better with words.

I swallowed. I had been so happy when I woke up, glad to have my power back. Fifteen ugly lemon-tree scrapes and scratches later, I felt nostalgic for my pre-power life.

I would love to have a good curse I could use over and over to spill off power in the least horrible way. To find it, though, I needed to do more experiments.

I dug a little hole and half-buried the banana, then curled both my hands around it. Red flame glowed around my hands.

"Be a tree, contained and small, dark and quiet below the wall."

The banana stirred inside my hands, grew. A short dark trunk sheathed in big stiff petally things shot up, and large feather-shaped leaves unfurled from its top. They were black. Flame flowed from my chest down my arms and into the plant, and it grew, but not too big, only eight or ten feet tall, leaves unscrolling from the top of its trunk in a black bouquet. The trunk, about three feet high, swelled in my embrace.

The power flowed out of me. When it was gone, I backed up and got to my feet, held a hand out to the tree, touched a glossy black leaf. It felt smooth and giving, and it didn't sting or make me itch. Not so bad.

A spike grew up from the center of the plant, drooped toward me. A huge, inverted teardrop-shaped bud with giant maroon petals swelled on the end of the spike, nodding down closer to my face. One of the topmost giant petals curled back, revealing a fringe of tubular flowers with thready yellow petals at their ends. A delicious smell came from them, banana, but floral, too, with an edge of vanilla. My mouth watered. Before the flowers could fruit, I backed away and ran to the house.

In the kitchen I got a Sharpie pen from the mess drawer and wrote a note. "Don't go to the orchard. There's a cursed tree there. Should be gone—" I checked my watch— "around four." I signed it and taped it to the double back-porch doors.

Upstairs, I wrote up my first two curses of the day in my curse journal, then went to find someone to drive me to a store. I listened at the doors in the kids' end of the house.

Mama and Dad had a huge master bedroom/study suite at the other end of the upstairs. Between the ends, the staircase rose, three sides of a square, to an open hall that fronted on two spacious bedrooms, one the guest room and the other Opal's old room, each with their own bathrooms. Opal's room opened onto the widow's walk on the roof, and Mama's study opened on the other end of it. They could go out any time they liked and watch the ocean and the weather from way high up. You could sneak onto the widow's walk from the guest room's bathroom window, but you had to make sure Mama wasn't out there first. She had creative trances there and hated to be disturbed.

The four of us still at home had had a number of discussions about who should inherit Opal's room now that she had moved out of it, but we all had good arguments, and even though she'd been gone six years, none of us had moved. We did sneak in once in a while, but we left her stuff alone, unless we were cursed. Sometimes I suspected Mama snarled our arguments about Opal's room so we couldn't find a clear answer just so we'd leave the room alone. Mama hoped Opal would move back.

Through Beryl's door, I heard the radio playing top forty, so I knocked, wondering who would answer, old Beryl or young Beryl?

Young Beryl came to the door. "You all right?" we asked each other.

"Yes," we said. Then we laughed.

"Guess the curse or the spell interpreted 'day' as that thing which ends in sleep," Beryl said. "I woke up me."

"Me, too. Thank God."

"Seriously?"

I thought about the banana tree. A quiet curse. I could live with that, even if I had to do it every two hours. There could be a little grove down there, one tree disappearing as I planted another one. If I got bored, I could plant an orange, or maybe a brussels sprout. I could make this work.

"Something smells great," Beryl said.

"I'm baking cookies, but I ran out of tins to put them in. You have time to run me to the store?"

"You're not driving?"

"Afraid I'll curse somebody."

"Oh, yeah, I forgot." She glanced over her shoulder. "Just let me get dressed and find my shoes."

"I'll get my wallet."

WE reconnected five minutes later. "Those curses I put on you yesterday?"

"Yes," she said.

"How was that? Are you still living with Ultimate Fashion Sense?"

"Naw. I liked it. I redecorated my room, and I spruced up some of my accessories, but eventually I realized I was spending all my time and energy on what stuff looked like, and I kept wanting to fix everybody against their wills, so I undid it."

"There's a way?"

"It acted like just another spell. You missed a lot of our training about spells, I know. Tobias taught us how to unweave spells put on us by other people, and it wasn't a particularly difficult or nasty spell. The old-age one . . ."

We headed down the stairs while she thought about it, stopped in the kitchen long enough for her to grab a handful of cookies. Then we went out the backdoor, down the steps, around the guest house to our hidden parking places under the giant fig tree.

Beryl had a vintage dark blue Volkswagen bug. She had gotten it cheap and totally fixed it up. She warded it so tree drips wouldn't touch its skin, or bird shit; it always sparkled, and everything in it stayed in tune. She was good with engines when she wanted to be.

We climbed in and she started that chugging engine, and finally she said, "Being old was interesting and scary. My body didn't work very well, and lots of things hurt— my joints, my fingers and toes. My eyes saw everything blurry. I tried to go with it, feel what it was like, but after a while I couldn't take it anymore and made some improvements. Then I went to the supermarket and tried that out."

She took off the emergency brake and backed out of her space, drove out of our yard and onto the little ragged-edged road we lived on. Bosquecito had many giant expensive houses, and, paradoxically, lots of small pot-holed roads paved in gray asphalt with white and gray rocks in it. People weren't interested in making their houses easy to get to.

"That was shocking," Beryl said. "Worth the experience. You have white hair and wrinkles and look eccentric, nobody wants to make eye contact. You ask questions and they don't even hear you. I bought some groceries, and those bag boys, the ones who always tease me when I go in there as normal me, no connection at all. 'Help you to your car, ma'am?' They didn't even listen to my answer. One of them carried my groceries out even though I said no. I felt like I was encased in Jell-O."

*Welcome to my world*, I thought. "Wow," I said.

"I went to the library. The librarians pay attention to everybody. So then I felt better. I went home and had fun with Tobias and Daddy and then, when Mama got home, boy howdy."

"How'd that go?"

Beryl frowned. "As soon as she figured out who I was, she started spelling at me. She was going to uncurse me without even asking. Completely against rules she made up herself."

Right. The let-us-sort-everything-out-ourselves, no-parental-interference-unless-things-got-severe rule. My favorite.

Beryl said, "Mama gets kind of fractured about how we look."

"No kidding."

We stopped at a red light, and she turned and gave me a searching stare. "So that was educational too," she said after a moment. "More than I knew. That's what she's always like with you?"

"She's kind of resigned, or at least she controls herself pretty much, but when she's ticked and wants to yell at me, that's the first thing that comes to the top."

"Guess I knew that," Beryl said. "Guess I've heard some of those fights. . . . Where are we going, anyway?"

Cookie tins at the bakeware store in the mall, a store I adored, would be way too expensive. "Let's try the drugstore. I bet they have a bunch of holiday stuff."

"Or Thrifty's."

"That would be good, too."

No store along the Old Coast Highway in Bosquecito carried anything cheap. Beryl hit the freeway for the short drive into downtown Santa Tekla, to the low-rent district, which had the best inexpensive stores, bodegas, panaderias, and the best branch library if you wanted to check out kids' books.

"So anyway," Beryl continued, "I told Mama to leave me alone. I think she was pissed that I looked like that while we had company, though."

"Yeah! I've been meaning to ask. What happened after I fell asleep? I cannot be*lieve* I brought Ian home and then just crashed. Was he okay? How long did he stay? Was he mad that I fell asleep? Who put me to bed?"

"He's really nice, Gyp. Where'd you find him?"

"At Claire's."

"Lucky! Mama invited him to Christmas Day."

"Oh, God."

"I think he's going to come, too. He doesn't have family around here, and he doesn't have enough money to fly home, he said. He survived us pretty well. There's a guy who'll make eye contact with a little old lady. You started snoring—"

Oh, God. Could this get any worse?

"—and he and Daddy carried you upstairs. I put you to bed after they left. Ian went back downstairs and finished his brownies, and charmed Mama, and said good night. He didn't even seem like he was rushing away."

I covered my face with my hands. I couldn't believe I'd ever see him again.

"He was *so* much better than Opal's dates."

"Sure," I said, feeling wretched. "How hard is that?"

She poked me. "Quit worrying. You'll be okay with him. And it's harder than you think to do better than Opal did with guys. Ever notice that I never bring anybody home?"

Now that she mentioned it. Huh. "I never meant to bring him home. He was just supposed to drop me off at the top of the driveway. Only, that curse. . . ."

"I think you're going to be okay." Beryl pulled into a parking space by the Thrifty's and turned off the engine.

Most of the Christmas stuff was already ten percent off, so I was happy. I found many, many Christmas tins in very dubious taste. Currier & Ives scenes on the lids of people at ice-skating parties or riding in sleighs through snowy winter landscapes were the prettiest ones. How relevant was that to Southern California holidays? I ended up buying all they had of those, and even some Coca-Cola Santa tins. What the heck.

I drew the line at tins with cartoon reindeer and snowmen, though.

I met Beryl at checkout. "Whoa," she said. "You need all those?"

"Probably." I had had to get a shopping cart so I could really load up on tins.

She had scored some purple wisteria shampoo and a kit of holiday nail polish & lipstick, both with candy-apple-red glitter in them. She flashed the nail polish at me. "Wanna have a girl date?" she asked. We had done that when we were younger, sat around painting each other's nails, tried on lots of different colors of lipstick and wiped them off again. Red glitter. Ultimate Fashion Sense would probably say no.

"Sure," I said.

We bought our things and left.

On the way home, Beryl said, "So I'm going up to the mountains to do my annual tree talk, maybe this afternoon." Beryl was responsible for summoning our Christmas tree. She had to wander through the wilderness talking to trees until she found one who agreed to come home with her. She shifted her shoulders. "Hope it works." She had brought us a good tree every year of the past six, and she still wasn't sure of her tree-calling skills.

"Can I come?"

"What?"

For a minute I didn't say anything. "I never got to go." There were a number of family traditions I had gotten shut out of because I didn't have powers. I had never particularly wanted to go find a tree and ask it to come stay with us for the holidays, but I had wondered what it was like.

"Oh." She drove in silence. "It's kind of a personal and private thing. I don't know how it would work if someone else were there."

I fiddled with my seatbelt.

"Maybe it would be okay. We could try it. If it didn't work, I could go out again on my own."

"Never mind. I've got baking to do anyway." Mama hadn't gotten around to assigning us holiday chores yet this year, but I assumed they would be the same as last year.

Come to that, it was odd that she hadn't told us what to do yet. Usually she was ultra-organized and gave us our chores at least a month in advance. Had she even gotten Christmas cards this year? We hadn't had an evening session of going through the cards that had come in, copying the return addresses into our card book, addressing our own cards to go out. Usually that was a family thing: we did three or four nights of card work together. Mama wrote all the messages in our cards, and she and Dad signed them. I did most of the address work, as I had the best handwriting. Flint had perfected an unreadable scrawl just to get out of it, I sometimes suspected.

We spent a few uncomfortable moments as Beryl navigated the maze of Bosquecito streets toward home.

"I'm sorry, Gyp."

"It's okay. Really. I shouldn't have asked."

"That's not right. I mean, we've got to be able to ask. I just have this feeling."

"You can say no. It's all right. I understand. It's your special thing."

"That's it."

When we got home and I carried my bags of cookie tins into the house, I found Flint and Jasper sitting at the kitchen table with glasses of milk, eating cookies.

What? Before I'd even had time to assemble the cookies, give Jasper his batches, sort the others into various tins so I could add other kinds later and we'd have gift baskets? "Hey!" I yelled. "Stop eating!"

I wasn't even conscious that I had any power to spend. I hadn't planned anything, hadn't worked out a rhyme. My words came out with a curse anyway, a flash of red fire from my hand to my brothers' faces. Their mouths closed, and their eyes widened.

"No!" I dropped my plastic bags full of tins and put my

hands over my mouth. "I didn't mean that!"

Jasper and Flint looked at each other. Jasper worked his jaw, but his mouth didn't open. Flint pressed his fingers to his mouth, then shook his head. He smiled at me, but with lips only. No teeth.

"What!"

Jasper got up and fetched the phone message pad and pen. "Good one, Gyp," he wrote.

I shook my head. "I didn't mean it. I didn't mean it! I'm sorry!"

Flint shrugged and offered me the plate he had been eating from. There were six cookies left. I glanced at my cooling racks. Lots of cookies gone.

I guessed Jasper had decided not to worry anymore about eating sweets. His plate still had about eight cookies on it, and lots of crumbs.

Jasper wrote another note and showed it to me. "Time limit on this?"

"Six point seven hours? That's what it was yesterday. God, you guys. I'm so sorry."

"Quit apologizing. It happens," he wrote. "At least we've got full stomachs." He tucked the pad and pen into his pocket, tapped Flint's shoulder.

Flint stood, made his best sheepish face, added a shrug, and followed Jasper out of the kitchen.

I sat at the table, staring at half-eaten cookies, half-drunk glasses of milk. For a short time I laid my head on the table and let tears drip onto that smooth surface. No. I was never going to be like the rest of my family, flinging power here and there, hurting people without thinking it through. I was going to be careful and kind, no matter what sort of power I had.

Gyp, get a clue.

My sister had given me the face of a witch. My brother had broken my leg (though not on purpose). I'd been a pawn in a variety of ways when they were really feeling their power, their desires. Sometimes they still made me do things against my will. Sometimes they made me do things without my even being conscious of it. Sometimes they made me do things, and made me feel good about doing things, so that I wondered why I bothered with free will; sometimes being directed felt better.

I sniffled and rubbed my nose and sat up, poured the leftover milk into one glass, grabbed the cookies that were half-gone or broken, and treated myself to a snack. I was a member of this family. Now I had the power to make scary mistakes, just like everybody else. My family was strong. They could handle it. They might even be expecting it.

My cookies tasted like tears at first. Then I got to the full flavor of melted chocolate chips, butter, flour, sugar, vanilla. Delicious.

I cleaned up everything that was out of place, washed a few dishes, checked the coffee thermos, started another pot of coffee, and went back to baking.

"So, we're not allowed to touch these now?" Tobias asked me when he came down to the kitchen around eleven.

"You may have three," I said. I had already filled some of my new tins and felt less volatile.

Tobias checked the racks carefully and selected the three largest cookies. He got coffee and sat at the table, watched while I stirred pineapple filling on the stove. For a while neither of us spoke. He must have run into my brothers if he knew I was being strict about letting people eat the cookies. Was he going to get mad? Tell me how to remove curses? What?

I hunched my shoulders, tried to ease the tension in them. Time for another banana pretty soon.

"That was a nice boy you brought home last night," Tobias said.

"I can't believe I fell asleep!"

"Sometimes a spell will knock you out. You can never tell ahead of time if that's going to happen." He bit into a cookie and smiled at me. "Sometimes you cast the spell, and the results dismay or disturb you so much you knock yourself out because that's the best way to get through it."

I sighed.

"You've been learning a lot, haven't you?"

"I hope so." I set my spoon on a plate on the stove and turned to face Tobias. "Beryl said I couldn't curse myself back to normal because I was never normal to begin with. But, Uncle—"

His eyes narrowed. "Perception is a factor. What you believe, you can achieve, whether your belief is based on fact or false speculation. What you don't perceive, what you don't believe—those things are much harder to work with. You believed you were normal. I think that makes it possible for you to go there. What did you discover?"

"I hate normal! Not only that, it makes me sick."

Great-Uncle Tobias smiled at me. His eyes twinkled. "Welcome home, Gyp."

I turned back to my pot and stirred some more. Hating normal! That was not a noble sentiment, and I wasn't sure I wanted to celebrate it. I had a lot vested in being noble. It had been all I had for a long time. "Normal's not so bad."

"Normal's not so bad when it's your only option," he said. "Time to recognize you've left normal behind."

My pineapple filling thickened up, and I took it off the flame, poured it into a bowl and put it in the freezer. I got cookie dough out of the fridge, kneaded it a little bit, then floured the butcher block table and rolled the dough out thin. I got all the cookie cutters out of the back of a drawer and set to work cutting out shapes, two of each.

"Do you want to go back? Gyp, seriously now. You've had time to try your wings. Do you know what you want?"

"What if I wanted to turn back into my old self?"

"There might be a way."

I wiped my forehead, felt flour stick to my face. "You tell me that now? Not before?"

"I found some new information yesterday. Now I see a path you could take away from your power. I wanted to check with you, but it seems to me that you're doing fine."

I set cookies on a greased baking sheet: stars, bells, hearts, angels, trees, rabbits sneaking over from Easter, scotty dogs. I got the pineapple filling out of the freezer and set a spoonful of it in the center of each cutout cookie, then pressed their top layers over the filling and tamped down the edges with fork tines. "I don't know about doing fine. I'm doing something, anyway. I know enough to know I don't want to go back."

"Good."

I put the cookies in to bake and started another sheet. I had cut out half a sheet's worth of cookies when I noticed red light gloving my right hand.

Tobias saw it, too. "Now what?"

"Time to curse something," I said.

"You have a visible tell?"

"If I don't act on it soon enough, yeah."

"You might want to train it not to do that."

I set my cookie cutters aside, put the filling and the unused dough back in the refrigerator, and clenched my hands into fists.

"Do you have anything in mind?" Tobias asked.

"I didn't mean to curse the guys. I better go outside and figure out something. Will you watch this for me? Take those cookies out in a couple minutes? They should be a little brown; dark brown is burnt."

"I will take care of them."

"Thanks. Or I could stay here, watch the cookies myself, and curse you."

"You could. You could try."

I looked for his shield, but didn't see it. "Back in a few," I said.

At that moment, the kitchen door opened, and Mama walked in, completely naked. In her left hand she held a bunch of red bananas, and in her right hand she held a single one, half-eaten. She smiled at us.

"Anise?" said Tobias. He stood.

She strolled to him, her hips swaying, and held out the bunch. "Have you tried these, Uncle? Amazing."

He opened his mouth, held out his hand. I could smell them from where I was, and, oh, I wanted one, too. "Shield yourself," I said to Tobias. "I made those."

His fingers flickered. A shield, almost invisible except for glints, formed around him.

Mama frowned. She set the bananas on the table, reached out and jerked the shield off Tobias. "Don't be rude." She handed him the half-banana in her hand as I grabbed the others.

I was suddenly hungry, and they smelled delicious, promised me every taste I could ever crave.

I opened the oven and stuffed them in on top of the baking sheets of cookies.

Tobias fought his hand. It brought the banana toward his mouth, then, with effort, pulled it away again. I clenched my fist, formed an image of my intention, pointed toward the banana, and said, "Damn." The fruit cindered into nothing.

"Gyp." Mama's eyes glowed.

"Mama, why did you eat those? Didn't you see my note?"

"Gypsum." Her voice was full of freeze. "How dare you?" She pumped her hands open and shut, and blue flame gathered above her palms, so bright it seared my vision. She flicked her fingers. The power shot toward me.

I screamed and shielded myself with my arms. Red light flooded from me, clashed with Mama's blue light. There was a strange stillness around us as our fires devoured each other and disappeared.

"Anise," said Tobias. He gripped Mama's shoulders, stared into her eyes, and said something in a low, chilling voice.

Mama straightened, blinked, peered at Tobias. "What?" She glanced down at herself, paled, then flushed. "What happened?"

"Sit down. Both of you."

My heart raced. My arms were trembling. I couldn't get myself to move at first. I shuffled across the floor to a chair and collapsed.

Mama sank down beside me.

Tobias reached into the air and grabbed a bathrobe from somewhere else, handed it to Mama. She blushed again and wrapped up in it.

An enticing smell was filling the kitchen. I bit my lip, got up and went to the oven. I patted my chest. I didn't think I had any fire left, but I opened the oven door and damned everything inside it, and a faint flash of red answered my call. All anything smelled like afterward was burnt.

"What was the curse, Gyp?" Tobias asked after I sat again.

I told them about planting the banana and summoning a tree. "I didn't know what it would do. I just thought if it was someplace away from the house—"

"I was lying on the chaise after my morning laps," said Mama, "and I smelled this wonderful smell."

"I put a note about avoiding the orchard on the porch doors."

"I didn't go out that way."

Sometimes, when she was sure no one was looking, she drifted down from the widow's walk to the backyard. I had forgotten.

"Do you remember what you just did, Anise?" Tobias asked.

"Not really. Last thing I remember was that taste on my tongue, so luscious. It made me feel good all over."

"You tried to kill me," I whispered.

"Oh, no. No. I couldn't possibly have—" Mama gazed at Tobias with anxious eyes.

He cupped his chin in his hand and studied her. "I believe it was more that you didn't care what consequences your action had."

"What are you saying?"

"You ate fruit of a cursed tree. It affected your world-view. You were irritated with Gyp, and you cast all the fire you had at her."

Mama's wide violet eyes fixed their gaze on me. Tears ran out of them. "I'm sorry. I'm sorry. Oh, lord, Gyp, I—"

I swallowed. "It's my fault. I made those bananas." I looked away from Mama. She ate my curse, and it bounced back on me. I didn't think I had ever seen anything more terrifying than my mother's cold eyes as she threw potential death at me.

She wept and hugged me. I sank down inside myself, away from her. I thought of Great-Aunt Meta. I understood her better now.

"Those bananas," I said. I pushed out of Mama's hug. "What if someone else eats them?"

We ran out back, down the new staircase and over to the old vegetable garden.

The tree looked as though it had been carved from obsidian, except for the three heavy flower spikes, with their blood-red hands of fruit and deep maroon petals with creamy insides. A raccoon was eating bananas at the tree's base. It turned and snarled at us, but didn't leave.

The smell was light and seductive. Mama gripped my arm. I glanced at her face. The tip of her tongue traveled slowly along her top lip.

Tobias spoke something that clunked from his mouth as though each word were a brick. The air around the tree glistened. A shield formed around it, cutting off the scent. "Time of creation?" he asked me.

"Nine-fifteen."

He spoke some other words, and the shield turned opaque, rendering the small black tree invisible. The raccoon, still snarling, came out through the shield, then turned back to glare at it before trundling off. "Should hold for eight hours or so," Tobias said.

"Thanks," I said. "Can I change my mind about going back to the way I was?"

"Not yet."

"Tobias," Mama said. "What is this?"

"I've been researching matters of power to see if Gypsum might have some options, or at least some help. I found a seventeenth-century grimoire in my collection yesterday. It had some interesting spells in it. There might be a way for her to give up her power without dying. Gyp, I don't think you're ready to decide yet. While it's true that Anise could have killed you, it's also true that you saved yourself."

"Did she?" Mama asked. "I just assumed—"

"That I took care of it?" he asked when the pause stretched. "I hadn't time to take care of it."

Mama looked at me, and I stared back. Her lower lip trembled. Then she straightened and smiled. "You can defend yourself against me now? Good."

Heat curled over my breastbone. I had cast all my power out to protect myself, but more was coming.

Mama glanced at the black bell jar Tobias had placed over my curse tree. "Now I just have to learn to defend myself from you."

*Twenty*

"WHAT are you doing?"

I looked up from my curse journal. Opal stood in my doorway, her arms crossed over her chest and her feet crossed at the ankles as she leaned against the door-jamb.

"Hey, Opal. Welcome home."

"Hey, kid. Thanks."

"You talk to anybody else yet?"

She leaned back and looked out at the sitting room, checked around for other signs of life. Shook her head. "Snuck up the back way. Wanted to get a feel for the place before I ran into Mama."

It had been almost a year since I had seen my older sister. She worked on one movie project after another; once people saw what she could do with special effects makeup, word went around, and she was hired solid.

It made Mama mad that Opal had so many jobs and didn't make time to come home for more frequent visits. Opal's jobs were on location: Mexico City, Seattle, Florida, Toronto. After one of these jobs when Mama didn't know where Opal was, Mama laid down the law: I know you're working sixteen-hour days and you don't have time to talk to your mother, but you *will* leave me a phone number where I can contact you, or I'll do something disruptive and you'll regret it. If Mama was desperate to find you, she could reach right down your bloodline and pull you home whether you wanted to go or not. So Opal let us know where she was. She usually didn't tell us what she was doing, though.

My sister looked worn-out, painfully thin and tired.

"I've got some cookies to get back to." I'd begged Tobias's help in cleaning out the oven, then left him in charge of the kitchen before I came upstairs to write the latest curse news. "You want some?"

"You made the snickerdoodles yet?"

"Yeah."

"Oh, boy. I'll come with you, Sis." She glanced around my room. "How come it smells like magic in here?"

I pushed past her and shut the door. "Okay, that's kind of a long story, but the short version is, last weekend? When I was too sick to go to L.A. and meet Gerry? Transition."

She grabbed my arm and pulled me to a stop. "No lie, Gyp? Holy shit. Holy shit!" She hugged me tight.

I relaxed into it. When I was little and Mama was busy, Opal took care of me. Mama was always busy. Opal took care of all of us. She cared about us even when Jasper and I got old enough to tease her for being who she was. When she moved away, I was so upset. How could Opal leave us? And she really left. She didn't keep in touch with us, not till Mama forced her to. Seemed like she was glad to get away.

"Okay, okay," I said, and pushed back. "And the other news is I got the power of curses instead of regular power."

"What?" She gripped my shoulders and stared into my face.

"Stuff I do comes out twisted and mean."

"Oh, Gyp." She hugged me again. I closed my eyes. She smelled faintly of her favorite essential oil, October Rain, a scent she almost always wore. I pretended that she could take care of me again, make everything all right. I gave it about twenty seconds, then sighed and let go of her.

"Are you doing all right with this?" she asked.

I shrugged. "Working on it." Opal didn't live here anymore. I was technically almost grown up. It was my problem.

I wished I was a little kid again, before any of us had transitioned.

"If there's anything I can do to help, tell me, okay?"

"I will."

We studied each other. Finally exchanged smiles.

"Is Mama home?" Opal asked.

"She was about twenty minutes ago."

Opal looked at nothing for a few seconds, then shrugged. "Might as well see her."

We went downstairs.

Tobias was studying my cookie book on the cookbook stand, where clear plastic shielded the page from random ingredients. He had rolled out more dough, and was cutting out pairs of shapes with the cookie cutters.

"Hey, Uncle! Domestic streak?" Opal asked.

Tobias smiled at her. "It occurred to me I hadn't tried anything new in a while. This is interesting. How nice to see you, Opal. Welcome home."

"Thanks." She kissed his cheek.

I got a cookie tin down from the top shelf and opened it, held it out to her. She selected some snickerdoodles and headed for the coffeepot.

"Thanks for taking care of things, Uncle." I put away the tin, grabbed the spatula, and transferred the finished cookies he had taken out of the oven from the baking sheet to the cooling racks.

"You didn't mention that detail."

"It's a small one," I said. "You're doing great."

Flint came in, carrying index cards and a Magic Marker. He dropped everything when he saw Opal, and went to hug her.

"Hey, little brother. How are you?"

He smiled and smiled. Then he went back and picked up his cards, sorted through them. Held one up. "Cursed," it said.

I hid behind my hands.

"You cursed Flint?" Opal asked.

"I didn't mean to," I said through my fingers. "It just popped out. They were eating the cookies without asking."

"So he can't talk? That doesn't make sense."

"I think he can't open his mouth."

Flint nodded.

"For how long?"

I lowered my hands and checked the kitchen clock. "I cursed them around ten-thirty. Now it's two hours later? So another four, five hours?"

"Harsh!" said Opal.

"It's awful. Uncle, how can I take off a curse?"

Flint found a blank index card and wrote on it, held it up. "Never mind. We won't starve. Steak for dinner?"

I went to the money drawer and checked the grocery envelope. Mama and Dad put money in it every week, and I spent most of it for dinner stuff and the day-to-day things that everybody ate; I checked out the cupboards and the refrigerator often enough that it was easy for me to keep track of what we were running out of. There was a shopping list magneted to the refrigerator, along with a pencil, and people wrote new things on it, and I bought them. I left money in the envelope for people to buy meals on the nights when I didn't cook; usually they bought pizza or Chinese takeout or someone picked up something at the supermarket deli on their way home.

We didn't have any steaks on hand, but there was enough money left from the week's cache that I could buy a big family pack of steaks. Plus, I owed Flint, and steaks were his favorite. I didn't make them very often, because they were expensive and didn't make good leftovers (not that there was ever anything left over after a steak night). "Sure."

He held up another card, this one already written out. "Gyp, will you help me?"

"How?"

He turned the card over for another prepared message. "Mama says I should make the lights again this year."

"Okay," I said.

Next card. "I screwed up so much last year. But if we worked together, maybe I could get it right."

I felt my own smile. "Oh, yeah! That would be great!" Another curse I wouldn't have to worry about casting, and something Flint really needed.

He grinned. He wrote a card. "When?"

I checked the clock again. "A couple hours? I just used up my energy, but I should be recharged in a couple hours. Can we do this if you can't talk, though? How about we wait until your curse wears off and then do it?"

He held up a prepared card. "OK."

I smiled at him. One of this evening's curses was spoken for. I was totally happy about that.

"What's that about? How can you help Flint?" Opal asked.

I explained that to her. I could filter power through Flint, and through Altria, and it came out clean. At first I thought it was just Flint. But since it worked with Altria, too, and, come to that, my UFS self, maybe it would work with anybody? I needed to do some more experiments.

"Have you tried setting time limits on your curses?" Tobias asked.

"How do you mean?"

"If you built a time limit in instead of letting them run their course—which, I should warn you, may be more variable than you're giving them credit for; it depends on how much energy you put into it. More oomph, longer curse— if you specify a limit, that might help. Say you were mad at Flint and Jasper for eating the cookies, but you just shut their mouths for an hour."

"That would be great, if I had been thinking when I did it. If I had been thinking, I wouldn't have done it, though."

"How much oomph did you put into it?"

Flint and I exchanged glances. "I was pretty mad. But I didn't rhyme," I said.

"Good observation. Maybe without the reinforcement of rhyme, the curse will be weaker. All these things factor in. Flint, keep track of when the curse wears off, will you? Gyp can add that information to her curse journal."

Flint held his thumb up, waved it.

"You cursed Jasper, too?" Opal asked. She sounded surprised.

"Yep."

Tobias said, "That might be a factor, too. You spread the curse between two people, which might make the individual curses less powerful or shorter."

"You cursed Jasper," Opal muttered. "You made it so he can't talk?" She gave me a brilliant smile. "I'm going to find him."

Just then the phone rang. Opal was closest, so she picked up. "Afternoon. LaZelles," she said. "No, this isn't Gypsum. This is her sister. No, not Beryl. Opal." She glanced at me, mouthed B-O-Y. "She didn't tell you she had a sister Opal? Well, I just got home half an hour ago after a year away. You're fascinated, right? Gypsum's home. She's fine. She's right here. I'm just torturing you both. Hey, Gyp, it's for you."

I took the handset from her, heat in my face, and turned away from my family. "Hello?"

"Hi. Are you all right?" Ian asked.

"I'm fine. How are you?"

"Great! I just wondered if you recovered from last night."

"I am so mortified. I've never fallen asleep in front of company before."

"Stress makes people do weird things."

"Did you survive all right after I conked out? I guess I should warn you I'm talking in the kitchen, and a bunch of my family are listening. So you can say whatever you like, because they can't hear you, but I won't be able to ask you the questions I really want to ask. If you can just imagine what I want to know and fill me in, that would be great."

"Hah! Everyone was really nice."

"I find that hard to believe."

"I like your dad."

"Me, too."

"Your mom is very . . . impressive."

"Hmm."

"The brownies were great."

"Good."

"Beryl was hilarious. What does she normally look like?"

"Very cute."

"Anyway, it made me nostalgic for my own family."

"Beryl said Mama invited you over for Christmas Day?"

"Is that okay with you?"

"Oh, yeah, great with me. I'm making a turkey. You like turkey?"

"I love turkey. What I called about, though, other than to find out if you're okay, is, Claire's having a party tomorrow night. Want to go?"

Claire was having a party and she hadn't invited me

herself? I wondered if she was mad at me. Usually she told me when she was having parties, even if she didn't have room for me to come, so I wouldn't find out later from somebody else and be mad that I didn't know. "Is it okay with her?"

"She asked me to ask you."

"No kidding?"

"She said she sent you an e-mail about it on Wednesday but she hasn't heard back yet. So I said I was going to call you anyway, so—"

"Jeeze, I haven't checked my e-mail in a week. I forgot all about it." Too busy cursing things. "Anyway, yeah, I'd love to go. What are we supposed to bring?"

"Snacks. Want me to pick you up?"

"That would be great."

"About five okay?"

"Yeah." I wondered where I would be in my curse cycle at that point. I should curse something at 4:45 just to be on the safe side. "If I have to leave suddenly, are you okay with that?"

"That's fine with me."

"Kewl. See you tomorrow."

"Right." He hung up.

Doubts assailed me. I wondered if Ian would have asked me to the party if Claire hadn't asked him to. D'oh! Was he *really* okay with all the things that had happened last night? If he wasn't, he wouldn't have called me, right? Was he interested in me because he liked me? Or was he just interested in what I could do? Remember all those non-dates, though. He had invited me to go lots of places with him before I grew into my power. He hadn't minded when I asked him not to bring other friends this time. That was before I cursed anything where he could see, too. Maybe he did like me.

If he was interested in me, was there something wrong with him? Nobody else had ever been interested in me that way. It wasn't like I was beautiful, or shaped like people on TV, or anything.

Well, whatever happened, I was getting some experience now, I guessed. Even if it didn't work out, it was experience.

I hung up the handset and turned around. Opal was grinning.

"Shut up," I said, with no heat behind it.

She laughed and left to look for Jasper, maybe.


A couple hours later Tobias had done a whole batch of cookies by himself, without cheating. I had made two more kinds of cookies and mixed up the pfeffernüsse dough. I should have made the pfeffernüsse a couple weeks earlier and stored them so they could get just the right kind of stale, but I always forgot that until cookie baking day. People just had to eat them fresh.

My right hand was glowing red again.

"I'm ready to try something with a time limit on it," I told Tobias.

"What did you have in mind?" Tobias asked.

"I could curse you."

"No."

"Why not?"

"I know the most about unweaving spells. If you do something dangerous, I want to be up to capacity to deal with it."

That made sense. It had certainly come in handy with Mama. I could go find someone else in my family to curse, or curse something around the house. Or—

"I'm going to the orchard for an hour. Tell people to stay away if you see them." I put the dough in the fridge, went up to my room to get my curse journal and protection stone, and headed to the orchard.

I settled near the shielded tree and made plans.

I wrote down my idea before I said my curse aloud, because I wasn't sure how it would work, or even whether I would be able to write afterward. Then I sat for a while and thought about it.

I had made promises: promised Flint a steak dinner tonight, and I hadn't even bought the steaks yet. Promised Flint I'd help him with the lights. Promised Ian I'd go to Claire's party with him tomorrow.

Part of me wanted to play with fire, though. I was tired of being careful. Even when I was careful, horrible things happened. What would happen if I wasn't careful?

I reached into my pocket and pulled out the protection stone. I held it in cupped hands. It felt warm, though not with curse energy. I spoke to it. "Altria, for an hour, do what you want to me with my power."

Heat flowed from my chest down my arm, out of my hand; all of it I had went into the stone. Then my twin sat beside me in the dirt, dressed the same as I was: a black T-shirt with a Tlingit design of a raven in red and white surrounded by white painted-on buttons, jeans, black socks, and black ankle-high Reeboks. "That's a lovely invitation," she said. "So many fun possibilities. I've missed you." She trailed her fingertips over my shoulder, then nudged me. "I've been watching you, too. I like your boy."

"You're not going to mess with him, are you?"

"I couldn't do it directly under this particular spell, but I could make you do it."

She could make me do anything. Just the edges of the ideas that swept through my mind sent fear prickling through me.

"However, how smart would that be?" she asked, after letting me think and grow cold. "An hour's not very long. You are my sweet thing, my love, my goose, and if I upset you too much, you may not call on me or make offerings to me again." She stroked my hair. I remembered what she had said about our differing definitions of kindness, how she thought pain could be helpful. Why hadn't I remembered that before I crafted this curse? "So let's do something we both want." She swept her open hand up, and I rose in response like a marionette, floated a few inches above the earth. For a second I windmilled, confused, but then I realized I wasn't going to fall—I couldn't even get back in touch with the ground. Altria rose beside me, took my hand. "Let's go flying."

We shot up into the sparkling afternoon sky, so quickly I felt like I left my stomach and my breath behind. Then we stopped, higher than any building in earthquake-conscious Santa Tekla or the suburb of Bosquecito, but not so high we couldn't see details. I gasped and tried to quiet my terror at being up in the air without a plane.

"I won't let you fall," Altria said. Then she dropped my hand, and I fell like a stone. The ground rushed up at me. I had time to envision crashing down feet first and breaking both my legs, and then she swooped down and captured me again, dragged me up. "Or only a little bit," she said. "Don't worry."

"Don't worry!" Adrenaline pumped through me. I gripped her hand as hard as I could, hoping I'd give her bruises.

She pulled me close, fitted herself to my back, and clasped her arms around my waist. I closed my hands over hers, tried to lock myself into her embrace. "All right," she said, her breath warm in my ear. "Just a little wakeup call to remind you I'm not nice. Now let's go do something interesting."

We flew. With her arms tight around me and my hands over hers, I was no longer afraid she would drop me. Afternoon air rushed past us, cold because of our motion, until Altria stroked my stomach and red flame rose at her touch and wrapped us in warmth. I had given her permission to use my power on me for whatever she wanted. It hadn't occurred to me that we could use it like a heater. I liked it.

We flew out over the freeway, over the cemetery, above the bird sanctuary and the zoo and the broad beaches where people played volleyball when the weather was right, over the high-priced beachview hotels and convention centers, and along the beach boulevard toward the pier. Sábado y Domingo, the weekend open-air market under the line of palm trees beside the boulevard, was in full swing below us, artists and jewelers and potters and others selling wares. Christmas shoppers thronged the booths in search of gifts. It flashed by, and so did the pier, the harbor, and the breakwater where Ian and I had been last night. We flew across the boulevard and the Speare Beach parking lot, over the STCC campus and right to the Learning Center.

Campus was deserted for the holidays. Altria dropped us down next to the bench where I had waited for Ian the night before. No one was around to notice our descent.

She let go of me. I swayed and staggered. I had never flown like that before, and didn't know if any of my siblings had. I had loved the view, but feared the fall; the whole distance I had been terrified and elated, and now I just felt shaky as hell.

Altria, distracted, flapped a hand at me. A short tongue of orange flame flew from her fingers into my face, and I breathed it in without meaning to. It slid down my throat, hot and sweet and smooth, settled in my stomach, and warmed and steadied me.

Altria leaned over and sniffed at the bench.

"What are you doing?"

"We're going to find that man," she said, "and decide what to do about him."

Suddenly I felt excited. Who was Dennis Ralston, if that was even his name? What did he want? Did he really threaten people, or was that just my paranoia talking?

With Altria on the case, I felt like we could actually find out about him, and resolve my own unease.

She stroked the bench, then sniffed at her fingers. I wandered over to look at the hole in the row of cement stanchions where the one I had atomized used to be. A moment later she came up behind me and slid her arm around my waist. "Oh," she said, following my gaze, "that." She touched my chest. "Have you got something more for me, my sweet? Ah, yes." She drew her hand away, and a trail of red power followed. "We'll fix that first, just to be nice." She flicked her fingers three times, and a new cement stanchion, identical to all the others, spun up on the stump of the old one.

"How can that be?" I asked. "I used up a whole load of curse energy to destroy the other one. You can make a new one with just a little?"

"A fraction. You're wasteful, but you don't know better yet. I know how to use this gift. If you call me back again, I'll teach you. I'll feed you knowledge a fragment at a time. Are you happy now?"

The pillar was repaired. "Yes," I admitted.

"Good. Let's go." She dropped her arm to hold my hand again, and led me over the bridge above the road to the east side of campus. "He walks," she said, "mostly at night, but he comes here sometimes during the day, too. He has secret places."

We crossed most of campus, walked to the opposite side, which looked down over the edge of a cliff at a city park below, its baseball diamond and tennis courts and swing-sets. Clumps of trees dotted the park, and there was a bandshell and a concrete amphitheatre for concerts, too. Altria went with the confidence of someone familiar with the area to a place at the edge of one of the walking paths, then pushed off the path through some bushes, following a faint trail or none at all.

Dennis had a little carved-out earthen nook three feet

below the top of the cliff, where he could sit in comfort with his binoculars and watch things happening in the park below.

Altria pulled me to the edge just above his head, tugged me down beside her. We squatted there, watching Dennis as he watched other people. He was riveted. I stood, trying to see what he was looking at. Altria gripped my ankle so I wouldn't slip.

Below, sheltered, or so they thought, by a thick screen of eucalyptus trees between them and the park, and the cliff between them and the rest of the world, a boy and a girl were hard at it. She lay on her back on top of her dress. He still wore his shirt. Her head thrashed from side to side. Her small short gasps were almost swallowed by traffic sound and the cries of children chasing each other on the nearby lawn.

I ducked down. Altria smiled. I sat back and raised my eyebrows.

She leaned forward. "So," she said in a low whisper. "You like to watch."

Dennis jerked, would have dropped the binoculars, except they hung from a strap around his neck. He turned to stare up at us, then teetered in surprise.

Altria leaned over and grabbed a handful of shirt, steadied him.

"Get back," he whispered.

We went back through the bushes to the path. He followed.

"What are you doing here?" he asked when we were far enough from the cliff that nobody below could possibly hear us.

"Checking you out."

"Why?" He looked at me, then at Altria, then back at me. "Cripes, you're twins? I didn't know that about you. I mean, I've watched you before—one of you, anyway." He stroked his mustache. His eyes narrowed. "You. Gypsum."

He nodded to me. "I had no idea there was another one. I was just trying to help you last night."

Altria put out her hand.

Dennis ignored it. "What can I do for you?" he asked me.

I checked the campus. It was broad daylight. It was Christmas Break. There was no one on the mesa but us.

"Look, you came to me," Dennis said. "One might almost say you stalked me. Something wrong with your boyfriend?"

"No."

"What is it you want, then?"

"*Are* you the campus rapist?"

"I already told you I wasn't." He frowned. "What if I said I was?"

"Well, I—" I turned to Altria. What were we doing?

She stepped behind me, fitted herself to my back, her arms around my waist, her chin on my right shoulder. She was warm against my back.

"Two of you," Dennis said. He glanced around too, then focused on us. "That's more interesting, even though you're still not my type. You want to come home with me?"

"Is that a line that works?"

"You'd be surprised."

"So suppose we say no."

"You still have your keys to the Learning Center?"

"Sorry, didn't bring them."

"That's all right. I've got the keys to one of the portables." There were several prefabricated buildings on campus that had started as temporary classrooms and were now permanent, though they were still called portables. Dennis dug a key ring out of his pocket and jingled it. "Want to check it out?"

I glanced at Altria's profile. She smiled. "Okay," I said.

"Now, look. Are you seriously interested in me, or are you just teasing me?"

"I'm serious," Altria said. "My sister is scared."

Dennis pursed his lips, then turned and walked toward the nearest portable. Altria moved to my side, grabbed my hand, and followed. "Guard walked past here about ten minutes ago," Dennis said as he unlocked the door. "He won't be back for another half hour. Time enough?"

"For what I want," said Altria.

Dennis gave her a wicked smile. We walked in past him, and he closed and locked the door behind us. He set his binoculars on the teacher's desk by the blackboard, then dug his hands into his jacket pockets and pulled out some nylons. "Restraints?"

"No," Altria said.

He shrugged and stuffed them back in his pockets. "What is it you want?"

"I want to know if you hurt people."

"Is that what you like?"

"Sometimes. Right now I want to know if I can use you to teach my sister a lesson."

"Kinky, but okay."

"Lie down."

He took off his jacket, folded it, and lay on the floor with the jacket under his head. Altria stood over him, her feet planted on either side of his waist. She lowered herself to sit on his stomach.

"Not comfortable," Dennis said. "You weigh a ton."

She put her knees down at his sides and raised herself off of him a little. "Gyp. Come here."

"What are you doing?" My voice quavered.

"Come on," she said. Dennis looked up at me and laughed.

I squatted beside them, scared and uncomfortable.

"Watch carefully," Altria said. She stroked my chest, pulled a streamer of fire from me, and, as Dennis gaped, placed her red-cloaked hand on his forehead.

"Do you hurt other people against their will?" she asked.

"What?" He tried to pull her hand off his forehead. He struggled, kicked his legs, gripped her arm and pulled. She didn't move.

"Do you rape people?" she asked.

He convulsed, arms and legs and neck straight and stiff, his head back, mouth stretched in a silent scream. Then the fit left him and he relaxed. "Only special people," he whispered. "Only the exact right one. I don't find her very often."

Altria lifted her hand from his forehead and turned to me. "Here." She placed her palm on my chest. Fire poured out of her into me. "Some of what you gave me. Curse him."

"What?"

"You don't want to curse the people you love. I heard you talk to Tobias after your mother ate the fruit of that beautiful tree. You'd give this up if you had to hurt people you love every day. Why not curse someone who deserves it?" She took my hand, guided it down to rest on Dennis's head. "It's not hard. Give him something to pay him back for what he's done to others."

"But he—but you—but I don't really know—"

"Your hand's so hot. Hurt me," Dennis said. "You're turning into my type."

"Nothing twisted gives you pleasure," I whispered. Heat poured out of my hand, flooded into Dennis.

He began to weep.

Altria stood up, leaned to pat his cheek, then grabbed my hand and dragged me out of there.


SHE hugged me from behind again, and we rose up into the air. Wind chilled the tears on my face. Would he be all right? Did he deserve to be cursed? I didn't even know who he was, or if he'd really done what he said. He hadn't hurt us, hadn't even come close. Guilt twisted and burned in my belly. This time I'd cursed someone who had no defenses. How could that be right?

We flew fast above the boulevard for two miles, over the people at Sábado y Domingo, past the convention centers again, over the point that stuck out into the ocean, past the part of the cemetery that was on the cliff above the sea, where our family has had plots for years in preparation for the ultimate, and down to the narrow, unimproved beach in Bosquecito that Jasper and Flint and Beryl and I walked to from our house, Mariposa Beach. At high tide, the waves lapped at the rip rap and there was no beach; at low tide you could walk along the beach past a tar hill to where the cliffs curved out and away, and below them were the magical tide pools where I had been searching for treasure since I was a little kid.

The tide was halfway in or out, and seagulls flew along the strand, crying. Grown-ups and kids and dogs walked or raced or swam along the water's edge, leaving footprints in wet sand that shone for a moment before all the water forced to the surface by the pressure of the feet sank down again. The air smelled of sea, with a touch of dead fish.

At a moment when everyone faced away, Altria dropped us to the sand with a soft thud not too far from where the dark rocks that sheltered and formed the tidepools began.

The air was warm in this stretch of beach where the shore wind was diverted by the cliffs. Heat rose from sand that had been baking under afternoon sun for several hours.

I took off my shoes and socks and dug my toes into the sand, wishing I could crawl under it and bury myself. Altria sat close, her arm draped over my shoulders.

Not far off, a man and his dog played fetch the driftwood stick and throw it. Out in the rocks twelve-year-olds poked sticks into tidepools, and one stooped to pick something up. Three teen girls in bright bikinis walked along the water. A woman with her pants rolled up held her little boy's hand, and they waded in the edges of the waves. Farther back, where the beach was just a beach and didn't have rocks in the water, people swam, bodysurfed.

"You're not happy," Altria murmured.

"I wish I knew what was right," I said. "I have no sense that that was right. I feel like you forced me to do something awful."

"I do that. You knew that."

"I do now."

"But I was trying to help, Gyp. If you can open up your head a little, you'll see that you have treasure. Open your head. You don't even know how to curse right. And it's all so close." She gripped my head between her hands and stared into my eyes. So strange, this view of my own face, which I usually saw in the frozen moment of a photograph, or with planned expressions in front of a mirror, never just serious and searching and frustrated. "I want to get this right, but I don't know my job yet, either. Will you give me more chances?"

"I don't know."

She caught one of my tears on a finger and tasted it. She took my hand, turned it over so she could read my wristwatch. "I have fifteen more minutes."

"I can set time limits and you'll respect them?"

"Today. Hmm. Fifteen minutes." She stroked her hand across my head, warm and gentle, and looked down the beach.

A bathing-suited mother played with her two naked toddlers in the surf.

"Let's try that," Altria said, and laid her hand on my back.

It was like the earlier diminishing had been, a collapse and collection down into a smaller self, pulling tighter and losing pieces of myself—bone length, muscles, all the growth and change experience had written on my body. In a moment I had dropped down into the cavern that my T-shirt became, arms and legs pulling up out of my clothes.

I sat in a dark cocoon of fabric. I had the urge to wail.

Altria lifted the edge of the T-shirt. Her face—my face—was suddenly the most beautiful thing I had ever seen. It promised comfort and security. I held out my arms to her.

"Hey, little one," she murmured in a soft voice, and lifted me, cradled me against her breast. I reached my arms as far up toward her neck as I could and laid my head on her chest. I could hear her heart beat. The sun blazed on my skin. A breeze brushed my back. Both things felt like touches.

She held me tight for awhile, and it was all I wanted. I didn't think about who or what I had turned into. The warmth of her chest against my front, a smell like campfires and sagebrush and fresh bread, her breath across my head, ruffling what little hair I had, her arms around me, tight and warm.

"Hey," she murmured. "You want to go wading?"

I didn't want to move.

Her arms shifted around me. Her hands cupped me under my arms, and she set me on my feet on the sand. I sensed each grain of sand against the bottoms of my feet. I took a step and stumbled, landed on my butt, sand printing its story against my skin.

"Too small, maybe. I don't know human children." She got to her knees in front of me, took my hand, helped me back to my feet. "Can you walk?"

I tottered, even with her support. She let me sit down again, rose, and stooped to lift me. Sand formed a gritty layer between her arm and my body. "Come on. Let's see if you want to get wet."

She walked down to the water's edge and held me up on my feet on the wet sand. A wave rolled toward us. It looked like a tidal wave from so low! I screamed, and Altria lifted me above the surge line; the water ran up and washed around her knees. "Oh!" she said in a surprised tone.

"Cold." She lowered me into the water as it washed back out. "What do you think? Do you like that?"

It wasn't as scary as a wave racing toward me. The water felt cold, and I liked the pressure of the rush of it past my legs and waist. It smelled salty. I danced a little, felt the pressure change as I turned my body.

Altria laughed. She lifted me again and walked into the water in all her clothes. Waves broke around us. As long as she held me tight, I wasn't afraid. I loved how the water moved around and against us.

The water was cold, but the sun was warm. Sometimes the water embraced us, and sometimes it let us go, and then I felt colder than when I was down in it; breeze chilled me. Altria moved around in the water, cradled me against her, jumped up as surges swept past us, stood when the level dropped. She moved farther out to where we could float.

Then—something talked to me. Something deep and low and thrumming, something speaking about time and change and how things repeated, always different and always the same. Something about the power of water, the water washing in and out of the power in me, the power that had formed Altria. Something that was too big and old to be either a curse or a blessing, something that was a constant surge and retreat. It called to me. I pushed at Altria's chest, ready to answer the call, to float away into that deeper power and forget who I was.

"What are you doing? Shit," she said, and ran out of the ocean.

My mind was half engaged with the call; even though we weren't in the water anymore, I still heard it. Altria set me on top of my T-shirt and grabbed something shiny out of the sand, stared at it. The sun sparkled on it, and it looked pretty. I reached for it. In the grip of my desire for the shiny thing, I lost my connection to whatever it was that called.

"Shit," she said. She snatched me up, grabbed my clothes, handed me the shiny thing, and held me tight. She closed her eyes.

A moment later we were in my bedroom.

She set me on my bed.

I put the shiny thing in my mouth. It tasted sandy, salty, gritty against my tongue, but there were smooth things under the grit, and I liked the feel of it.

"My hour is up, Gyp," Altria said. She kissed my forehead.

I took the shiny thing out of my mouth and shook it. I sucked on it some more, then looked around and realized that Altria was gone. A green stone nudged my knee. I held it. There was a song inside it, like the song of the deep water. It was a home song, a comfort song, but it faded. I opened my mouth to cry.

Then I grew. My arms and legs shot out, my spine extended, lengthened my torso; flesh spun out around me to match the pace of my skeleton's growth; strength and knowledge, muscle and bone and blood vessels all stretched out, knitted a new me, a full-grown me, naked and sticky with seawater and sand. I took my watch out of my mouth and sat on my wet bedspread for a while, the protection stone in my right hand.

What *was* that?

She'd turned me into a baby.

She wasn't much of a mother.

I smiled.

She wasn't much of a mother, but she hadn't let go of me, and she had brought me home, and honored her commitment to play with me for an hour and that was all.

Jeeze! I'd been a baby!

Strangely, I had loved that. As long as she didn't let go.

But what was that sea-call thing? I had trouble even thinking about it. I put the stone up to my forehead, caught a thread of promise, lost it.

I put on one of my sleepshirts and crossed the sitting room to the bathroom for my second shower of the day.

*Twenty-one*

I looked up Dennis in the phone book. He was listed. I never wanted to talk to him again, but I was worried, and I felt guilty. I dialed his number. "Hello?" he said in a hoarse voice.

"Hello? Dennis? Are you all right?"

Silence. Then, "Gypsum?"

"Are you okay?"

"No."

"I'm sorry," I said.

I heard him breathing.

"It's very odd," he said presently. "I'm not myself. I don't know who I am. I ate an apple, and just the taste . . ."

I waited. Then I said, "Are you okay?" again.

"No. I don't know. I've got your phone number now, anyway. Caller ID. I'll call you." He hung up.

He couldn't have the right number. Mama blocked that. Still—

My heart was still shocky and unsettled. I got out the journal and wrote down the facts, then what Altria had said to me, and what I felt.

I stared at her words again, the ones about curse people who deserved it, and I had something to treasure. Open my head.

Flint knocked on the door, poked his head in. "The curse wore off at three-forty-five," he said.

"Oh, good." I flipped back to an earlier page where I had written about cursing Flint and Jasper, and in the "duration" field, wrote "five hours."

"You ready to do lights?"

"Still building up after my last curse. Would you take me to the market to buy steaks?" I asked.

"Sure."

I handed him my car keys and we drove to the market.

After we returned with dinner ingredients, I finished up more batches of cookies. Tobias had done several sorts and lost interest, leaving me to clean everything up.

Somewhere in there, I went to lean over the retaining wall in the backyard to check on the banana tree. It had vanished, and Tobias's shield had, too; the only thing left was a scrap of yellow in the dirt, the original banana.

Thank God there was a time limit.

Around six, the sun dipped low and evening fog moved in. Good weather for making Christmas lights.

Flint and I went out in the front yard, where there was an ornamental garden in the middle of the roundabout with a bench we sat on. "Did you figure out a spell to keep your hands cool?" I asked.

"Damn! No!"

"I'll wait." I felt the power in my chest, warm, heavy, ready to be called. Building. See how this one went. Maybe it *was* treasure. Why couldn't Flint and I work together all the time?

Flint muttered to himself. I looked at our big yellow house. Lights were on in upstairs rooms. In mine, in Beryl's, in the master bedroom. Light shone from the kitchen windows, from Dad's study. A light glowed in the upper room of Tobias's tower, and over it all, I could sense the wards woven to protect us and our place, faint traceries of blue and green lines.

The family van pulled into the driveway and drove right to the front door. Flint and I jumped up and went around the van. Flint opened the side door. All the seats had been taken out of the back. Beryl, muddy and scratched but happy, sat there with this year's tree, a bushy lopsided pine with dense, short needles. It was tall enough that it had bent to fit in the van. It smelled wonderful. We helped it out. "Welcome, welcome," Flint told it. It straightened its top.

Mama came around the van. "Beautiful tree," she said, "may I help you?"

I strained to hear if the tree responded, but I guessed I didn't speak tree; I couldn't hear anything.

Mama held out her hands, palms up, and something streamed from them that I couldn't quite see. It wrapped around the tree's roots, and then the tree floated. Beryl climbed out of the car and took hold of one of the tree's branches, and we all went in through the big front door, turned left in the great hall, and proceeded to the living room, where a tub of enriched earth and a watering can waited.

The tree drifted up and settled down into the earth, moved its roots, dug in. Beryl watered it and tamped the earth. "Thank you, glorious tree. Welcome to our house."

I had a sense of things happening all around me. They teased at my energy, but I couldn't see or understand them.

"Did you figure out how to use just a bit of the energy?" Flint asked me.

"Not exactly." I had established a time limit, but Altria had used everything I had in her allotted hour. I remembered how we built the staircase: she had been in charge of the draw, had taken it more slowly than Flint knew how. Maybe I could control the flow. That would be useful.

"Should we experiment before we dress the tree?"

"Yeah. Welcome, tree. Thank you for gracing us with your presence," Flint said to the tree. We went back outside and sat on the bench again.

He took my hand. "I'm not sure about whether I can keep it cool."

"Let's just try to go slow. Colored lights or white lights?"

"White lights for the front of the house and the tree," he said. "We could put colored lights on the hedge."

"Do you have an image of what you want?"

He pointed at the house. "A line of lights at the eaves. A line of lights around each of the windows. A line of lights around the front door. What do you think?"

"Sounds nice."

"Pretty much what Jasper did a few years ago, before I got this job."

"So we should add something fancy."

We grinned at each other. "Let's do the easy part first," Flint said.

"All right." I gripped his hand and closed my eyes and thought of feeding my power to him slowly so he could shape it. White lights, or maybe slightly yellow lights for warmth, safe and gentle on the outside of the house, to go on at dusk and turn themselves off and rest during the sunlit hours of the day. I imagined lights in each of the places Flint had mentioned, and let energy flow in a smooth thin stream from me into my brother's hand.

Flint squeezed my hand. "Look."

The house wore lacy lines of light, not straight lines but strange weavings and patterns; an embroidery of lights around each window, along the eaves.

"Wow."

"You thought them safe? I felt that. I love that. On at sunset, off at sunrise? Thanks for thinking that."

"You made lace!" I turned his hand over and looked at it. "I didn't burn you."

"Yeah. We're getting good. I should never say that, because that's what I always think right before I mess up big-time. Dang."

"We did all right. Let's go talk to the tree."

The tree had settled itself. It was a bigger tree than we had had in some time, a proud bushy tree, dark green and fragrant.

"You have to do the tree talking," I said. "I don't understand the language."

"All right." Flint went to the tree and put his hand on a branch. "May we dress you in light?"

I almost heard an answer.

"Thank you." He held out his hand to me, and I stepped forward and took it.

Safe lights, cool lights, shine and don't burn, shine and feel good to the tree, I thought. I felt our power flowing gently and slowly.

Flint squeezed my hand. I opened my eyes. He had laid a lacework of lights over the tree's branches.

Mama gasped behind us.

"Thank you," Flint said to the tree. He let go of my hand and we turned around.

"Beautiful," Mama murmured. "Wonderful."

Flint smiled. "We were going to do the hedges, too. You want that?"

"That might be a bit gaudy, don't you think?"

"Yeah." Flint nodded and grinned. "Colored lights."

"Just say no to colored lights!" Mama said.

"I love colored lights," I said.

Mama frowned. "Tasteless!"

"I bet we'd make them nice."

She looked at the tree. "Give it a shot."

Flint and I wandered outside. "How you holding up?" he asked.

"Power to burn."

"That is so cool. Okay, she challenged us to make it tasteful."

"I leave that up to you."

We faced the pittosporum hedges that walled our front yard off from the little street, except for right in the middle. In the center of the yard, there was a landing with a stone railing, and a double staircase descended to the roundabout across from the front door.

I held out my hand to Flint and closed my eyes again, imagined safety and timing while he did all the creative work with lights. This time it took longer, and drew enough power that my charge was nice and low. I wouldn't have to curse anything for a while.

"Done," Flint said eventually.

The lights glowed faded colors, in spiderweb patterns that flickered as though wind blew on them; they weren't gaudy. You had this sense you were seeing fairies, and that if you looked away it would all disappear. Mysterious, faint, lovely.

"Wow," I whispered.

Mama stood in the doorway. "All right. You managed it. Flint, I'm so proud of you."

"Me and Gyp."

"I'm proud of you and Gyp. You did a wonderful job."

"Thanks, Mama. Did you look at the house yet?" he asked.

She stepped out into the driveway for a look. She did us the honor of not saying anything for a good minute. Then she came and hugged us.


WHEN I woke up Sunday morning, Altria was sitting on my bed. She still looked like the me of yesterday, black raven T-shirt and jeans. I felt this longing to have her hold me. She was my half-remembered safety in the midst of sun and water when I was small.

She smiled.

I remembered there was something wrong with this picture. "I didn't call you," I said.

"You're leaking." She waved at my chest. A blanket of red light lay over me. "And you called me in a dream."

"Can you come into people's dreams without asking?"

"Dreams are where I spend most of my time. But I didn't need to sneak into your dreams. You invited me."

How could I help dreaming about things that had happened during the day? She had been a big part of my Saturday, so it didn't surprise me I had dreamed about her. Still, it made me suspect strange things. I still didn't know who she was or where she came from. She spent a lot of time in dreams? One of the few pieces of information she had given me. "Are you a nightmare?"

"Of course." She dipped her hands in the red blanket of energy over my chest and smiled. "So lovely. You make the best." She scooped up my power in cupped hands. "What do I want to do with this today?"

I sat up, held out my hands, and sucked my power back inside of me. My shoulders locked up, so tight with power that my elbows locked, too. "No."

"Cough up a little of the red stuff. Come on, Gyp. Give." She tickled me. I couldn't help laughing. I tried to cover all my ticklish spots, but she found others, and I lost hold on the power. There was a pile of it, anyway; I hadn't cursed anything after Flint's lights last night, and I had slept—I managed to catch a glimpse of the clock—until nine this morning. Hours of power. We rolled around in a red haze, hot with it, but not sweating, either of us; only the smell of campfires that she brought with her, and bread. We were both acclimated to my power. I tickled her, surprised when she fell prey to laughter too. I tickled her into helplessness. "Stop! Stop," she gasped. "All right. You win."

"Whoa!" I didn't know it was possible for me to win.

She poked me. "You always win, don't you?"

I thought about our relationship. In every encounter, she had given me strange gifts, and she had saved my life once and my brain another time. She had given the yard a new staircase without asking for anything back. She had given me the opportunity to experience myself in strange ways, and she had taken care of me even when I was afraid she wouldn't. "I guess that's right."

"Well, of course, I win, too. I get to play with you." She lifted red in her hands, shaped it into a ball. "Why won't you give me some? What do you need it for?"

"I don't want to change today. Not until after the party, anyway."

"Give this to me now and I'll save it until later."

"You can do that?"

"Of course. Simple. I might use some. A girl has to eat."

"Use it how?"

"I could arrange not to bother you."

"Would you be bothering someone else?"

"I might. I've never capitalized sufficiently on my relationship with Jasper, for instance, and I haven't even touched the rest of your family yet."

"Forget it."

"Give me what you've got now, and I'll save it for later," she said again in a resigned tone.

"You promise?"

"I promise."

I wondered if she considered a promise binding.

"My word is my bond," she said.

"How can I trust you?"

"Realistically, you can't. Yet you do, again and again. I call that a fine basis for a relationship. Don't you?"

"You always say scary or threatening things, and do scary things, but you soften up afterward."

"It's all part of my diabolical plan. I'll string you along until I get what I really want, and then whoosh! You'll find out you shouldn't have trusted me that last time, but it will be too late."

"Is that true? What do you really want?"

She lay back on the bed and stared at the ceiling. "This is too much like work." She faded.

I sat in the welter of sheets and blankets, haloed and heated by red power, so much power my shoulders couldn't tighten any more than they already had, and wondered what to do. I thought about Altria saving me when the computer had turned me into a girl droid, Altria repairing that pillar yesterday up at the Center just to ease my mind, trying to teach me a new direction for curses, holding a tiny, helpless me safe as we rocked on the ocean.

I could fly to the Antarctic and blow off power there, but I might just make the hole in the ozone layer bigger. "Altria?"

She materialized on the bed, raised an eyebrow.

"Hypothetically, could you take today's power and keep it until I get home from the party tonight, and not torture my family with it?"

She sighed and nodded. "But after that, we do something major."

"We would have to, wouldn't we?"

"Yep. Something huge."

I outlined my next step in my head, and then aloud. "Altria, would you take the curse energy I generate today and save it for me so we can use it when I get home from Claire's party? And I mean *we*. I get to direct it. Okay?"

"Mmm." She ran her fingers through the red glow, drew out scarves of it, released it so that it flowed back to me. "All right. I agree." She opened her arms, and all the red in the air around me flew to her as though she were a vacuum. It melted into her chest. More red came out of me; she drew it slowly, so that I was conscious of the tension leaving my shoulders. At last I relaxed enough. She hugged her stomach and lay back. "Oh, glorious," she murmured. "I'm drunk with power! I love this!"

She sat up after a while. Her face was flushed, her eyes bright. "You are the best," she said. "Oh, and while I'm drunk, I should tell you a secret about later."

"Yes?"

"It's good you told me we'll work when you get home from the party. Because if you agreed to let me save the power until later, like I promised, well, it's always later. Could have taken it now and used it in ten minutes." Then she whispered, "Everything people say has a loophole, if you know where to look." She leaned forward, hugged me, kissed hot cinnamon on my cheek, and disappeared.

SUNDAY pancake breakfast was the one meal a week that Dad cooked. He brought the electric frying pan to the dining room table and made pancakes to order for everybody who wanted them. When we were little, he made pancake shapes: animals, our initials, mystery shapes we were supposed to guess—clouds was always a safe guess, though usually wrong. I got him a book of pancake recipes, and now he experimented with batter instead of shapes. This morning we were having blueberry pancakes, a favorite.

Today everybody was at breakfast, even Aunt Hermina. When everyone had a plate with pancakes and syrup on it in front of them, Mama said, "We need a family meeting tonight."

Four or five people sighed.

Mama glanced around, but it was too late to tell who had done it. "Come on," she said. "Give me a break. Christmas is only three days away, and I've fallen down on the job of planning for it. I don't know what's the matter with me this year. I'm grateful to everyone who went ahead and did their chores without my asking them to. That's worked surprisingly well. We still need to do some planning, though, and we have new factors to consider."

Everyone looked at me.

"That's right. Gyp is still settling. We've never had a transition this close to a major holiday before. She doesn't have as much room for mistakes as the rest of us had. The mistakes she makes cause different kinds of problems, too." Mama lifted her shoulders and shuddered.

"What happened?" Jasper asked. "Something else?"

"More evidence that what she has is not benevolent," Mama said.

"You couldn't tell from what that computer did to me on Friday?" asked Hermina.

"Sorry, Aunt. It came closer to home for me yesterday. So anyway, everyone please meet in the living room tonight after nine, all right?"

Everyone nodded.

I had a thought. "You guys, will you think up curses all day and bring them to the meeting, too? I could use some new ideas."

"Curses," said Opal.

"I'd like to have a bunch ready to try. So far my own ideas haven't worked out that well."

Beryl smiled. "Curses."

"Sure," said Flint.

After breakfast, I said I was going to the mall to shop, and did anyone else want to come? Provided we could separate for the actual shopping part and meet up later.

"You driving today?" asked Beryl.

"Yeah, if I need to."

"You're not afraid you'll curse somebody on the freeway by mistake?"

"I'm storing up my power for later tonight."

Tobias's gaze sharpened. "How?"

"Are you putting it into something?" Opal asked.

"Sort of," I said.

"Gypsum," Tobias said.

"Uncle."

"Are you sure what you are doing is safe?"

"Nope."

"Nothing is ever one hundred percent safe, and we survive it all," Dad said, and gave me a plate with a giant pancake on it.

I had such a normal afternoon that I felt weird.

Beryl went to the mall with me, and then we split up.

I loved that afternoon. The air was clear and warm; the shops swarmed with other last-minute Christmas shoppers, and I wasn't afraid I would turn them into doorstops or statues or mutes, because I didn't have the power. Every once in a while, Altria appeared, brushed against me, and pulled curse energy out of me. I hadn't felt so relaxed in days.

I went down my list of people and found gifts I thought they would each like. Maybe I hated some things about being normal, but I enjoyed this time I spent not worrying about power.

Beryl and I met for lunch at a place with sidewalk tables and big umbrellas, where they served forty-seven different kinds of wraps and roll-ups. She was toting big shopping bags full of stuff too. After lunch we stopped at the car to drop off bags and went out shopping again. We finished by three-thirty and drove home, full of secrets.

Then I went upstairs to figure out what to wear to Claire's party.

I'd never paid much attention to that stuff before. But this was almost the first time a boy who wasn't a member

of my family was going to pick me up and take me somewhere, and I wanted to look decent.

I had three shirts I thought of as "good" shirts, and one
pair of black jeans that I considered formal enough pants.
Or, that was what my closet had looked like before UFS
me had gone through it.

Now I had a bunch of clothes I didn't even recognize,
and they all looked good on me for weird reasons I could
no longer understand. How had UFS me known to make
this shirt that color, or to decorate the collar of this one
with those silver pointy things? Who knew. I stood in front
of the closet mirror holding things up and being surprised.

Opal knocked while I was still deciding. She came in
and sat on my bed. I held up two shirts, one after the other
in front of me, and asked her which was best.

"The red one with the pirate sleeves," she said. "Since
when do you wear red?"

Good question. I remembered Opal's poppy-red dress,
my first venture into red. I put the green shirt away and
hung the red one on the closet doorknob. "Opal, Friday I
was under a curse, and I went in your room and wore your
clothes and stole your makeup. I apologize."

"I could tell you'd been in there. What, you cursed yourself?"

"I cursed something else, and it cursed me."

"And that's your excuse for messing with my stuff?"

"I'm sorry. What can I do to make it up to you?"

She smiled. "Let me make you up for your date."

"That'll do it?"

"That'll do it."

I dressed in my red shirt, black pants, and black cowboy
boots with the pointy toes, then went to Opal's room and
sat at her vanity. She draped a thin towel over my shirt
collar, and did things to my face and hair. Then she did
my fingernails, made them longer, colored them a glittery
red that matched my shirt—all without compacts, bottles

of foundation, eye shadow, lipsticks, blush, or nail polish. Makeup was what she did for a living, though on the job she used props—she waved store-bought makeup around and pretended she was using it.

She could be turning me into a movie monster; she wouldn't let me look until she was finished.

"All right. You can open your eyes now."

She had turned me into someone else, and not really a monster. I wasn't as nervous about this self as I would have been before my various forays into fashion on Friday. Dark brown lines around my eyes made the hazel of my irises look intense, and on my eyelids she had blended shades of green and gold and pink. My lips looked larger, in a color that was my natural color intensified. She had styled the curls on top of my head taller, and clipped the other curls to the sides of my head with red sparkle star-shaped barrettes, giving my head less width, more height.

"Oh, Opal," I whispered. Last week I would have been terrified of this new self. I was still a little scared, but I was ready to actually leave the house looking like this. "Thank you."

She opened a drawer in her vanity table and took out a brown leather-covered box. She opened it. Her pretties. When I was a little kid, she had sometimes let me look through her pretties. I had loved to sit on her bed and take each thing out, cherish it, long for it, put it away again. Sometimes she had let me try on the necklaces and bracelets and rings.

Now she lifted out the top layer of the box, which was covered in white velvet and divided into lots of little compartments for rings. She rooted around in the lower compartment. "Here we are."

She held up a pair of dangly earrings, bunches of tiny papier mâché strawberries dipped in red glitter. She handed them to me and I put them on.

I stood up and we both studied me in her vanity mirror.

This red and black garbed stranger might have posed for a fashion shoot in *Mode*. I cocked my head, tried to see myself under the surface. Would Ian know me? Would Claire?

"Too much?" Opal asked.

"Did you change me a whole lot? I mean, like, my features?"

She shook her head. "Just the colors."

"Weird. You're amazing."

"Thanks." She cocked her head. "Maybe it is a little too much. I could tone it down a touch." She lifted a hand toward my face, and I backed up a step.

"No, let's leave it. Try it out on Mama, see what she says."

Mama was astonished. She hugged me carefully so she wouldn't smear anything—though when Opal did makeup, it was smudgeproof. Mama took Polaroids of me. "It might be overkill," she said after considering both me and my photographs.

Opal drew her fingers across my face and removed a layer of sophistication. I ended up looking like my UFS self. I felt more comfortable that way.

"Thanks," I said again.

"My pleasure."

I went downstairs, grabbed one of my gift cookie tins, and went out front to wait for Ian.

Altria appeared next to me on the bench. She looked like present me now, though earlier in the day she'd looked different from me. Still a twin, but wearing different clothes and attitude.

"Love the boots," she said, sticking her legs out straight and studying her footware.

I opened the cookie tin and offered her some.

"This is what you were working on all day yesterday."

"Yeah."

She selected a cookie and bit it. "Oh! Nice. Not what I usually eat."

I ate a chocolate chip cookie. I had maxed out on bites of cookie dough yesterday, ate enough that I got sick of it by dinnertime, but I hadn't had a cookie yet today. Delicious.

"Want more?" I asked. She took two more and I closed the box. "How are you doing?"

"I'm floating." She smiled. "You know what we could do with all this power? Anything we want. I had to develop a new way to store it so I wasn't just drifting around out of my mind with joy." She stroked my shoulder, drew another ribbon of power out of me.

"Are you going to loophole your way out of our bargain tonight?" I asked.

"No. I'll be very interested to see what you do."

Ian's car pulled into the driveway just as the sky darkened enough for the house and hedge lights to go on. Altria vanished.

Ian parked in front of me and jumped out of the car. He was wearing dark pants and a gray-green sweater with no holes in it. "Wow," he said. "You look great."

"Thanks. You do, too."

"Wow," he said, turning around to study the lights, "the house looks great, too."

"Thanks again."

"You did that?"

"Flint and I collaborated."

"Hey! Ian!"

We both looked toward the house. Beryl was leaning out my bedroom window. "Hi!" she yelled.

"Hello?"

"I'm Beryl! This is what I look like uncursed!"

"Nice to meet you again."

"What are you doing in my room?" I yelled.

"Leaning out the window, what does it look like? Hey,

this is Opal, she's our other sister. She told me you were coming over and we should spy on you!" Beryl dragged Opal out of the shadows and made her lean out the window, too.

"Hi, Ian!" Opal called.

"Hi, there. We spoke earlier."

"Yeah! You're as cute as your voice!"

My face burned.

"Thanks," he said.

"Opal did my makeup," I said, even though I was embarrassed. "She's a pro."

"Uh," Ian said, then yelled, "Nice makeup!"

"Cute and complimentary," Opal said. "Nice combination!"

"Let's get out of here," I muttered.

Ian walked me around the car and opened the passenger door. I climbed into the car.

"Ooh, polite, too," Opal said.

"See you later!" Beryl yelled. "We're going to the Griddle House for dinner!"

"We had pancakes for breakfast," I said. The Griddle House was a restaurant, the first of a chain of pancake houses that had been popular in the sixties and seventies, and the last of the chain, too. All the others had been chased out of business by IHOP. The original Griddle House hadn't changed. We had been going there since we were too young to talk. It was a very silly restaurant, designed for families with young children, and it felt kind of weird for us to go there when we all looked like grownups, except we knew everyone on the staff, and they still talked to us as though we were kids.

"It's a long time until next Sunday," Beryl said.

"Have fun."

"You, too."

Ian closed my door, went around the car, got in, started the engine.

"I am so sorry about that," I said.

Ian laughed. "I don't know. Makes me wish I had more than one sister."

"You're welcome to mine."

He glanced at me and smiled. "Might take you up on that."

At Claire's, people whistled at me. Mainly Claire and July and Orion. At first I was startled. Then I held out my arms and posed.

"You look so much better!" July said.

"Opal did my makeup. But I feel a lot better, too. Thanks again for rescuing me last week. You saved my life."

"Oh, Gyp." She hugged me.

"What's this? Mom saved your life? Opal's back?" Claire asked. "Hey, are those the annual Gyp Christmas cookies?"

I handed her the cookie tin, then glanced around to see who else was here. "Is this a family party?"

There were five other people, only one of whom I had met before—Claire and Orion's older brother Tim, who hadn't lived with July while we were growing up; he'd stayed with his father in the mountains to study communal witchcraft after the divorce. I had met him maybe three times before. He might actually be a decent witch, in which case he could sense stuff about us that we hadn't told other people, so LaZelle family policy was to stay away from the Rhodes's when Tim was visiting. Policy hadn't embraced me, because there was nothing magical he could sense from me, until now. So I'd had more contact with him than anybody else in my family. Still, that didn't amount to much.

If I had known he was going to be here, would I have come to the party now that I had changed? Maybe not.

"It's not specifically a family party. It's a solstice party," Claire said. "Didn't you get my e-mail?"

"I'm sorry. I haven't been checking. Things have gotten totally weird for me lately."

"Ooh. Tell me later." She took the cookies into the kitchenette, then introduced me around.

Ian knew a couple of them already.

"This is Lenora, one of my roommates from Idaho." He introduced me to a very pale girl with black hair and clothes and nice black eyeliner around her eyes.

"From the Goth days," I said.

"Lucky guess," said Lenora. She smiled.

"Hey, Gypsum. You've changed," Tim told me.

"Thank you," I said to be confusing.

"You have a doppelgänger," he said, maybe to confuse me back.

"What does that mean?" The word sounded familiar, but I couldn't remember ever using it. I knew I'd read it, but I hadn't looked it up.

"A double walker. A shadow self."

"Tim," Claire said, her tone scolding.

"What? Wouldn't you want to know if you had such a thing?" Tim spent a lot of time immersed in his occult studies up in the mountains, and not much time with regular people. Claire corrected him when she thought he was being too weird in company, and he was usually a good sport about hearing from her.

"I know about her," I said. "She's a friend."

His gaze flicked past me, fixed on something just behind me. "Are you sure?"

I glanced back. Nobody visible there. Cool fingers touched the back of my neck, though, let me know that Altria was behind me even if I couldn't see her. Maybe she had followed me invisibly all day, only popping into view when she needed to draw power from me. "I'm pretty sure," I said.

Ian studied me, eyebrows up.

"Long story."

Claire looked frustrated. "Take your coat?" she asked.

I wasn't wearing a coat, though I should have brought one, since the nights were chilly. Claire took my arm and led me across the living room/kitchenette past the other guests into her bedroom, where she closed the door.

I glanced at the pile of coats on the bed. Then at my hostess.

"Tim isn't just being weird?" Claire asked.

I held my hand out behind me, and Altria slid hers into it. She stepped up beside me, visible now.

Claire paled. "How did you do that?"

"Magic. It's in my family, Claire. I didn't inherit it until Wednesday, though, so it wasn't an issue before. Now I've got a lot of things to work on. Altria, this is Claire, my best friend. Claire, this is Altria. I don't know what she is, but she's been helping me."

"Hello," Claire said in a shaky voice.

Altria smiled. She set her hand on my chest, lifted it, drew a swoosh of red light from me. For a moment it formed a glowing ball above her open hand. Then it melted into her palm. "Hi, Claire," she said. "Later, Gyp." She vanished.

"What? What? What!" Claire said.

"We need to talk."

"You bet we do."

"Now?" I asked.

"Um—well, I've got this party to run."

"Later," I said.

"Right." She opened the door and we rejoined the others.

It was a party like many of Claire's parties, friendly and funny, with good food. Everyone was interesting, and they had great anecdotes. There were few enough people that we could all listen to the same thing at once if we wanted to, and enough people so that we could break into small groups to talk about other things. Most of the time Ian and I sat next to each other on the couch. Occasionally our thighs bumped into each other, and I would smile at him, and he would smile back.

He got up to get us drinks, and Tim dropped onto the couch beside me. "Seriously," Tim said.

I raised my eyebrows.

"Your aura is totally different now."

"Okay." I felt ready to share more with Claire, but I didn't even know Tim.

"And there's the doppelgänger."

"Uh-huh."

"Are you a good witch or a bad witch?"

"That's kind of personal."

He studied me for a long moment, then smiled. "That's right. If Claire was listening, she'd tell me I was doing something wrong, wouldn't she?"

I smiled at him.

"But this change in you was sudden, right? It's hard to handle something like that alone. I guess what I mean is, if you need some help, you know where to find us. We'll do whatever we can."

"Thanks," I said, touched. If I were alone in the wide world and went through transition with no Uncle Tobias, no family to help me figure out what was going on and to forgive me when I messed up, this would be a much more difficult thing. I would probably be relieved to find some people who called themselves witches.

Around eight-thirty, I touched Ian's shoulder. The family would be home from dinner by now; it was almost time for the family meeting; and I'd been getting more and more restless and distracted, worrying about what Altria and I were going to do with a whole day's curse energy.

"Gotta go curse something," I whispered to Ian.

"Oh. Okay."

We made our good-byes and he drove me home.

"Thanks," I said, my hand on the doorhandle of the car. "That was nice."

"We could try something with fewer people next time," he said.

There might be a next time.

He took my hand. I sat feeling the warmth of his hand on mine, the strength in his grip, even though it was gentle. I stared out at our yard, draped in fairy lights, and listened to the palm of my hand as it told me about connection with someone else.

I looked at Ian in the darkness of the car, and he looked at me. He leaned forward and kissed me, a brief touch of lips on lips.

Oh no! Now what? Was I supposed to do something else? What did I say? Wait, where were all those feelings people always had in books and movies when this happened? His lips had been warm and not wet. Before I had time to experience anything else, he sat back. His fingers tangled with mine.

Should I ask him to try it again?

Too pushy!

Now we had to have another date so I could try this again. Maybe next time I'd realize it was happening before it happened and I could hold his head or something, make the kiss last a little longer, see what it really felt like.

"Okay," I said, breathless and confused, "Thank you. Good night." I slipped out of the car before anything else could happen.

I was already unlocking the front door when Ian called, "See you Christmas afternoon around three, right?"

"Right!" There would be lots of people at the Christmas party, not an optimum time to try kissing again, but we'd be at my house, so if we really wanted to talk or experiment, we could go down to the orchard, hide in one of the basements, sneak up to the widow's walk or even the roof. Or we could go to my room.

I should clean up my room before Christmas, just in case.

I waved to Ian and went inside to find my family.

I heard people noises in the house—TV talking in the great hall, conversation in the kitchen, footsteps from upstairs. Warmth and comfort. Sunday evening at the La-Zelles's. Home.

I walked in. Flint sat on the big easy chair in the TV alcove of the great hall with the remote control on the chair arm, watching Fox TV. "Is it time?" he asked.

"Almost."

He flicked the TV off.

"I want to get my curse journal. I'll be right back." I went toward the staircase.

"I'll tell Mama and Dad you're home." He headed for the kitchen.

## Twenty-two

I went upstairs to my room. I closed my door and locked it, then sat on the bed, holding the protection stone. I set it on the bedspread.

"Altria?"

She sat on my bed facing me. "Is it time to figure out tonight's big curse?"

"First there's a family meeting."

"We could do it there."

"Oh, no!" I shook my head. "I don't want to curse my family."

"You do. You just won't admit it."

I leaned forward, checked to see if she was serious. She smiled. I couldn't tell.

She put her palm on my forehead. "Take a look."

Something ripped open in my head, and rage came roaring out. Rage at years of being weak in the face of their power.

"Your legs don't work. You can only walk on your hands," Flint told me.

"But I can't walk on my hands."

"Then you can't walk," he said, and strolled away.

True, I had just pounded him so hard I left bruises. His power was new, and I had forgot he had it. But a beating had a beginning and an end. Not like being left on the living room floor for hours, and needing to go to the bathroom without being able to get there. I was a mess by the time Opal found me hours later.

Or the time I chanced to enter the kitchen while Jasper and Flint were having a spell fight, and they decided to challenge each other to turn me into the strangest thing possible. That fight went on for way too long, and most of the time I was things that couldn't protest.

The fights I always lost. The only time I got to sit in the front seat of the van was when it was just Mama or Dad and me going somewhere. The only time I got to choose the TV show was when I was home alone. Even if I knew I wanted to see something else, a couple minutes after I sat down I'd be convinced I wanted to watch what whoever was strongest at the moment wanted to watch. I suspected that I lost track of my own tastes more often than I knew.

*We* always included me, whether I wanted it to or not.

The special things the rest of them got to do because they had transitioned. The sense that I was always going to be second-class.

All the things Mama had done to us down the years without thinking twice. I remembered being five years old. I was on the back porch floor, sitting next to Beryl, who was two. She was strapped into a rocking seat. She was crying and sobbing. Tears ran down her face. Nothing she did made a noise; Mama, playing cards with some other adults at the table, had been irritated by it, and silenced her. I kept patting Beryl's cheek, but it didn't help. She screamed her face red, and no one heard. I didn't know what to do. It took me way too long to realize I should find Opal.

I did want to cast curses on my family for every careless or mean thing they had ever done to me. I wanted to fill my hands with red light and send it everywhere.

Altria lifted her hand from my forehead. She still smiled.

"I don't want to curse my family," I repeated.

Altria sat back and waited.

"One part of me would love to curse them. But *I* don't want to." Well, that wasn't as clear as I had thought it would be. "What good would it do me to hurt them for things that happened a long time ago? Things they might not even have known bothered me? It's over."

"It gives you a focus for your power. If they don't know why you're mad, *make* them know."

I sighed.

I picked up my curse journal and flipped to a back page, where I'd been working on a spell during my spare time all day. "I'd like you to come with me to the meeting. I want them to know you." I confused myself. Why was this important? Because she was important. She was helping me figure out how to handle my new life, even if I couldn't always tell it was help. I wanted her to stay my friend, if that was what she was. "But if you do come, I need to put a spell on you first."

"You want to put a spell on me?" She grinned. "Why didn't we think of that? You could have been cursing me all this time."

"What?"

"Maybe I'd like it. Whatever it is, I could probably survive it. What kind of spell?"

I showed Altria my spell for her. She narrowed her eyes, frowned, then added a line and showed it to me.

Her handwriting looked nothing like mine. It was spiky and wild and somehow old-fashioned. I was more interested in that than in what she had written.

Focus, Gyp.

I looked at her line, "For the length of this meeting," and nodded.

We set the curse journal sideways between us. I held out my hands, and she put her hands in mine. Heat roared into me through our connection, flared like wildfire through my chest. *Too much*! I thought, and then I thought, *get used to it. It's all from me. I need to own it and use it.*

*Be my aid and my filter so this comes out clean*, I thought to Altria. Then I said my spell.

> *"Altria:*
> *For the length of this meeting,*
> *Care for us as I do.*
> *Love us as I do.*
> *Protect us as I would.*
> *Help us as I would."*

Altria shivered and shook, closed her eyes and turned her head. Finally she let out a loud breath. "Eww."

"Sorry," I said.

"You love them. You actually love them, no matter what they do or say to you."

"Family."

She let go of my hands, scratched her nose, stretched. "Yes. I didn't understand before. I've never been this close to one. It's interesting."

"Besides, it's not all awful. Most of it's wonderful, don't you see?" I thought of Flint and me holding hands, crafting lights to embrace our house, our yard, and the tree. Leaning into Jasper's leather-clad back as we rode his motorcycle. Holding my hand still as Beryl painted red sparkle nail-polish on my fingernails, the brush flickery and cool, her hand warm under mine. Mama's voice reading us the Mowgli stories. Dad teaching us chess. Opal brushing my hair.

Altria hugged me, and that, too, was strange. I had

hugged her before, and she had hugged me, but I hadn't been so conscious of hugging someone my own soft, solid shape.

*Love us as I do.*

I guessed I loved myself in addition to everybody else in my family. Sometimes. Hoped that would hold true for the duration of the spell.

"Never mind," Altria said. "I'll handle that part on my own."

I pulled myself together and stood up. "So how do we work this? You want to come downstairs with me in visible mode?" We were both still wearing our party clothes. Might be strange if they couldn't tell which of us was which.

"Let me think." She stood in the center of my floor and stretched her arms toward the ceiling. She took shape as Mama, smiled, flowed into Dad's shape, Jasper's, Flint's, Opal's, Tobias's, Hermina's, Beryl's. Then she turned her back on me, hunched her shoulders. A moment later she faced me. Now she was someone else: my hazel eyes, Beryl's slender teenaged shape, Jasper's nose, Opal's mouth, hands like Flint's, but heavy long red hair like none of ours. She wore a tight melon-green dress with a short, many-layered, scarf-pointed skirt, tights with narrow horizontal black and white stripes, and black cowboy boots like the ones we had worn to Claire's party.

For a moment I saw her as a collection of parts, and then something clicked and she looked like another member of our family—a cousin we hadn't met yet.

"Okay." I picked up my pen and curse journal and unlocked the door.

Beryl and Opal were standing in the sitting room outside.

"I told you it smelled like strange magic," Opal said to Beryl. "Gyp, what are you doing? Who's your friend?"

"This is my curse child, Altria," I said. "She's been helping me sort things out." Had Beryl met Altria before? I tried to remember and couldn't. I was pretty sure Opal hadn't seen her.

"Hello, sweet things," said Altria.

"You look familiar," Beryl said.

"I am familiar." Altria smiled. She glanced toward Tobias's tower as a key sounded in the lock. Tobias emerged, stared at her.

"Uncle," she said.

"Shade."

Jasper came out of his room, rubbing his eyes. He saw Altria and straightened, gave her half a smile.

"Jasper," she said. "Oh. Jasper." *Love them as I do*. She knew he was my favorite; if my spell had worked, she felt the same way about him as I did, in addition to whatever she had felt about him before. She darted over and gave him a hug, kissed his cheek. He looked surprised and worried. He hugged her back.

"Like the new look," he told her when she let go.

She laughed. Then she said, "Gyp put a spell on me so I won't hurt anybody." She glanced at Tobias.

He blew out a breath, nodded.

We went downstairs.

Across the living room, the tree glowed in its lace of lights.

Flint had set out tins of cookies and brownies on the coffee tables in front of the living room couches, and even fixed a coffee tray. Or, with any luck, Mama had fixed it.

Mama and Dad sat on the love seat in the square of four couches that faced each other in a conversational grouping to the right as one came into the living room through the double pocket doors. Flint was in the middle of the big couch facing the love seat, the one that could seat four, and often did during parties.

All three looked up when we came in.

Mama jumped to her feet. "You brought that thing here?" she asked me, glaring at Altria.

"Anise," said Dad.

Usually when Dad said that, in that tone of voice, Mama stopped what she was doing and took a moment for reflection. Dad was the only one who could slow her down, even stop her, when she was about to tirade. This time Mama stayed agitated. "Miles, this is something you can't understand. Gyp has made—contact with that—creature, an amoral creature, who, while it may not wish us ill, hardly wishes us good. In fact, it may only want to play with us, and its powers—" She ran out of words, something that almost never happened, and resorted to arm waving. I wondered what she was trying to say—some kind of warning—and whether it was true.

"Really." Dad stood. He studied Altria. "Hello," he said, then looked confused. "But you look—" He glanced at the rest of us, then back at Altria.

She went to him. "I'm a shapeshifter," she said. "The perceived connection is illusion."

"Purposeful illusion?"

"Of course."

"Not a lot of Bendixen there." Bendixen was Dad's last name before he married into the LaZelles. It's a rule; anyone who wants to marry one of us has to take our last name.

"Yes. I'm sorry." She held out her hand, and he clasped it.

"Miles! You shouldn't let it touch you," Mama said, but she sounded resigned.

He watched Altria's face. A moment later he laughed. She turned to me, and I saw that she now had a cleft like Dad's in her chin. Her eyes danced.

"Did you meet Flint yet?" I asked her. She had taken the shapes of all my siblings, but I could only remember her meeting Jasper before. Then again, she had been shadowing me all day today, and maybe yesterday, too. She had

had time and opportunity to observe everybody.

And she could visit people in their dreams.

She turned. "Flint." She smiled.

"Huh—hi," said my brother.

"This is Altria," I said.

Altria and my brother shook hands.

Mama pulled herself together. "Altria." She held out her hand. "Oh, well. Might as well meet you, since we seem to be going this road."

"Anise." Altria held Mama's hand a moment. Neither of them smiled.

"You're here because . . . ?"

"Gyp asked me to come."

"You said we're going to discuss the problem of me," I said as the family settled onto the couches in the conversation square. "Altria's helped me in lots of ways since I came into my power. I hope she keeps helping me. Whatever we decide about me, it'll probably involve her, too." I dropped my curse journal on the coffee table. Altria snuggled against me on the gray couch, which made me feel strange, as though we had declared something momentous to the family. "Today, for instance, she's been storing my power so I can access it later instead of having to curse things every two hours."

"So you could go Christmas shopping," Beryl said. "Oh! And to the party."

"Right," I said.

"Store your powers in a person? How does that work?" said Opal.

"Don't even ask," Tobias said. He and Jasper sat on the couch across from Altria and me. Opal, Flint, and Beryl chose the big couch in front of the window that overlooked the pool yard to my right, and Mama and Dad returned to the love seat.

"Why not?" Opal asked Tobias.

"It's ridiculously risky."

"Why did you teach it to Gyp, then?"

"I didn't. Gyp has been teaching herself."

"Altria's been teaching me," I said.

"No. Uncle is right. You've been teaching yourself," Altria said.

Was that one of those loaded statements where she was really admitting that she was part of me, despite the fact that her personality was different from mine and so was her handwriting?

"No," she said, and thumped my head. "Get over it."

"You've been teaching yourself," Mama repeated. "You've been struggling with all kinds of things while the rest of us have been preoccupied."

"That's not true. Everybody's helped me." Jasper had rescued me from school, and had tried to rescue me from Altria, and had definitely rescued me from the computer, with Altria's help. Beryl had encouraged me to curse her. Flint had shared his power with me. Tobias gave me pointers and broke some of the worst spells. Hermina forgave me after I screwed up. Dad accepted me, and Mama left me alone.

I grabbed my curse journal and a pen, opened the journal to a blank page. "And I could use some more help. Have you guys thought of curses I can do?"

"Am I too late?" Aunt Hermina came in through the pocket doors and looked around the circle. She sat down beside Tobias, across from me and Altria. When she noticed Altria, she sat up straighter. "Gyp?"

"This is my friend Altria," I said.

"A nightmare is your friend?"

"Yep."

"A better friend than enemy," she muttered. "Maybe." She grabbed a couple cookies.

"Have you ever thought about cursing people who need it?" asked Flint.

"Who needs it?"

He shrugged. "People who did something wrong. You could go to jail and curse people who killed other people."

"How can I be sure they're guilty?" I asked. "All those DNA tests turning up innocent people in prison. I could never be sure."

"We tried that kind of thing. It's hard for her," Altria said. She held out a hand, and a cookie jumped into it. She took a bite. "She closed the door on the self who knows how to be mean. Opening that door makes her miserable."

"You could stick with the playful curses," Beryl said. "Turn us into toads. Children. Dogs. Furniture. Strangers."

"Strangers?" I said.

"Gyp?" Dad said.

I turned to him.

"We *are* strangers now," he said slowly. "Something happened, and you sent me away. I left, because I didn't want to make things harder for you. Curse me with knowledge of what happened after I left."

Altria sat up straighter. Her red hair grew redder—glowing. My fire coming out of her. "Knowledge is a curse," she said. "That's right." She took my hand. "Give them your memories, Gyp." She stroked her fingers across my palm. Red fire danced from her hand to mine. She spiraled an index finger, drew up a scrap of flame—baby Beryl, sobbing and sobbing without sound—and flicked it at Mama.

Mama straightened, her eyes wide, then slumped back against the couch. She pressed her hands to her cheeks. "No. I didn't. No. I couldn't." She stared across at Beryl, and Beryl looked at me and Altria, her eyebrows up. Mama pulled her legs up to her chest, hugged them. Tears ran down her cheeks.

"Miles," said Altria, rubbing her fingers against her thumb and drawing up another spiral of flame. She blew it toward him, and he frowned as it melted into his eyes.

"Oh." He sounded more interested than upset.

I closed my hand into a fist and stared at Altria. She touched my lips so that I tasted the memory she had sent to Dad. It was me walking into Hermina's house Friday morning, to find her trapped in a welter of plants and computer. Just what Dad had asked for.

"What's she doing?" Jasper asked.

"Want to see? Open up, Gyp." Altria teased my fist open and stirred fire on my palm again, flicked a shred toward Jasper—the time he sneaked a girlfriend home when he wasn't supposed to, and I was on the couch and saw him before he saw me, and he sent me silence and invisibility and froze me until he was ready to leave again. He left me tongue-tied so I could never tell anybody. Not that I would have. He could have just asked.

"Oh," Jasper said, his tone dismayed.

"Stop it," I said to Altria.

"This won't get us very far," Altria said. "It's too incremental. Knowledge. Hmm."

"What *is* she doing?" asked Flint.

"Just what she said," Jasper answered. "Gyp's memories. Not the happy ones. Sorry, Gyp."

Beryl leaned forward. "You could curse yourself with the knowledge of what to do with your curses."

Altria turned to me, her eyes wide and glowing, her hair a flaming halo around her head and shoulders, her hands raised to shoulder height, each hand swallowed in a red cloud of light, my power, rendered untwisted and less limited by its passage through her. "Gyp . . ."

"Personality bending," Tobias said. "It could change you beyond recognition."

Altria's hair lifted, alight with a wind and power she was generating from material I had given her.

I heard the footsteps of my heart in my ears. All along, what had bothered me most about my power was not knowing what to do with it. Maybe—

"Come on," I said to Altria. "Let's do it."

She leaned into me, gripped my head in her glowing hands, pressed her forehead to mine. Her hair wrapped around us, snaky and full of static and heat. All I could see were her eyes, glowing golden now, and all I could taste was her breath, so close to mine, chocolate chip cookie and woodsmoke. Something grew like a mushroom inside my head, swelling, pulsing, rising like bread dough, and all the while we were wrapped in robes of red heat together.

The mushroom burst, a thousand thousand spores of spinning facts and speculations, a shuffle and fall of stacks of images, a supple squirm of memories and imaginings, only a few of them mine. Altria released me and I sagged back against the couch, my eyes tight shut, as things snapped and snorted and sorted in my brain. Too much of everything.

So much. Was that what Mama had been like when she was fourteen? Had her older sisters really done all those mean things to her? And her mother—that wasn't Grandmère. Who was it who had left the house when Mama was only six and never come back? Who had left a hole in Mama's heart so big that she never wanted to let anyone else leave her that way? Left fears that stirred her sleep with terror every night? Left a hurt that lasted so long Mama had spelled us all to stay home, not to leave her?

Was this really Dad at eighteen? Standing in the front hall of a house I had never seen, talking to two cold-faced people I had never met, saying if that was how they felt, he would say good-bye now. If they ever wanted to see him again, they would have to call him. The door closed behind him with a sound like the crack of a continent falling into an ocean.

This must be Tobias, in his twenties, hiding on an adobe rooftop with a brother, spying on the hated father in the courtyard below, the father who had protected himself against all forms of spellcasting applied directly, and with reason, so many of his children hated him; Tobias, thinking of shifting stones beneath his father's feet—

A young and beautiful Hermina, standing in family council beside a stork-awkward young man, watching as one after another of her parents, aunts, uncles, grandparents, shook their heads no, denying her petition to marry, the youngest of her elders holding out a cup of forgetfulness to the prospective bridegroom—

A shuffle and fall of humiliating, disturbing memories from my brothers and sisters: Opal at fifteen, pre-transition, smiling at someone who misread her, caught her, trapped her, tore off her shirt, grabbed at her breasts; Jasper turning away from the hopeless love in his best friend's eyes; Flint staring down at a dead, spellmarked squirrel in his hands; Beryl covering her ears so she wouldn't hear something she had hidden to listen to—

And this, a strange oily memory full of hunger, the slide of coil on coil, unblinking golden eyes, a long forked tongue that slid out, tasting and testing for the wine of fear, the nectar of terror, which could be pressed out of almost any moment, induced if not already present, the finest taste there was, and never enough of it—

The sea song, below everything, still whispering that all things came from it, all things could return to it, changed and unchanging—

A strange matrix spun in darkness before me, lines visible and invisible, colored threads of light weaving through it, a diagram of kinds of power and how they acted on each other. If I could focus long enough to learn it, I could change everything.

"Gyp? You okay?" asked Opal. I felt her near me, her energy, her heat, her scent.

"Wait," said Tobias.

I lost the grid, though I had printed some of it on my memory. I frowned and opened my eyes, stared up toward the ceiling. Altria's face eclipsed it, her eyes still golden, her mouth sad, her hair hanging in my face. She touched my cheek.

I lifted a finger, aimed it at her. Her hair twisted around itself, retreated from her front to lie against her back. She smiled: dimples in both cheeks. I thought of the ancient hungry serpent I had seen, alert for terror, tried to fit it into my image of her, could not make them match. She touched foreheads with me again, and then there were layers over layers, shifting and shining, wider than I had known, and older, darker, yet with tasty red rivers running through them, touch points and desires and connections, new and ancient currents flowing, mixing, washing some things in and some things away.

Here was the spell we had said before we came down to the meeting, restraining some of her appetites and changing the course of others, suffusing her with feelings she had never known before. Here were all kinds of new marks on her, each contact she had had with me, cuts and colors, shocks to the system one after another, new desires—

Altria sat back, her face troubled.

"Gyp?" said Opal.

I blinked and rubbed my forehead. I pushed up from the back of the couch. Altria gripped my shoulder and helped me sit up. Her touch had echoes and magnifications. I clutched her hand, afraid she would slip away before I could find out who she was now.

The world looked different. Strange, ghostly colored cobwebs draped everything. "Do you see that?" I asked Altria.

She stared at my face, then toward where I was looking—at Mama, actually, because so many of these cobwebs had strings that led to her. Altria lifted an eyebrow.

"What did the nightmare do to you, Gypsum?" Hermina asked.

"Bent my personality, probably." I touched the nearest web, a green string that led from Mama to me. It melted.

I felt a click in my head, and realized there was nothing to stop me from moving out of the house.

Well, except sense, love, lack of money, and fear of the unknown.

I reached out for a green string that ran from Mama to Jasper. My fingertips glowed red as I touched it. It snapped. I glanced at my big brother. "What?" he said.

I checked Mama.

"What are you doing, Gypsum?" Her voice was midway between fear and anger.

*What you perceive, you can affect.*

Even if I didn't know what it was, apparently. What this had to do with curses, I wasn't sure.

Mama signed something on her palm, flicked her fingers. Green lines spun from her to me and Jasper. When the line touched me, I felt the faintest flow of soothing, comfort, and even fainter, the persuasions. *Don't leave. Never leave me. Stay young. Stay unsure. Let me take care of you.*

I wondered how Opal had gotten away from home. I looked, saw that there was no green line from Mama to Opal, but there was a turquoise line unlike any of the lines she had bound the rest of us with.

"Gypsum," said Tobias.

"Uncle."

"What are you doing?"

"Just looking." I stared at him. He was wrapped in a cocoon of silver and gold lines. Faintly through them I saw a skeleton. I rubbed my eyes, but the vision didn't go away: I couldn't see his face any longer. I grabbed Altria's hand again. "What kind of knowledge did you give me?" I asked her.

"I don't know."

I studied Dad. Dad looked like himself—the only one in the room who wasn't tangled up in strangeness. Mama had lines to him, but they went to his hand, where he held the ends. Mama's other lines plunged from Mama right into our hearts.

Then there were cross-lines between us.

Some of it resembled the grid I had seen in the darkness, but mostly it just looked tangled and messy, as though it would take a lot of time to figure out.

I looked down at my chest, and saw the deep pool of red power at my core, saw that there was a matching pool in Altria, that it traveled between us in another kind of connection.

Something inside her puzzled me, a small black invitation that was also a doorway. I reached in and touched it. Everyone in the living room except Altria gasped or cried out loud. Altria just studied my hand. Then she smiled.

The door described itself to my fingertip. It led somewhere wide open and vast, where power could wait safely without suffering, without hurting anything. Maybe it was the same place power came from.

I lifted my finger from the door and touched my sternum. An image of the door printed there, sank into my center, turned from thought to reality. The door opened, and more power rushed out. I was breathing hot red light, swimming in it, drowning in it. Yet it was intoxicating, too.

I tapped my chest. "Reverse," I said.

The red ran down into the doorway as though it were a drain. Before it was all gone, I tapped once more, and the door closed, leaving me with a small pool of power.

When I looked up again, the cobwebs were gone: everybody looked normal. Well, horrified. But they had faces instead of webwork.

"Gyp," Beryl said.

"What?"

"You stuck your hand in her heart!"

"What?" I glanced at Altria.

She smiled at me.

"It was disgusting!" said Opal. "You stuck your hand right into her chest."

I stared at my hand. I stared at Altria's chest. "Did it hurt?"

"No." She took my hand and kissed it. "You went insubstantial."

"What did you do, Gyp? Suddenly the threat potential dropped," Tobias said.

"Altria taught me a technique for managing power." Was that what had happened? She said she had developed a new way to store power today—

"Did the curse work, Gyp?" Beryl asked.

"I guess it did. I'm not sure." I opened the inner door and called some power out, let it gather in my hands. In the course of the curse, I had seen and shelved a thousand thousand dark memories and torments. It felt different, this power, still red and strong, but somehow tamer, as though we had domesticated each other. "Mama, may I curse you?"

"What did you do to me before? It hurt."

"This won't be the same. I'll limit it, so you can see what it's like and decide if you want it to be permanent."

She sighed, looked at Dad. He took her hand. They both faced me. Mama's free hand was a fist. "I guess it's time I let you curse me, after the way I cursed you. Go ahead," she whispered.

I didn't speak to my power. I formed specific intent, thought it through three times, and sent the power down into her memories, told it to eat out the night terrors and leave her free of them, save them unhurt behind the door where I could retrieve them and restore them if she wanted them back. It was delicate and intricate; everything connected to everything else, so each cut had to be considered carefully.

At last I finished. Altria's arm was warm around my shoulders, and my forehead was wet. I had no heat in my chest, and I had taken all the heat she had on the surface, too. I glanced at the others, wondering how much time had passed. They all stared at me.

Mama drew a deep breath. "I feel so strange," she whispered. Her face twisted, settled into a new shape, the edges softer.

"What did you do?" Dad asked me.

"Mama? Did it hurt?"

"No." She put her hand over her heart. "I feel—so light."

"Gyp," said Tobias.

"I cursed the things that make it so she can't sleep at night," I said.

"Bent her personality," Hermina said.

"Yes." I wiped my forehead with my red pirate sleeve. "I'm keeping them safe for you, Mama. Tell me if you want them back."

"All right." She let out a shuddering breath. She straightened. "All right. Sounds like you've learned control." She stroked her knuckles across her chest, frowned. "Feels like you've learned control."

"Yes. I think so. Yes."

"Tobias?" Mama said.

Tobias shook his head. "I don't understand it, but I think you're right. She doesn't broadcast dangerous anymore. Gyp, you've settled?"

I stared down inside myself to the door where power waited. Nothing knocked. I felt comfortable, almost normal. "I guess so."

"Good," said Mama. "The Gyp Factor part of this meeting is over, then. Let's move on. Jasper, have you written us a carol yet?"

## *Twenty-three*

BY the time the meeting ended, we all knew what we were supposed to do in the two days until Christmas. We broke up around ten-thirty. Altria followed me upstairs, her hand warm on my shoulder. Things were still shifting around in my brain: I kept noticing new and strange information, and trying to deal with it.

"Phone, Gyp!" Beryl said as I walked past her in the sitting room.

I hadn't even noticed the ring. I took the handset. "Hello?"

"Hi. You still awake? Is this too late to call?" Ian asked.

"No, it's fine." I turned to Altria. She had vanished.

"How'd the curse go?" he asked.

"Pretty well. I think I've got this curse thing under control now."

"Wow! Great! Congratulations."

"Thanks. Did you go back to the party?"

"No, of course not. Just wanted to call and find out if you were okay. Are you okay?"

"I'm fine."

"Good."

Silence stretched.

"Hey," Ian said at last. "See you on Christmas."

"Good," I said.

LATER that night I walked down to the beach. If anybody tried to hurt me, they would regret it. I only had to open the little black door to access my power.

Fog made the air visible, kept the night pale by trapping light close to the ground. I knew the air was cool, but my energy kept me warm.

Shards of glass clinked away from my shoes as I walked the dark tunnel under the freeway, below the ocean tides of traffic. I was halfway across when I heard the echo of someone else's steps. I stopped below the grating that showed a barred square of sky between the southbound and northbound lanes of Highway 101, and waited for my follower to catch up.

She walked barefoot across the glass scattered concrete, all of her a shadow here in the dark, a silhouette against the light at the far end of the tunnel. I held out my hand. She took it, her fingers warm and strong around mine. We walked on into deeper darkness, and then up into gray night.

The tunnel let out at the dead end of a beach road, bordered with tall, skinny eucalyptus trees reaching toward the sky. We walked two blocks and came to the beach access, crumbling asphalt-and-rock stairs the ocean kept wearing away.

The tide was halfway out, stroking the shore with a constant rush and tumble, occasional waves breaking with crashes that rolled into roars. Foam hemmed the waves, rushed up across the beach, pale against dark water and wet sand. Salt breeze gusted along the shore.

We knelt in the lee of a drift log where the sand was

dry. She faced me, pressed her knees to mine. She reached across the space between us and touched my breastbone with her fingertips. I opened the door to my power and let some rise from the holding place, flow from me into her, a gift I was comfortable sharing with her now.

She lifted her hand away from my chest, then joined it with her other hand and rested her cupped hands on our knees. Clear white light pooled in her hands, my power, changed on its journey through her. She stared at me, her face lit from below, light caught in her butter-amber eyes.

"Marry me," she said.

"What?"

Her gaze lowered to the light, then lifted again to meet mine. "I love you."

Thoughts startled up, stuttered, subsided. But marriage was—a man and a woman? A church, a ceremony, a dress? A promise of eternity? A physical bond?

"But Altria—"

"I want to stay with you. I won't hurt you. Maybe scare you once in a while, shake you up so you remember you're alive. I'll protect the ones you love. I can be whatever you want."

"But Ian—"

"I can be Ian." She shifted shape: his blue eyes, his half-shy square-jawed smile, his wiry, slender body.

"Don't do that."

She tossed her head and turned back into a honey-eyed self with long ruby hair. Her face looked more fey than human. "You can marry him, too. I don't mind."

"I don't want to marry Ian. I don't know what I want. It's all new to me. I just want to see what happens if I keep seeing him. He's the first—"

The first what? The first one outside my family to see me clearly and come back later? Altria had done that, too. In the last four days since I had opened the way for her to come into my life, she had helped me again and again, even if the help came guised as torture. She had acted as my mother and my sister and my friend, my helper and my director and my dark side.

I stared into her eyes, the one my uncle called Shade and my aunt called Nightmare and my mother called Creature. I thought of how she had stepped out of nowhere to save me from falling, how she had blown cobwebs out of my brain to restore me to myself, how she held me in her arms, stroked warmth into us with my own power, and took me up into the sky. She was the first one to help me fly. I had felt safe with her, even when she was threatening me.

She had seen me in different forms. She had sent me into different forms. She knew my power. She had seen me fail, watched my weaknesses. She still said she loved me.

I had had a dream, one I had never let myself have on the surface, but still, one that had dreamed itself down deep inside. Could anyone love me if they really knew me? I had found someone who could.

Maybe two people. Ian had seen me at my lowest, and he called back the next day.

I cupped my hands around hers. The pooled light shimmered, colors shooting through it, then steadied.

"See Ian all you like," she said. "Just let me stay with you, one way or another. I can take any shape. What do you want me to be?"

"Yourself."

"Oh, no. You're not ready for that."

We stared at each other.

"I love you," I whispered.

"Good."

"Don't you think I know you?"

"What do you know?" she whispered.

I lifted one hand from the nest we had made for the light and touched her forehead, red flowing from my fingertips. I showed her all the ways I had seen her during my curse: the ancient serpent, hungry for fear; the night-mare spirit trapped in a vessel I had offered it, shaped by the protections and love Jasper had set in the sea stone, sculpted by every encounter with me and my family into something foreign to itself, spelled by me into reluctant love for my family. The spell was over now. Traces of the love remained. Perhaps, having tried it, she found she liked it. Still, I had seen the self she owned that walked through dark dreams and made them darker. That self still lived inside her, strong in its terrifying desires.

"No. You were never supposed to know," she whispered.

I closed my eyes, wished I could close my eyes to all the things I had seen that I was never supposed to know. Knowledge was a curse. I knew my family better than I had ever wanted to.

I knew I had a self like Altria's, better hidden but hungry.

I filed the dark memories away. That worked. I didn't have to focus on them all the time. Knowledge was a curse, and it was also treasure. I could lock it up or take it out to look at. Now that I knew so many strange things, I had a flickering idea of a future. Maybe this would be my work: find people's bad memories, the scars on their souls, and change or remove the ones that tortured, the ones hardest to bear. I could do that with a curse.

I wasn't sure it was a good thing. Mama would tell me tomorrow, after a good night's sleep, maybe.

"Is there any part of you that you want me to curse?" I asked.

She frowned. Her face went remote. "Not yet," she said.

"Not ever is okay with me."

She lifted her hands, broke the cup. Light spilled out over our legs, laps, stomachs. Some drained into the sand. Some slicked her palms like a radioactive skin. She put her arms around my neck. I hesitated, then embraced her.

She kissed me. It was not the brief touch of lip on lip

I had experienced with Ian. There was more pressure, movement of her lips over mine, searching, tasting, wet heat, tingling, the touch of her tongue, a taste of chile and woodsmoke. She turned her head and hugged me closer, her cheek against my ear.

We sat entwined in the darkness. I listened to her breathing, and the waves. I teetered on an edge between wonder and terror. The warmth of another person pressed against me, wrapped around me. Where did we go from here?

After a while the fear faded. Something else seeped in.

What had I heard here yesterday, when I was a baby? What was that sound under the crash of waves, the rush of water?

It still called, a sea song.

I stroked one hand down her side. She lifted her head and nodded. We untangled, and she helped me up.

We sat on the log and I took off my shoes. We walked down across the cold dry sand to the cold wet sand. I felt the cold now, but it didn't bother me. It told my feet something about their shape.

We walked out into the water. Its cold was intense and shocking. Altria stroked my chest and summoned power to warm us. We swam out beyond where the waves broke, and the sea carried us. We held onto each other.

After a while we drifted to quiet water.

We floated, holding hands, and I heard again the murmur of something old and undivided, something early and ever. In the presence of this vast, ancient, unjudging energy, I understood that no matter what she was, no matter what I was, we were enough alike to be twins, soulmates, together.

"Yes," I whispered.

She hugged me. "Yes," she whispered.

We floated.

Eventually we drifted home.

NINA KIRIKI HOFFMAN won the Bram Stoker Award for First Novel for *The Thread That Binds the Bones*, and her second novel, *The Silent Strength of Stones*, was a finalist for both the Nebula and World Fantasy Awards. Her other works include novels *A Red Heart of Memories* and *Past the Size of Dreaming*, and the short story collections *A Legacy of Fire*, *Courting Disasters and Other Strange Affinities*, and *Time Travelers, Ghosts, and Other Visitors*. Her young adult novel, *A Stir of Bones*, came out in 2003. She lives in Eugene, Oregon, with three cats and a mannequin.

BRAM STOKER AWARD-WINNING AUTHOR
# NINA KIRIKI HOFFMAN
# Past the Size of Dreaming

"SURE TO PROVE TO BE ONE OF THE BEST
FANTASIES OF [THE YEAR]." —*LOCUS*

Matilda is a witch with the ability to speak with
inanimate objects and see into people's dreams.
Edmund Reynolds is her companion, a young man
who is only beginning to come to grips with
his own magic.

The two travelers come to the town where Edmund
grew up and settle for the night in a haunted
house—a house with plenty to say to Matilda.

"HOFFMAN WRITES ABOUT MAGIC CREATIVELY
AND WITH GREAT FEELING...HER INGENIOUS
PLOTTING EXPLORES MEMORY, THE NATURE OF
RECOLLECTION AND PERSONAL GROWTH."
—*KIRKUS REVIEWS*

0-441-00898-4

**Available wherever books are sold or
to order call 1-800-788-6262**

a167

**Available in Paperback**

National Bestselling Author of
**THE LOST YEARS OF MERLIN**

# T. A. BARRON

"A superbly likable book."
—Brian Jacques, New York Times bestselling author of Redwall

## heartlight

0-441-01036-9